SANDRA

ALICE M CURRY-FRANK

ISBN: 1475030959
ISBN 13: 9781475030952

Library of Congress Control Number: 2012904792
CreateSpace, North Charleston, SC

Acknowledgements:

I want to thank my parents for giving me life as well as my son Charles, daughter Alicia, friends, relatives and co-workers who have all but beat this second novel out of me. I thank you all for your support, and words of encouragement.

I would also like to send my most indebted gratitude of thanks to the Ngubane family; who's life-style of peace and tranquility was able to help me write the ending of this novel effortlessly.

Without the solitude, which was given without question; this novel may still be in the works. There is nothing more precious than a peace of mind, and they deliver it by the platters in South Africa…..I love you all.

DEDICATION:

To my husband: A Beautiful Man

I prayed for someone to love me, and God sent me you,

To be a father figure to my children,
someone to look up to.

I never wanted for anything; I never had a need,

God sent me someone so perfect, you fulfilled
my every dream.

Our love could be matched by no other,

People know what I'm saying is true,

You're the most beautiful thing to have ever touched me,

I got my strength through you.

It's too early to say goodbye, or even speak in past tense,

Your love will forever be held inside of me,

Everyday of my life you will be missed.

Forever your wife——Alice

SPECIAL THANKS

Special Thanks To my sister-in-law Resser Ingram-Williams: There are not enough words in the dictionary to express what you mean to me. You listen quietly even when I have nothing to say.

Your brother; my husband, left behind something that can hold no price tag. A friend. A confidant. A sister. Is what he blessed me with in you. I love you!

CHAPTER 1

*R*unning at full speed, she was momentarily caught off guard when she was swung off her feet and into the air.

"Homework?"

"Check!"

"Lunch?"

"Check!"

"Are you ready?"

"Yep!"

"Get set...and...go!"

She was released in one fluid motion and bolted for the door. Things could get no better for little Sandra Hansley. She had on her favorite pair of socks, a new book bag, and a bright yellow summer dress with a matching bow around her pigtail. Nope, it simply didn't get any better than this!

School brought boundless amounts of joy to the curious eight-year-old, mainly due to her not having any siblings, which made seeing other kids very exciting for her. Sandra's interacting vibe was always in full peak mode when she walked through the doors of Kickamoore Elementary School in the mornings. The teachers marveled at her intelligence level as well as the underdeveloped natural beauty within the child. Even at the tender age of eight, she was a force to be reckoned with.

As she skipped down the street, Sandra waved to Mrs. Whitmund as she passed her by. She was the elderly widow on the block, or at least that's what the adults in her neighborhood referred to her as. Sandra had no idea what it meant to be a widow, but she did know that the blue house on the corner with the busiest flower garden ever is where all the kids went for the best homemade cookies in the world! These famous cookies were being sold three for twenty-five cents all day long, which just made her even more popular in Kiddy Land. If you told her your favorite candy, she would try to make up a recipe with the sweets inside the cookie.

Sandra's cookies had a huge, gooey caramel square sitting right in the middle of a butter cookie. On the days where homework was scarce or nonexistent, Sandra would do small chores for her elderly neighbor in exchange for the little treasures she loved most.

Sandra would bring cookies home to her mother, in which most times she didn't eat, but she would place them on a plate for her none the less. Her mother's appetite wasn't as great as it use to be, but she didn't seem to lose much weight because of it. Dorothy could be found nibbling on chips every now and then, and on good days, she would eat an entire plate of food.

Sandra would never complain to anyone that her mom doesn't eat. She was merely happy to be at home with her mom. They didn't go out to play like Lillie and her mother, but she also didn't get whoopings all the time like Jack mom would do, so she felt she was in between the two, and that was just fine with her.

CHAPTER 2

*B*efore entering the school, Sandra looked up to the sky and sent a silent prayer, hoping that this would be the day that God would hear her. Since the age of four, she had been in the habit of praying daily. One Sunday morning, she heard the God man on the television say, "Ask the Lord for help and guidance, and he shall give you what you need." So whether it was in front of the school or at her bedside, she always kept the faith that God would finally hear her little whispers and heal her mother from her medical condition and the sickness of her medication.

Sandra couldn't remember a day in all her young years that she didn't come home to find her mother in a sick state. For quite some time, she had no idea why her mother slept so much or couldn't keep the basic functions of life in order, but as she got older, it was explained to her that the medicine her mother took for her heart condition caused her to sleep a lot so her heart could rest. Her mother, Dorothy, explained that without it, her heart would stop. It didn't seem very fair to Sandra that you had to choose between the two, but considering the choices, Sandra would prefer her mother to be sick and sleepy than to be dead. What eight-year-old wouldn't?

Her father had left them four years ago and had since remarried into a ready-made family. She could remember talking to him on the phone a few times, but no real communication between them existed. He paid child support on a regular basis, and Sandra molded herself to be eternally happy for that. On the days when the check would arrive in the mail, she would remind her mom not to take her medicine until after they went to the check cashing place. She never asked much more than that from Dorothy, always fearing her heart would cease to beat if she tried to accompany her to the grocery store or run any other errands outside of cashing the check.

When food ran low or there was something special Sandra wanted, she would go down to the convenience store and buy it with the spare money that she left under her mattress. The landlord thankfully handled all the bills for them and would bring the change back to Sandra. Over time, the amount she received back was beginning to increase, so she always paid herself two dollars, which she would also place under the mattress. By the time she was ten, she was counting money fairly well on her hands and knew her way around a calculator, so she would always give the landlord the correct amount for each bill, which for some reason left her with more money than she had during the period when he was in charge of their finances.

CHAPTER 3

At the time, there was really no difference in school from one day to the next. Sandra was always a good helper and finished her work earlier than most of the kids in her class, so she was always chosen to go to the copy lab and make printouts for all the teachers at the end of the day. She was well-known in the building, from staff to classmates. Everyone knew of her, but a few of her teachers were concerned that they had never met the joyful child's mother. Hearing about her illness, mostly through the grapevine, calmed some of the inquisitive thoughts and ideas, but not all.

One quiet morning, the principal requested that Sandra come into his office for a one-on-one conference, which pleased her because she absolutely loved Principal McLaferty. He was nice to all the kids and even gave out winter coats last year to those who didn't have one. So he ranked quite high on her list of top-notch people. His seat, in her world of heroes, definitely ranked up there next to her mom.

"Come in, Sandra, and have a seat."

Full of bounce, she plopped into one of the overstuffed chairs on the other side of his desk.

"You want me to make you some copies, too, Mr. McLaferty? I going to make some for Mrs. Wright and Mr. Noel if you…"

"Ahh, thank you very much, Sandra, but that's not why I called you into my office this morning. As you know, parent-teacher conference is coming up, and we will need to see your mother. Now I know that she is very sick and has medical problems, but the board has discussed this issue, and it was decided that we need to have some form of verbal communication with your mother. Since you don't have a phone at home and your mother is ill, we are more than willing to come to your home where your mother will be able to remain comfortable throughout the meeting. We just need a few questions answered."

"But she's really sick, Mr. McLaferty! What if her heart stops?" Sandra stated this with all earnestness. Her blue eyes were the size of buttercups, and the principal could easily read the fear in her expression. She really believed that a visit from the school would kill her mother. He didn't want to scare the child to death, but her mother had been ill for such a long amount of time that the school feared she may be in need of a full time nurse or a relative to live with them for a while until she was able to take over the responsibilities of the household. Then again, it was one of the main reasons they were having this conversation in the first place. If her mother was as brittle as she proclaimed, then who was running the house? Surely not a child?

"Are you telling me that no one comes to your house to check on you?"

"Well, Uncle Bill comes by when he's not driving his truck, and a few of the adults from the neighborhood stop by every other day and give Mommy her medicine. They don't really say much to me, but Mom says they help her while I'm at school, and sometimes when I come home they are there, too."

"Sandra, forgive me if I really don't understand what you are telling me. I don't mean to make you nervous, but do you know what kind of medicine your mom is taking?"

She sat back in her chair and thought about it for a little while. She wanted to give the right answer, but going through her memory bank, she just couldn't remember her mother ever telling her the name. Maybe if she could describe what it looked like, then Principal McLaferty would know just what it was.

"I'm sorry I don't know the name, but I could describe it for you, if that would help."

"Yes, that could help me, I guess."

"Well, it's a powder, and…"

At that precise moment a knock sounded at the door, and the secretary bustled into the room looking frazzled.

"I'm sorry Mr. McLaferty, but we seem to have a problem in hallway four. It requires your immediate attention, sir!"

Without hesitating, he rose from behind his desk and followed her to the door. Pausing, he turned back to Sandra, "You may go back to class, Sandra, and I'll think about what we have discussed. I'll notify you about the decision on the home visit in a day or two."

He bolted out the door, never giving the home visit a second thought when he laid eyes on the mini-riot in hallway four. There were kids screaming and crying clear down to the exit door. "Oh my God!" was the only sentence he could muster as he went head on into the catastrophe.

Sandra and her mother were quickly forgotten as the local news media picked up the story of a five-year-old spraying mace on school grounds. It made the top headline for the next week. The onslaught of parents wanting to remove their children from school in concert with the lawsuits being filed put Sandra and her home visit beyond the back burner.

CHAPTER 4

By the time she entered the fifth grade, things were becoming a little more transparent to Sandra. She now knew that the "people from the neighborhood" were not just stopping by to give Dorothy her medicine but that they were also on the same medication. After walking in on her mother and the "pharmacist" having sex, she started to pay a little more attention to the comings and goings in the house.

She instinctively became a little more frightened by the company that was being kept and even more skeptical of her mother's illness. In the mornings as she went to school, her mother would either be in a self-absorbed daydream, or you could find her at the kitchen sink with three cottage cheese buckets filled with different solutions to clean syringes. The smell of the bleach was the strongest and most overpowering. It would filter through the house like mold, clinging to everything, smothering out all other aromas.

The morning conversations they used to share were all but forgotten, and the number of visitors increased, along with the length of time they would stay at the house.

In the past when she would return form school, her mother would be alone, most times waiting for her. But things were changing into something a ten-year-old couldn't attempt to understand. Sandra noticed that her mother's appearance was not like it used to be; the silhouette that that could turn the most faithful of men's heads was deteriorating. It seemed as if Dorothy had become frail overnight.

The slender but full size six she used to be had drifted to an unsightly size three. It made the weight loss that much more apparent when Dorothy would halfheartedly pin her old clothes around her skeletal frame. Her pants would be pathetically twisted to the extent that the zipper placed itself diagonally from her hip to her pelvic area. Forget about a bra for her now-sagging b-cup breasts. She would simply turn all v-neck sweaters or shirts she owned around and wear them backwards.

Bathing and grooming, which she had so relentlessly instilled into Sandra, were also forgotten acts. For days she would wear the same clothes, but when Sandra found her sleeping in the nude, she would toss the over-worn items in the laundry hamper.

Sandra realized that the medicine was affecting her memory even more when it came down to bathing. Because her body odor sometimes became too much to bear, Sandra would run her mother a bath and insist that she got in. She would take the time to wash her hair and scrub her back, always being gentle around the unsightly ridges of her spine.

Dorothy was fading quickly, and this worried Sandra. Who would take care of her if something happened to her mother? She was too young to see that for the last two and a half years, she had been the one running the house and taking care of Dorothy.

CHAPTER 5

Sandra ran into the house with her book bag dragging, hair in disarray, and a happily flushed face. She had been playing red light/green light with some of the other kids on the school grass until she the sun had begun to fade.

Sandra came to an abrupt halt when she entered the house and noticed Bill and her mother kissing on the couch. What was going on? Surely her mother couldn't have two boyfriends. What had happened to the pharmacist?

"Hi, Mom."

Dorothy was looking a little perkier than usual, and Sandra briefly believed that it might be okay for her to date Bill. "Hi, honey. Why are you running for your life? That black-and-white dog isn't chasing you again, is it?"

"Nah, I just remembered that today is laundry day and I didn't put the clothes together for Allen."

"Oh, shit! I'm sorry, Sandra. I didn't even realize that today was the day he would come by."

Dorothy got to her feet to help organize the clothes. Sandra was surprised by the amount of energy her mother had. She was so used to coming in and finding her completely exhausted from the side effects of her medication that to see her mom in an upright position and moving at a normal pace caught her off guard.

11

"Wow, Mom, it looks like you're doing better than ever!"

Dorothy gave her outfit one quick spin and saw in her daughter's eyes that she approved of the new dress she was wearing.

"Well don't just sit there with your mouth open, little girl. Tell me if you like it."

"You look beautiful, Mom."

Sandra hugged her mother but instinctively held her breath. She didn't want to smell the oily sweat that usually seeped from her skin, but when Dorothy wouldn't let her go, Sandra had to exhale. Her nose caught a whiff of a sweet vanilla aroma.

"Oooh, Mom, you smell like a cake!"

Dorothy couldn't help but smile from ear to ear. She was feeling very good. She didn't know how long it had been since she was able to operate outside of a haze, but she knew it had been long enough. She was so angry at herself for what she had become but even more enraged that her daughter had to see her day in and day out that way.

*

She'd met Bill a few years ago but had never done much outside of sleep with him for a little cash every now and then if he had a load to dump in a neighboring town. But for the last few weeks or so, he had been coming by more regularly and spending almost the entire day at the house. He would drink his beers and maybe toot a line or two of coke, but he was always calm and, for the most part, a generally nice person to have around.

When he was at the house, he wouldn't let any other visitors drop by. He didn't like the crowd, and he always said, "What I do I do in private." Dorothy could appreciate that because the quiet was always better than having groups of people around doing God knows what in her house while she was out of it. Someone had stolen their television not too long ago, and when Sandra came home from school, she'd told her that it was being repaired. She had to admit even to herself that the people stopping by were getting worse and worse. Sometimes they would just flat out refuse to leave when Sandra came home from school. If Uncle Bill was the alternative, she was happy for it.

"Bill bought me a few gifts today, and guess what. You have a few of your very own in your closet, too!"

Sandra ran over to the couch and gave Uncle Bill a hug. "Thank you!"

For the first time since she came rushing through the door, the six-foot-four visitor spoke.

"You're welcome, princess. What kind of uncle would I be if I didn't buy my favorite little girl something?"

Dorothy beamed at him wishing for once that he didn't have a wife and daughters of his own so maybe he would be able to spend even more time with them. But she knew a woman in her condition and predicament didn't have a chance of competing for Bill or any other man, for that matter.

"You go ahead and look at all the great things Bill has bought you, and I'll finish putting the clothes together for Allen."

"Don't forget we have to pay today. It's Friday."

"Don't you worry about that, okay? Bill took me to cash your father's check, and everything has been taken care of. I bought all the cleaning goods and food for the month. I've been busy while you were playing after school, so just go, go, go."

Sandra didn't hesitate another second. She bolted to her room and closed the door. She couldn't wait to see what hung in her closet.

Dorothy started to get the clothes together as promised and didn't realize she was crying until her hand rubbed across the wetness on her face. She silently wondered how she had become the worst mother in the world and at the same time the proudest. To Dorothy, Sandra was a prized possession. What other child could be raised in such an unhealthy environment and still manage to be so pure and innocent, untouched by life's harsh realities? She knew Sandra's turnout was no thanks to her nurturing abilities. Her happiness had to come straight from God and maybe a little from the four years of closeness Sandra had with her father before the divorce, which was another thing Dorothy wanted to kick herself in the butt for.

Michael Hansley. Who could have asked for a more honest man? They'd met during their first year of high school and were envied by all. Who wouldn't be jealous? Dorothy was beautiful, and Michael was exceedingly handsome. Not that big in the intelligence department, she thought, but in the end, he was the one with enough sense to see that their marriage wasn't worth saving.

Dorothy had been secretly using drugs since their first year of marriage. They married very young, which made her believe they had more than enough time to play "the old married couple" roll. She felt they should still be able to party and hang out with the in-crowd, while on the other hand, Michael wanted a family in the real aspect of the word and wanted to take his father's machinery shop to the next level.

Time after time, when Michael would find out that Dorothy was using again after promising to quit, he would immediately send her to the nearest rehabilitation center. She hated going to those places and always promised to be good when she got out.

On her third visit there, she met a lady who really inspired her to try to make it work, and that was the longest she had ever stayed clean: nine months.

After that, it was three to four month intervals, and then back on the merry-go-round she would go. He had exhausted all of his avenues and had done the best he could. She didn't want the future he sought, and it took him six years to realize that before he gave up on her.

For quite some time she believed he had given up on her and their "miracle child" (his private nickname for Sandra, since she was born in the middle of one of Dorothy's many rehab stints) as well, until the furious custody battle began three months after they went their separate ways.

They were constantly in and out of court, which became nerve-racking to Dorothy, and because of the tension and stress she was undergoing, it only made her want to get high that much more. On the morning of their fifth hearing, Dorothy had made her mind up to stop the fight for Sandra and relinquish all of the custodial rights. She decided to be the parent who would get the visitation privileges and be happy with that.

She could longer keep her appearances up and pretend as if she had everything in order when it came down to Sandra. It was mental warfare. She would have to stick notes everywhere to remind herself that she could not get so out of it that she would miss a court date or a meeting with the attorney. She constantly borrowed court-appropriate out-fits from friends and neighbors, and it was just becoming overbearing. Dorothy didn't want the hassle anymore. Her mind was set, and she was ready to explain it all to her attorney and the judge that morning, but Michael had called in his change of heart first.

He left a note to be read by his representative specifi-cally stating that he was giving up all rights to his daughter and would pay the amount of child support deemed fair by the court.

For the next few days she called him on his job, at home, and even phoned his attorney a few times, trying to find out if the decision she heard in court was final or if Michael was somewhere regrouping in order to attack her from a differ-ent angle. She never heard back from him, and every line of communication was completely severed. His attorney no longer took her calls after a week, his job notified her that he was no longer employed there, and his home number had been changed. He cut them completely off from him, almost as if they were a cancer surgically removed from his life.

She had no idea that during one of their father-daughter meetings Sandra informed her father that Dorothy had been to the doctor and was told that she had a bad heart and had to be on constant medication. At first Michael chalked it up to the side effects of her frequent drug use and felt very little remorse for the course of life she had chosen when he had offered her so much more.

He wanted to provide for Sandra no matter how their relationship had turned out, but he couldn't find himself to be cruel enough to rip the child from her mother's arms when he knew she would need someone to be with her during her time of illness. He felt if she was now under the care of a cardiologist, then she would definitely have a more substantial reason to kick the street drugs.

He went with his decision, and felt pretty good about it. He had been seeing Dorothy several times over the last few months, and she looked clean and sober to him. A little weak, but now with the medical condition Sandra had just explained to him, he knew why. He left word for his attorney to set up the child care account, insuring that each check given was personally signed by Dorothy.

He wanted to be notified immediately when one of the payments was returned unopened or if someone else was cashing the checks. Only, with one of those indications, would he then move in on Dorothy's turf and check on his daughter.

He knew ending things in the manner that he did was not right for Sandra, but it was what he needed at the time. He did not want to be drawn back into the web that had been spun around him since he was in high school. He knew Dorothy had the power to have him believing whatever came from her mouth at a moment's notice. She had a certain aura that drew him, even in her drugged state. He had to get away from her and try to start fresh. His mind had become just as boggled as hers during their marriage.

He had met a beautiful woman who had two little boys the last time Dorothy had been admitted to rehab, and for the first time in his life, he saw another option, the light at the end of tunnel. He got a small glimpse of what his life could be like without all the drugs, without coming home to find syringes strewn all over the place and his wife so out of it that she couldn't tell him what day of the week it was if her life depended on it.

He fell in love with the new idea of a real family and a solid foundation. On his last visit with Sandra, he told her he would keep in touch, and he felt he kept his word. He called her on every birthday and holidays and kept the checks rolling.

In the last two years, his business had been going so well that he opened a new shop and increased the payments he was sending to Sandra. The checks always arrived on time and seemingly when they were needed most, but he never put a return address on the envelopes or included a phone number.

His new wife asked about Sandra a lot when they first got together, but when no child surfaced and the discussion was always one-sided, she dropped it altogether and rushed to tell her friends that she had found a father for her sons and that he had never been married and had no children.

It nagged Michael the first couple of times her heard her talk about his past life in that manner, but eventually he let it go and allowed her fantasy to become his reality.

Dorothy was a little shocked by his behavior and the way he chose to handle things, but she had to let it go. She couldn't keep wondering why or when he would come back to her. She had to move on, and she had no idea how to do that in a positive way. Every time a man smiled at her or gave her a compliment she tried to convince herself that she was getting over Michael through them. It didn't take her very long to see that she was being frequently used and discarded.

She never recovered from the fact that he would no longer be around to push her to get clean just one last time. Dorothy had to admit that she didn't volunteer to go to rehab at any time, but just the thought of being out here alone with no one truly caring whether she was an addict or not was a situation she found to be terrifying.

She realized quickly that she was alone in the choices she would make for her and Sandra's future, but she never in a million years thought she wouldn't be ready for parenthood and the life of being a single parent.

She allowed Michael and their life with him to drift slowly by and without giving thought to herself or Sandra, she decided to never step foot in another rehabilitation center again.

CHAPTER 6

*S*ince the day she took the vow to disown the twelve step programs, life had not been kind to her, but she never complained. She could look up at Sandra and see that God was giving her more than she probably deserved. Sometimes when she would come home from school, Dorothy couldn't bear to look into her angelic face. She had been lying to her for so long; it just seemed natural to call her drug of choice a "medication." How else could she get her daughter to understand that she was a drug addict who would sleep with—and practically had slept with—every man who came in and out of their home?

Brief stints passed where she believed she was in a relationship with a man, only to see him at the house two to three weeks later asking her to sleep with him and his friend. What child could understand that her own mother selfishly destroyed a family because of an ongoing addiction that mattered more to her than being a mother and a wife? Thinking of one miserable thought after another, Dorothy hurriedly put the clothes in the laundry bag just as the doorbell rang.

*

Allen had been picking up and delivering their laundry for the last two years, ever since he ran into Sandra at his Laundromat trying to do a load of clothes on her own. Naturally, she told him of the bad heart her mother was suffering from, and he readily offered to pick up their laundry and return it in a day or two for a small fee. It was Sandra's nature that made people want to jump in and help. Not many could avoid the clarity of her eyes or the sincerity of the words she spoke. Everything she said came straight from her little heart, and to know that every move she made was in effort to make her mother's life as uncomplicated as possible had them jumping in even faster to assist her in anything and everything she may need.

Allen was about to speak when he also noticed the change in Dorothy.

"Oh my God, you look wonderful Mrs. Hansley!"

She blushed. It had been a while since she felt this good. Why couldn't she just stay this way? How could she enjoy the time she was having but still feel the need to rush him out the door in order to get the drugs she knew Bill had waiting on her?

"Thank you, Allen. The clothes are all ready, and I want you to know that I appreciate everything you have done for me and Sandra."

He wanted to linger on in conversation, but Dorothy quickly paid him and began to have a bout of spasmodic coughs until he decided that he had better leave. He paid her an additional compliment and took a closer look at her appearance. It was covered well, but with determined attention he could see the jitteriness in her eyes, along with the twitching in the corners of her mouth. He knew he was looking at a made-up junkie, but he had to admit that despite her flaws, she did clean up well.

Dorothy wanted to push him out of the door using bodily force as it was becoming more and more difficult to stay calm and reserved at this time. Bill had been there since earlier in the day, and they had run errands and even gone shopping. He had her take a bath and clean herself up before they took off, so all of that time had to be accounted for. She was well overdue.

Bill didn't allow her to go out of the house with him if she was not presentable, and she couldn't be under the influence, walking zombie like while she was in his presence. Dorothy tolerated this from him because in many ways it reminded her of her ex-husband, and she liked the strictness of his demands. It seemed as if her cared for her, but if he did, it was never mentioned.

Her hands had begun to shake, and she could feel the tiny vibrations accumulating inside of her. Her little clean episode was beginning to take its toll as her endorphins continuously screamed to be released from the confines of her sobriety. They needed to be calmed and soothed in some way. Dorothy's palms were sweating and she craved a straight line to get her back on an even plane.

"Thank you again, Allen, for everything you have done for us. I have company now, so if you'll excuse me…"

"Oh, sure. No, I understand. I'll be on my way."

He turned with the laundry and headed out. Dorothy prematurely closed the door on him, clipping the heel of his shoe.

CHAPTER 2

*T*he things that went on in the house were no longer a secret to Sandra. She knew. She had turned eleven years old over the summer, and at the same time the blinders came off. Drugs and their effects were now being introduced in her health class, and the reality of what she was beginning to understand sickened her. All this time she had feared her mother would die in her sleep from some form of heart malfunction; was a lie.

Although she never confronted her mother on her findings, she paid more and more attention to the comings and goings of the house. If her mother was zoned out on the couch, she would lock the doors and pull the curtains. This usually deterred the other junkies from stopping by, but the stubborn ones knocked anyway, and Sandra would not answer. The control she felt over the house grew daily. She was in charge in so many ways and did everything she could to handle the pressure and hide what she felt was a degrading embarrassment: her own mother.

Dorothy had very little to do or say majority of the day, and Sandra had to look past that in order to go on to the next day. She would play little games with her psyche, fooling herself with the notions that her mother was sleeping or just not feeling well.

When she went to the room with men, Sandra now understood that was how she was paying for her drugs. She never took any money from the child support checks, and Sandra decided that as small of an action as it was, it had to account for something. She didn't use their only income for her own personal needs. So she wasn't really a drug addict, was she? The kids at school said drug addicts stole a lot and lied about everything. She could never say that Dorothy had stolen anything from her. They also said prostitutes walked the streets at night, begging men for money, so comparing again, Sandra wasn't able to put her mother in that category either. She did not walk the streets at night. She was at home all the time.

So with these comparisons out the way, she felt very secure in knowing that her mother was not completely the person they described in class or out on the playground, but she could not deny that there was something truly wrong with her mother. Dorothy was slowly withering away. A pound surely dropped from her frame on a daily basis. Her clavicle protruded boldly from her upper chest, and her spine was now a prominent feature in her back. Right before her eyes, she was wasting away, but Sandra refused to give up on her mother. Dorothy needed her to keep the house in order as much as she could while making things run as smoothly as possible; she would not bail out on her. No one needed to know what went on inside of their home, and if she had to smile and skip every day to prove her life was just as good as her friends', then that's what she would do.

Sandra found herself having to hand-feed her mother in bed when she would let two or three days slip by without eating. It was almost as if she was taking care of one of her baby dolls that had come to life. Dorothy would be so weak she could just barely get herself out of the tub, so Sandra would help her with everything she needed until she went to bed at night. She was so consumed with the upkeep of the house that in the mornings she fell asleep at the table while trying to finish her homework before school. Ultimately, she came to know and accept this as her life. It was the hand that God had dealt her. She could do nothing but succumb to her environment and adapt—quickly.

The older Sandra became, the worse things got for her. She never did approve of the company her mother kept. They would generally give her a bad feeling, but being a young girl surrounded by women and men strung out on drugs scared her even more than she cared to admit.

On the days when her mother was alert and able to entertain (if you could to call it that), it seemed as if her role switched from caretaker to servant, and her mother never once objected on her behalf.

"Get the door, Sandra."

"Get me a beer, Sandra."

"Clean the needles, Sandra."

"Change the linen on the bed, Sandra."

The list went on and on, and she became more involved with their lifestyle than she was comfortable with.

Sandra began to hide in her room when the house started to fill up, and when she heard people coming her way she would either get under her bed or hide in the closet.

Sandra was getting the sense that she was being used. Dorothy didn't stand up for her anymore, and it hurt her in ways she could not express. In the beginning, she would say, "No, Sandra is not an errand girl," and she would send her to her room before she would allow one of her guests to tell her to do something, but now the ballgame had changed, and Sandra didn't like the outcome.

Her role as the dominant of the two was changing drastically. Dorothy was introduced to marijuana by one of the new comers, which had been a blessing in the beginning because she began to eat more and pick up a little weight. But now her mother was getting so high from the mixture she was consuming that Sandra could no longer get her to bathe. The thought of her mother going at it alone terrified her; but the last time she had lost her grip, and the way

Dorothy began to flail around in the water, Sandra, thought she was surly close to drowning.

Sandra did everything a child could do in order to hide the catastrophe that swelled inside her home. She wouldn't let any friends come over for a visit, nor would she return outside after coming in from school. These were big no-nos for her because when she did go over a friend house after school, their parents would always ask her about her mother and how Sandra got by with no help. Who cooked her breakfast, lunch, etc.? The questions were getting to be too much for her to bear, and she began to feel embarrassed by the entire situation. Even though she wasn't old enough to voice her concerns in the right way, she knew what she was feeling was very painful on many levels.

She had no idea how to get out or even just get help, for that matter. She knew that if things were not going right she could always call the police and they would assist her, but didn't they also put people in jail? She knew drugs were illegal.

This was perplexing to her. She didn't quite know how to go about it, and she wasn't sure if she could reach out to them or not. She loved her mother and didn't want to see any harm come to her, but at the same time how much more could she take? The entire dilemma was causing her to have nightmares and dreams that she didn't quite understand.

Dorothy's entire personality was transforming, and she acted as if Sandra had become a bother overnight.

"Not right now."

"Go to your room."

"Can't you see I have company?"

She wanted out now more than anyone knew.

Sandra came home from school in a complex mood. Nothing seemed to be going right for her, and yet this was something she had to keep bottled inside. There was no outlet for her to express what had happened to her today or what she was going through emotionally. It was as if she was circling in a maze of confusion with no chance of getting out. A girl who she had believed was a good friend of hers decided today would be the day that she sided with the new girl by coming to tease and push her in the hall.

Sandra was so stunned by the turn of the events that she didn't how to handle the situation. She had never before experienced bullying of any nature. It was totally out of her scope of knowledge.

She asked her friend repeatedly what she had done to her or to the new girl, but there was never an answer given.

Mrs. Baker came and tried to diffuse the situation, but it was too late. The bond between them had been broken, and she still had no idea why.

Things were spiraling out of control in her life. Life had been much simpler when she was younger, when a lot of things were overlooked because of her lack of exposure. At this stage in her life, she knew more than anyone her age should.

Sex, drugs, and addiction were the things she knew well and feared at the same time. She wanted her mother to stop having strangers in and out of the house and get a job like everyone else's parents. But that was not going to happen. Why did life have to be so difficult for her? That was the new song that rang in her heart.

CHAPTER 8

*U*ncle Bill was sitting on the couch when she came in, so she spoke to him first. "Hi, Uncle Bill."

"Hello, honey. How was school?"

She didn't know how to answer, so she just kept walking to her room. He instantly noticed the difference in her attitude and that she wasn't her normal bubbly self, so he called her to his side.

"Come here, honey. What's the matter with Bill's little woman?" Sandra had never had the opportunity to confide in an adult about any of the things that went through her mind, and for him to even inquire was like a cloud opening up upon her. She rattled on and on about her day and the fact that she couldn't really talk to her mom because she was always out of it.

She felt the weight on her chest get that much lighter, and for the first time, she felt really free. She wondered if her classmates felt this way every day because their parents listened to their stories and sat them on their laps while they talked.

"Do you want Uncle Bill to go and talk to the girl's parents? There is no reason for her to have treated you the way she did. I mean, you didn't provoke her or anything, did you?"

"No. I was just walking down the hall."

"So do you know where she lives?"

"Yeah, but…"

"I know you don't want to get them in trouble, but what she did is wrong. I'll tell you what. Go to school tomorrow and see how she treats you, and if she is still acting in the same manner, then we will have no choice but to go and speak with her parents. Okay?"

"So you'll go with me if I have to go?"

"Sure. I'll be in town for the next couple of days, so we'll see what happens."

"Thank you, Uncle Bill!"

Sandra hopped off his lap and smiled all the way to her room. God was taking some of the pressure off of her, and she couldn't wait to get to her room, get on her knees, and thank the good lord for all that he had done.

The next day of school no longer frightened her. She was ready to face it head on.

Dear Lord, thank you for sending Uncle Bill into me and Mommy's life. I was really worried that you didn't hear me when I talked to you, but now I know that you do. I am sorry for being mad at Mommy when she has her friends over, but I am scared of them. I want to thank you again for Uncle Bill, and I'm not being ungrateful, but could you also help my day at school go a little smoother tomorrow? I don't want to go to my friend's house with her parents if I don't have to.

Also, God, please let Uncle Bill come more often. I feel happy and safe when he is here. Oh, and one more thing: please help my mother stop using drugs. Okay, that's all. Amen

The next day went surprisingly well for Sandra. She was called into the office by second period, and there she ran dab smack into Shelly and her mother. Mrs. Baker called her in to the school after their altercation yesterday, and Shelly readily apologized for what she had done. God was cooking with gas now, as far as Sandra was concerned.

She knew without a doubt that by the time she got home, her mom would be drug-free, and she would have a home environment just like her friends. There was no way God would just grant a few of her prayers when he was on such a roll. Nope, none all.

The rest of the day she practically floated on air. She breezed through her English test and was chosen to represent the class at the science fair the next month. To wrap it all up, for lunch they even served her favorite: hamburgers and fries! Life was fantastic!

She didn't stay after school to play with the other kids, even though Shelly told her she would buy her some cookies. Under normal circumstances, she would never turn down those famous cookies, but today wasn't ordinary by any means. She was on a mission. She was anxious to fly home and witness her mother cooking her famous pasta with white cheese sauce, totally drug-free. Well, she'd never asked God for the meal, so she wouldn't be too upset if she wasn't cooking. But just to see her as she was the day she had on that new dress would be good enough for her. She smelled good, and her eyes were bright, and she actually spoke to Allen when he came to pick up the clothes instead of hide from him.

Sandra swung the door open very slowly, and peeked her head into the living room. "Mom?" She didn't get an answer. She was unaware of how God granted miracles or answered prayers, so she didn't want to get in the way. Cautiously, she entered the house and noticed right off that she didn't smell anything cooking, but she didn't let that get her down because after all, she hadn't include it in her prayers.

Eyes closed, prepared to see the miracle firsthand, she encountered her mother's voice first.

"Why are you walking around like that? You want to be blind?"

She opened her eyes to find her mother sitting on the couch with Uncle Bill, obviously under the influence of some serious narcotics. Her eyes looked unfocused. She was leaning heavily on Bill, and he looked upset to have her to do so.

"How was school, baby?"

"Fine, Ma."

This conversation was over! She needed to go to her room and talk to God. This is not how her day was supposed to end. Her mom was should be drug-free, not drugged up!

Sandra began to believe she may be at fault in some way. It was impossible to think he would have gotten everything else right and left the most important thing out. There was just no way! Did she say it the wrong way to God? Was she mumbling? Did she not speak clearly? Somewhere along the way, their lines on communication had gotten crossed, and she needed to figure out where. Sandra headed to her room and kneeled at the foot of her bed. She had to try again before God moved on to someone else and she would never get her final prayer answered.

CHAPTER 9

*D*orothy had been borderline high for most of the day. She was just coming down a little when the guy from up the street left. He'd wanted oral sex in exchange for the little bit of drugs he had given her. Under normal circumstances, she would have done it without batting an eyelash, but with Bill in the house, it felt different.

He had a hollow look in his eyes for the better part of the day, and she knew it had everything to do with her. She had asked him several times over the last few years to leave his wife, but he had made no effort to do so. Then again, why would he? She had just walked out of the room after performing oral favors on a stranger, and this wasn't the first time he has witnessed such behavior from her.

Where in her right mind did she think that he would want anything more from her than the next man did? Dorothy began to feel sorry for herself all over again as she plopped down on the couch.

Bill didn't share her drug of choice and preferred cocaine over anything more hardcore. When he was in town, it was the only time he would toot a line or two. He had never attempted heroin and had no plans on graduating to that phase. He had to admit that he'd liked Dorothy when he first met her, but at this stage in the game, he thought about not stopping by her house at all when he came to town.

It was so depressing to walk into her dim and sparsely furnished house. If it weren't for the slipcovers that Sandra threw in the laundry bag every Friday, the entire couch would smell like sweat and sex.

There were a bunch of whores and drug addicts who would frequent the house. Sometimes they would just want to use her bedroom, and she allowed that as well, for a fee.

He needed a new venue, an entire new scene. He had met quite a few women on his travels who offered a variety of things he was interested in, but he found it hard to leave Sandra in such despair. He had grown very fond of the little blonde-haired princess, and he had no plans of deserting her. He wanted to be more than Uncle Bill, but a father figure was not exactly in the cards for him.

His wife had left him years before he had ever laid eyes on Dorothy and Sandra, but he still wore his wedding ring and used it as a ploy to keep too many questions from flowing his direction. He did have two daughters, that much was true, but he had no visitation rights, and he had no idea of their true location.

He had just been released from prison prior to becoming a truck driver. He used to be the corporate supervisor of a big marketing firm in Texas, but that came to a crashing halt when allegations of misconduct ripped the life he had known right from up under him.

Sandra was all he could think about when he had a delivery in Colorado. Sometimes he would take a detour in his routes just to check on her wellbeing. She was becoming more than enough reason for him to stop by. She depended on him. She trusted him. He began to believe that he needed her just as much as she needed him. It felt good to see her getting ready for school or see how excited she got when he was there when she came home. That felt good to him, and he wanted to explore their awkward relationship further.

*

Bill accepted the kiss Dorothy offered when she sat next to him, but he had grown more than a little tired of her. She wasn't a bad-looking woman when she cleaned herself up, but he just had no use for her anymore. Any way you could think of having a woman, he had accomplished that with Dorothy already. She was more than willing to degrade herself for a fix.

During one episode when he had tooted three lines consecutively, he brought two more men in the room with them. She asked him several times if this was what he wanted from her, but after he popped her with a straight line, he no longer had to convince her of what he was after.

*

"I got a line I want to do. Get me my mirror" She readily obliged to his request, knowing that he would get her high as well. Dorothy came back to the couch with what he wanted and then asked, "What about me?"

"I think you're getting a little too expensive for me. I can't afford to get you and me high all the time. You're going to have to use some of mine." This statement alone sent her into minor tremors. Bill had money to buy what she needed, and she didn't have time to play games with him. She needed a fix. Everyone had been coming by with pieces here and there, but it only took the edge off. She never felt the complete warming sensation that she sought.

"What do you mean, Bill?"

"You know exactly what I mean. Your habit is too high for my pocket. I'm going to liquefy this coke for you, and you will have to try to shoot that."

"It's not the same thing, Bill, and you know it. It's a totally different high. I never even shot up cocaine before. Can you even do that?"

"Well, you will today, otherwise you can go without. The choice is yours."

"Okay, okay. You don't have to talk to me like that, Bill."

He got up from the couch and went into the kitchen. Bill glanced over his shoulder to see what Dorothy was up to. She sat dumbfounded on the sofa, rubbing her arms in a rhythmic trance.

"Try to find a vein while I mix it up."

Dorothy jumped at this. She knew she had blown the majority of the veins in her arms out. She took a hit a few times in her hands but found it to be extremely painful and something she would rather not do again unless absolutely necessary.

If she let herself get too anxious while she searched, it could take up to thirty minutes for success, and she wasn't in the mood for that. She immediately pulled off her pants and panties, pulling the belt securely around her upper thigh so much that the buckle rubbed her pubic area.

She was so thin now that she could see veins for miles in this area. She marveled at the fact that she could even see them appearing in her hip area. She had gotten this idea from one of the many drug users who frequented her home.

Dorothy couldn't believe what she was seeing at first when Bill began to drop his pants in the kitchen while he held the needle she so desperately needed in his teeth. It was fascinating on a sick level, but his high was always instantaneous and appeared to have a lasting effect in his bloodstream.

Now Dorothy wasn't sure if this was a hundred percent true or if she had just imagined it, but she was more than willing to give it a try. To know she had a fresh area, with more than one shot at entry, made her relaxed and eager to enjoy the experience.

"I found one, Bill. Hurry up."

He took his time at the sink. He mixed such a small amount of coke in the solution he prepared that even her daughter couldn't get high off of it, and that's exactly what he wanted.

"Here it is. You're going to shoot it, or you want me to do it?"

There was no way she would trust the last high of the night to be given by a none-shooter. She didn't have the patience for amateur mistakes.

"Naw, I got it. Just let go of the belt when I tell you to."

Dorothy injected herself, and it went so smoothly she couldn't help but to release a sigh of release.

Bill sat next to her and did two more lines. He didn't want to get up looking wild, so he just took it slow and relaxed back into the cushions. His main focus was on Dorothy and her reaction to the hit she had just received, and it didn't take long for the complaints to start kicking in. "Bill, I don't feel anything! I mean it's like I'm sitting in church or something."

"Well, I let you shoot yourself, didn't I? Maybe you missed and got it into your tissues again."

"Don't you think I would have known if I'd wasted a shot? I didn't start this yesterday, you know."

"Oh well. I've got to hit the road. I have a load to pick up on the other side of town."

He got off the couch, redid his pants, retrieved his jacket from the back of the recliner, and headed for the door.

"Bill, seriously, you can't leave me like this! I feel like I have fire ants crawling all over me. I will literally be skinless the next time you see me if you don't help me out."

"I'm running late, Dorothy. I have to go."

"Bill, no!"

Dorothy put herself between him and the quick exit he sought. He would have to physically remove her in order to get out of the house.

"What is your problem? Don't cause a scene!"

"I need it, Bill. You know I do. Please don't make me beg."

Tears began to well up in her eyes, which blurred her vision. She knew she must be a sight to behold, standing naked from the waist down, in front of the door, with a belt trailing from around her ankles, but at the time she could care less. She needed the drug so bad at this point that she was willing to do anything.

She wanted to try to convince Bill to help her, but if all else failed, she would have to hit the streets! She could not go without it tonight. This was definitely not a good place in her life to be trying cold turkey, not at all.

"Calm down. You sound like a lunatic!" He turned away from the door, rubbing his fingers through his hair. He stared Dorothy in the eyes as he asked, "What are you going to do for me?" She couldn't believe her luck. He wanted sex? He could have said that a long time ago. They could have been done by now. Dorothy's respirations began to decrease as she relaxed a little.

As he continued to look at her, from his left breast pocket he pulled out its contents, and held five little pink packets in front of him. She knew exactly what it was. It was from the dealer around the corner.

Ever since he moved into the neighborhood, he always sold his stuff in the pink packets. He said that way his customers would know "The bunk from the skunk." And he was definitely right. His product was so strong you would literally be knocked off your ass from a sitting position. He sold his heroin for a little bit more than the regular vendors, so Dorothy had only been able to sample it twice before.

On introduction, he personally came to her house since it was considered the "hot spot" in the area, introduced himself, and demanded a blowjob for him and his partners. They declared they were the new guys on the block with the hottest bangers.

Dorothy was glad that there were two more women at her house when they came with their demands because there was no way she could have satisfied all eight of them and still been left in one piece.

They pounced on them as if they hadn't seen women in years. They snatched them by the hair, ramming them continuously past their gag reflexes, causing one of the women to vomit. The lady who threw up was slapped viciously across the face in return, and for payback, he grabbed two more guys and trained her until she collapsed from exhaustion.

The entire time, they didn't utter a kind word to them. It was "bitch this," and "slut that," but she endured long enough to get what she was after: the promise to freely sample the pink packet. To this day she would not admit it out loud if someone paid her to, but she wouldn't think twice about doing it all over again. She had never felt a high like that before. It hit her so fast and hard she didn't have time to take the needle out. The first push of the syringe warmed her all over instantaneously.

When she woke up some thirty-odd minutes later, she was still so high she couldn't walk. She felt cold and hot all at the same time, so she crawled to the bathroom and lay her face on the base of the toilet, which is where Sandra found her when she returned home from school. Dorothy was lucky that the needle wasn't still in her arm at the time.

Her body was sore from the uncomfortable position she nodded off in and from the sexual battle with her neighbors. They had given the other ladies one packet each, but they gave Dorothy two since it was her house and she promised to spread the word for them.

She'd only had the fortune of the pink packets two other times since then. For Bill to be standing there holding them in his hands took her breath away.

"What are you willing to do for these, Dorothy?" She wanted to feel that rush consume her body so badly she was ready to denounce God and claim atheism at the sight of them.

Greedily, she clung to his waist trying to un-buckle his pants, but Bill shoved her quickly to the floor. She knew he liked it rough at times, so she jumped into the role.

"Oh yeah, you know I like it like that! Give it to me, Bill. Give it to me!"

She wanted to waste no time in getting him off. Her only desire was to get to the packets he held in his hands.

Dorothy pulled off her shirt, baring her skin and her dignity for the taking.

"Get up. Let's get on the couch." That was a good idea. At least she wouldn't fall to the floor or be found in an awkward spot after she received her dose. Bill came to stand in front of her, and she hungrily nuzzled his crotch.

"Oh yes, yes, I'm so ready for you."

He looked down at her but never moved. She began pulling and tugging at his pants in hopes of exciting him, but her hands were pulled away, and Bill sat on the couch next to her.

"What's the matter?"

He didn't answer her at first but placed a hand on her knee and looked her straight in the eye.

"Let's get high first."

"I won't be any good for you, Bill, once I mainline. Let me make you happy first, baby."

He allowed her to fondle him through his clothes, but then he eased back and returned to the kitchen.

"Let me get it together."

Dorothy no longer argued the point with him. If he wanted to sleep with a zombie, then so be it. As long as she got what she was after, he could play with her until the cows came home. She would never know it.

Bill returned to the couch with the needle ready for her. She quickly darted to retrieve the belt form the floor, and re-tie her thigh.

"Are you ready, baby?"

"Yes," she huskily replied.

"How bad do you want it? Tell me. What will you do for it?" Dorothy was ready to say, "Anything!" when she felt the tip of the syringe prick her skin. He was teasing her, and it was driving her wild. If she didn't know any better, she would think she was close to reaching a once-in-a-lifetime orgasm. Dorothy clutched Bill's manhood and squirmed under his touch.

"You want to go to the room?"

"Yes, I do, but not with you, sweetheart." Bill roughly pushed her hands away from him and stood up. "You're old news, sunshine. I'm looking for something new."

"New? What are you talking about? Did you bring someone with you?"

He had been there for the majority of the day. If he had brought someone with him, they would have come in the house by now. What did he mean by "new"? Did he want to bring another woman over? A pang of jealously ran through her briefly, but she let it go as her eyes focused on the dark brown solution in the syringe. At this point she couldn't bring herself to deny him what he wanted. If he felt that bringing another woman would give him the satisfaction he desired, then that's what she would do.

"No, I didn't bring anybody. What and who I want is right here."

"What are you talking about?"

Even as she asked the question, she could feel the bile rise in the back of her throat. Why hadn't she seen this coming? Sandra was blossoming into a strikingly beautiful girl, but never in her wildest dreams did she think Bill would be the one to look at her in such a way. He had daughters of his own, for heaven's sake! How could he even think…?

"Are you out of your mind? Are you crazy?" Bill zipped up his pants and headed for the door.

"Where are you going?"

"To get me something to eat. You have my cell phone number. Call me when you change your mind. I need to be on the road in the next twelve or thirteen hours."

"Don't you ever come back here, you sick motherfucker! Never!" Dorothy leaned forward to spit in his face and was quickly smacked to the floor.

"A whore will never spit on me!"

His change in behavior frightened her. He told Dorothy that he enjoyed her company at times and the sex as well, for that matter. She thought he wanted to be a father figure to Sandra. She had no idea where it went all wrong, but him coming to the house again was not something she would allow.

Dorothy felt so stupid and so humiliated. How could she not have seen the signs? What in the world was wrong with her? For the first time in a long time, she wanted to call her ex-husband. She was not capable of keeping Sandra safe any longer. Her mind just didn't operate the way a caring mother's should. Who would have missed those signs in a sober state?

The front door slammed, and Dorothy balled up in a fetal position and cried. The nausea she felt drained her energy, and she thought she would never be able to get up from the floor.

Minutes later, through the layers of tears; her eyesight zoned in on the sofa and the exact location of where their altercation first began. She wanted to get high so bad and forget the last ten minutes of her life that she crawled to the couch in search of the syringe Bill had loaded for her. Did he drop it during their altercation? She prayed for that to be the case. Dorothy removed the pillows and ran her hands over the sofa cushions. She came up empty and quickly moved to the floor. Nothing!

She was so frustrated and angry by the turnout that she just screamed. A pure, raw, guttural release escaped her to the point that her chest burned from the force of it. She knew without a doubt the bastard had taken it with him. He knew what state he was leaving her in. She sat by the couch and watched the front door, hoping that the Bill she had known, or at least thought she had known, for the last few years would return to give her what she so desperately needed. But as time ticked painfully by, he did not come back.

➤ ——ᴜᴜᴜ—— ✦

CHAPTER 10

*D*orothy was near hysteria as the evening slowly progressed to the night. Bill had not returned, and no one had stopped by with even the scarcest trace of a drug. She decided she would hit the streets and find what she was looking for. It wouldn't be that difficult. She had slept with men for far less, and her dignity was way beyond repair.

She went to her room in search of some form of attire to prepare herself for the outdoors and stopped by the phone on the wall in the kitchen. She wanted Michael to come and get Sandra whether she was able to get a fix tonight or not. Her safety was in danger, and her mind was clear enough now to do something about it. In the bottom of one of her dresser drawers, she pulled out all the information she had on Michael, which she had held onto over the years. She knew some of the numbers may not coincide, but she decided to give it a shot anyway. Anything would beat a failure to try on her behalf.

The first call ended with him no longer being employed there, but she imagined from the sheer desperation in her voice, the reason they gave her a list of the numbers they had on file for him. The second and third calls were to disconnected numbers, but the fourth one was the jackpot.

"Hello. May I speak to Michael?"

"Who is calling, please?"

"My name is Dorothy. I'm his daughter's mother, and I really need to talk to him. It's a matter of urgency."

"Michael doesn't have a daughter."

This statement set her back a little, and she thought maybe she had reached the wrong Michael entirely, until she heard his voice in the background. He was asking the lady who was on the phone, and before she could get another word in, she heard her say that the caller had the wrong number.

"No! No! No! Hello? I need to speak with him! Hello?"

She was met fiercely by a dial tone ringing in her ear. She called back approximately ten times in a row, but the phone only rang once before going straight to voicemail, and it was his voice.

Dorothy left one message after the other, but she knew what she was doing was useless. The other lady was not going to tell him who was on the phone, and she definitely wasn't going to let him call her back. Without a doubt, it had to be his wife, but why would she think he didn't have a daughter? Is this what Michael went into the marriage telling her? Did he deny Sandra to everyone except the child support agency?

The phone call enraged her to the point where if he had been standing in front of her at that moment, she would have gouged his eyes out! She decided there wasn't anything she could do about the turn of events at the time, but she would definitely be giving Mr. Hansley another call tomorrow.

CHAPTER 11

Dorothy could do no more than drag herself back into the house. It had begun to rain as soon as she left, but she braved the storm without question or complaint. Up and down the streets she went in search of someone, anyone, willing to pay her for what she was offering, but she found no takers. It was the most exhausting, mind-consuming journey she had ever taken. Her conscious wouldn't rest. The thoughts of Bill and those pink packets he possessed ran rapidly and uncontrollably. She knew if she was to call him, he would have them. He didn't use heroin at all, and just the mere idea that it still lingered in his possession, unused, disturbed her psyche.

She could tell that Sandra had woken up during the time she was out of the house because the remainder of her sandwich was on the counter, and she had run water in her glass of milk to keep the remainder from sticking to the bottom.

This sight alone caused her to well up all over again. How could she even consider doing that to her? Why did she let the drug consume her to the point of no control? She wanted so badly to be able to walk away from the whole thing and just start all over again, but the ache was too deep. The drug called her continuously, over and over again. It was as if a magnetic force was pulling her to the brink of destruction. There was no breaking free for her, no form of escape. Once again, she placed the blame squarely on her, and her ex-husband's, shoulders.

The sight of the needles on the kitchen counter was just another reminder she had to come to terms with. It was just unbearable. She didn't know when or how she ended up with a knife in her hands, but the moment was there, and she was ready to take it to completion.

Her hands shook profusely as she tried to steady them. Tonight was the night she would end her life, and she knew her daughter would be better off for it. Someone more qualified would come along who would do a far better job than her. At this point it was the only choice she had. There was no other option.

She slid to the floor and wept as she tried to find the vein across her wrist. She didn't want to miss. She didn't think she would have the nerve to try it again. She prayed for the safety of her daughter as she placed the knife along the edge. "'Please forgive me, God. I am not strong enough for this world." Dorothy pricked her skin with the smooth edge of the blade, and she felt the warmth of her blood run over her hand and drip to her thigh. For a moment she seemed mesmerized by the sight.

It held her in a trance as she watched the path that her blood flowed. It hit the upper part of her thigh and then curved sharply to the right and ran over her inner thighs, where it began to puddle on the floor. It was almost magical to see. The brightness of it reminded her of her favorite dress, so she touched it...then tasted it. It was warm and salty.

Dorothy found herself licking her arm and enjoying the sensation that it brought her. It was almost like seeing her blood being drawn up in the needle, just before she hit the plunger, but brighter somehow.

She had no idea of the time that lapsed as she continued to sit in the corner. The blood on the floor was now dry, right along with the blood on her lips. Her entire mental focus had changed, and she was now fully concentrated on Bill and the pink packets again.

Dorothy had a plan. She would overpower him when he came. She would hit him over the head and take what she needed. She knew he would be angry to the point of no control, but she couldn't worry about that right now. She had to get what she needed, by any means necessary. The desire to get high had taken full control of her. She was no longer Dorothy the mother of a beautiful daughter or Dorothy the cheerleader. She was strictly Dorothy the drug addict who was ready to take the chance of a lifetime to get her dope.

As she dragged herself to the phone, she asked God to please forgive her for the phone call she was about to make.

CHAPTER 12

*D*orothy sat on the couch and awaited Bill's arrival. She had removed the baseball bat from behind the couch and had it resting against the wall. She was more than ready for him—at least that's what the addict inside of her said. "I'm going to knock his ass out and take his shit! And if he has some money, I'm taking that, too! Who the fuck does he think he's messing with? I'm going to show his ass!" She couldn't wait for him to get there. He seemed to take forever, even though it was less than thirty minutes before he came through the door.

He walked with an air of cockiness, and Dorothy wanted nothing more than to knock that cheesy grin off his face.

"I see you changed your mind."

"Yeah well, I see you're still the same sick motherfucker that left here."

"Look, Dorothy, you called me back, okay? I didn't come looking for you. I put my offer on the table, and it was a take-it-or-leave-it situation. It's not that I don't care about what you think or how Sandra is going to feel because I do. I just want her to know that you guys can always come to me for anything. It's like making what we have…permanent. Do you think I would go in that room and hurt her? I love her. I love you."

Bill leaned in and kissed her on the cheek. His look had totally changed from the time he walked in the door to now. At first he had told himself that he would walk in, demand what he wanted, and make sure nothing stood in his way, but that brought an immediate problem. Dorothy still wanted to protect Sandra. So he had to take the alternative approach.

He had waited down the street from Dorothy's house ever since he left. Sandra was all he could think about. The thought of touching her smooth skin in the most secretive of places brought him an arousal so strong he was almost embarrassed by it. He knew that little girls needed their fathers in their lives for far more than just financial reasons. They wanted to be loved completely and utterly by them. This is the exact thing he had done for his daughters until the oldest one began to listen to the outside world instead of what her own father was teaching her.

The day he went to her room and she said "no", he should have caught heed that something between them was changing, but the hunger for her flesh overruled his common sense. She was his creation. If it were not for him, she would never be. He wouldn't come right out and say that he owned her, but in many ways he felt that God had placed his daughters in his life to fulfill the desires that his wife couldn't.

After his oldest daughter began to change, he moved on to the youngest one, but he never quite had a chance to mold her into the submissive being she was supposed to be like he had with the oldest one.

One day when he came home from work, he noticed two police cars in his driveway and immediately thought something was wrong with one of his girls. He slammed his car into park and fled from the vehicle. His new Armani suit caught in the door and ripped as he slammed it shut, but he did not notice. Two neighbors were standing in their front lawns and asked him what was going on, but he had no answers.

He bolted up the front steps and practically kicked the door down. When his eyes and mind finally adjusted to the scene, he wished he had never come home but instead had vanished into thin air, hopped on the nearest plane, and started over.

The police were standing guard as soon as he entered the foyer. One officer flanked each side of the entryway, giving him no chance of escaping. There was another officer farther inside the house, and he could see right away that things weren't good for him. The one obviously in charge was a female officer, and she held his youngest daughter on her hip, while the oldest daughter sat on the couch next to her mother with her head on her shoulder. Neither of the children would look at him, and he knew without a doubt that whatever was about to take place was the fault of his oldest daughter and outside influences.

He couldn't believe the harsh sentence of thirteen years that was unjustly given him. He was at the prime of his life. He was grossing six figures easily, and his home was worth more than half a million dollars! He was living the dream! He'd worked hard in college and was proud of the outcome. His dad Jerry stayed on his back the entire time he was enrolled, and it worked out well for him. He was diligent in his studies and aimed for the top. This was not the way his story was supposed to end.

He made several attempts at contacting his wife and his girls when he was released, but the letters were always returned unopened. The only reply he received came from their attorney, stating that further charges would be filed if he tried to contact them again.

The fact that they continued to live in his house punished him daily in his sleep. She was a housewife, for heaven's sake! Granted, she was beautiful, but her good genes were the only reason he married her. He knew his kids would be gorgeous and brilliant, all wrapped up in one package. The remainder of his trust fund was released to them, and his father paid the monthly mortgage installments. He had learned everything from Jerry, how to run a company, how to advance in one's career, and everything else under the sun, but a lesson he should have paid closer attention to was how to make your daughters keep quiet!

Ever since he was six he knew what his father was doing to his sisters. It wasn't until he was eleven that his dad made him stand in the room and watch. His sisters didn't look fearful to him, but they did move in a robotic kind of way. His dad had total control over them and the situation at hand, and this intrigued him. They never said, "Stop," or "Please don't," so in his mind, they must have enjoyed it.

When Jerry had a stroke, Bill was seventeen and a senior in high school. One sister was a freshman and the other a sophomore. They seemed relieved and even made fun of him behind his back until Bill decided he wouldn't stand for it any longer. He began to tell his dad what they were saying about him, and his father told him it was his job to put them in their place, so that's just what he did.

The next time he heard them snickering, he burst into the room and slapped each one until their faces were as red as Christmas lights. They called for their mother repeatedly, but he knew she would not come. She had been passed out on the couch since he came home from school. She was useless, and they knew that as well. The men were the strong ones in the family, and he would make sure they didn't forget it.

When he would come home from school mad or frustrated about anything, he would instantly seek out his sisters and make them pay for whomever or whatever had ticked him off. Bill was stronger than the two of them put together, and being captain of the wrestling team had many advantages.

He used his older sister for oral sex only because his father had already been with her for many years, and for some reason it bothered him to be second.

The younger of the two is who he honed his skills on. He tried everything and every position he had ever heard of in the boys' locker room, and most times he would have both sisters together. His last year in high school was the most memorable and enjoyable to him, and when he went away to college, he never forgot his sisters.

He met his wife while she was still a sophomore in high school and he was a junior in college. He had been dating younger girls all his life, and he enjoyed being the first to ever touch them in intimate places, although he must admit he did run across a few who claimed to be virgins but were able to show him a trick or two in the backseat of his car.

The wife he chose was strikingly beautiful but totally empty-headed. He knew when he met her that he had found just the person he was looking for to have his children.

The first thing he did was take her to the doctor for confirmation that she was indeed a virgin. Bill dropped her off, and waited in the parking lot. He had been fooled in the past, but this was too important to overlook even the smallest of details. The day he found that out she was pure, he took her to a fancy hotel and wooed her with an expensive meal and plenty of champagne. She had told her mother that she was spending the weekend at a friend's house, and so he used the entire weekend to mold her. She was deeply in love with him by Sunday afternoon, and he dropped her off Sunday night.

He married her when she graduated high school and immediately removed her from her mother's clingy influence. He blamed the sudden relocation on his job and stated that he would be making more money in a bigger city and they would be able to live a celebrity kind of life. She fell for his pitch, hook, line, and sinker.

He had to prove his intentions, and he spent hundreds of dollars on her weekly and spoiled her with "just because" jewelry. Six months after her graduation, she reluctantly let go of her mother's apron straps and followed her husband where he led.

It took him quite some time to completely rid himself of the in-laws. Her mother, in fact, chose to fly down and see them every month, and she stayed for days on end. When he would get off work and see her on his sofa, his stomach would flip and gnaw at itself internally from the very sight of her.

Two years later, his lazy, hen-pecked father-in-law was diagnosed with prostate cancer, which seemed heaven-sent for him. For a while he didn't know if he could take the lady much longer and thought of more than one way in which to dispose of her body.

With her it was always, "Bill, honey, could you please get me some water? Bill, could I have an extra blanket? It's a little chilly in here. Bill, honey…" Anyone on the outside looking in would have thought he was married to the mother instead of her daughter. He came very close to just walking away from his wife, her mother, and the whole scenario altogether, until his father-in-law's ill fate became the family's focal point. The visits went from once a month to twice a year. On the holidays he would fly his wife down to see her parents, but he would always be too busy or off on some business trip of his own to accompany her.

His wife never paid attention to his attitude or demeanor when he was around her parents, and for that exact reason: she was his wife. She had two unlimited credit cards and a Mercedes that she upgraded every three years, so she was blinded by it all. She was into her women's club, shopping and dining out with the girls, and he let her have every avenue she desired, for he was a very busy man with many locations to frequent as well.

There was one holiday in which he did go with his wife for Christmas, but he opted to stay in his own hotel instead of at his in-laws' home. He told his wife that he had taken the trip just for her but he needed peace and quiet to catch up on all his work that he had brought with him, so dutifully she left and went to her parents' home.

He was on a mission that holiday season. He had heard from his father that his youngest sister was going to be married, but she was trying to do so without either of them finding out. Bill could care less about her or the wimp she was going to marry, but his father was enraged. He wanted Bill to find the ceremony location, cause holy hell, and disgrace her in the process. Bill had planned on bursting into the church and shouting explicit and vulgar slurs until a new idea entered his head as he headed to the church on Sibley Boulevard.

*

"Sarah, Sarah, Sarah." Hearing her brother's voice froze her in place. She thought he had moved to another state, found a wife, and forgotten about his two sisters, whom he left tormented by their past. Why was he here? She didn't have the strength to face him, so she stared at his reflection through the mirror.

"To think you were going off to get married, yet we never received an invitation. How very, very rude of you. Did you not want me and Father to attend? Or did the invite get lost in the mail?"

Bill was only inches from her, and he watched the small wisps of her hair move with his every breath. She was shaking all over, and it almost looked as if she was having an out of body experience.

She had made no move to even acknowledge his presence. She stood virtually still in her white lace wedding gown, trembling. The fact that she had on white made him smirk. White was for virgins, and his sister definitely was far from that. He ran his hands down the length of her and couldn't believe the electricity he felt. He molded himself against her so she could get his meaning without saying a word.

"Please, Bill."

He pressed her against the dressing table and continued to grind methodically against her. "He will never be this hot for you, Sarah. You make me want to explode every minute."

"Bill, please...no." He ignored Sarah until the frenzy building in him begged to be unleashed.

He grabbed her breasts and savored the roughness of the material beneath his fingers. He locked eyes with her in the mirror, which only intensified the feelings that boiled deep inside of him.

"This is the last time we will be together. Once your husband finds out just how good you are…" His last words caught in his throat as he licked and sucked her neck, taking in her scent.

He couldn't hold out much longer, and wasting himself in his pants was not an option. He had been with Sarah so many times, but never did he feel the urgency that commanded him at this moment. The fact that it was her wedding day and he was soiling her before the husband could get the chance brought him to the brink of blindness.

The many, many layers of her dress frustrated him. He wanted to take her from behind while he watched her face in the mirror, but the material wouldn't cooperate.

"Get on your knees."

"No."

"Now!"

Roughly he spun her around to face him and bit down hard on her lip. Sarah's tears wet his face, and he loved the taste of them. He had no idea why this moment with her was so intense, but he didn't want it to end. Never before had he felt anything like this. Even when he took his sisters together, the heat had never before matched what he was feeling at the moment.

"Get on the floor."

"Bill, please. I—"

"Do it, Sarah. Do it right now!"

He watched his reflection and was charged to the point of no control. The back of Sarah's head could be seen in the corner of the mirror, moving rhythmically up and down with him. He could no longer hold out. Bill removed the crystal clip from the back of her head, watching the blond strands cascade down her shoulders. He let out a small roar as he smeared her face with his remnants, before roughly zipping his pants back up. He felt as if he had just been on the fastest ride in the amusement park, and never before until that day, did he wish it wasn't illegal to marry your sister.

"By the way, congratulations!" Bill tossed a two thousand dollar check at her and made his way toward the door. "The money is for services rendered, darling." With that, Bill left. He hadn't seen either one of his sisters since then, but he dreamed the same dream often.

*

"I'm just going to talk to her. I won't scare Sandra. You have to believe that."

"But why can't I do what you want, Bill? She's just a little girl, my little girl"

This conversation was getting him nowhere, and he was becoming angry and anxious all at the same time. He pulled the packets out his pocket and sat them on the coffee table. Dorothy eyes followed them, and he knew it was only a matter of time before he would succeed in his approach. "Forget I said anything, okay? Let's just get high." She wanted to trust him, but the mama bear inside was screaming at her not to let her guard down.

"Are you sure, Bill? Because I can't let you—"

"I said forget it, didn't I? I just wanted to make sure you would protect our little girl, even from me. You know? Don't let this drug consume you to the point where you forget that you're a mother first."

"I would never do that."

The relief she felt from not having to attack him or worry about him going after Sandra was almost all the high she needed. She had truly overreacted to the entire situation. He was looking out for her daughter's best interest, and she had turned it into something far more sinister than it should have been.

Dorothy had been so consumed with getting her next fix that it had never occurred to her that this was some form of test he was bringing to her attention, but now that he had brought it to light, she would have to watch out for the company she let just roam through the house. She was going to have to do more to keep Sandra protected.

"Get the belt. I'll help you." Bill removed the syringe he had filled earlier for her and then removed the safety cap.

"Where is yours?"

"Let's get you feeling better first. It takes the longest. I have mine on me too. Lay back."

Dorothy removed her clothes and lay back on the couch. Bill tied the belt around her arm, in search of a vein.

"Tie it on my upper thigh, my arms are gone."

He did as instructed, and Dorothy pointed to the area. He stuck her several times before he had success.

When he found the flash of blood she told him he would see, he plunged half of the contents inside of her. Dorothy removed the belt and reached for Bill. He began to caress her breasts and kissed her on the mouth.

"Make love to me, Bill."

Make love to her? The thought was sickening. His manhood didn't so much as stir in his pants, but for the moment, he played the role. He climbed on top of her, fully clothed, and pretended to enjoy the session. Within minutes, Dorothy was nodding off, stuck in her high.

Bill waited a few minutes and then got up. He went in the bathroom and brushed his teeth with Sandra's toothbrush. Giving Dorothy one more look, he headed into her daughter's room.

She couldn't get up from where she lay, but her eyes had become focused on Bill. She saw him head to the bathroom, but when she opened her eyes again, he was gone. Dorothy had no idea if he'd left or was still in the bathroom. Time had been stolen from her, and it was time that she would never get back.

CHAPTER 13

S andra was sleeping soundly in her bed, and Bill allowed himself the pleasure of taking in the smell of the room. The baby powder she used fragranced the air, but he could still catch hints of baby shampoo and other girly things swirling around him. The sight of her lying there so innocently reminded him of the first time with his daughter Bianca. It was very intense and erotic. He couldn't wait to recapture that moment. He knew Sandra would be frightened, but he would be able to calm her. He knew many, many practiced techniques to quell her fears.

Stealthily, he removed his clothing and slipped into the bed beside her. She stirred a little, but he didn't think she noticed the intrusion. Her little body seemed so tender and soft. He wanted to just devour her until he could feel her heart beating inside of him, but he knew he had to be patient. He had to establish a bond with her, and that took time. She was beyond beautiful, and so very innocent.

Sandra felt Bill climb onto her mattress, but she didn't know why he was there or what he wanted. He had never entered her room before, and she felt equally violated and confused. This was her Uncle Bill, and she loved him very much, but at the same time, she knew he did not belong in the bed with her.

Bill rubbed her thigh, and he knew when she jerked from his touch that she was awake. The next move was very important, and he would have to be very careful. He didn't want her to get up and run, although he would chase her if she chose to do so. Under no circumstances would he reconsider what he was about to do. He had watched Sandra long enough to know that he could not just walk away. Physically he ached for the touch of her, and he would not deny himself. The thought of another decade-long prison term deterred him slightly, but he convinced himself that Dorothy was a drug addict who he could easily control. If Sandra didn't put up too much of a fight, he would win all the way around.

"Sandra? Sandra, are you awake?" She didn't answer him, but he knew she could hear him. He allowed his hand to venture further up her thigh, and she stiffened. The ruffle of her panties almost rushed him, but he reined his emotions in. Without looking under the cover, he knew their color. He had purchased them for her.

"You smell like an angel. Did you know that? Angels are priceless and beautiful just like you."

Still no response from her, so he continued on. Bill reached in front of her and began to caress the small buds of her adolescence.

Sandra was humiliated by the touch. He told her to call him uncle, but he was fondling her like he did her mother. She didn't want this. She didn't want to be anywhere near him. She had no idea what her next step should be, but she knew she wanted him to stop.

"Mom! Mom!"

Her screams startled him. He had his eyes closed with his head embedded in the scent of her hair. It took him seconds to realize she was calling for help, but he was quick to react. Bill placed his hand over her mouth, but he didn't apply much pressure.

"Shhh. Please, Sandra. I'm not going to hurt you. Okay? Now I'm going to uncover your mouth, but don't scream again.

"Mom! Mom!"

Bill jumped into action, planting himself on top of her. Sandra began kicking at him and trying to claw his face. He grabbed her wrists and forced them to her sides. The weight of him alone crushed most of the air from her lungs, and she feared he would suffocate her. She tried to roll from underneath him, but she was totally immobilized.

"Sandra, Sandra, listen to me. Please. Calm down. I'm not going to hurt you. I'm not trying to frighten you, and if you relax a little, we can talk, okay?"

Bill's eyes blazed into her, and she no longer saw the man she had called uncle. He looked like a killer in one of the scary movies she'd seen on television. Panic was slowly engulfing her, and she tried desperately to gather enough breath for a scream, but only shallow bursts of air came out.

Please oh please, God, where are you? I need you! Why is he doing this to me? What does he want from me? Tell him to go away. Make him go away, please. I've been good. I really have. I'm scared of him. He's like a monster! Take him away. Please oh please. Where are you, God?

Sandra closed her eyes and continued to try to communicate with God. She thought of nothing else but getting through to him. He had been on her side and helped her with most of the challenges she had met in life, but she had no idea if he could just respond in an instant. She never had to call on him in a demanding situation, but she gave it her best shot. He had to know she was terrified, and that alone should have him moving at warp speed to rescue her, or so she prayed.

She stopped moving under him, and he took that as a sign that she was willing to talk or at least hear him out, so he began to explain.

"I know you are wondering what is going on right now, and I'm trying to tell you the best way I know how. I love you in a way that I have never loved anyone else. Do you understand that?"

He waited for her to respond in some sort of way, but her eyes had lost their luster, and she seemed to be mumbling to herself.

"I want to show you just how much you mean to me, and this is what men do to show people their love. I'm going to be so gentle with you. I will never hurt you. I'm going to bring a new form of love to you, Sandra."

Bill leaned down and kissed her lips. He could feel the instant quiver flowing through them. Delicately her licked the top one and was lost immediately in the tenderness of it. Bill proceeded at a much faster pace than he had originally anticipated. The animalistic need grew so powerful that he felt like he wanted to peel away her flesh. But he knew it took a real man to be able to control himself the way he did.

Sandra had decided not to talk; she just lay there and continued to chant, which was fine with him. She was not a willing participant at this time, but he knew how to get her to be more interactive in the long run.

God, please send my mother in after me. She doesn't know what's going on in my room. There is no way she would allow this to happen to me. If you can't come yourself, then please send my mother. Please, God. Time is not on my side right now. I need you. I need you. Please help me!

Her anxiety level had begun to rise again, and Bill knew the fight would be a little longer, and a little stronger than the last, so he decided not to try to woo her with words. That step would be skipped for now. None too gently, he opened her legs with the force of his knees and pushed his weight down. His muscles were wound taunt as cable cords as he prepared for her to resist.

She was his prize, and the time was now. It would hurt, he knew, but he would make it up to her in the long run.

In less than thirteen minutes, with multiple attempts, he entered a place that is usually saved for a first love. A warmth of satisfaction and fascination engulfed him. Sandra bit his face when he entered her, and she nearly removed a portion of his cheek. Her teeth actually met through his flesh. Their screams moved furiously in the air, and slammed together.

God! God! God! Where are you? Why didn't you come for me? Why did you let this happen?!

Bill continued to silence her with his mouth. He constantly shoved his tongue deeply into the back of her throat, where her screams were gagged and swallowed. Sandra had turned stiff as a board beneath him, but the tears she shed flowed in streaming paths down her face. He released himself inside of her, knowing Sandra was not fully a woman yet. When she would begin her cycle, he would wear a condom like he did with Bianca. Getting a young girl pregnant was definitely not something he wanted to face again.

Sandra was burning all over. She couldn't believe the pain that throbbed and stung between her legs. Her arms were shaking, and she had no idea what if anything to do next. Bill was talking to her again, but she had shut him out. What had just happened still seemed like a mystery to her. She could comprehend the gist of the situation, but to know this level of betrayal was at the hands of someone she looked up to and trusted hurt worse than the pain between her legs.

The realization that her mother hadn't answered her screams terrified her, and for a minute she believed that Bill may have killed her in order to achieve access to the room. She would have to live through this moment and whatever else Bill had in store for her because checking on her mother became her number one priority. She didn't want to let on to him that she had a plan or that she was focusing on anything other than the humiliations he continued to put her through, so she just lay there and listened to him.

"I know that you're in pain, and I'm not going to leave you like this, okay? I'll be right back."

Bill got up from the bed and headed for the bathroom. Sandra contemplated running out the door behind him but dismissed the idea rather quickly. Not only did it feel as though she would have to live the rest of her life lying with her legs apart for air, she was afraid he would return before she had the chance to escape. Bill stepped back into the room, and she quickly looked away.

"Okay, now, this is a little warm, but it'll take the sting out."

He delicately applied the warm washcloth, being as gentle as possible. Sandra still had yet to speak a word to him, and he was desperate to hear her voice after what they had just experienced together. "Is that better?"

Sandra nodded her head, and a flush of relief filled him.

She wanted him to think that she was coming around to accepting her fate, but she was far from that. She wanted to check on her mother, and she would pretend to be a docile squirrel if that's what it took.

"How do you feel, Sandra?"

How on earth did he expect her to answer such a question? Her vocabulary did not extend to the level of words she would need to conjure up something to say to him. He didn't know of the things that roamed freely in her mind, but she wished desperately that she could voice them. She was alone in this world from this moment on, and she knew that. She would be the one to run the house and take care of her mother. There was no longer a God, as far as she was concerned. She had no plans on consistently praying to someone who never appeared when you needed them. God had allowed her to foolishly thank him for sending Bill into their lives, knowing full well what kind of person he was inside. Why would a kind God do such a thing? The truth as she now knew it was that he was not so kind and loving after all. People wanted to believe there was someone or something out their protecting them and looking out for them, but in reality, they were on their own. She wanted to go to school and make the biggest poster in the world and let everyone know they had been made fools of. There was no God!

At the time, she was clueless about what she could do to make him stop, but she knew that it was left up to her to do so.

She briefly thought of her friends in school and wondered if they would be able to see in her eyes what had just happened to her. She hoped not. She would attend class and talk to the teachers just as she had before. Her pain would not be appearing on her sleeve like a runny nose kid. She was stronger than that. Her time to handle the situation in her own way was not in the immediate future, but she knew Bill would not win in the end. Sandra vowed not to let that be the case.

The monster beside her began to speak again, and she felt nauseated from the sound of his voice.

"Sandra, I want you to take a nice warm bath, okay? I ran the water for you and put some pajamas in the bathroom. When you come back to your room, there will be a nice present for you."

"Thank you."

Bill stared at her in awe. For her to be speaking to him now, so soon after the incident, was something to be admired. He was usually given the silent treatment for at least the first five to six sessions before they would even look him in the eye or have a conversation. Sandra was different. He had never run across her kind before, but he knew he had made the right choice with her. He would never doubt that.

CHAPTER 14

S andra did as she was told and went to take a bath. Bill stayed behind her the entire time, even volunteering to help bathe her, which she quickly declined, as she closed the door behind herself. She wanted to get to the living room and check on her mother, but he blocked every step she made. He was done with her, wasn't he? He was hovering as if she was going to bolt from his sight at any moment, and she would have if the opportunity had presented itself. He had to leave the house at some time, and she tried not to appear anxious over the state she may find her mother in.

Once inside the bathroom, she locked the door and collapsed to the floor. God never came for her, nor did he send her mother. He let those terrible things take place, and they could never be taken back. They would be forever stored in her memory. The tears threatened to come again, but she refused to let them. She would not cry again over this. She had to get around what had just occurred to make her stronger somehow.

It didn't seem as if this was the first time he had done something like this. He was very controlled and precise in his movements, but then again what rapist wasn't? She couldn't allow herself to think if there was a list of terrified girls in the past that may have trusted and adored him as she did. She could now testify to their fear and pain. Sandra knew that he would come back for her again and again. Men like him never thought about the victim's feelings or what they may be putting them through emotionally. It was all about them, and since this was just their first encounter, she knew there would be more.

Sandra climbed into the tub and once again stopped the tears that her spirit so desperately wanted to shed. Her body flexed and constricted from the emotions that raged inside of her. She fought the internal battle for more than five minutes before her body relaxed itself from the tension. She was tired, but she did not weep or feel sorry for herself. She was instead angry and very determined at this point to see that she would survive this.

Bill had changed her way of thinking dramatically. The world was no longer filled with cookies and ice cream cones, It was a place where the faces you came to trust the most could turn on you in an instant. It was a place where children were forced to take the roles of adults to satisfy the desires of pedophiles, a place where the phrase "survival of the fittest" should began to be taught in elementary school, long before society had a chance to wreck you with it.

This world didn't have a safe place for children to grow and have a happy life. There was no separation between the good and the bad; they were all blended in together, and it was left up to you to decipher what was inside of whom.

Sandra sat in a trance, replaying the rape over and over again in her mind. She didn't want to miss a movement, didn't want to forget a word. This, she would have carry with her for the rest of her life, so she wanted to make sure not one element of it was left out. All the lies and the "Uncle Bill's were long gone. He tore the very fiber of her being, and she could not, would not, forget that.

She heard the front door slam, and she quickly jumped out of the cold water and made a break for it. She grabbed the towel, wrapped herself, and eased out the bathroom.

She had to be sure he was gone. She didn't want to risk running into him and not being able to check on her mother.

Quietly she tip-toed into her room and stuck her head in. Bill was gone. Sandra looked for the package that he told her would be left behind, but she saw no wrappers of any kind. A part of her really did want some form of apology from him, something that would clearly say that he was sorry for the pain and misery he had caused her, but she saw nothing. As a matter of fact, the room looked identical as before she went to bathe.

She saw her panties crumpled on the bed, and she wanted nothing more than to set them and the bed on fire. The memory of him touching her in her own bed, on her own sheets was enough to make her want to die, but she knew she could never kill herself. Bill had to pay for what he had done, and she would be the judge and the jury in his court.

One day her death would come, as sure as day turns to night, but it would not be at her own hands. She wanted to make sure Bill knew what he was doing to little girls was wrong, and he should not go unpunished.

Sandra tipped out of her room in search of her mother. Her first instinct to remove the sheets from the bed was something she dismissed. She would not try to hide what happened. She would not pretend to herself that this was some horrible nightmare. No, she was not a frightened child but a survivor. She decided to leave everything as it was, a constant reminder of what had taken place in her sanctuary, in her house, and in her bed. It permanently singed a corner of her brain, and in the future if the thought of forgiveness or forgetfulness ever crossed her path, she would replay the horror of this day.

Sandra closed the door on the memories of the destruction of her youth and forever sealed the chapter of her childhood as she knew it.

Dorothy lay sprawled across the sofa in an awkward position, and Sandra was afraid to approach her. From the distance that she stood, it didn't seem as if her chest was rising and falling. Sandra tip-toed a little further into the living room and stood by the wall.

"Mom? Mom, are you awake?"

Dorothy didn't stir, so she ventured closer, inches at a time. She didn't know what she would do if her mother was dead. She didn't know how long she could live on her own or who she should contact, for that matter. She would be placed in the home she heard her friends talk about when you are bad or your parents give you away. She would be alone, on her own. The fear of being shipped off somewhere propelled her toward the sofa, where she began shaking her mother viciously. "Mom! Mom! Wake up! Wake up! Please be okay, Mom. Wake up!"

Once again those stubborn tears pushed to the surface, and it infuriated Sandra. Angrily, she wiped them away and went to the kitchen. Sandra filled a glass with cold water and returned to her mother. On cartoons a glass of cold water could wake up anybody, so without hesitation she forcefully splashed the water in her mother's face.

Dorothy attempted to sit up and talk, so Sandra helped her into a sitting position. "Mom, are you all right?"

Dorothy wiped her face and tried to focus on her surroundings. Things were very blurry for her, and she was nowhere near coming down off her high. The feeling of floating into the abyss consumed her, and she enjoyed the euphoria of it all. She could hear her daughter talking to her, but it was almost impossible to respond. She wanted to tell her to leave her alone, but she couldn't voice that statement either. So she tried to focus on what Sandra was saying, but the warm darkness continued to consume her until she slumped back down onto the couch, appearing to be asleep.

Sandra turned from the sight of her mother and headed for her room. The fact that her bed was still soiled did not concern her. The last hour of the day was lost upon her. She could not breathe or think. She let the tears explode from her, and she did nothing to contain them this time.

She pulled off her pajamas and clawed at her skin, using her nails to rip and pull at the top layer until a small red stream ran a path down her leg. From her kneecap to her ankle it traveled untouched, except for Sandra's gaze.

The room was spinning as Sandra began to hyperventilate. She lost her balance and ended up on the floor, staring up at the ceiling as the color began to fade from the corners of her vision. She grabbed at her chest to try to prevent the inevitable, but it smothered her and left her motionless.

*

The sunlight danced through the curtains spreading a beautiful amber glow throughout Sandra's room. The night had fallen, and the day took its place with a sense of serenity and peace that the inside of the house could not match.

Dorothy stood in the doorway, watching her daughter sleep on the floor. The vicious red welts zigzagged across Sandra's body looked painful and permanently etched into her skin. She didn't want to decipher what the bloodstains on the bed meant, nor did she have the stomach to visualize how they appeared there. She had allowed herself to be fooled and manipulated by Bill, and it burned her to the core to know what he had done. She'd had an idea that he was lying when he reappeared as the concerned father figure, but knowing he held those precious packets in his possession took precedence over the instinct to protect her daughter.

There was no way to turn the clock back, and there was no way to erase what had taken place. Her stomach churned inside, and she tried to fight the wave of nausea that swam in the back of her throat but failed.

Dorothy escaped to the bathroom and dry heaved into a fit of convulsions while holding on to the sink to steady herself. She somberly swallowed her sobs and went back to the living room, where she found the pink packets resting on the cushion of the sofa and was slapped again with the gravity of the situation. She had sold her daughter to feed her addiction.

If she'd taken the time to be honest with herself, she knew what Bill was up to. Maybe not in the beginning, but she knew he cared about Sandra and showed her a little more attention than anyone else who came to her house. She tried to chalk it up to him missing his own daughters when he was on the road, but she noticed that as Sandra got older, his visits became frequent and longer. He was establishing a predatory bond right in front of her face. She could see it. She could smell it, yet she had allowed it come to this.

Dorothy would not be able to face Sandra at this time, and she knew it. The words would not be able to form in her mouth; she had no idea what to do about what had taken place. She could call the police, she thought for a split second, but tell them what? She had let a known drug user into her home to rape her daughter? And when they asked what she was doing at the time of the incident, what story would she then be able to tell? "Oh, I didn't see it for myself, Mr. Officer. I was too high to get off the couch."

Her hands were shaking so badly that she was unable to prepare the fix she desired. She tried repeatedly to pick up the spoon, but it fell continuously from her grasp. Dorothy wanted to be as far from reality as the heroin could take her.

He ex-husband had known she was a drug addict when he left her. He'd stopped fighting for Sandra and decided to leave her behind with a dope fiend. The fact that they had survived all this time on the lonely child support check should count for something. She'd made it work to support her daughter.

Dorothy felt the entire blame should not rest at her doorstep. Sandra's father should be here with her to face his daughter. He claimed her financially but disowned her physically. His new wife had told her as much with a snide smirk in her voice. She knew who was calling, just like he did. Dorothy had remembered hearing his voice in the background, and not once did he reach for the phone. She could have been calling to say Sandra was hit by a car today or that she was in the hospital for some reason or other, but did he pick up the phone? No! He turned the other cheek and decided to act as if he had no idea they existed. So be it!

Why should she have to face the problem alone? She wasn't strong enough. She could not, would not, look into Sandra's blue eyes and know she had failed her as a mother.

Dorothy pulled the belt as tight as she could and slapped herself repeatedly until the line to freedom formed on the inside of her thigh. She had broken out in a sweat, but she paced herself and inserted the syringe. The immediate heat she felt was all too consuming. She wouldn't have to talk to anyone. She would not have to look into the innocent face of her daughter. She was in a place that was un-reachable to many and un-heard-of by most.

She had just enough time to untie the belt and remove the needle before she would be in total darkness. It took less than five minutes to achieve the maximum effect, and she relished it. She eagerly let go of life and drifted. By the time she would come around, Sandra would be in school, and she would be in the clear.

Ideas of how to handle the situation would arise. She was sure of that. All she had to do was avoid her now and think of what to do later. The dope nod smothered out all of her existence, and she didn't fight it. Dorothy slumped over in a sitting position, oblivious to the sight of Sandra standing in the corner of the room.

Sandra watched her mother's every move. She heard her repeating to herself that what had happened to her was not her fault. She witnessed her tying herself up and putting the drug in her veins, and she felt betrayed by the one person who was put on this earth to protect her.

She no longer wanted to be made a fool of. For all of those years she had told the principals and teachers that her mother was on medication. She knew what it was now, and she also knew that her mother liked using the drugs in order to escape from her everyday life. She wanted to get away from Sandra as well.

Just to think that she had told her father that her mother needed her made her want to punch a wall. But in the end, he didn't want her either. To know that her mother had a number to contact him brought a nervous jitter to her stomach, but she didn't know what to do with the information. Would he pretend not to know her if she was to call him personally? She didn't know if she would ever be able to face rejection again.

Bill had taken advantage of her, using her for his wants and desires. Her mother wished she could be shoved off to her father, yet he denied her. The betrayal at the hands of her parents and Bill was just too much to bear. She had to get away from it all.

So Sandra headed for the one place she knew she had always felt safe and loved. She got dressed and went to school.

By the time her third class rolled around the enormity of what she had suffered and the fact that she didn't want to return home began to take its effect on her. One of her favorite teachers picked up on the change in her instantly and held her after class to talk to her. She usually took pride in the pigtails she wore in her hair daily, but today her hair hung limply on her shoulders in a tangled mess. She had on the exact clothes she had worn the day before, and that just wasn't like the Sandra she knew.

She was worried about her in more ways than one. "Sandra, honey, I need to speak to you for a minute okay?" No, this was definitely not okay. She wanted to go to her next class and get the day over with. She thought she'd wanted to be in school with her friends and teachers, but it didn't make her feel any better. She wanted to hide in a corner and forget her life as she knew it, but Mrs. Smacker was blocking the opportunity.

"I need to get to the next class or I'm going to get a tardy."

"Oh, it's okay. I'll walk you down myself. Have a seat."

Sandra retreated to her desk and awaited the questions she would be bombarded with.

She knew she should have taken the time to clean herself up, but she just didn't have the energy or desire to do it. She was angry at herself for not being able to cover up her situation. She'd told herself that she wasn't going to discuss what was going on with anyone, but how did she expect to avoid questioning if she couldn't keep things looking normal on the surface?

She vowed to herself that she would get through this interrogation, and would not sit through another one. She would keep up her appearances and smile at all the corny jokes being told in the classroom.

She would not allow herself to be cornered like this again and placed on trial as if she had committed a crime. At that moment, something changed deep inside of her, and she felt it. It might have been considered an awakening of sorts. She wasn't sure of the word, but she felt reborn and empowered. No one would be able to see what went on inside of her. She would be like a two-way mirror: she'd be able to look out, but no one would be able to see inside her. She would learn the game, and she would play along.

She sat a little straighter in her chair now as she covered herself in the strength that was growing deep within. "Well, Sandra, I just wanted to ask you if there was anything at all you wanted to talk about. You know I'm here for that, right? I'm not just your teacher, but I'm also like a counselor for you. You can tell me anything, and I will try to help you out the best I can."

Sandra weighed what was being said. She wanted to be able to have someone to lean on, someone to confide in, but at this time she just didn't see adults as being someone she could trust or count on, so she shut her out. "Nope. I'm fine, Mrs. Smacker."

"I was just wondering because you usually look so pretty and bright, and today you are wearing yesterday's dress, and you hair is tangled."

"Oh! My mom did the laundry, and she said she didn't wash this dress because she didn't see it in the hamper. I really like the color. It's one of my favorites, so I wore it again since it didn't have any stains on it. I'll be sure to put it in the laundry when I get home, though." Sandra paused for effect and a quick breath before continuing on. "I thought I would wear my hair like this because this was how Madonna wore it in her last video, but it takes a long time to comb through it, so I probably won't do this style again."

Mrs. Smacker was a little surprised, but Sandra had a logical answer for every question. The little girl was indeed one of her best students, and she was never known to be a fibber, so she had to take what she said at face value. She had no reason to doubt her, and she knew the girls in the school were fast approaching their teenage years and were trying to express themselves in different ways.

"Well, I'm just so glad to know that you are all right. I was really worried about you today. I didn't know if I should have sent you straight down to the principal office when I saw you and requested a conference with your mother or what, but I'm sure glad now that I took the time to talk to you first. It could have ended up being quite an embarrassment!"

Her teacher let out a nervous laugh and put her arm around Sandra's shoulders. Then she got up in order to escort her to the next class. Sandra falsely put spring in her step and followed her out the door.

She had been her favorite teacher all year, but she now wondered how that was possible. Didn't she see what was really going on? Did it have to be spelled out in order for her to catch on? She was hurting inside, and no one could tell by the surface, but a teacher should know you by more than just appearances, especially your favorite one. She was content to know that she had gotten away with the lie, but at the same time, she thought Mrs. Smacker would be able to see what she feeling.

Once again she felt let down and disappointed, but she swallowed that pain as well and followed Mrs. Smacker down the hall.

CHAPTER 15

*H*er life as she knew it was officially over. She no longer relished in planning tea parties with her dolls, nor did she sing the love songs on the radio to her teddy bears. No, things had changed for her, and she was too young to do anything more than go with the flow.

Bill began coming by the house one or two days a week to see her, and she had no idea how to stop it. When she said no he would just profess his love to her and take what he wanted anyway.

Her mother was no longer in the dark about what was happening between the two of them. She tended to turn her head in the other direction. The first time Bill returned Dorothy put up a fuss, but it couldn't be considered much more than that. She said a few harsh words to him, which turned into a shoving match, but eventually she took the drugs he offered and didn't give her daughter's door a second glance.

*

Sandra was in her room lying across the bed one day when he arrived at the house. The sound of his voice brought her to full attention and poised for flight. She quickly put on her shoes and headed for her window. She no longer wore pajamas to sleep. She layered herself in clothing; two pairs of pants, a T-shirt, bra, and socks made up her nightly attire. She was dressed for escape at a moment's notice, and that moment was now! Unfortunately, the front door as she had always planned was out of the question.

Her window latch was difficult for her to manipulate, and her fingers fumbled clumsily with the mechanism. She concentrated with all her being and tried to turn the lock again. It moved just a fragment, but it was stuck. The lock and window had been painted over, and it made the task extremely daunting. Sandra began tapping on the glass. She didn't want to break it, but she wanted it to be able to release her somehow.

She ran to her closet and removed the spatula from her Easy-Bake oven set and ran back to the window, dragging the chair from her vanity table with her. She climbed onto the chair and began scraping at the paint that not only held the window pane in a death grip but also restrained her from her freedom.

"Sandra."

The vibrations radiated to her inner ear and caused an immediate shift in her equilibrium. She fell from the chair, landing harshly on her right ankle. "Ow!"

"Look at my little girl. What were you doing at the window? You have to be careful or you might hurt yourself."

"Mom! Mom, please!"

Bill lowered himself to the floor and began massaging the ankle that she held. "Shh, it's okay. Let me take a look."

"No!" Sandra roughly pushed his hand away and tried to stand. She was scared to put any pressure on the wounded leg, so she tilted to one side. "I don't like you! I don't want you to touch me."

Her anger didn't settle well with him, and he tried not to show his irritation. He was going to weaken her in time, but he would not tolerate her erratic behavior in the process.

"Sandra, I am not a stranger here. You have known me for quite some time now. I don't expect you to act like this when I come to see you. This is a difficult situation for me as well. I'm trying to help you understand my feelings for you, but we can't talk when you are so riled up like this. Come and sit next to me." Sandra didn't move. She stayed locked in position by the window. She glanced at it from time to time and wished it would just fly open and suck her out of her room. Her ankle was beginning to throb, and she really did want to get off her feet, but sitting next to Bill was not something she desired to do.

She knew he would catch her if she tried to bolt from the room, but she didn't want to just walk into his web willingly either, so she sat on the floor instead. "Is your leg still hurting?" She didn't answer him, and he started to get up from the bed.

"It's my ankle that's hurting."

"Can I see it? You might need some ice on it."

"No, it'll be fine."

Bill watched her carefully and tried to judge what was going on in her head. Sometimes to conquer her was an easy task, and other times like this she would rebel against him and make the fight a little longer.

He'd thought he would have to go through the same crying spells that he did with his daughters, but he had never seen her shed a tear since their first time. Sandra was a strong one, he would give her credit for that, but her entire demeanor was changing, and he didn't like what he was seeing at all.

Bill went to the floor and sat next to Sandra; in response she scooted closer to the wall. "I have bent over backwards being nice to you, and it seems as if you don't appreciate my efforts. You are not in control of this situation, and I think it's time I show you what that means."

Bill grabbed a fistful of her hair and yanked her onto his lap. She yelled out when he first grabbed her, but other than that, she didn't make a sound. He didn't deserve a conversation with her. He didn't deserve to touch her or put his tongue in the foreign places he desired.

Everything he did was for his own satisfaction, not hers. She could mean no more to him than a mattress to a frame, and she knew that. She wondered if she had been a boy if he would also rape and soil her.

She looked into his face as he grabbed her breasts and forced himself inside for what seemed to be the hundredth time, and she realized that boy or girl, this animal would just as eagerly shred it.

CHAPTER 16

By the time Sandra was a junior in high school, she was unrecognizable to those she had attended middle school with. She requested that all the teachers call her by her last name, and this was honored without much hesitation. She was a different person altogether, and it suited her just fine. She was now five feet seven inches and stood powerfully in her 155-pound frame. She had been in the military program at the school, and she relished in the discipline and hard work they required of all the cadets. She was always the one they called on when the class needed to be shown an example of new exercises or how to do strength training without weights.

They were pushing the marines and the army pretty hard at her, but she continued to reject all offers. She wanted the training, and she loved learning the maneuvers for defense and attacks, but she had no desire to enter into the government program. What her future held she was not sure. College didn't seem like a place she wanted to spend the next four years of her life, and her childhood dreams of being a kindergarten teacher were just that: dreams.

She hadn't looked at her life the same since the age of eleven. From that time on, she no longer played with dolls—or anything, for that matter. Life became a black tunnel that she walked through day in and day out, without light. She didn't know how it felt to kiss a boy for the first time, as her experience was with a man three times her age. She watched the girls her age smile and blush as the boys walked past them, but she was oblivious to such flirting.

No boy had ever asked her out, and she never wondered why. They all knew that she was used goods.

She had never worn a dress again since fifth grade, and she couldn't imagine herself pinning up her hair and putting make-up on. She just wasn't the same as the other girls, and she knew it. She was sure she was the only one who had been sold by a parent for drugs.

*

Sandra had not seen Bill for the last fourteen months, and she began to briefly see herself in a new light. She felt a small light of hope had been cast her way, and she took a little more pride in herself and really began to focus on all aspects of her life. There was a light behind her cloud, and for the first time, she could see it. She considered what the rest of her life may be like without him, and it actually made her smile.

There was a rumor that he was behind bars, and she couldn't be happier, but her mom seemed to slip into some form of depression during his absence. She was no longer getting drugs on the ready, and it became more and more difficult for her to accomplish anything. She was agitated all the time and downright cruel to Sandra. It was as if she blamed her for Bill being in jail instead of being thankful that he was no longer the dark cloud that hung over their house.

Sandra would come home from school, go directly to her room, and close the door. She could not bear looking at her mother. They had grown so far apart over the last couple of years; it was as though they were strangers when they passed each other in the house. Sandra hadn't been able to define her feelings toward her mother since her sweet six-teen summer ended and she was to begin her junior year of high school, but now as second semester had gotten under-way, she knew the exact words that described how she felt about her "pimp."

This was the new title she had given her mother when she realized that she would stop at nothing to get high and trying to send men into her room was just the tip of the ice-berg. Most of them would leave after Sandra threw a shoe or some other object at them, but on some occasions, she would have to yell and bolt her door to get them to stay out.

She didn't consider it a blessing in any shape of the word, but Bill was mildly better than the litter her mom continued to "accidentally" send at her; at least Bill bathed. Most of them seemed as if they hadn't seen water in months, and she hid under the bed or in her closet most nights to avoid them.

Sandra felt she must have been spared because they were not true molesters in some sense of the word. A few would go and swear at her mother when they entered Sandra's room, seeing how young she was, and one man even cried when he opened the door to find her reading in her pink room. She had been saved by the bell more times than she cared to mention.

*

Sandra knew that the apparently drugged and delirious man she was now looking at had made a wrong turn into her room when he stumbled over to her bed. She immedi-ately jumped up and took a defense stance.

"You're in the wrong room. The bathroom is the next door over."

"I'm not looking for the bathroom, darling. I paid your mama a pretty penny to be with a pretty penny."

Sandra was briefly clueless about the "penny" he was speaking of, but she didn't like the sound of it at all. She knew her mom would pretend she didn't know that her company was making advances on her daughter in order to get getting high, but to know that she is now taking money for it, was inconceivable.

"You've made a mistake. This is not her room." She was standing inches from him, and the foul smell of his breath assaulted her senses. She tried to grab him by the elbow and escort him out the door, but she was not prepared for his strength. He clasped onto her arm and spun her around to the bed.

Sandra could feel him pressing against her, and she fought as hard as she could from the awkward position she was in. She repeatedly kicked her leg back in hopes of landing a blow solid enough where he would relinquish his grip on her, but she could not.

Sandra's hair was almost waist length, and he used it against her. He took a handful of golden strands and wrapped her wrist with it. "Now I know you're not some prized virgin. Hell, your mama done told me that, so I suggest you stop acting like this is your first time and I'm the school principal."

She could feel the layers of clothes peeling away, and she was powerless to stop him. All of the strength training in the world could not get him off of her as she was forced to succumb to the vile things he had in store for her.

The assault seemed to last for hours, and she felt as if she had been placed in a clothes dryer the entire time. He pulled and tugged and did anything and everything imaginable to her.

The chance for her to fight came up again somewhere along the way, and she took it. She sideswiped him with a fierce elbow, which made him loosen his grip on her, giving up a little more space to maneuver.

She knew she wouldn't be able to make it to the door, so her only option was to stay and fight. They were about the same height, but she was not strong enough to handle his extra weight or his altered mental state. Sandra concentrated on bringing him down and aimed for his knees.

He saw it coming before it happened, and she began to wonder if he had been in the military himself in the past. He was quick on his feet, and his eyes could read hers before she even considered a move.

Sandra was caught again, but this time she was on top of him. This would have been an advantage point for her had it not been for the fact that he had her hair twisted several times around her neck. He was demanding that she grab his manhood and put it inside of her. She refused and lashed out at him with the heel of her hands. He pulled so tightly on her hair that the next breath was taken from her.

She was at a loss. She had no idea what to do. She knew she should not panic, but what they'd failed to teach her was how she was to go about getting her next full breath of air. She was practically immobilized and locked in place. He looked her in the face as he held her hips in place with one hand and pulled roughly on her hair with the other. He was beginning to gasp for air as well, and just for an instant she thought he was going to pass out right along with her, but he didn't.

He jerked under her releasing himself, and Sandra watched his eyes roll to the back of his head. It was a very scary thing to witness. She had never seen Bill look this way when he finished with her, so she was sure that she was witnessing someone having a heart attack. She wanted nothing more than for him to die, but she didn't want to go along with him. She grabbed his hand that held her hair and tried to pry it loose from his fingers. It was not difficult to do. As a matter of fact, her hair slipped out of his hand like butter. He was breathing very hard, and his face had turned red, but other than that, he didn't appear to be in any form of medical distress. His body had turned slack, which was a total opposite from the rigid force she had just gone up against. Seeing how weak a man becomes after sex was new for her. Bill would always just roll over and become silent.

She never watched his face, or touched him if she could help it. She stored this new information in her data bank, and took advantage of her current situation.

Sandra began pounding his face with her fist, which landed squarely on the corner of his nose with precision, sending a spray of blood into her eyes. He rolled over and tried to cover his head from the downpour of pain she was unleashing on him, but he could not avoid it. She gave him everything she had until she, too, was exhausted from the efforts.

She rolled off the top of him and sat panting on the floor. She wanted to do much more to him, but didn't. She got off the floor, walked out of the room, and headed for the bathroom. Her first thought was to clean up and wash the blood off of her, but feeling as she was, she headed for the living room where she heard the voice of her mother entertaining some visitors.

She didn't think twice about her nakedness, and why should she? Her mother was boldly sending men into her room to feed her high, so why shouldn't she advertise on her behalf? She hoped they would enjoy the drying blood on her skin as an added touch. Her mother liked to play blind and innocent to what went on behind her door, but it was not a secret to be hidden anymore. She wanted everyone who came into contact with her mother to know she was for sale at her mother's requested price. A grown man would soon emerge from her room, and what would they think then? Would they just hold their heads down and pretend as if it didn't occur or that they were not seeing what they were really seeing? She would not allow them to hide either!

Sandra walked over to her mother and stood in front of her. "The man you sent in my room is going to require your help." Dorothy found her mouth hanging open as if captured in a still moment. Embarrassment was an understatement. She leaped up from the couch and landed a powerful slap across her mouth. "You will not speak to me like some slut! Go to your room!"

"No! I am not six years old. Look at me. You have allowed men to rape me for your own selfish needs, and I thought I would let you know that I don't like it. They make my skin crawl. I feel like a disease! And you just sit here and zone out on the couch. You are using drugs while I'm being raped for the product. You're a monster!"

She leaned back and spit in her mother's face. Dorothy did not move. How could she? The realization of what her daughter had just accused her of came as a point of awakening. Sandra punched her crisply across her lower jaw, which sent her spiraling. She jumped down on top of her, slamming her head into the floor. She wanted her to feel the humiliation and disappointment she felt. She wanted her to know the pain that she had hidden inside for years. She wanted her mother to listen to her cries, the ones she pretended didn't exist. She was fed up and wanted her mother to know it.

There was no talking to her at this point. Not once had she ever asked Sandra how she felt or if she would like for her to make Bill stop what he was doing. No. She looked away. Well, she would not be able to turn the other cheek from this! She relinquished all her hatred into a fiery force and unloaded on her mother.

She didn't feel herself being lifted off of Dorothy, nor could she figure out how she was now sitting in the corner of the room crying.

The man who was in the house with her mother had apparently pried them apart at some time, but that instant was lost somewhere. Her mother looked horrible, and she relished the sight of it. He was helping her to the couch, and for a split second she thought about attacking him, too, but then she realized how she had been overpowered by the man in the room, so she held her composure. She wasn't sure when the shaking had begun to consume her body, but she felt chilled to the bone and disoriented.

Her bedroom company decided at that precise moment to venture out to where the commotion was, holding a washcloth to his face. His gait was a little unsteady, but once he saw Sandra in the corner, he dropped the rag and headed her way.

"You little bitch, you broke my nose."

He swung his leg back and aimed for Sandra's head, but was met with a solid thump across his back. He turned to see the stranger standing behind him.

"What the fuck, man? This bitch—"

"She's a child, man, and you just raped her. I suggest you take your broke-ass nose and get out of here!"

"Fuck you!"

He took a step in his direction but thought better of it. He stormed out of the house and into the street, leaving the door standing wide open behind him.

The stranger went over and closed the door before heading back to Sandra. She was not feeling powerful anymore but drained and afraid of what may occur now that she was alone with him. He looked down at her, and the expression he held on his face hurt her far more than the physical wounds. He appeared to be battling to keep from crying. He reached his hand out, intending to help her off the floor, but she shrunk even further back in the corner.

He advanced no closer but instead headed to her room. She had no idea what he was about to do, or what he wanted her to do for that matter, so she just stayed where she was, frozen.

"I'm going to put this blanket on you, okay? I'm not going to touch you." Sandra looked into his eyes and tried to judge if what he was saying was true, and she saw the tears streaming down his cheeks. She didn't know what to make of the helpful dark-skinned man. She was puzzled and confused by the emotions on his face, but she would not allow herself to believe that he really cared what happened to her one way or the other, so she kept silent. "I didn't know anything like this was going on here. I swear. I don't even know what to say right now. I know you don't trust me, and I don't expect you to, but what he did to you was wrong."

He stood there, torn between calling the police himself and just physically removing her from the environment, but he had no idea how she would respond to him. She had been though a traumatic ordeal, and from what he was hearing, not for the first time. He had no inkling of what she would say to the police or if they would think he had something to do with what happened here, and he couldn't risk it. He was out on parole, and finding himself under these circumstances would not sit well with his reporting officer. He felt he had done nothing wrong by coming to the house to smoke a little weed, but in his world it could easily become twisted into something sordid.

"I'm going to leave now, and I won't be back. Go to the school tomorrow, and report your mother. The proper authorities will know what to do for you, okay?" He turned to pick up his jacket and headed for the door. He gave a last look at Dorothy as she sat wounded and dumbfounded on the couch, but he didn't speak a word to her. He just kept walking.

Sandra watched the figure walk out of the door, and she still did not feel safe. He had turned the mechanism to make sure the door was locked and that no one could get inside, but in doing so he had locked her in with the most sinister one of them all. She watched her mother for the longest of time and still could make nothing of her. She hated her, and her stomach boiled from everything she had exposed her to. Just thinking of how she had taken care of her since she was old enough to walk and all the lying she did to cover what was really going on in their house brought her to an intense rage.

She did not want to be anywhere near her, but she knew at the same time she did not want to end up in a group or foster home either. She had one more year of high school and one more year to figure out her next course of action.

CHAPTER 17

S ix months had gone by before the two of them were even able to be in the same room together, but the time for talking things out with one another had never risen in the air. Dorothy would brush up against her in a gentle fashion, but Sandra would not use it to initiate conversation. By this time she had totally tuned her out. She was operating in a different mode now. She no longer looked at her mother as her comforter or someone she could rely on but instead as someone who was a hindrance to her future and the things she desired to do. Her mind was made up, and she would not stray from course.

In eight months she would be eighteen, and she could cut the umbilical cord from her mother, the house, and all the devastating memories. Sandra would walk away with her head held up high. She didn't know her next destination, but she knew her mother would not know of her where-abouts. She vowed to pay her father a special visit before shedding them both like a winter coat.

Her teachers had been talking to her constantly about college and how to apply for certain grants and things of that nature, and she had to admit that it now sounded appealing because she would be able to live on campus, but she wasn't totally ready to commit to anything as of yet. She wanted to keep all of her options open. She was due to graduate one month before her eighteenth birthday, and she was planning to have everything figured out by that time. If college was her future, then she definitely needed to start applying. She had heard all the other students at the school talk about applying for colleges nonstop for the last five months or so, so she knew she had to get on the ball.

Sandra went to her guidance counselor about her chances of getting into a college, and she was told that with her GPA of 3.8, it should be no problem for her. That had to be the first good news she had ever received in her entire life. Sandra stayed in the office for over an hour and asked any and every question that came to her head. She found out more about dorms and living on campus and how since her mother was unemployed she would qualify for grants and loans from the government. She had no idea that her window to a new life was in her control if she would just utilize it.

Within days, she knew without a doubt that she be going to college. She would be able to get away from her mother and at the same time get a degree that would support her and make sure that she would never have to lay eyes on her parents again. She was very excited, and her counselor was just as excited for her.

Many of the staff wondered about the student whose mother had a heart condition and was unable to leave the house. This story carried on from elementary school up into the high school. It was the same scenerio year after year, so most of the teachers knew the story, and the kids would repeat it for those who didn't.

It wasn't after they began Sandra's college preparations that Mrs. Washington incidentally drove pass Sandra's house and saw a woman on the porch talking to a gentleman that she realized just what condition her mother had. She was often to be seen panhandling in front of the grocery store or at the gas station. She had no idea that for the last four years she had been living practically a stone's throw away from the student with the sickly mother.

She'd thought the story was heartbreaking when she first heard it, but now she thought it even more so because her mother didn't have a condition but an addiction.

She had never told anyone at the school about her discovery because she knew that she wasn't the only one that had a parent on drugs, so what would be the reason to point her out to the staff or the principal? She knew what it was like, and she also knew how difficult the situation was to overcome. It seemed to be much easier for families with one or more siblings, but Sandra was an only child. For her to make it in life without turning to drugs and alcohol herself should be commended and not turned into a public display.

She had been covering for her mother and her living conditions for years and was still able to have a sparkle in her eye when it came down to her future. She was actually looking forward to college and living the dorm lifestyle. Mrs. Washington would not let her down or let the system fail her. Whatever was required to get her into the door she was willing to do, and she started by typing the most sincere and heartfelt recommendation she had ever composed.

*

Sandra practically floated out of the office. She held onto her counselor's words as a prayer book. She remembered everything she'd told her, including keeping her grades up this year and focusing on taking the ACT again next month. She was even kind enough to give her a study guide to go by, and that would help her figure out what type of questions were to be on the test. She looked over the study guide as she walked home, but then she detoured to the library. She had to get online. Mrs. Washington told her the sooner she filled out her applications; the better her chances would be of getting accepted. Of course that would ride greatly on her test scores as well, but she wasn't concerned about that.

Sandra had not had a very difficult time in school at all. Her home life was the biggest task she had to conquer, but right now her mother was not winning.

She would be going to college, and she decided she would do that alone as well. By the time her mother realized that she walked out the door and was not coming back, she would be long gone.

She knew planning was the most critical part of the process for her, and she didn't want to miss a step. She stayed in the library until closing time, checking out all of the colleges that were at least a thousand miles from her mother. Arizona State, Florida State, and UCLA were the ones that jumped out at her. They were all hot and sunny places, and she would have a reason to smile every day.

The campuses were all huge and looked very well-maintained. She knew she would have to do very well on the ACT, but her counselor also told her she would be able to take it twice more after this one.

Sandra decided to study the guide and the online ACT questionnaire she printed out. She signed up for the next test date before leaving the library. You needed a higher score to get into UCLA than her other two choices, but she decided to aim high and not think negative. Sandra headed home with her bundle of papers in her hands and her future in her heart.

CHAPTER 18

S he was called down to the office two weeks before graduation, and she felt as if she were walking in quicksand. She knew Mrs. Washington had promised to call her down as soon as she got the results from the test. She had no idea what the outcome would be. She'd found the ACT to be difficult in some areas. She thought she came out all right toward the end. But now that the results were here, she wasn't so sure of herself anymore.

This was a huge deciding factor for her, a make-it-or-break-it situation, and she could not afford to lose. She had mentally placed herself in college ever since the day she'd started to seriously discuss it. She liked school; it was like a comfort zone for her, somewhere she could find peace in the midst of chaos, and it soothed her.

She sat in the general office, and waited for Mrs. Washington to call her inside. Her stomach was doing flips, and she felt a very strong urge to vomit right where she sat. "Ms. Hansley." She was being summoned to her destiny, and she was in no way sure of the outcome.

The counselor sat behind her desk with a yellow folder conveniently closed and placed in front of her. Sandra could easily make out her name on the front, but that was the only visible information the cover held. Her nerves were jumping all over the place, and it became very difficult for her to sit still or concentrate. She had never felt like this before, and she found it to be stimulating and disheartening at the same time.

"Well, I know you are very anxious to hear the results of your test, and I don't want to hold them from you any longer, but let me just say this. You are a beautiful person, and I have never seen anyone want something as much as you and go after it with such a vengeance. I applaud your efforts, Sandra, as I'm sure anyone else would."

Her spirits just hit the floor, and she now felt only despair. She knew the "I'm sorry" speech better than anyone. Damn! She had no idea how to focus on what she was being told or what she should do from this moment on. Taking the test again was an option, but at the time, it felt as if she was being rolled up in the rug and taken out to the trash. She couldn't be optimistic now if she'd wanted to.

"Your financial aid papers were approved, and they were sent to the three schools of your choice. Since you used the school and my office as your address for your correspondence with these schools, I also have the letters they have sent to you in response to your application. I have not opened them, but I will do so now, if you want me to."

Sandra didn't utter a word. Fear planted itself inside of her was very visible across her face. She had gone blank and was no longer in the office with her counselor, but some empty place instead.

"Sandra? Sandra, are you all right?"

"Uh, yes. I was just, uh…"

"Well, let's not delay any longer. Would you like for me to read the first letter?"

"Yes, please."

Mrs. Washington opened one letter after the other, but she never said a word, just continued to read. Sandra's eyes bored into hers, praying for some form of confirmation, but she held a steady poker face.

Sandra waited patiently for her to reveal the contents to her, but instead she turned the letters around and faced them in her direction. Sandra didn't move to retrieve the papers.

"Go ahead and read them. They were sent to you, and so you should read them for yourself."

With fingers that shook worse than a fall tree losing its leaves, she grasped the first letter, and the letterhead informed her that it was from Florida State. The first sentence started with, "We are pleased to inform you..." and her eyes blurred and reddened at the sight of those beautiful words. Never before in her life had she ever felt so complete.

She moved the letter to the side in search of the UCLA letterhead. She knew she must have scored high enough for Florida and Arizona State, but UCLA was a different ballgame. No matter what they decided, she had to admit she was not sad at all. She was getting away from her past, and she had done it on her own!

Bravely, she began to read the letter from the college that she really wanted to attend, and her heart skipped a beat. "We are pleased to inform you that your application for this fall semester has been accepted."

"Oh, oh, oh!"

She jumped up and down, screaming and shaking all at the same time. She could not believe it!

"Congratulations, Sandra."

"Oh, thank you so much, Mrs. Washington! Thank you!"

She ran to the other side of the desk, drowning her counselor in hugs.

"You scored high enough on your ACT to go anywhere you want to. You did an excellent job, Sandra."

For the first time since she was a child, she did something she had never done before: she sat in class and did absolutely nothing all day.

Most of the kids were putting the finishing touches on their senior projects or cramming for extra credit, but not her. She had everything done, and she was ready to go.

Sandra hadn't planned on going on any of the senior field trips, so on those days she stayed in the library, reading anything and everything she could about California. She looked at the pictures and read about all of the celebrities. She would soon be a part of that world, and she could not wait.

*

Graduation came and went without too much fuss. She gave her extra tickets back to Mrs. Washington just in case someone had a big family and didn't have enough tickets to have them all there. She did not want her mother anywhere near the school, or her, for that matter. They had been speaking, but barely, and she preferred to keep it that way. Dorothy continued to get high and have some of the least desirable people over, but Sandra just walked past them with a butcher knife in her hand, and they pretty much stayed where they were.

She had not had another encounter with anyone, and her mother didn't even consider sending someone into her room since she started carrying the knife. Dorothy demanded that she put it back in the kitchen drawer when she first saw it, but when Sandra blazed a hateful look in her direction, she decided not to say anything else to her about it.

Dorothy knew her daughter hated her, but to what extent she really had no clue. She also knew Sandra had graduated from high school, and she cried for half the day knowing her daughter did not want her to attend the ceremony.

She had every reason to hate her, but she also felt that she was her mother and should have been included in such a big event. Sandra treated her as if she were a total stranger, and they just happened to be roommates.

She would prepare herself something to eat and walk right past her with the plate, making sure not to leave any extra in the kitchen. She took her own clothes to the laundry now, and Dorothy's belongings were never considered in the process. She could spend the whole day walking around her.

Dorothy no longer spoke to her daughter unless it was absolutely necessary, and that was only two to three times a week.

Dorothy started tooting heroin because her veins were little more than scarce. If no one was able to find a vein for her, she would call Sandra from her room to do it. She knew her daughter would come, but she would take her sweet time. The first time Dorothy needed her during their no-talking spells, Sandra walked right past her as she was going through withdrawals on the floor. She didn't bat an eye as she stepped right around her and headed to the kitchen. It wasn't until she heard Dorothy still crying and begging in agony hours later that she got up out of bed to help her.

She found her mother withering on the floor with bleeding needle sticks all over her. She was curled up, naked and moaning like a cow that needed to be put down.

"Please, Sandra. Please help me. I need it, baby. Really, I do."

For some reason, to see her mother in this bad of shape vibrated her heart strings. She obediently went about tying her mother's thigh and trying to find a vein, but after thirty minutes, she grew weary and frustrated.

"You don't have any! You need to go to rehab!"

"No! No! Please, Sandra! Try it again, okay? Just try."

Sandra was very angry by this time, and she didn't want to do anything but call the police to come and get her!

"Tie it by my knee. Somebody got it there before. Please!"

Sandra grabbed the belt and yanked it as hard as she could just above her kneecap. She didn't see anything popping up. And she was about to call it quits when a vein surfaced behind her knee. She was surprised to see it. She thought surely they were all blown by now, but then again, she was more than happy to shoot her and get it over with.

*

The weeks were winding down, and she kept a count on her calendar in her room. She had forty-nine days to go, and then she would be putting herself and her belongings on the Greyhound. Mrs. Washington was nice enough to purchase the ticket for her, and she also organized some-one to pick her up at the other end of the trail and escort her through the campus and to her dorm.

She had been packing for the last couple of months. Ever since she found out that she was accepted, she has done nothing but prepare for her departure. She would collect her child support payments, pay some of the bills, buy a little food, and spend the rest on things she would need for the trip. Her mother never came into her room, so she felt perfectly safe in leaving a few of the shopping bags lying about.

On average, she spent three to four hours a day packing and unpacking her belongings. She didn't want to forget anything, and she had to make sure not to take too many things from the house either.

Sandra didn't pack any photos of herself from her school years, when she really believed her mother was sick. Every time she would look into the eyes of her youth, she would feel more and more manipulated by her mother, and it made her think of using that butcher knife on her, so she decided not to take any of those with her. She didn't need dark reminders looming over her anymore. She was going to be a new person, reinvented in most ways. College and a career were her new start, and she would not be taking the memory of Dorothy along with her.

*

Everything was going as scheduled. She had twenty-six days left, and she was ticking them off as they went. She no longer needed the calendar; it was all in her head. She went to bed early to catch the sun when it appeared in the morning. That meant another day had gone, and she was getting closer.

She had met with Mrs. Washington on several occasions during her wait, and they shared lunch quite a few times. Sandra must have appeared anxious or nervous because Mrs. Washington asked her if she would like to come and stay at her house for the last few days before her departure. Sandra declined her offer at first and then had a change of heart. She told her that she could come and pick her up when she had three days left. That way she could check out her belongings, and make sure she had everything she needed.

She also wanted to give Mrs. Washington the address to her father's house that she got by giving the operator his phone number she found in Dorothy's room, in hopes that he would answer the door to receive the letter she had written him. Her first mind was to make it as mean and as nasty as she possibly could, but she knew it didn't have to be hurtful in order to get to the point. He would know from the words she chose that her life had not been easy and that she blamed him for not doing anything to make it a little better for her.

She then told him about her acceptance into college (although not which one) and that she was thinking of taking up sign language for the deaf. She told him that she knew he no longer claimed her and that she had no idea why he would do that. Sandra spoke silently in the letter, but anyone reading it would be able to see the hurt in her words.

Even if she'd only visited him on the weekends, she knew it would have made a difference in her life. But that chance was never offered to her, and for that, he would only have the letter to look at with no photos. He didn't deserve better.

In one breath she hoped he would answer the door when she knocked just to see if there was a resemblance between the two of them or if he would be able to decipher who the stranger before him was. In the next breath, she wanted to just place the letter in the mailbox and leave. She would decide once she arrived at the house. She would let the spur of the moment depict the outcome.

She knew her father had to care for her in some form or fashion because of his constant child support payments. He never quit his job in order to duck his responsibilities, nor did he fight the increase that was approved by the court when her mother wrote a letter to the judge describing the hardships of their lives (if that judge only knew the half of it).

He never stopped the money from coming, but then again, he never came to check on her to ensure she was getting it or if his ex-wife had gotten back on drugs and if so, how his child was doing All of these things had played with Sandra's mind constantly during her life, but she wouldn't let it bother her anymore. Out with the old and in with the new.

She would no longer ask the question "Why me?". She was not going to wonder if someone on this hateful earth had any love in their heart for her. No. Sandra resolved that she loved herself more than anyone else could, and that would have to be enough to get her through most anything.

CHAPTER 19

$\mathcal{T}$he days ticked by without much going on in the house, but the excitement bubbled inside of her to the point of boiling over. Mrs. Washington called in the morning. Her mother happened to answer the phone, but she didn't say much, just called Sandra to come pick up the line. She was more and more out of it as time went by, but Sandra couldn't allow herself to focus on her or the dilemmas she would soon be facing when Sandra left. She had no control over her mother ruining her past, but she would not allow her to intervene in the future she had planned for herself. She knew that Dorothy would not last more than a few years after she left, but that also did not blur her mindset. She would have to leave the past behind, and that included her mother. She had to find a way to forgive her for what she had put her thorough—or at least that is what Mrs. Washington told her when she laid the story of her life out to her.

Once Mrs. Washington got over the initial shock of it and Sandra was able to stop the well of tears that flooded her face, she was embraced and told that everything would be okay. It was the best feeling Sandra had ever known. Her counselor stroked her hair and dried her tears repeatedly. It was such a warm feeling that her heart seemed physically sore from the pain that squeezed out of it.

Mrs. Washington explained forgiveness to her and how it was an important part of her healing process. She needed to forgive her mother for her own wellbeing more than any other reason. She explained that if she was to hold on to the hurt, then it would eat at her and dampen the prospects of her future. Sandra listened to what she had to say, and she wanted to do as she was asked, but it would definitely take time.

She had to try to ease the hatred out of her in order to let the forgiving process in, but her mind played repeatedly with her past. Without wanting to, she would see her mother slumped over on the couch with a needle loosely hanging from her fingertips, and she had strong a desire to set the couch on fire. If she saw her in the kitchen, she would instantly think of drowning her in the sink or pulling the butcher knife out on her.

Those thoughts constantly swirled in her head, and the only piece of sanity she had to hold on to was the fact that she was leaving and closing the door behind her.

*

"Hello, college student! How are you?"

"I'm fine."

"Good. Good. Are you ready for tonight? I can pick you up when I get done grocery shopping. I'm going to pick us up some Rocky Road ice cream and some scary movies. I'm giving you an introduction to girls' night on campus. It's what my sorority sisters and I did every Saturday for our first three years. We would get in our pajamas, and… Sandra? Hello?"

"Yeah, I'm here, but I don't think I can come today."

"What's the matter, Sandra? Do you need my help? You want me to come over there? What do you need me to do?"

She sounded so concerned and scared for her. There wasn't a real reason as to why she couldn't go, but yesterday she found one of her mother's visitors roaming around in her room, and when she asked the lady what she was doing in there, she pretended to be looking for the bathroom.

Sandra had spent all summer getting her things together for her departure, and she wasn't about to let anyone steal all of her belongings. She knew that she would be able to take them to Mrs. Washington's house, but she had already done so much for her that she couldn't find herself to be even more of a burden than she already has been by lugging tons of bags into her counselor house, so she did something that she had never done to her before: she lied.

"It's nothing major at all. I just need to get a few more things together and I'll be ready."

"Do you need my assistance in some way?"

"Not right now. It's just a little work."

Her counselor decided she didn't want to press the issue. She knew she was there for her, and that's about all she could do at this time.

"Well, I won't open the ice cream until you come. Call me if you need anything."

They hung up, but it left Sandra feeling empty inside. She didn't want to lie, and she didn't want to spend another day looking at her mother either. She thought constantly about calling her counselor back, getting her things together, and leaving.

She was clueless as to what held her back, and she didn't want to dig too deep in trying to figure it out. Dorothy was a pathetic excuse for a mother, and she had no desire to spend another moment with her, but she still couldn't seem to make herself leave.

Not wanting to think on it anymore, she headed for her room to go over her checklist one more time.

*

On the third day, Mrs. Washington called to ask how she was doing, and Sandra could hear the anxiety in her voice.

She was begging Sandra to let her come and get her, but Sandra wouldn't budge.

"You can come and get me when it's time to go to the Greyhound station. I have a few more things I need to finish here, and then I will be free to go."

Her counselor hesitated for more than a minute. She had no idea what was going on, but she didn't like it. It seemed as if Sandra was starting to pull away from the idea of leaving for college altogether. She didn't know the right words to say in order to get her to leave the house, but she was almost tempted to tell her she was ill herself and needed her help. She knew Sandra would come then, but she didn't want to make things seem more drastic than they were.

Maybe she was taking her advice to heart and was really trying to forgive her mother and make some form of connection with her. It was not her place to interfere in that aspect of her life. She had already stepped around so many teacher-student boundaries that she had allowed herself to be consumed with Sandra and helping her start a new life.

Sandra was a very independent girl. She had been taking care of her mother for years and was exposed to the grimmest parts of life at an early age. Sandra knew how to handle herself, of that she was sure, so she backed off and gave her what she asked.

"Okay. Your bus leaves at eight, so I will be at your house early. How about six o'clock? That way we can go have breakfast, and you can sleep for the first few hours of your two-day ride."

"That sounds good. I will have my stuff at the door."

"Well, I'm counting down. Are you?"

"Yep. Three to go! When I wake in the morning, it will be two, then one, then none! I am so ready."

Mrs. Washington heard the voice of the Sandra she was used to, and this satisfied her greatly. She could hear the energy coming from her, and this put her at ease.

"So I will see you at six o'clock, in less than eighty hours."

"Well, when you say it like that it sounds like a long time. Three days, and I'll be throwing my junk in the back seat of your car. How about that?"

"Okay, three days it is!"

They had laughter in their throats as they hung up, and Sandra did a quick spin and bumped into her mother.

"What's happening in three days?"

She was momentarily caught off guard, but she got a hold herself effortlessly.

"I'm going to the movies with some friends."

"Since when did you start having friends? You've never brought anyone over here."

Sandra was about to blow her top, but she couldn't allow her to steal what little joy in life she had. She refused to stand there and define her friendships or anything else to her mother.

"Excuse me."

Sandra bumped her on her way out of the kitchen. She headed for her room and thought again about calling Mrs. Washington back.

CHAPTER 20

When Sandra woke the next morning, she found herself a little edgy and out of sorts. She quickly got out of bed and took inventory of her things. She thought she may have been robbed in the night, and maybe that was the cause of her nerves jumping all over the place, but all of her things were there. She had two suitcases in the back of her closet, and she threw a pile of clothes on top of them. Her duffle bag was under her bed, and that's where she put all of the feminine products she had purchased.

She went to the grocery store to get some snacks for the long ride and more batteries for her headphone set. She put the items in the duffle bag but forgot to throw away the plastic bags in which they came. It no longer mattered whether she hid the wrappers anymore. She was on her way out the door, and if her mother were to stumble across something now, she could care less.

She got out of bed looking at the clock and was surprised to see it was nine o'clock. She could distinctly hear voices in the living room, and the sound raised the hair on the back of her neck instantly. She knew the sound of that voice, even though it had been a very long time since she had heard it.

She knew she had to get out of there, and fast! Sandra ran to the closet and tossed all the clothes to the side in search of her suitcases. She then dove headfirst under the bed to retrieve her duffle bag. She dressed in a fleece jogging suit, even though the temperature was well into the upper seventies. The material was loose fitting and comfortable. Sandra checked her pockets for change, and made sure there was enough to call Mrs. Washington when she got to the store.

Sandra slid back her curtain and opened the window. After her last episode, she'd chipped away all the paint that held it shut and sprayed the sill with cooking spray. If she ever needed to escape again, she didn't want the window to be her downfall. One by one she heaved her belongings out the window. Once her duffle bag made it to the grass and she got ready to climb out, a chilling sound vibrated her ear.

"Hello, Sandra."

Bill stood less than three feet away from her, and she hadn't even heard him approach. There wasn't a plan of action at the time, but she knew she was getting out of the window one way or the other.

In a blink, she tried her escape route. Sandra bounced up unto the edge of the window sill and began pulling herself through it. There was no more than a six-foot drop beneath her, and she knew she could land in practically any position and not be too badly hurt. Her feet were the last things to clear the window, but they were stuck on something. She couldn't tell what it was from her position, and it was impossible to try and kick loose.

She kept wiggling, in hopes of being able to free herself, but she couldn't get her legs out the window. She was in such an awkward position that she had no balance or coordination to do anything but hang upside-down.

The blood began rushing to her head, and she feared she would get some form of brain injury if she couldn't get her legs to follow the rest of her body. She tried again and again to shake her feet loose, and it wasn't until she felt the fingertips digging into her ankles that she realized she was being held and was not actually caught on anything.

She tried to turn her head upwards, but it was no use. She was getting dizzy. She wished he would either push her out or pull her back in. One way or another, she would be in a better position than she was currently in.

She had no legs to fight with, and her arms were of no use to her either. They just dangled above her head, while her fingertips began to tingle. She had to get him to make a move; just hanging there was not getting her anywhere. She needed to be on solid ground in order to fight this battle, so she did the only thing she could to get him into action. She screamed.

"Help! Help me! Help!"

It was early in the morning, and someone was bound to walk by and see her there.

"Help! Help!"

Sandra continued to scream in hopes that someone would hear her, but instead it got her pulled back in through the window. She could feel his hands clawing at her legs and tugging with a strong grip. She used this opportunity to try to free herself. She wanted to move around in hopes that he would lose his grip on her. She really didn't want to end up back in the house. She wanted to hit the ground and start running.

The war seemed to go on forever. She was losing her pants, and it became useless to try to keep reaching for them. She didn't care if her panties were showing. She was hoping someone would pass by and see her. The tension in her legs was getting the better of her. He had leverage by being in the house. He could put all his strength in his arms without worrying about falling or anything else.

The fight was slipping away from Sandra as she continued to swing side to side. He was going to be able to get her back in the house, that she was sure of, what she would do after that became the big question.

The butcher knife was under her mattress. She knew she wouldn't have a good chance of getting at it. She tried to think of a plan B, but her head was swaying, and it felt as if someone were drilling her temples with a hammer.

The more she fought, the worse she was beginning to feel. She allowed her body to go limp and give him the chance to pull her back into the house. It was the only option she had at the time. He was not going to let her go, so she had to give up in order to get out. She was clueless as to where her mother was, but she was sure she knew what was transpiring behind her door. She would not come to help her, and once again Sandra found herself on her own, fighting a battle that was bigger than her.

"Where in the world were you going? I take it by your leap of faith that you are not happy to see me?" Sandra said nothing. She allowed her head to hang down, and she just relaxed. She needed all of her senses to help her get out of this situation. She had no idea what route to take. She wanted to fight until the bitter end, but she wasn't sure if she would win. He had overpowered her before, and she didn't want that to take place again. She must outthink him. She couldn't allow her anger to control the situation. She had to be smarter than the last time.

"Hi, Bill."

"Ah, now that's better. Act like you're happy to see me, at least. I thought about you every day I was gone. Do you know that?"

She was sitting on the floor just beneath the window sill, and he had begun to massage her leg. Bill was on his knees in front of her, and the hungry look in his eyes scared her more than anything. She didn't want to be his victim anymore. She didn't want him to touch her. The anger that she tried to hold at bay would not stay buried. It simmered and stewed inside of her until she was no longer in control of it.

Sandra leaped at him, clawing at his face the entire time. The rage that poured out fueled the intensity of her actions, giving her the strength she needed.

She had caught him off balance, and for a second she was holding the better hand. She quickly crawled toward the door when he fell on his back, but he grasped her ankle before she had a chance to get a good grip on the knob.

Sandra used her other foot to kick at him, but he never relinquished his hold on her. He was trying to stand up, and she knew he would definitely overpower her if he was standing.

Quickly, she reached for the lamp on the nightstand in hopes of smashing it over his head, but he yanked the cord that dangled from it, and the lamp landed clumsily on the floor. He was still behind her, and he only had a hold of one leg, so she continued to kick. It satisfied her to see the blood running from one of the scratches over his eye, but it was not enough damage.

She twisted over to sit on her butt so she could aim more accurately at her target. She brought her heel down with expert precision on his forehead, and he let out a bursting groan. She tried to repeat her last step, but he was ready for her.

When she raised her foot, he leaped on top of her, bending her leg into a skyward scissor position. His weight pulled fiercely at her hamstrings, and she felt as if her muscles were tearing from the inside.

If it wasn't for the nightstand, he would have pressed her foot beyond her head. Her other leg was flat against the floor, burning from the separation. Sandra's left arm remained free, so she tried punching him in the ear over and over again.

He was getting angrier by the second. The longer she extended the inevitable, the rougher he became, but she knew she could not and would not give up. He was so enraged by her rejection that he began to spit in her face.

"Whore!"

Drool fell from his mouth after every expletive he hissed at her. She could feel it on her lips, but she tried not to think about it. The continued boxing of his ears was getting the better of him, so she kept on that path. Bill tried ducking his head between his shoulders, but she kept swinging, and landing her punches in the same spot until he thought he would lose his hearing in that ear. She could not flip him. She was wedged between the bed and the nightstand. Her knife was close but also so useless at the time. If she were to go for it now, she knew he would be able to easily obtain it from her.

Bill was so overcome with bitter resentment that he aimed for Sandra's throat with the thought of choking the life out of her. He didn't care if she died or not at this point. He was blinded by rage, not thinking twice about his actions.

The moment her air supply became restricted, she went for his hands. She no longer slammed her fist into the side of his face. She couldn't breathe, and her next breath became top priority. Her feeble attempt to free his hands became an act of desperation. Her vision was beginning to blur, and she could feel every nerve ending in her body begging her to let in some form of oxygen, but Bill didn't even consider letting up. Veins were extending from her temples to her forehead. Her face turned crimson red and looked hot to the touch. She was losing focus, and he knew it.

It took less than twenty more seconds for her to totally give up the fight. Her arm fell to her side, and her eyes began to roll. She could think of nothing but the hatred she held for this man and her mother. To know that she was so close to getting away, and then to have this happen to her, made her want to fight her fate that much harder. She knew she was in a lose-lose situation. There was no way she could get this two hundred-and-some-pound man off of her. With all of the things she wanted to accomplish and all of the things she'd been able to overcome, Sandra was furious that this was to be the end of her beginning.

For the briefest of moments she thought about Mrs. Washington and what she would think of the ending to her life story. She knew without a doubt that she would always wonder why she didn't do more or why she never called the authorities about Sandra's home life situation. She probably would dwell on it for quite some time, and that brought a new feeling of guilt to her. Why hadn't she just packed her stuff and left? Why did she allow herself to stay in the house a minute longer than she had to? If she just would have taken her counselor's advice, she would have been eating Rocky Road ice cream and listening to her reminisce about her college days. But it didn't matter now; it was over.

It took Bill only five additional seconds to realize he didn't want to return to prison for a homicide. He released his hold on her neck, but she didn't move. There was a blue tint to her lips, and her eyes seemed to be permanently embedded in the top of her head. He had no idea what to do. He didn't know CPR, so he had no inkling what his next step should be in order to restore some color to her face. He did what he thought was best, and he smacked her with as much force as he could.

That caused her eyes to close, and he was grateful for that. Some reaction was better than none. Sandra coughed once, but that was it. Bill was standing over her now, with no plan B. He thought about bolting out of the house, but he could hear more than one voice in the living room. He didn't want to risk someone trying to play the hero. Absently, he looked at the same window Sandra had tried to escape from, and that became his number one option. Bill peered out the window, hoping the street was clear so he could jump out. He spotted one elderly woman walking on the other side of the street, but she was almost past the house. He decided to wait for her to go by and then count to ten.

He was so focused on the movement outside of the house that he didn't notice the movement within until it was almost too late. A change in the atmosphere made him turn in the direction of the shift. He was just able to catch Sandra's hand going under the mattress. She was sitting up against the nightstand, but her hand could no longer be seen.

The bruising around her neck was visible even from across the room, and her cheek was swelling from his faint attempt of reviving her, but other than that, she was very much alive.

He was ecstatic in one aspect that he had not committed a homicide, but at the same time, he was almost too slow to catch her intensions. Her movements were not as quick as they would have been had she just not been deprived of oxygen for the last forty-five seconds or so, but she was still going after something under the mattress, and he knew it wasn't a love letter.

Bill was quick to react, clearing the five feet that separated them in seconds. He reached for Sandra and was more than surprised to feel sharpness in his thigh. Sandra let out an animalistic howl simultaneously as she plunged something into his flesh. She twisted the knife into the upper part of his leg, intent on ripping his thigh to the bone if she could.

Bill leaned down to grab the knife out of her hand, but he was too slow. The twisting motion she had initiated almost made him black out. He had never felt a pain as blinding as what he was experiencing at the time; it brought him to his knees.

Sandra had brought her nemesis down. She was operating in a way that she no longer had control over. She could not think of it as an out-of-body experience because she was not exactly capable of defining herself. She was no longer sane by any meaning of the word, but she was very active in the scene that was in progress.

Sandra pulled the knife out of his thigh, rose to her knees with the knife held high overhead, and immediately aimed for his chest. He tried to put his hands up to block her but was only able to deflect the arch of her swing slightly. She met a resistance under the blade when it came into contact with his flesh, so she pushed downward with all the might she possessed.

The blade sliced through whatever had tried to hinder its path, and she began to twist again. Bill spun and writhed on the floor in pain. He reached for Sandra's leg and was met with a firm kick in the chin. She was dominating the entire situation now and was functioning in an eerily mechanical state.

She did not stand over him but instead stayed on the floor very close to him. She seemed to be feeding off his misery. While it drained him of his strength, it fueled her. He continued to try to fight her off even though he was unable to use his right arm. She had stabbed him under his clavicle, and the blade angled itself toward his armpit. She dug deeper into the wound, but it didn't seem to change his appearance of pain. Sandra retracted the knife, and without thought or hesitation stabbed him again.

Bill was panting and groaning while she unleashed her vengeance on him. His breaths came in short bursts, and he couldn't seem to get enough air. He was on his side, balled up in a fetal position, crying. "Please, Sandra...please...I'm sorry! I'm sorry! I swear to God! Please!"

For the slightest of moments, she considered opening her door, telling her mother what she had done, and maybe even helping him in some way, but another part of her could not trust what he was saying.

She had looked to him as some form of a father figure when her own father decided not to be around. He had shown her attention and catered to her like a devoted parent, and the entire time he was waiting for her to become a little bit more mature, a little riper, a little more developed. He was a predator! He had no respect for women, and he viewed children as little disposable pawns in his game.

He didn't deserve a second chance. She didn't need Dorothy, a courtroom, or a judge to help her reach a verdict. She would be his judge and jury today!

Without an inkling of pity, she started to slice into him repeatedly. Sandra was blinded by the years of fury and the disgust she held for men. The days of walking the fine line and smiling to ensure she was liked were over. Long gone were the pigtails and bobby socks. She had now emerged from a life of abuse and neglect that at one point she thought she had only a slight chance of escaping.

All of the vivid dreams that crossed her mind as she slept were now right in front of her, in reality. She was putting her helplessness to rest. She would no longer sleep facing the door and jump at everything that moved. She didn't have to cry herself to sleep and wonder why no one ever loved her. Bill would not crawl all over her skin and make her feel like vomiting every time she bathed her own body.

Her mind involuntarily skimmed back to the first time Bill raped her and how she was unable to eat for days. She was weak and terrified daily of going home. He came for her every day for the first four days. It wasn't until a week had gone by without seeing him that she stopped hiding in the closet until dark. When one of her teachers began to question her rapid weight loss, she had to endure the bouts of nausea and keep the food down in order to keep the questions at bay. In a way she was protecting him, and it sickened her.

She had been through so much, had seen too much, and now she was facing the point of no return. The rationale in her head pleaded constantly for her to back off and do the right thing, but she was unable to obey such a simple command. She couldn't turn off the sheer impulses she was operating on. A clinging film of exhaustion covered her, and she took a moment and a few breaths to reflect on what had taken place.

Bill was breathing, but he was no longer fighting her as before. His voice came in whispers as he pleaded and cried for her to get him some help. There was blood everywhere. She looked at the walls and was temporarily transfixed by the splatter patterns that consumed the area by her bed. Some of the droplets were dry, while others glowed bright from their freshness.

Sandra looked across the room, and the window seemed to stare back at her tauntingly. It spoke of the destiny she had so carelessly abandoned. Her life stood frozen in the gentle breeze that wafted into the room. She would never be able to laugh again. Her eyes would not twinkle at the touch or feel of something new. The opportunity had escaped her, and she would not be able to grasp it again.

Her mind allowed itself to close off from the outside world and the possibilities and options it held for her. She could no longer conceive it. It was as if it wasn't there and never had been. Sandra got up off the floor and walked around her room. The bed held the most disastrous memories and nightmares for her. She looked in the closet at the wire hangers that dangled loosely there and knew her clothes would never hang there again.

The last items she purchased still remained on her bedside table, where they had been forgotten when she tried to leave hastily. She fingered the little can of feminine deodorant spray that Mrs. Washington told her to buy. She had never used it.

She popped the top off, pressed the plunger, and the room was hit with an instant scent of powder and cucumbers that brought tears to her eyes. She had never used anything to make her feel like a woman, or even considered it, for that matter, but now that the scent clung to her nose and permeated the air around her, she ached for it desperately.

But Sandra knew that her life wasn't meant to be that way. She wasn't one of the girls with the good parents and supportive siblings. She was very much alone. Soft and gentle things were not for her. It was rough and hard, and it would never get any easier.

She wanted to believe what Mrs. Washington was telling her, and for the briefest amount of time, she did. But now that her life had taken on its second phase, she knew exactly who was to blame: God. She thought of all of the time she'd wasted praying to him, only to be fooled in the end. She thought he was working on her mother and going to make her life just a little bit easier, only to find out he had no such thing in store for her.

The constant prayers to make Bill and all the men like him disappear went unanswered. The begging, the pleading, the tears, the torture! There was no God! Sandra dropped the can to the floor and watched it roll away, smeared with her bloody fingerprints on its surface.

She removed the two sticks of deodorant and tube of lip gloss that remained in the bag and dropped them on the floor along with the spray. She held the bag in her hands and felt her soul was now just as empty. She stood by the side of her bed, utterly confused, and no matter how hard she tried, she just could not get a hold of reality.

There was a war going on inside of her head, and she had no choice in the winner. It was as if she were a pawn in a chess game not knowing who the opponents were. She was being physically and mentally manipulated by the battle that went on, and she could do nothing. She had lost control of all voluntary functions and was now propelled by something darker and deeper than herself.

She didn't know what force was driving her, but she decided not to fight it. She didn't want to feel sorry for Bill or her mother. Let their future be as it may. Why should she give them a second chance? Where was hers?

Her counselor could not fit the shoes of a savior because that was not the role she was meant to play. God had placed her there as an illusion of some sort, a diversion. God had allowed her to believe that she was going to be saved from her life as she knew it. He dangled Mrs. Washington in front of her like a carrot. Sandra took the bait and was led around feverishly. She wondered if Mrs. Washington knew that she was never meant to succeed or if she truly believed wholeheartedly that she had saved a child. Either way it went, the plan would not come to fruition.

She knew that God was somewhere, waiting like a thief in the night. Every day she tried to push it out of her mind that he was coming soon to take away everything she had hoped for, especially when it had gotten so close to her departure time. His presence continued to nag at her. Even if she were able to get to the bus depot, she knew her trip would be hindered by some form of accident; a gunman on board or some other misguided fate would be thrust upon her.

It had taken days on end to convince herself that she was going to make it, she was getting out. She forced herself to throw out the negativity and think positive. It put a strain on her psyche, but she continued to break through and show Mrs. Washington her determination. It was daunting and time-consuming, but she did it. She felt she had a real chance. When she'd started the ten-day countdown, a veil had been lifted off of her.

Things that she had never taken the time to notice before became the reason she woke up in the mornings. God had forgotten about her. She'd breathed in the air of her future and cried tears of relief every night. She'd allowed herself to be overjoyed and empowered by her journey, until she'd heard Bill's voice behind her.

God had come back for her, and he did so in the worse way. He sent the man who had used her first. He sent the man who had taken pleasure in the ripping and shredding of her very soul, the animal that gave her nightmares and caused her to wet the bed on several occasions from fear of leaving her room. God had sent him!

Sandra blinked out of her reverie when the sound of Bill's voice broke through the trance she had been in. She looked over to see that he had made his way to the door and was trying to reach the knob. There was a huge saturated puddle from the spot he left, but he still had enough gusto to try to escape. For a moment, she was in awe. She watched him until she saw the door open and let out a sliver of light that led to the living room.

She leaped across the bed in time to push the door closed. He started to get louder in his croaking, and she wanted to silence him quickly. She didn't know if her mother still had company or not, and she didn't want to chance someone coming into her room and her not having an explanation for the scenery.

It took her less than a second to place the plastic bag over his head. Sandra sat on his back and pulled the handles tightly around his neck. Bill started to pant and puff profusely, and it seemed to inflate the bag instead of suffocate him.

With seemingly skilled professionalism, she smoothed the bag tightly over his face and re-clamped her hold around his neck. The inflation stopped instantly, and seconds later his body began to shake and buck tremendously. Sandra had never ridden a horse before, but she was sure the ride would be close to what she was experiencing now.

He was shaking his head wildly from side to side as he reached back to claw at her hands. Nothing could faze her at this moment; she felt no pain. Instead, she was exhilarated to the point where she felt an electric tingle jolt to life deep inside and take control of her body. She was sure that her hair must be standing on end from the currents going through her. Sandra was feeling a rush that she had never known, and she wondered briefly if this is what the first hit of a drug felt like.

Her fingers began cramping as she continued to hold her grip on the bag. They were slipping because of the blood that was already on her hands combined with the steady seeping from the gash in the upper part of his shoulder. Bill fought with everything he had, and the more he did, the more blood he lost.

The fight was lasting longer than it should have. Sandra had no idea how long it took a person to suffocate, but she did think Bill was over-extending himself somehow. She was already fatigued from the battle earlier and the life-preserving strategies Bill was using against her now were adding to her weariness.

On instinct, he began tearing at the bag that restricted his air flow. He needed to breathe. He used his finger to try to poke a hole in the mouth area, and this infuriated her. He should be dead by now. He deserved to die, yet he desperately tried to cling on to his miserable life.

Sandra leaned forward and bit his hand as he started to reach for the bag that had abruptly cut off his air supply. She could almost feel her teeth meet between the gristle of his knuckles, but the fight persisted. They tussled back and forth until his movements became less and less forceful.

She knew that without a doubt he was dying. Bill's legs no longer kicked and moved sporadically, but they took on movements similar to shivering. His feet jerked every now and then, but other than that, he was not moving anymore.

*

Bill also knew the fight was over. He could feel her pressing into him with her entire body weight, as his neck was being reined back. If he'd had even the slightest idea that his day would end like this, he would have chosen to go with the prostitute who'd begged his for attention instead of going to Sandra's house. He should have never come back once he got out of jail. He was free again and was still able to drive trucks. He should have taken that as a sign that he needed to start his life over, at least in a new venue.

He hadn't actually planned on seeing her for another two weeks or so. He had a long haul to do in Texas, and from there he had to go upstate. He wasn't going to be in the Denver area for at least the next ten to twelve days.

It wasn't until he'd called Dorothy that the conversation spurred him into action. He really had just dialed the number to see if it was still a working number, nothing more, but she answered. She had told him that Sandra was leaving soon for college. Dorothy had gone on to tell him that she had missed him terribly and that she could really use a good fix. He didn't want to go that route with her again. He could tell by the sound of her voice what she must look like. He told her he would be there in under an hour, but really he hadn't planned on it.

The thought of seeing Sandra again was a dangerously succulent morsel to dangle in front of him. She knew all along he would come to see her daughter eventually, but by throwing in the fact that she was leaving for college, she knew he would show up. In his mind's eye she was a worthless and despicable excuse for a mother. He felt a parent's job was to protect their kids before all others, but Dorothy, his mom and his wife had failed miserably in that department.

He blamed both of them for the things that happened to their daughters, just as he had always blamed his mother for what happened to his sisters. They chose to turn the other cheek instead of believing there was a monster living under their roof. His mother was so submissive to his father and his demands that somehow what she wanted from him and the marriage was lost in the shuffle.

There was no way she didn't know the danger her daughters were in or the way they were suffering at the hands of their father. She knew, and yet she did nothing. She hoped it would go away, but did it really matter if it continued? His older sister came to their mother and told her in as many words as possible what they had been subjected to and what they were going through, but nothing changed. They felt betrayed, and he felt vindicated in his actions.

Bill's wife was a different story, but not totally. She was so into shopping and making good appearances that she didn't notice anything if it didn't have a hundred dollar or better price tag attached to it. She would dress his daughters in the finest clothes and most expensive shoes the store sold, but that is all she paid attention to: their outer layer. She didn't take the time to notice how hollow their eyes had become or how withdrawn they were until it was too late. Even then she fretted for almost a year before she decided to call the authorities. It was all about image to her. She didn't want the outside looking in, especially if the dirty laundry was about to be aired.

Bill knew the exact day that she found out something was going on. She was such a surface person that it didn't take a rocket scientist to read the emotions across her face. She no longer slept in their bedroom, yet she did nothing to protect her daughters' room. She would stay out all night and drink with her girlfriends, which Bill took as an indication that she knew but didn't want to face it. So he continued to do just as he pleased. He never thought for one minute that she would have the guts to call the authorities on him. Not for one second would his ego allow him to see that in his near future. He had miscalculated, and it cost him dearly.

That was so long ago, but now he had misjudged his final outcome again. To think that Sandra would have somehow overpowered him was ridiculous. He'd planned on seeing her and rehashing some of their old memories.

Although his original thought was to get a hotel room to deal with the street walker he had picked up, he went against his first instincts, kicked the lady out of his truck, and headed for Dorothy's house. He would never be able to chastise himself for the error in judgment he'd made because he had lost control of the situation, and he would not be able to recover from it.

He guessed this was payback for all the things he had done. He knew there was no such thing as heaven, but he'd always believed in hell, and he knew he was now experiencing it in its purest form. His chest burned as if Satan himself was jabbing him continuously with a poker from the fire. With every sip of air he tried to inhale, the burning sensation grew more and more intense. He would swear that he could feel the capillaries in his eyes rupturing one by one.

His mouth had already filled with blood long before he was being suffocated, but the agony of not being able to swallow it or clear his airway sent him into a stage of panic. He flipped and flopped uselessly on the floor and even tried to use the last of his strength to bring some kind of pain to Sandra, but it was all in vain. She had him in a savage grip and had no plans on letting go. No matter how he bucked, slid, or clawed, the pressure on his throat was intense and unrelenting.

Bill didn't want to face it, but she had won. He no longer could feel his toes, and the sensation in his upper body had left him long ago. His body went slack, and he knew he would never stand, walk, or talk again. The most basic aspects in life were now forever out of his reach.

*

Sandra felt the fight escape him, but she refused to relinquish her hold on the plastic.

It wasn't until her fingers were locked and her wrist seemed to be flexed in a permanent position that she began to un-wind the handles of the bag. Bill did not move. It was as if time was sitting still, never to be started again. She didn't think about the past or her future because she was deeply enchanted with the right now and what she had accomplished.

She was free. The demons that chased her in her sleep, followed her up and down the halls of her school, and screamed constantly in her mind were quiet now. The stillness of the moment brought her a calmness she had never known. Sandra could not remember a time when she was at such deep peace within herself. She was acutely aware of her surroundings and everything about herself.

Sandra stood up and stretched her legs to relieve the cramps that invaded her thighs. She had no emotions going through her at this time, and she left it as that. Not for one moment did she want to look inside and see the animal that had enabled her to do what she had done. She focused on right now, not what might have been.

She didn't know how to go about cleaning the mess in her room, but she knew she didn't want to wake up every day and see Bill blocking her door. No, he would have to go.

The concept of what had really taken place seemed to evade her. She was no longer thinking of the consequences of her actions but of carrying on with the daily activities of her life without the presence of Bill looming over her. She felt absolutely vindicated in what she had done, and her mind wouldn't allow her to think any other way.

Sandra bent over and grabbed him by the legs to move him out the path of her door. She guessed she should feel some form of disgust from touching and manipulating a corpse, but she didn't. She felt nothing at all. It was no different than if she were moving a load of laundry. She managed to get him flush with the wall, and she was satisfied with her efforts.

The bag had slipped from his head during the repositioning, and he was now staring at her. She leaned down close to his face and spit in the eyes that stared back at her. The blood that seeped from the corners of his lips maddened her for some reason, so she stuck her hands in his mouth and scooped it out. She didn't want to see him dripping all over her floor. She would not clean up after him anymore. She would not cover the tracks of the things he left behind.

She was so upset by the mess his body was now creating that she kicked him repeatedly. Sandra stomped him about the head and continued to abuse his lifeless body.

"Sandra...Sandra are you okay?"

Dorothy was at the door, and Sandra didn't know what to do. If she came in and saw the bloody mess, she could not deny what she had done or how it happened.

Sandra slumped down on the floor beside Bill and felt her anger and humiliation soar beyond her control. She yanked his head up and slammed it against the wall, despite the fact that her mother may walk in at any given time. She felt the fury consume her and motivate her movements. She began ranting to herself and was surprised to hear that it was her very own voice whispering in her ears. She couldn't just sit in one place; she had to plan out her next steps, what they should be, and the process by which she should carry them out.

Sandra slowly and methodically began to picture her next couple of moves and the way they should be incorporated into the immediate future, but the insistent buzzing would not allow her to focus on a continuous basis. The sound was more persistent than her concentration. It beat in her mind at a pace that became too fast to keep in check. She began to listen to the noise, which took on the sound of a desperate hissing, and then a voice just as crisp as her own emerged from her throat and planted itself on her lips to be spoken.

"You have to move him, Sandra. He can't stay by the door where he will be seen when it is opened. Drag him to the closet. Quietly!"

She was surprised to hear the noise, and even more so to find herself following its commands, but that is exactly what she was doing. It seemed to be stronger than she was, and it came across with such calm, she knew by listening, things would have a better outcome. It took all the tension out her body. When she listened closely, everything else was silent. This was her savior, this was her God, and this is what would help her make it to another day.

Sandra felt almost ecstatic in her demented situation. Just when she had begun to believe she was alone, she was not. There was someone with her, and of all time's she was thankful for the company.

Without question or hesitation, she grabbed Bill's legs and headed for the closet. She had voluntarily relinquished her hold over the situation. She couldn't come up with the next steps on her own, so the voice became quite helpful to her at the time.

She knew eventually she would have to leave the room, but then what? Sandra knew she would have to face Dorothy, and how to handle that was not clear to her, but her inner self seemed to know just what to do and how to go about doing it, so without question, she moved to its barking orders.

"Push him in the back and hide him with some clothes. We don't want to see poor Bill anymore, do we? You need to clean off your bed. There is no way we can sleep on it the way it is. Remove the linen, roll it up, and put it under the bed."

She was feeling better about the situation all around, almost bubbly, in fact to know that she was not alone in this mess. Something bigger than her was tapping into the very center of her intellect, and carrying because she could not stand on her own. She had help, and it was smart and precise under pressure. She was feeling more than thankful.

After the sheets were removed and placed where she was told to put them, she was at a loss. She had no idea what her next step should be, so she sat on the soiled mattress and waited for some sign or for the voice to return and tell her what to do.

"Sandra?"

"Don't just sit there. Lock the door!"

Sandra leaped into action and locked the door. Within seconds of her twisting the lock into place, she could clearly see her handle jiggling from side to side. Her mother was trying to get in. Dorothy tapped on the door, lightly calling Sandra's name again.

"Answer her! Don't act like a mute."

But the words would not escape her lips. She put forth all the effort she could muster, but nothing came of it. Her mother continued to tap on the door, and the tugging on the knob became more urgent, judging by the force she was using.

"Answer her, damn it!"

It felt as if someone had punched her in the back, and the air, along with her voice, exploded from her mouth.

"Yeah, Mom? What is it?"

"Oh, um…it's been a while for your umm…company, and I was wondering…"

"I'll be out in a minute."

"Oh, okay. The package that Bill brought me, is it in there with you? You can slide it under the door and—"

"Get away from me!"

"I need it so I can—"

"Get away!"

Sandra heard her feet shuffling away from the door and down the hall. She knew she was cutting it close. She had to get out of the room and past her mom so that she could run away from this disaster. She didn't know how long she could hide in plain sight, but she definitely had to get out of the house, and fast.

She allowed her mind to drift again without an immediate plan of what to do to keep her mother at bay and still survive.

"What are you waiting on? Check his pockets."

The voice sprouted through the trance-like state she was in and brought her to full attention. It was demanding that she get into action and do as she was told. But things were getting to be more than she felt she could handle.

Sandra had no plans of going anywhere near Bill again in life. She did not want to look at his face ever again, if she could help it. She fought the voice that urged her to go into the closet and frisk the very corpse she had just disposed of. She had to find her own voice of reason. She couldn't allow herself to be driven by some unforeseen force. She had to think, but her mind was so fuzzy and out of sync that her next steps were puzzling to her. Sandra went to sit on the mattress and was instantly bolted upright.

"Get up! Go to the closet. What are you doing? There is work to be done! Get the little packets your mother is craving. She will not stop coming to the door until she gets what she wants."

Sandra was beyond furious and stressed by the entire scenario. She didn't want to do the things that were being demanded of her, and her mother would not stop pestering her for one minute. She wanted the drugs that Bill had brought, but why hadn't she gotten them when he had first arrived there? Why would she wait until now to start protesting about it?

She had never knocked on the door when someone would pay her to go in and mutilate her daughter. She always played the innocent who had no clue of what was going on beyond the walls of her room, and now out of the blue, she was demanding entrance into the hellish scene?

Sandra began pulling at her hair as her nerves got the best of her. She wanted to scream to release some of the pressure building inside, but didn't want to bring attention back to her doorstep. She paced back and forth until the soles of her feet burned from the friction generating off the carpet. This is not what she planned on doing. She just wanted to get out and be free.

At the very thought of the word, she looked at her window as it remained open like the dangling fruit from the Garden of Eden. She did not hesitate in her movements; not once did she look back.

Sandra charged for the window. She desperately wanted to get out and into the open before that voice could rein her back in. She couldn't hear anything except the beating of her own heart racing inside her chest. She put her feet on the ledge and prepared to jump but didn't. She wanted so badly to be outside and away from the sight of Bill and the smell of his blood, but something wouldn't allow her to go.

There were no physical restraints in place, yet her feet were stuck in a fixed position. She was beyond fearful at this point, and once again, she lost focus and could not make a concrete decision on what her next steps should be.

"Get down from there and finish what you started! You didn't run as you stabbed him like a psycho! Why are you leaving now? Isn't this what you wanted? To be in charge? You killed a man, and now you run like a coward!"

"He was trying to rape me! He wanted to rape me!" Sandra screamed at the voice that taunted and teased her.

"Yes, yes, calm down. You handled that. You were able to come out on top, but now we have to finish the job. We can leave no stone un- turned. You have to get the packets."

"No. No, I can't"

"You can, Sandra, and you will. We have to keep going."

Sandra stood, shaking, as she held on to the ledge. She didn't want to go back into the closet. She didn't want to ever enter the house again, but slowly and as if from no will of her own, she started climbing down from the window sill. She didn't go toward the bed to sit on the mattress, but went directly to the closet. She had to finish the job. This is the one step she had to put before her escape. If she could muster up the strength from somewhere inside, she may be able to get rid of Bill and the voices all at the same time.

Sandra thought for a brief moment that she could blame the murder of Bill on her mother. If she was the only person in the house when the police came, then why wouldn't they think she was the cause of his murder? Surely they wouldn't go looking for her while she was in college.

Maybe this is what the voice was trying to tell her all along. Maybe it took some talking to in order for her to see the bigger picture. She would give her mom the packets, make sure she was high and in no condition to get off the couch; then she would be off. She would call her counselor form the corner store phone booth, and the rest was history. She would be in college and living the life that Mrs. Washington had told her so often about.

The mere thought that she still had a way out, moved her feet in such a way that she felt as if she was floating. There were no second thoughts anymore. No more doubts. She knew what she had to do, and she was very determined to do it.

She no longer dreaded looking at his body. He had something that she needed, and that is the way she continued to look at the situation.

Without hesitation, she opened the door, and was met by Bill's legs. They didn't flop out the door the way they had flopped in but instead sat stiffly in her way.

Sandra didn't want to look into the cramped closet, so she just felt her way up his pant leg until she could feel his pockets. She felt inside the first one and found it very moist but empty. The smell of urine permeated the closet and whiffed up her nose.

Sandra stayed calm and focused. She reached for his other hip and found the pocket. She crammed her fingers inside and felt the moistness again, but there was something more. With the precision of a surgeon, she removed the packets her mother had been asking for.

Sandra wiped the bloody residue from the outside and just held them. These minute things had caused so much damage in her life. They had taken her father away and left her with a heartless dope fiend for a mother. She wished there was a way she could kill the packets as well, but it was a useless thought. Sandra balled the packets up in her hand, and headed for the door.

"You have to go to the bathroom first. You can't let her see that you have blood on your hands and clothes. Take a clean set of clothes to the bathroom with you. Things have to look normal. You don't want to sound the alarm before you've had the chance to escape."

Once again, she was thankful for the guidance her subconscious was giving. She had not thought that far and would have more than likely gone out into the living room looking like something out of *Night of the Living Dead* if the voice had not warned her otherwise.

In almost a robotic way, Sandra went to her drawer to get a change of clothes. It was only then that she realized that all of her belongings were in the duffle bag she had thrown out the window.

"Get one of the shirts that you used to cover Bill. You left a pair of shorts in the bottom drawer. Be careful leaving the room. Timing is everything."

Once again she ventured into the closet and retrieved a shirt. The first one she pulled out had to be tossed back in because it was stained just as bad as the one she was wearing, and the second one was too wet. The last shirt that was the closest to his feet was the one she decided on. It had a little blood on the tail of the shirt, but she thought she could tuck that into her shorts.

She pulled her T-shirt over her head and tossed it into the closet, along with the pants she had on, and then changed into the new shirt and shorts. Sandra made it to the door with no more instructions. She peeked left, then right, and then made a quick dash down the hall. She made it successfully and was thankful. She felt as if she were living out an episode of *Mission: Impossible*.

As quietly as she could, she closed the bathroom door and began to wash her hands. The blood rinsed from dark red to clear, and she started to feel a little better. She glanced in the mirror and caught a glimpse of her face, with a smudge of blood on her cheek and tiny splatters all over.

Suddenly she realized just what she had done and who she had done it to. Walking around in a haze was no longer an option. She was now being slapped with the harsh reality of it all, and it consumed her totally. She felt her body involuntarily constricting and tightening, and she began to feel nauseated.

It took less than a minute for her to begin retching in the toilet. Her body convulsed and shook with tremendous force, and she shed tears as she emptied her stomach. She was drained and not sure if she had the strength to go on. She wanted to give her mother the drugs and leave the house, but she just didn't think she had the strength within her. Her arms were shaking in a terrible way as she tried to hold on to the back of the toilet. She flopped on the floor and wept.

Everything she had ever wanted had been cruelly ripped away from her, and now she sat on a cold floor, contemplating how she was going to fix the mess she created. Actually, she didn't know if blaming it on her mother would even work. Would she be able to get out of the city before the police hunt her down like a stray dog?

Sandra sat in an inconsolable state of isolation and despair until there was a knock at the door.

"Sandra?"

Why couldn't she just let her be? Why did she have to follow her and hound her at every step?

"Sandra?"

She was growing more and more resentful and angry by the minute. She wanted nothing more than for her mom to leave her alone, right now and forever.

"Sandra?"

"Answer her!"

"Sandra, are you in there?"

"If you don't say something, she will either bust down the door or worse, go to your room."

"I don't care! I don't care! I don't care! I'm tired! Let her go in the room! Let her see what she did!"

"Who are you talking to? Is Bill in there with you?"

Sandra was in a frenzy of torture. Her mind was struggling to hold onto the gravity of the circumstances as well as comply with outside influences. She had reached her breaking point and she could not rein herself back in from the severity of it. She gathered herself from the floor, trying desperately to take steps in the right direction.

She faced herself once again in mirror, turned on the cold water, and began splashing it in her face. The coolness felt remarkable, like a medicated salve on a burn. She just needed a few more minutes to herself, and she would be able to get through the worst part of this scenario. She was almost convinced of that.

"Sandra?"

The knocking was unbearable and distracting. No matter what she did, her mother would not let her rest. Just when she was getting a hold of herself and the situation, she would break through with her whining voice. What could she possible want? She asked the question to her reflection, and then she saw the little forgotten packets on the sink. She had placed them there when she first entered the bathroom and had totally forgotten about them. Of course that was what she wanted. It was what she always wanted. A life with a husband and child did not take precedence over the packets. No, everyone was second in comparison to what the drug could give her.

"Sandra..."

"I'll be right out, Mom. Go wait for me in the living room."

The calmness of her voice surprised her. She didn't know in what corner of her mind she was able to come up with such serenity to her voice, but it was there. She could hear her mother once again retreating to the great abyss of the sofa, and this helped her gather herself before she exited the bathroom. She was on autopilot, but she couldn't hear the voice this time. All was silent in her mind. The sole driving factor was determination and the desire to get out.

No one had ever been there to help her remove the demons from her life or to take the addiction from her mother. No one told her father that it wasn't right to leave his child behind without a father figure or a protector. The world had turned its back on the little girl named Sandra, and now it was her time to turn her back on them. She would not listen to reason. She would not allow society to judge what was right or wrong in her life. Society was not there. No judge, no lawyer, no court came in to make things a little bit better for her, and now she wasn't sure she should try to make things okay in their eyes.

Sandra walked from the bathroom with the tail of her shirt hanging askew against the waistband of her shorts. She had buttoned the shirt wrong but hadn't noticed. Dorothy looked up from the couch and caught a glimpse of her attire.

"What happened to you?"

Just above a whisper, she answered, "I got in a fight with Bill."

"Oh."

That's it. That was the parental statement of concern: "Oh." Sandra went and stood directly in front of mother and allowed her to scan her body from head to toe. She wanted to see if Dorothy would comment on her total appearance or if her eyes would immediately focus on the tiny packets Sandra held before her. The tightly wound packets put a glimmer in her eyes. The corners of her mouth turned up just ever so slightly. She was salivating from the mere sight of the drug. Her eyes never left her daughter's hand as she reached up and picked the packets out of her palm.

Dorothy bounced up from the couch and headed for the kitchen, leaving Sandra in the exact spot in which she stood. The sound of spoons clinking together along with the water from the tap provided the house with some form of activity.

Her mother returned to the couch, belt in hand, needle primed and ready. When she was younger and her mother still insisted that the drugs were medicine that helped her heart, she would never allow Sandra to witness her getting high, but now it was a different story. There were no more lies to be told, no more secrets. She had thrown her daughter into the adult world of drugs, sex, and prostitution without much hesitation or a second glance.

Sandra's mind lingered from one incident to the next, but her eyes never left her mother's face. Her stares went unnoticed because Dorothy never blinked from the task at hand. Her main concern was to see the red flash appear in the syringe, which indicated that she had indeed hit a vein. Not once did she take the time to see the deep emotions etched across her daughter's face.

She no longer cared for her as a mother should but only saw her as a tool to be used in order to get what she was after. Her motherly instincts died a long time ago, and she could not find it inside of herself to be there for her only daughter anymore. Her addiction had taken over every aspect of her life, and she became incapable of feeling the emotions of a nurturing or caring mother. She was consumed by the drug, the high, and the constant need to be higher.

"Do you need help with that?"

Dorothy had stuck herself more than six times, leaving little bloody pricks on her arms and legs. She took off her pants and once again tried to hit the vein in her groin. It was painful, and she swore under her breath as she stuck herself continuously.

"Goddamn it! The needle broke!"

Blood was flowing down her legs now, and it reminded Sandra of Bill for a brief moment.

"Sandra, you're going to have to help. Go to the kitchen and get another syringe. Better yet, take this one with you, put it back in the spoon and use the other needle to get it out of the spoon. You know what I'm talking about, don't you?"

"Yes."

"Hurry up. My hands are shaking, and I'm feeling real bad now."

Sandra walked into the kitchen with the used needle and did as she was told. She retrieved another needle out of the jar on the counter and rinsed the bleach from it. She emptied the broken needle into the spoon and then picked up the clean one. She hesitated in this next step, and stood paused at the counter.

"Do it! She has done nothing for us! Why she should be spared!?"

Her voice of reason had returned. Sandra used the needle to get the solution out of the spoon, and when she was satisfied that she had it all, she filled up three more syringes and placed them in her waistband.

Dorothy was a jittery mess by the time Sandra returned to the couch. She was deeply scratching herself, causing more marks to appear on her flesh than the needle trails she had left.

"Shoot it right here. Come on! It's a vein there."

Dorothy was pointing to the same area she had just been trying. Sandra did not want to poke her anywhere near her pubic area.

"Why are you just standing there, damn it? Give me the needle!"

Dorothy went about poking herself several more times with no success. She was so frustrated by this time that she had begun to swear at Sandra and cry at the same time.

Sandra stood there and watched her mother in her tormented state for well over two minutes before she decided to help her out.

"Turn over, Mom. I'll try the vein behind your knee."

It seemed as if God had opened up the heavenly skies and welcomed Dorothy right into them. She had not used that entrance in quite some time and had nearly forgotten about it because it was so hard to reach. She was sure Sandra would be able to get a line going back there.

She flopped over on her stomach and allowed her leg to dangle off the edge of the couch. This position flexed her knee tightly, and she hoped it would make it easier for her daughter to see the vein.

Sandra released all three syringes from her waist and set them on the floor beside her. She used the belt to tie the upper part of her mother's thigh and began searching for a site. It took less than thirty seconds for an opportunity to appear. It showed itself just above the crease of her knee, and Sandra prepared herself to inject the drug. Dorothy was squirming all over the place, and she had to tell her to be still on more than one occasion.

"I'm going to miss if you keep jerking. Stay still!"

Dorothy calmed herself and waited to feel the prick of the needle and the rush of the drug as it entered her system.

The stick came first, and she was more than happy to know that Sandra had been able to find a port of entry so quickly. She allowed her body to relax as she waited to be taken to the next level. She adjusted her head on one of the cushions and inhaled a deep breath. She had her eyes closed initially, but then she opened them slightly so she could witness the room as it began to blur.

*

That had always been a telling moment for her, a sure sign that she was about to experience the ultimate high. The first time she saw the room take on another shape was when she experienced heroine in high school. That was the only aspect of the drug that she was able to match again and again.

Her first encounter with harshest aspect of heroin took place in the boys' bathroom her junior year. The initial shock of it to her system was so extreme that the principal called the ambulance to come and get her off the floor. Dorothy was high for more than eleven hours. She was hooked instantly and spent the rest of her life chasing that multiple-hour high.

She knew now that there would never be a first-day experience again, but the fact that she could still witness the room fading in and out gave her the illusion that she was about to experience the ultimate high.

*

Dorothy allowed her head to relax, and she waited anxiously for Sandra to give her the high she sought. The first prick must not have been successful because she felt her trying to prime her leg for another spot. She didn't want to move because she knew it would be that much more difficult to get a main line, so she kept relaxing and breathing deeply.

It was during this time that her eyes peered across the hall to Sandra's room. She slowly realized that Bill had never emerged from the room, even when Sandra went to the bathroom. She had not laid eyes on him since his arrival.

She would be lying to herself if she said she hadn't heard her daughter's cries for help through the walls, but at the same time, she didn't know what to do about it. As far as she was concerned, Sandra was far from virgin status at this point, and she should have been more familiar with Bill than any of the other men. She figured she was giving him a hard time, or maybe they were having a lovers' quarrel. Her mind couldn't grasp more than that. Sandra answered when she knocked, so all was well behind the door wasn't it?

Dorothy wasn't immediately alarmed by the pieces of the puzzle that were being put together because she was far more focused on hoping that Sandra would able to find one of the few veins she had left. But it was that mindless train of thought that had her realizing that something was terribly wrong.

Her leg began to burn, and it felt as if she had been set on fire. Sandra was now sticking her for a third time, and she could not fathom what was going on. Her entire lower body was now aflame, but she was not feeling anywhere near high.

Dorothy craned her neck to try to get a glimpse of what her daughter was doing, but she only saw the needles on the floor. There were two syringes, and they appeared to be empty, but Sandra was already inserting a third syringe into the back of her leg.

"Sandra, what are you doing? You're sticking me with too many needles."

She tried to move from her position, but her daughter held her firmly in place. She could not shift the lower part of her body at all because of the burning and the pressure that Sandra was applying. "Sandra, let me up!"

Sandra deftly jabbed her in the thigh before releasing her grip on her. She wiped the perspiration from her forehead and sat back on her haunches. She was so drained by this time that she had to take a breath before she was able to consider another step.

Dorothy turned over on the couch to face her, and for the first time since Sandra entered the living room, she felt very afraid. She now knew by the way her daughter was looking at her that something went horribly wrong between her and Bill, but did she really want to know what?

Sandra glared at her mother quietly, but at the time it seemed that she wasn't exactly looking at her but through her.

While Dorothy mentally battled out the situation that had led to the current circumstances, Sandra never said a word, just watched and waited. Their eyes locked in a silent battle, and Dorothy wondered just what her daughter had shot her with. Her eyes left Sandra's face and returned again to the syringes that were discarded on the floor. Her throat had begun to go dry, and she feared if she did not speak now, her voice would be lost forever.

"What did you do to me, Sandra? Did you give me more than heroin? What was in the needles?"

Her daughter tilted her head and looked at her as if she was seeing her for the first time. She had no reaction on her face, and she did not speak. Her emotions were flipping in a constant circle. One minute she wanted nothing more than to get away, and in the next, she would do anything to see her mother take her last breath. She couldn't decide the greater of the two.

The silence was unnerving for Dorothy, and she needed answers. She had to know if there was a possibility that she could seek help or if she was past the point of help. She was getting desperate.

"Sandra!"

The sight of her mother begging for answers irritated Sandra beyond belief. She wanted to shout in her face and stomp her chest out, but Dorothy couldn't read any of the rage she was holding because her face was blank. The voice emanating from Dorothy was no more than a croak, but it still sounded like nails on a chalkboard to Sandra. She'd had enough of her and thought it was high time she told her just what she thought of her.

"You are an undeserving bitch, and I hope you die a very painful death! You have officially just received your last high, Mother, and I hope it's all you've ever dreamed it would be."

Sandra stood up and leaned over her mother, despising every inch of her. She wanted to cut her open and let her rotten soul roam freely through the house, but instead she grabbed her by the hair and yanked her into a sitting position. Dorothy tried to put up a fight by leaning forward and biting into Sandra's abdomen, but it wickedly backfired. She was immediately assaulted with a flurry of fists that pounded relentlessly into her face and neck.

She was totally unable to defend herself against her daughter, and no matter how much she wanted to stand, her legs continued to betray her. She could see her blood running from her nose onto the floor, but that's all she could do: observe.

Dorothy's hands were beyond numb, and she noticed they had a purple hue to them. In her state of mind, she thought that Sandra may have bruised them somehow, but upon closer inspection she realized it was a small pocket of blood that had formed under her skin; taking a closer glance over her body, there were more of the pockets forming in a variety of sizes.

She was being dragged across the floor but didn't pay as much attention to that as she did the fact that her feet were totally purple. There seemed to be liquid sacks hanging loosely from them as well, and it reminded her of water balloons. When she felt carpet graze against her skin, she knew she was in her daughter's room, but even that couldn't deter her mind from the thought of her transforming skin.

Her eyes briefly took in the bloody scenery, and she could tell just by the trail and splatter on the walls that a fierce battle had ensued here. The blood staining the walls had long since lost its red luster and now held the look of rusty nails and the smell of some form of acid.

Sandra didn't hesitate in her steps and took her mother directly to the closet in which she had placed Bill. It was difficult to pick up her mother's dead weight, and Sandra became frustrated by the efforts. Dorothy's body hung limp and useless, as she flopped out of Sandra's grasp continuously. On instinct, she pictured herself cutting her up, and putting her in the closet piece by piece, but she didn't think she could bear to hear her mother's voice in her ears ever again.

She backed herself into the closet, dragging her mother with her, and when she could go no further, she let go of Dorothy's hair and stepped on her back as she exited the closet. One of the pustules ruptured from the weight, and she found herself with blood on her feet, which enraged her even more. The idea of snapping her neck became a prominent idea.

Sandra roughly grabbed her legs and flipped her up and into the closet. This position caused Dorothy head to be at

Bill's feet, while her legs were strewn across his shoulders. This deeply satisfied Sandra for some reason, and she actually smiled as she closed the closet door.

Sandra went back into the living room, picked up the needles from the floor, and returned them to the bleach jar in the kitchen. She had briefly looked up the consequences of bleach entering the blood stream when she was at the library, but she never thought she would be witnessing the gruesome effects she read about. Why she researched it in the first place was lost upon her until now. She realized her internal voice had been with her all along, and knew very well why she needed the information. The liquid sacks were popping out from everywhere, so she guessed her mother must be bleeding internally just like the medical site said.

She didn't know if it was painful, and in her current state of mind, she did not care. She was finally able to rid her life of the things that constantly tortured her, and she felt better for it. Sandra decided not to waste one more minute of her day on Dorothy or Bill.

She simply started to go about her daily chores as if all was right in the world. She cleaned the kitchen and bathroom and then prepared herself something to eat. She was feeling very light and carefree at this point, and if someone were to say she was calm and serene, she wouldn't have disagreed.

Sandra sat in the recliner and ate a sandwich. She didn't turn on the television or radio; she just sat in the silence that she had come to enjoy. It was as if she could finally hear her ideas and desires as they floated lazily through her mind. She was able to hear the sound of birds just outside the window. It brought color to the inside of the house that was brighter than any paint or television screen.

Sandra was far hungrier than she'd initially believed, so she went to the kitchen to make herself a second helping. It was then out of the window that she saw her packed bags sitting beside the house and decided to retrieve them. The whole concept of what she was supposed to be doing with the bags or where it was she was going was lost upon her. It was as if a light had been turned off, and she was now in the shield of darkness. Her mind was fused against the possibility of a tomorrow. She saw the here and now; beyond that did not exist.

She found herself going out the door, venturing to the side of the house to get her luggage, and then dragging it back inside. It was as if her entire past was a bad dream and she had just awakened new and refreshed. The wire connecting to her history had been severed, and there was no possibility of a reconnect.

⤖ ——— ⤗

CHAPTER 21

S andra fell into a heavy sleep in the chair when her mind could no longer fight off exhaustion. It was the most peaceful sleep she had ever experienced and one of the first where there were no nightmares. She didn't toss and turn and she didn't sleep facing the doorway. There was no knife under her pillow, and the loud voices of her mother's friends weren't playing in the background. There was silence. The hum of the refrigerator was the last thing she heard when she dozed off, but it was a totally different sound that woke her up.

Someone was tapping at the door while simultaneously calling Dorothy's name. Sandra was a little disoriented and out of sorts as she rubbed the sleep from her eyes. Looking out the crack in the curtains, dark had fallen, and what time it was exactly was questionable. The stranger at the door grew more intense as the knocks turned to a persistent pounding. She had no plans on getting up from where she was and hoped that the irritation would stop soon.

A couple of minutes later, Sandra readjusted herself to a suitable position as the noise subsided. Whoever it was had given up and left. It wasn't difficult for her to drift back off, and she was almost in a state of oblivion when she detected a slight scratching noise coming from behind her head.

Sandra sat up and looked over the back of the recliner only to find her mother had made it out of the closet and was in the doorway of her room.

Dorothy slithered her way out of the doorway and was reaching for the doorknob, but she couldn't quite get a grip on it. She tried over and over again to grab it, as if it was some form of life preserver. Sandra didn't make a move in her direction; she just watched in a mixture of fascination and irritation combined.

Dorothy was a solid form of purple from her fingers to the upper part of her chest. Her face and neck were ghostly pale, but her eyes were red as fire. There were streaks of blood streaming down her cheeks and Sandra could only surmise that it had come from her eyes, seeing as she wasn't bleeding from anywhere else except her back. Her body was moving in segments of fluid, which sickened Sandra.

She glared at her mother a couple of minutes longer until the sight of her alone became unbearable. Sandra leaped from her position, cat-like, and was upon her mother in seconds. She no longer reached for the knob but instead held her hand out to her daughter.

Dorothy didn't know if she could speak or not. The pain she was in was so excruciating; there was nothing in life for it to be compared to. She needed medical attention.

She couldn't see out of her eyes, but she sensed that Sandra had moved closer to her, and she decided to reach out her hand almost as a form of a peace offering and a sign to show her daughter that yes, she had won. She just hoped that it was seen that way. The struggle that she went through to get out of the closet with Bill was astronomical in itself. She almost gave up on several occasions, but she wanted her daughter to see her and maybe get her some form of treatment.

"San...dra?"

Her voice did not sound like her own, and she tried to muster up a little more strength to say it once again.

"Sandr...a?"

"Shut up!"

Sandra had placed her hands over her ears to block out the sound, but the sight of Dorothy sent her mind into a demonic frenzy. Blood oozed from her mouth every time she tried to talk, and it made matters worse than if she had said nothing at all.

Sandra didn't understand why her mother wouldn't just die, lie down and simply cease to exist. Why did she have to taunt her even as her life ticked away? She called her name as if she were her savior or she had tried to kill her accidentally. Why wouldn't she just give up? Why did she want to haunt her even now?

Dorothy continued to slide and scoot farther and farther into the living room, and Sandra was paralyzed to do anything but watch.

"Are you going to let her just slide her bloody ass out the door? Put the mutt out of its misery!"

"I can't! I can't! Why won't she die?"

"Is it the dog or the veterinarian's fault if it lives through being euthanized? When did she ever say she couldn't on your behalf? Did she tell those men, 'No, you can't rape my daughter'? Did she say, 'No, I won't take drugs over my daughter's innocence'? What did she ever say no to for you?"

"But I put bleach in her veins, and she still is here, living and breathing. I thought she would die in the closet."

"She will die, but do you want to wait on eventually? Do you want to see if she can actually make it out the front door? What are you waiting for?"

Sandra didn't know what to say or do. Her mind was in a haze, and her mother was practically at her feet.

When Dorothy knew that Sandra wasn't going to lift a hand to help her, she began to plead in a voice that made a sound far worse than fingernails across a chalkboard. It seemed to be a higher octave than that. It touched Sandra somewhere deep inside, and it was almost powerful enough to send her to her knees. Sandra wanted nothing more than for her mother to shut up for good.

Dorothy heard Sandra whispering to herself again, and she became even more fearful than she had been. She wasn't talking to anyone specific but listening and negotiating with someone only she could hear.

She knew kids have make-believe friends all the time, but this was something totally different, something sinister. There was no use in trying to get through to her daughter now; she knew it was a lost cause. Maybe even trying to save herself was a lost cause. She was fighting an uphill battle, and if she had ever known that this is the way her life would end, she might have made a change. It didn't take her that long to come to terms with what was going to happen to her and by whose hands.

She released the air in her lungs, let her hand fall limply to the floor, and decided to let things be as they may. The whispering had stopped, and she knew her daughter had finalized her next steps. She silently asked for forgiveness and another chance, but she knew that she could do nothing more than wait for her demise.

Once again Sandra yanked her by the hair and turned her back toward the room, but when Dorothy's head was parallel with the door jam, she stopped. Dorothy was on her back, but her eyes were in an upward stare. Her pupils was no longer visible, and the blood that continued to leak from them made her appearance that much more ghastly.

Her arm impulsively reached up toward Sandra, and it made her want nothing less than to remove the purple limb from her body.

Dorothy knew her daughter was in a state of manic rage, but she was in a critical state herself. She needed emergency treatment, and time was not on her side. She gave it one last try.

"Sandra...ple...ase"

Her daughter looked down upon her and something snapped. She grabbed a hold of the door and began to slam it repeatedly against Dorothy's head.

"Shut up! Shut up! Shut up!"

Sandra was furious and inconsolable at this point. Her mother wanted to taunt her even as she died, but she would not allow it. She'd had a taste of peace, and she was not about to let her mother ruin that as she had ruined all other things in her life. She would be silent, and if it took all night to get her that way, then so be it.

Sweat was dripping freely from her chin and nose, but she wouldn't stop. She didn't know exhaustion at this time. She slammed her head with such diligent force that Dorothy's skull cracked under the pressure. Her head bounced back and forth against the frame of the door, but Sandra wouldn't relent. She didn't want to run the risk of her ever speaking again.

"Choke her! Snatch her vocal cords out!"

Sandra immediately jumped down unto Dorothy's chest and put her hands around her throat. Her hands were locked, and her fingers were cramped beyond belief. The ache radiated up her arms and into her shoulders, but she was determined to complete the task.

She held on for fifteen additional seconds before she released her hold on Dorothy. Sandra was not to be fooled into thinking that Dorothy was dead this time. She didn't want to hear her scratching, begging, or dragging herself back into her life. This had to end, and she wanted to make sure that's exactly what occurred.

Still pressed upon her chest, Sandra leaned down and placed her ear next to her mouth. No sound escaped from her lips, but Sandra could not be sure. She could not have her mother popping up on her later in life, healed and carefree.

Despite the blood that covered Dorothy's mouth, Sandra placed her hand over it, and pinched her nose. She held on to her mother like this for another minute until she knew for sure that it was done. Her tormentor had ceased to exist.

Sandra hummed a tune as she dumped her back into the closet. She knew now with certainty that she would not be disturbed in her sleep, and her mother's voice would never again be able to ring in her ears. Sandra went back to the chair, sat down, and began tapping her feet to a beat that only she could hear.

At two o'clock in the morning, she bolted up and ran to her room. She had dreamed that somehow her mother and Bill had escaped from the closet and had left the house. Sandra slowly opened the door to her room and peeked around the corner. She had to make sure they weren't behind the door ready to attack her. After ensuring that the coast was clear, she ventured further in and headed for the closet.

Sandra placed her hand on the knob and began to shiver from her feet up. She didn't want to deal with them again. She didn't think she had the strength to go another round with them. She prayed that she was having a nightmare and that the bodies would be exactly where she had placed them.

She took a deep breath and yanked the door open. The bodies were exactly where she had put them, no different, except they were stiff. They looked like grotesque wooden puppets. Sandra gave them a swift kick each and then closed the door for good.

⟡ ——— ⟡

CHAPTER 22

Mrs. Washington arrived two days later at six o'clock in the morning, and she was hoping she would find Sandra on the porch, waiting. The house held a dark gloomy look to it, and this made the pit of her stomach began to swirl. There were no lights on, no sign of movement on the inside, thus making the situation seem that much more eerie. She had never been inside Sandra's house, and there was no sign that anyone else was inside either.

She wished she had followed her instincts when she wanted to just pop over to Sandra's house the same day Sandra told her that she wouldn't be able to stay with her, but she was so afraid of pushing her and causing her to reject the college scene altogether that she decided to give her space.

She'd tried calling several times over the last two days or so, but no one ever picked up the phone. The mere fact that Sandra wasn't taking her calls raised her antennae a little, but she'd decided to that she was just calling at the wrong times, and Sandra was out picking up her last few items.

She could recall a few years ago when she had desperately wanted to get a student out of an abusive home. She had convinced him that college would give him the atmosphere to live as he chose, and that he no longer had to have the worries of the world on his shoulders. She had gained his trust, and he'd seemed so committed to the program that she mapped out for him that she did not see the other signs blinking in the background.

He had manipulated her into thinking he was a wounded soul with no direction, but it was all a lie. All of the alibis he had used her for were not because he was hiding from his parents but because he was sleeping with one of her colleagues. His parents were on to him and were going to the school board with the allegations.

She had talked to his parents on numerous occasions and had told them exactly what he had asked her to: "Yes, he was with me. Yes, we went looking at different colleges today," when all along he was nowhere near her but somewhere with the assistant principal Mr. Browning.

That had been one of the most embarrassing points in her career. It was devastating enough to almost make her lose her job and scandalous enough to make her want to change careers. She was suspended without pay for two months for her alibis. She was only able to return under a very strict probationary period. Neither her integrity nor her future would be able to suffer through another ordeal like that.

She believed Sandra just as she had her other student, but his time when the story was told to her, she never second-guessed if what she was being told was the truth or not. You cannot fake hollowness in the eyes or the emptiness of one's heart. It is worn on the sleeve as a banner and across the chest as a shield. Sandra had all the signs and symptoms. She was a loner. She had no real friends, and she had never dated, despite her striking beauty.

Her natural blonde hair reached to the lower part of her back, and she always kept it cut evenly as if she cared about having split ends. Sandra's nose wasn't small, but it wasn't big either. It fit her dimpled cheeks just right and was perfectly centered. Her eyes were deep blue, and always held the look of being surprised or innocent, whichever way the receiver took it.

She could not hide her emotions well because her face captivated her audience and drew them in. She may have easily been a model, and made it on the cover of the best magazines in circulation, but she was wounded, and those opportunities were not even in her thought pattern. She needed help, and this time Mrs. Washington was sure of it.

Her life goal was to help children get a better start than they thought they deserved, and she was going to succeed in that at all cost.

She knew she wasn't going to pull into the driveway and have her headlights flash through their curtains. She didn't want to startle anyone, and she didn't know if Sandra's mother knew that today very well may be the last time she saw her daughter.

She parked along the curb and cut the engine to the car. She didn't get out right away but just sat and waited. She could only imagine what was going on inside. If they were having last words, she didn't want to interrupt, but her gut kept gnawing at her to go and knock on the door. Mrs. Washington hesitated only a minute longer before she exited her vehicle.

She was going to find out one way or the other, and if Sandra needed her help in getting out, then she would do whatever was necessary to accomplish that. She walked up to the front step and was immediately assaulted by a smell that took her breath away. It was a mixture of rotting fish, road kill and bleach. The aroma was powerful, and yet again she felt a tremble deep inside of her.

She took the final step leading to the door and rapped on it. There was no sound coming from inside, no lights popped on; it was as if she had never knocked at all. She gave it a few more seconds and tried again, but louder. No answer. Mrs. Washington was beyond nervous at this time, but she didn't want to just walk away. She knew that whatever had taken place inside, Sandra may need her, and now was not the time to abandon ship.

Forcing a little more courage under her belt, she pounded on the door once more. She heard a light shuffling inside and felt relieved and anxious simultaneously. She could hear her heart beating fiercely in her ears, but she remained composed. She didn't want Sandra's mother to open the door to a skittish bird on the porch. She didn't know exactly what to say, except to ask for Sandra and take things from there.

The curtain in the window moved slightly to the side, and she thought she caught a glimpse of Sandra, but she couldn't swear by it. The odor continued to linger, as if daring her to enter, but she did not falter. She would get Sandra out of this house one way or another.

CHAPTER 23

Sandra could see someone on the porch, but the recognition was lost to her. She had not responded to the repeated intrusions since she had finally found peace. No one had entered her world, and she was content with that. If it wasn't for the mere fact that she was going to the bathroom, combined with the early morning hour, she wouldn't have gone anywhere near the window.

The lady she saw standing on the porch under the light was familiar to her, but she couldn't figure out how or why. The sight of her was not alarming, but at the same time, it was not welcoming either. She had no idea what she could want, and she wasn't sure if she was going to open the door to find out, so while she tried to make up her mind about what to do, she continued on to the bathroom.

Sandra walked barefoot through the bleach puddles that she poured on the floor, disregarding the burning and itching to her soles. Dorothy and Bill's bodies had begun to decompose, and they let off foul scents throughout the house. The odor was only slightly detectable at first, but then it seemed to come from under her door in strong gusts.

Sandra was almost at her wits' end of trying to calm the odor down to where it at least no longer woke her up at night. On many occasions she was tempted to drag them out of the closet and put them in the street, but the odor was so fierce every time she entered her room that she couldn't make it past her bed. She stomped around the house, tormented and angry that they still were able to torture her, even in death.

On the second night she'd had enough. She tied a shirt around her nose and mouth and went to retrieve the bodies. They could no longer be in the house with her, and she had no plans for leaving. Sandra went into the kitchen to get trash bags when she set her eyes on the bottle of bleach. She decided to pour the bleach in her room and by the door to see if it would make the smell less harsh, and if it worked, then she wouldn't have to move the bodies. But if by nightfall she still smelled them, then she would go to plan B.

The stench of bleach was so strong that it burned Sandra's nose and eyes when she lay on the couch. The fumes attacked her throat, and she gagged for most of the night, but she could no longer smell them, and that was her only concern.

Her feet were losing layers of skin because she did not rinse them after being splashed around in the bleach. She had been padding back and forth in the puddles, but that also didn't concern her enough to make her do anything about it.

Sandra had given up on her hygiene the moment Bill took his last breath. He was the sole reason she scrubbed herself everyday with such vigorous strokes that her skin was permanently scarred from her efforts.

She ditched all of the things she had been forced to do in direct response to something that had been done to her. She walked in a new light, and although she was alone, she felt vindicated.

Sandra flushed the toilet and headed back to the couch. She had forgotten all about the lady at the door until she saw her silhouette outlined in the window. She hadn't given her a second thought and to do so now brought a small line of irritation across her path. What to do with the lady outside she didn't know, but she knew that she did not fear her, so she detoured from the couch and headed for the door.

Mrs. Washington could hear the patter of feet heading for the door, and she almost acted on her instinct to bolt for the car, but swallowing her fear, she stood stiff as she came face to face with Sandra.

Her voice was lost. The words would not form to ask the right questions, and the first sound to come out seemed to be a puff. She didn't want to make any sudden movements because she worried about what Sandra would do at this moment. Gone was the youthful girl on her way to college. What stood before her now was a disaster.

Her hands were soiled, and her hair hung in oily clumps from her scalp. There were remnants of food around her mouth, and her clothes were mismatched and horribly stained. Mrs. Washington was mute for a moment; words were lost to her. Her voice had fled so she just stared at her and waited for the next scene to present itself.

Sandra felt that she knew this woman, but she couldn't figure out how. The staring competition they were in wasn't going anywhere, so she grabbed her by the arm and snatched her inside. She slammed the door shut, and then continued to watch the lady.

The fear that engulfed Mrs. Washington was intense and without warning. Sandra moved so quickly in snatching her into the house that she was not prepared to act. She was now staring at her, but she could not hold her focus. The aroma that held the air hostage was overpowering; the smells that mixed and drifted together made her stomach weak, and she could not bear it any longer. She covered her mouth with her shirt and tried to figure out what was going on.

The house was fairly clean, except for the area around the recliner. There were plates of old discarded food and empty glasses all around it. The arms of the chair looked as if someone had constantly wiped their fingers across the fabric, like a napkin of sorts. Mrs. Washington wanted to take in more of her surroundings to ensure her safety, but the smell and the constant glare of Sandra's unblinking eyes frightened her to no end.

She made a move for the doorknob in hopes of opening the door and letting in some fresh air, but just as quickly Sandra's hand came up and pressed against the frame. To see Sandra literally blocking her way out brought a new fear into her. She had no idea what had happened to Sandra, but she knew for sure that the foundation she was now standing on, was not stable.

She inhaled a shaky breath, trying to calm her nerves and get through to her.

"Sandra, honey, it's Mrs. Washington. I'm here to pick you up. Do you remember?"

Sandra did not reply to her, but she did see a glimmer of light filter into her eyes for the briefest of moments, so she latched on to that.

"Yes, you remember, don't you? I'm here to take you to the bus stop, and you're going to college. We're supposed to eat a big breakfast this morning because the bus ride is so long. I—"

Suddenly Sandra slammed her hands against her head, and screamed, "Nooooo! Nooooo! Stop it!"

She dropped to the floor and cried so deeply that her chest heaved with every breath until Mrs. Washington could no longer just stand by and watch. She let her purse fall as she kneeled next to Sandra to console her.

"Shhh. Shhh. It's okay. It's going to be all right. Tell me what happened, Sandra. Where is your mother?"

She said nothing as she pushed out of her counselor's grasp. She looked into Sandra's face, and the blankness seemed to waver just beneath the surface. She didn't want to lose her. She needed Sandra to tell her what had taken place in this house.

"Did you pack your bags, honey? Did you get your stuff ready to go?"

Once again the light came on, and she answered with a nod of the head. Mrs. Washington then took in the sight of packed luggage sitting by the recliner next to the television. She risked a chance, and judged her next words very carefully as she asked,

"Do you still want to go? You want to get your bags?"

Without a word uttered, Sandra went to the chair and picked up her luggage. Time constantly blanked in and out for her. Was she in the past? The future? She didn't know, she simply operated on auto pilot. The only voice telling her what to do was coming from the lady in front of her, so what she asked, is what she did.

She looked so tiny and wounded standing there that Mrs. Washington felt her own tears fall freely down her cheeks. She didn't speak another word as she got up from the floor and led Sandra to her car. She opened the trunk and helped her put her bags inside, and then she placed her in the front seat.

Sandra moved with instructions, but she was nowhere near her normal self. Everything was mechanical and very quiet, but she seemed to be trying to work through the things that were going on in her mind. Mrs. Washington climbed into the driver's seat with the intention of taking her somewhere they could talk, and figure some things out.

She knew Sandra couldn't board a bus or anything else in the condition she was in. Her silence had to be broken. She had to get her to open up and tell her what was going on and what had gone on inside the house. She decided to take Sandra to her residence, get her cleaned up, and start from there.

Mrs. Washington went to start up the car and realized she had left her purse inside the house. She climbed back out of the car and staggered up the sidewalk. Her head was just clearing from the powerful bleach smell mixed with only God knows what, and now she had to go right back inside the cave to retrieve her purse.

She looked back at Sandra, but she was just staring straight ahead it was like looking at a mannequin, so she carried on.

Once again from the porch, the smell slammed into her, and she covered her mouth. When she opened the door, she bent to retrieve her purse. Hesitantly, she took a few more steps inside. She was finally getting a glimpse into Sandra's life, and it was sparse, to say the least. There was only one couch and a recliner in the living room.

She found her feet moving further and further into the room as her curiosity lead her toward the kitchen. The linoleum on the floor was clean but peeling next to the stove and the refrigerator. Old cabinets hung loosely on the walls, as if another dish in their cavity would cause a sudden collapse.

There were a few dishes in the sink and open condiment jars lined the counters. It wasn't terribly messy, but it hadn't been tended to in some time. The odor tempted her to abandon ship long before she was even close to finding its source, so she grabbed a towel out of the kitchen, wrapped it around her face, and continued to the next room.

The floor was wet, and she knew it had to be bleach by the horrible stains that had been left upon the carpet. Someone had splashed the liquid all over .

Mrs. Washington figured she had seen enough and was more than ready to leave, but something about the stench, and the bleach bothered her immensely. She turned on her heels and headed toward the closed door with the towel pressed under the jam. The closer she got, the stronger the aroma became. In her mind's eye, she knew what she would find, but she didn't want to believe it.

The smell of death was overpowering in front of the door, and it wouldn't take a crime scene technician to figure out its source. She stood in one spot, reflecting on what she should do. She knew once she opened the door she would not be able to turn back. Her life as well as Sandra's would forever be changed. She didn't know if she had the strength to do that, but she also knew she couldn't just walk away now.

Her hands trembled violently when she reached for the knob. She cried silently, and for a moment the tears blurred her vision. She could not see or think as time ticked by. She thought painfully that whatever had taken place was solely her fault and should be placed upon her shoulders.

She'd had a chance to pick up Sandra despite what she had told her on the phone, but she didn't. She'd thought she would be too imposing, but deep inside it troubled her that she had changed her mind all of a sudden and voiced a change of plans. For two days she fought the urge to ride past her house and hope she would see her. She did none of those things. Instead, she went about her daily activities and counted the days down until she would be able to pick Sandra up. The day had come, and she felt as if she had walked right smack into a full-fledged nightmare.

There was no more time to reflect or regret, so she opened the door. She was met instantly by thick, putrefied air that swarmed around her and embedded itself into her clothes and hair. She pressed the towel tighter against her nose and mouth, but the smell continued to penetrate and shift itself down into her stomach where it disturbed the bagel and coffee she had just eaten. She turned her head back toward the living room and polished the floor with her meager breakfast. A faintness floated about her head, and she nearly blacked out, but she used everything in her power to hold on just a little longer.

Flies wisped past her head, aiming for what she had just left them on the floor. They were huge in size. She had never seen flies that even slightly resembled them. She hesitated in the doorway but didn't want to go a step further. Her feet were stiff as if she wore cement shoes. She looked down at them and mentally demanded that they propel her further into the room. The left one obeyed, and she went one step closer to the source that started her investigation.

When she was able to get her feet to act in sync with one another, she immediately wished she hadn't. Dried up blood hung on the bedding, the side of her nightstand, and the walls, almost like some form of eccentric artwork. There was a huge stain consuming the front portion of the carpet, and it was followed by an array of splatters. Whatever had taken place had been horrific and brutal. Sandra didn't look as if she had lost any blood. She would have to have quite a gaping wound to have cause so much chaos.

Mrs. Washington drug herself around the foot of the bed toward the closet and the majority of the activity from the flies. The stench was still overwhelming, but the slight breeze that came from the open window helped the situation a little. She was very careful not to step on any of the areas that were stained, and she didn't put her hands on anything unnecessarily. She covered the distance from the entrance to the closet faster than she would have liked, but she was there.

She prayed to God that she would find some old food or the family pet inside of Sandra's closet. She wanted everything to be all right for her. "Just once," she prayed to God. "Please let it be okay, just once."

Sweat covered her palms and caused her hand to slip off the knob. She had to steady herself before she was able to try again.

The buzzing alone was more than enough to make anyone turn away, but she knew she hadn't come all this way to turn around. The answer to Sandra's state of mind, as well as to the bloodshed that consumed this room, lay behind the very door in front of her. She had to proceed with the task at hand, and knowing this, she pulled open the door that housed the scene from hell.

Flies weren't the only insects that had manifested themselves inside the closet. There were a host of other insects, all using the corpses as a place to dwell. Mrs. Washington felt Sandra's mother's eyes watching her as she tripped over her own two feet trying to get away from the scene, but in actuality, it was the insects moving inside of her almost hollow sockets that brought her pupils to life.

She couldn't scream, run, or even move, for that matter. She had landed hard and could not get her feet under her.

The fact that there were two bodies, and not just one, just about broke her line of sanity. She had no idea what went on, nor did she care to find out. She wanted nothing more than to get out of the room and the house all together. When she was able to get her footing, she stumbled to the door, and began to instantly dry heave. She leaned over with her hands on her knees, trying to catch her breath, but it was almost impossible. She had left the door to the closet open, and she was incapable of escaping the fumes that now had stalked her into the living room.

Her shoes were planted in one of the designated bleach puddles, and it all made sense to her now: the stains, the odor, Sandra's odd behavior. She had killed those people. She was sure the lady had to be her mother, but why? She was so close to cutting ties with them that it seemed like a waste to go about ending things this way. Something had to have triggered this whole episode, and she now regretted even more that she had not come sooner.

When she felt she had enough air to at least make it to the door, a pair of bare feet landed themselves in her path, which instantly made her heart skip erratically in her chest. Sandra had silently re-entered the house.

Mrs. Washington surely didn't want to know what Sandra could be thinking. She carefully rose to her feet and looked her fully in the face, but Sandra wasn't looking at her; her attention was drawn to her bedroom. Mrs. Washington didn't know if she should make a break for it or try to leave as calmly as possible, but one thing she did know for sure: staying in the house was out of the question.

She turned her body toward the door without taking a step, just waiting to see if anything she did would cause a reaction from Sandra. She didn't know what she would do if she were to attack her or even open her mouth to speak. She hadn't thought that far ahead yet.

There was no plan of action for an episode such as that. She controlled her nerves to the best of her ability and decided she would give it a few more seconds before making her move toward the door and outside, but Sandra moved first, causing her to let out a little yelp in response.

Sandra moved slightly to the left and walked past her to her room. She went inside and headed for the closet. Mrs. Washington turned her head to watch her as she methodically went about closing the door that she had left open. She acted as if the flies were not buzzing in her ears and landing stubbornly on her face. She never lifted a hand to swat at them as they attacked her. She wanted the door closed, and that is what she did.

Mrs. Washington didn't know how to react to what she was seeing. She acted as if she were alone in the house. The mere fact that she walked around Mrs. Washington on her way out of the room and plopped down in the recliner was a sure attest to that.

Slowly, but without hesitation, Mrs. Washington walked behind the back of the chair, stopped at the door to pick up her purse, and stepped outside and into the fresh air. She glanced back at Sandra, but her body language had not altered in the least bit. She continued to stare blankly into space.

She pulled the door closed and headed for her car. There was nothing she or anyone else could do. It was impossible to turn back the hands of time to save her life, and it was devastating to know she'd had a chance to do so. Once again she looked back at the front of the Hansleys' home and wondered about the evil that her student had lived through. The daily torment that scorched her right down to the very last layer.

She felt the people in the closet may have gotten just what they deserved, but she knew that was not her call to make. She could not help her out of this, no matter what she tried. Sandra would not be able to attend any university now, and maybe ever. The damage had been done, and for her, the blame had been laid. The tears feverishly poured from her as she dialed 9-1-1 from her cell phone.

At the sound of the door closing, Sandra turned her head to face it. The only person, who had ever cared for her had now witnessed the massive destruction caused by her own hands. Words couldn't describe how she was feeling. The breath she had been holding as Mrs. Washington walked by her was released. There was nothing more for her to do, so she stared at the door.

CHAPTER 24

"Okay, ladies, listen up! You are now property of Winsor Marshall Women's Prison. You are to do as you are told so that we may get you processed and checked into your cells at a much faster pace than if you are uncooperative. Raise your arms above your heads, and turn around slowly. Lift your right breast…now the left one…"

One officer continued to give instructions while two others handed out bags and labels for their clothes.

There were ten women standing in a twelve-by-twelve room, lined up along the wall. The yellow stripe on the floor indicated the area for the prisoners to stand behind. If they stepped over it, they would be yelled at to back up, and before they could finish asking a second time, your face would be pressed into the floor.

No windows existed in the tight space, making the air hang thick and lazy. Some of the women had been in the county jail for some time, so they had a sour, musty scent clinging to their skins. Others were fresh from the courthouse and already resided at the prison.

"Back up until your back is against the wall. Then slide down the wall in a squatting position. I will repeat this one more time for those of you who are more special than others. Back up and place your backs against the walls…"

The orders came again, and the women did as they were told. Some of them had a few comments about why they were being asked to do such a thing, and one of the taller guards was more than happy to let them know.

"This is to ensure us that you are not hiding anything in your little safety deposit boxes."

The process did not seem legal or ethical, but they had lost their right to an opinion as soon as they became property of the state.

Eventually all ten of the women did as instructed, and the guards took a seemingly long time to check each and every one of them. The lady next to the last one seemed to pose a problem for the guards. They picked up their radios and began calling certain tiers and gates to come and assist them with the removal of some "contraband."

One of the officers held up a small red balloon that had apparently removed from the vaginal cavity of one of the women. When the women were instructed to cough, apparently she released more than a sneeze. She was a prostitute due to serve a nine months sentence, but now her time would be extended without question.

"Well, well, well what do we have here? It seems as if one of our ladies has a very nasty habit. What's your name?"

The lady did not answer immediately. The other guard picked up the clipboard from the wall hook and began to look it up, but the guard doing all the questioning slapped the board from her hand.

"No, this bitch will answer when she is spoken to!"

The lady was very hesitant to speak until a fist full of her hair was pulled, snatching her forward onto her knees.

"Janet. Janet Smothers."

"Well, Ms. Smothers, unless I stand corrected, there's at least three grams in this little balloon, which carries an exceptional amount of time that will be dutifully added on top what you're already here for. This was pretty stupid of you."

Handing the package to one of the arriving officers, it was placed in a brown paper bag and escorted out of the room with Janet and two more officers.

The processing scene was over after the last two ladies were probed. They were handed their grey-and-white uniforms to wear, which came with a permanent state ID number printed in the corner. Blankets, sheets, a pillow case, and a hygiene pack were handed to each of the women. Most of them were guided to cells with already established inmates, and some were lucky enough to be grouped with the women they had arrived with.

The prison itself was medium security; anywhere from selling drugs to attempted murder cases could be found in the Winsor correctional facility, depending on the severity of the crime.

Sandra Hansley had just turned nineteen but was about to spend the next seven years in prison. In the court of law, she was found guilty of all charges, after they declined the insanity defense weakly put up by her public defender.

She would have been looking at a harsher sentence if it weren't for the testimony of Mrs. Washington. She testified that Bill had raped and sexually abused Sandra for years and that the day he had been killed was only a couple of days before she was due to leave for college.

She presented the bus tickets and affidavits from professors and guidance counselors at the college stating that she had been accepted and was due to arrive three days after the death of Bill and Dorothy.

The case became a split decision on the two homicides. The judge conceded that she could have been temporarily insane when she killed Bill, but it did not explain the fact that her mother died almost a day later. They could not figure it out, and Sandra had not spoken a word since she was arrested.

They only reliable things he had to go by were the evidence presented and the words of a passionate guidance counselor, so he made the sentence as light as he could without seeming prejudiced to the courts. He could only imagine how treacherous her life had to have been for her to sit in a semi-catatonic state the entire trial. She would have to undergo therapy in the penal system, before she could be released into society. He added three years of mandatory therapy to her sentence, and it was so ordered.

CHAPTER 25

"*A*re you new here? Or did you transfer from another cell?"

Sandra consciously ignored her cellmate. She was silently trying to get a grip on her new surroundings. She didn't know what she was supposed to be doing or when she was to do it, but she knew one thing for sure: the sound of her roommate's voice was getting to her.

"Are you going to answer me or not?"

Sandra began unfolding her blankets and making the top bunk. She had already decided when she entered the cell that she would not be on the bottom. She felt it would make her too accessible for anyone who decided to walk into the cell. Being up in the air held a slight advantage to her.

She had just set her toiletries on the sink when she was called again.

Barbara was tired and frustrated. She felt she had been unjustly accused and sentenced for what she considered minor crimes, and now to be stuck in the cell with a mime, was agitating her greatly.

"Look bitch, I know you can hear me."

That stopped her dead in her tracks. Never in life would she be degraded or called someone's bitch again.

She had not spoken to anyone since she had been placed in handcuffs. It was all a lesson learned, and she was a fast learner. She knew the day would come. She couldn't sit in that recliner forever, but her thought pattern didn't include what was to happen after the police came.

This was all very new to her, and she decided to absorb it and learn from it. She had not heard from the voices in her head since her court date, and she felt she may be able to recover from the things that tormented her past, but first she would have to get her roommate in check.

Standing barefoot, she turned on her heels and faced her.

"I am only going to give you one warning, and then I will not be responsible for my actions. If you must address me, call me by name, I'll make it the last thing you ever say."

Sandra turned back around and continued to tidy up her side of the sink.

"Fuck you! Who in the hell do you think you are, scrawny little white bitch? You—"

Before she could get her next words together, her esophagus was caught between Sandra's thumb and forefinger. She applied a pulling motion as if she wanted to rip it directly out of her throat. The lady let out a gurgling noise as her eyes began to redden. Sandra stared fiercely in her eyes and watched as each breath she took came close to being her last.

The clanking of metal bars was the only reason she did not die from strangulation.

"Cool it in there, ladies. You'll be living together for quite some time, so let's get along, shall we?"

The guard continued to walk past banging on bars with her stick and making smart-mouthed announcements, as Sandra release her hold on her.

Moments passed before her roommate discovered her voice and asked, "What the hell did you do that for?" Again, she was ignored. She dared not push the subject for fear of igniting rage in the other woman. "Well, if you ever decide you want to talk, my name is Barbara."

*

There were special rules and certain zones in the dining room. You sat according to gangs, relationships, racial affiliations, and a host of other categories that the inmates had divided themselves into. You didn't just sit anywhere.

Many of the women sat on the floor with their trays in their laps, afraid to choose a seat or speak up for themselves, and the guards allowed this.

Sandra went through the line for her tray and sat at an empty table. In less than sixty seconds three women surrounded her.

"This is our table."

Sandra didn't look up; she just continued to eat.

"Can't you hear?"

Someone was leaning heavily over her shoulder; the body odor alone was almost unbearable. Her tray and utensils were knocked to the floor, but Sandra didn't move.

"Now let's see you eat."

The lady standing on the other side of her attempted to push her head in a downward motion, but Sandra turned her head quickly and sunk her teeth viciously into her nipple. Blood began to seep through her uniform before help arrived.

"Break it up, ladies. Break it up!"

Sandra wiped the blood from her mouth and went back into the line for a new tray. She was delivered one without hesitation.

She moved as if nothing had occurred, but her eyes flickered back and forth at a rapid pace. She would not be overpowered if she could help it. The guards were in no way there to help or save anyone; they intentionally let the altercation linger on much longer than it should have. When Sandra sat at the table, they knew trouble would follow, but everyone had grown tired of Beth and her crew, so they waited to see what the new girl was about. Beth had been a resident of Winsor for the last seventeen years, so she dominated everything she came into contact with. They lived for the moment where she would get her just desserts, and to them, that moment had arrived. But they also knew they would have to keep an eye on the newcomer's cell. Beth didn't take to kindly to those who tried to show her up. Broken arms, disfigured noses, and a host of sexual complaints landed in her folder on a regular basis. She was known for retaliation. For those who tried to stand up for themselves, there was always hell to pay.

That night, Sandra sat on her bunk wondering when the security guards would come and get her, but they never showed.

She was beginning to learn the ropes of the system pretty quickly, and most of them suited her just fine. She learned that if you were going to be called out by the guards, then it would be right there and at that moment; they didn't wait. Punishments were given out as the deed was done. You would not have to sit in your cell wondering if they were coming to get you.

*

The next morning was set in the routine style that she would be following for the duration of her stay. The only alteration she was able to make was how long she decided to stay out in the yard. The guards would lead you back into the building in fifteen minute increments, and they would allow you to stay out the entire time if you chose to do so.

At five o'clock in the morning they were led out single-file to the dining room for breakfast. At six thirty they were assigned chores, and from eight thirty until ten, they were free to exercise or just socialize in the yard. Afterwards they were allowed open cell for visits after everyone was accounted for, and then they were locked down again for lunch. They were allowed outside in the yard again after lunch, and then it was back to their assigned chores, open cell, lockdown, and dinner.

For those who were in groups, they weren't allowed to go to the television room or the yard after lunch. They had to go and see their counselor or therapist.

As she lay in her cell, Sandra went over the activities she had endured for the day and felt at ease with the establishment and the predicament she was in. The altercation at breakfast stayed on her mind because she heard whispers everywhere she went. A few of the women clapped as she walked by, while others told her that she would be dead or close to it by nightfall.

She didn't really fear death, but she also knew it would not be at the hands of Beth or her crew. She was not an all-out fighter, but she was more than prepared to defend herself by any means necessary.

She noticed that the yard had workout equipment and that some of the women who exercised there were bigger than most of the general men she had seen in public. She didn't want to be released looking like a man, but she did want to put on a few pounds and buff up.

She could not definitively say what she would be doing when she got out of prison, but she knew being taken advantage of did not fit the profile.

Her chores and gaining weight became her focus. She was not there to make friends, nor did she want to make enemies, so taking it one day at a time was how she decided to handle the upcoming years. She didn't know if she would ever verbally interact with her roommate, so she also put that on the daily roster. She didn't want to befriend her, but the space was so small there was simply no way to ignore her.

*

The next morning, she wondered what would take place in the dining room, but all remained clear. Beth and her crew stared at her and gave off evil glances, but other than that, they stayed at their table. Sandra went out into the yard heading for the exercise area. She stood by and watched the women pump iron.

There was a lady standing by to catch the weight just in case you were not able to lift it off your chest, and she was the first to acknowledge her.

"You want to get down?"

Sandra just stood there, not because she was trying to be rude, but she had no idea what "get down" meant. The foreign look she gave was not lost on the other inmate, and she realized that Sandra didn't know prison terminology.

"Do you want to try to lift some weights?"

"Yes."

The lady who was currently working out did not look happy that she was told to get off the bench for Sandra, but she complied.

"How much can you lift?"

"I don't know."

She slid two fifty pound weights on the bar, deciding to start her off with that.

Sandra arms shook with effort by the time she got to number ten, and she was more than happy to have the bar lifted for her. She took two breaths before she heard, "Again."

The bar was dumped back into her grasp, forcing her to lift again. She was made to do three more reps of the straight lifts, and then she was instructed to go to the parallel bar and work her abs.

She knew all about the parallel bars. She had encountered them many times before in gym. At the time she didn't know she was working her stomach muscles. She had never seen a difference, and she swung on them quite frequently.

"Get down."

The inmate from the bench was now at the bar with her. Sandra swung herself up top and looked down. Once again she had no clue as to what she could want.

"Get down. You're not doing it right. This is not a playground, and you are not at recess. Get down so I can show you."

Sandra jumped to the ground and moved to the side. The more experienced lady was bulky in size, but she climbed up on the bar with the ease of a cat.

Right away she noticed a huge difference in their form. Both of her legs were hooked onto the bar, where Sandra had only used one. She rose all the way up until her head almost met her knees. She was not jerking around but concentrating on every contraction. Just by looking at her, Sandra knew why she had never seen a difference in her stomach. Her form was way off.

The instructor jumped down from the bar and walked away.

She regained her composure and hopped back on. She hooked both legs like she had just seen the other lady do, and she noticed a difference instantaneously. She could not rise all the way to the top. Her stomach began to quiver, and she could just not find the strength to lift up.

She used her body to start a swinging motion, but that was only making her go back and forth, not up and down. She had to get in shape, and swinging was not going to get it.

When her body ceased to sway, she concentrated. She knew it may take some time for her to touch her toes, but she would give it the best shot possible to get up as far as she could.

Sandra closed her eyes, and concentrated. She wanted to do well, so she used everything inside of her and pulled up. Her stomach still quivered, but she ignored it. The burn she was now feeling matched the sensation she'd felt in her arms earlier, so that was a sure sign that she was doing it right.

She let her body relax after she completed ten contractions. She dangled upside down and breathed deeply.

Just before she was about to begin another set, a pillowcase floated over her head. Someone was standing right beneath her, landing what felt like steel fists through the material. Instantly, Sandra released her legs, grabbing hold of the culprit on her way down. The case was still over her head, and she knew she had a good hold on the other person, but her attacker wasn't alone. Several hands began clawing and tearing at her. Sandra was truly outnumbered, but she felt a few of her wild swings landed in good spots, too.

The squabble went on for several minutes before help arrived. They tore the ladies apart and handcuffed everyone except Sandra.

"You think you're smart, bitch? This shit is far from over!" Beth hissed.

The lady who instructed her during the workouts came over and pulled the pillowcase from her head. Once again, Sandra did not speak to her but simply walked off the yard. She was beyond furious. She had been punched, kicked, and stomped, and everyone waited until the end to lend a helping hand.

She inspected herself in their makeshift mirror and was surprised to see that her right eye was turning black, and her left cheek was huge. She had taken a few good licks in the fight, more than she ever wanted to, and more than she ever would again, for sure.

CHAPTER 26

*D*ay after day, Sandra sweated it out on the yard. She had one more altercation after the parallel bar episode, but no more since then. Many of the women tried to approach her in a friendly sort of way, but Sandra was a loner.

Her daily work schedule, which included her chores, was basic and mundane, to say the least. She was in charge of refilling the hygiene packs and doing inmate laundry.

*

Days soon turned to weeks, months and then fully a year. Sandra blended herself into the walls of Winsor very well. She did not stand out, nor did she try to. She kept her head close to the ground and her eyes focused ahead. She avoided contact with any of the other inmates, even though some of them would come and sit at what was now known as her table.

Sandra would eat and get up without even looking in their direction. Her roommate could often be heard telling stories about how she had found Sandra doing thousands and thousands of sit-ups in the middle of the night. She marveled how she would run in place for hours before lights out was called, and sometimes she would keep going well into the dark. Barbara bragged about her daily, and she had a devoted crowd that would listen.

She was in the middle of the routine of doing her chores when her number was called by one of the guards at the door. "Number one three seven two zero H, stand facing against your immediate wall for search." Sandra was thrown off track. This had never happened to her, and she had no inclination of what they could possibly want with her. She felt her pulse quicken up, and a small amount of perspiration formed under her arms as she complied with the orders given to her.

"What's going on?"

"Well, well. She speaks! Nervous, huh? You're going to see your therapist, honey. Today is your day."

"But the judge said I wasn't to see a counselor until my last three years here. It's only been eighteen months."

"You're going to see your therapist, not your counselor. The state just recently put that in the budget, so you are one of the lucky ones. You get two professionals to try and help fix you."

"But I don't want to go."

"Not a choice. Now place your hands out in front of you."

Sandra was led back to her cell, where she was allowed to freshen up and get ready for her two thirty appointment. No other details were offered to her, so she had no idea about who the therapist was, how long the sessions would be, and a million other questions that ran rampant through her mind.

She wanted to fake an illness or start dry heaving, something, anything, but nothing came. A different guard emerged in front of her cell with the same instructions as the previous guard. Sandra turned around and allowed herself to be shackled and led down a corridor she had never seen before. Her mind once again went to that blank state, and she did not know her next steps. She was unsure of herself again and unable to bounce back.

Her nerves were getting the better of her, and she deliberately slowed her steps, trying to delay the process. What to do and what to say ran consecutively through her mind, plenty of questions with no answers.

When they reached their destination, she was placed against the wall and searched once more, as if she'd picked up something along the way.

They stood in front of a thick wooden door that she assumed was supposed to give off the appearance that you were actually in an office setting and not a prison. The door was closed, but the guard had the key with which to enter. A metal table sat in the center of the room with a metal chair approximately three feet from the table, both secured to the floor by bolts. Sandra was placed in the chair and shackled to it.

"Someone will be in to get you in a minute." What more could she do? She sat and waited.

Time seemed to stand still. She didn't have any desire to talk about herself or her life. Her past was definitely out of the question, and she would not open up about it, no matter who was going to be asking the questions. She would do what she had become accustomed to and lived with daily: remain silent. She was not going to speak to the therapist, just stare. Eventually, she figured she would be written off as a lost cause and dumped back into her cell. She let out a deep breath and steadied herself. She was okay now.

Ten or so minutes had gone past before another guard came to un-shackle her from the chair.

"We are going in that door over there in the corner."

Sandra didn't notice another exit in the small room. She had spent so much time thinking about what her session would be about that she had not completely taken in her environment. She followed her to the door with no questions. They now entered another room and noticed how much different it appeared in comparison to everything else she had seen in the prison.

A neat and orderly desk sat almost in the center of the space. There was a leather chair placed behind it, while opposite sat a rather uncomfortably-looking computer chair with wheels attached to the legs. She would like nothing more than to take the wheels and roll the hell out of there, but she stood still, not making a move in any direction. "You need to have a seat, and don't touch anything. Someone will be with you in a second." The guard removed her handcuffs, before leaving the room.

Sandra did as she was told, but she was not comfortable. The buzzing started in her ears, and she became truly afraid of what her next action would be. She could feel eyes scouring all over her, and her skin began to burn from within. There was a huge mirror on the opposite side of her, and she knew without a doubt it was a two-way mirror. Someone was watching her every move. She tried to remain calm and not fidget so much, but the longer she sat under the microscope, the harder it became.

She started to shake her leg in an attempt to soothe herself, but it was not working. She was feeling very violated, and she didn't like it in the least bit. Sandra ran her fingers through her hair, trying to be patient, but also found that to be impossible to achieve. She had never been in the habit of it, but she found some solace in biting her nails. It tapered the buzzing down to a minimum, so she kept at it.

She briefly wondered if what the therapist thought of her would in any way hinder her stay at the prison or if this was just a note-taking ceremony.

She had been caught off guard, and she didn't like it. There was no telling what they would say to her, nor did she have any idea what she was supposed to say in return. Hashing up her past was unnecessary and, as far as she was concerned, a dead subject. From her arrest up until now, she hadn't discussed it with anyone. A few of the guards would make sly comments to her about it, indicating they were granted access to her files or had be told by the gossip train, but she never replied to the cackling remarks. She never defended or denied the allegations.

She was as contained as she was going to get, and she just wished the crank of a doctor would come on, ask the stupid questions, and leave. She was sure she could make the entire session an unpleasant one, where they would need time to consider bringing her back in. When that happened, she would be prepared.

"Ms. Hansley?"

She was in no way ready for what she was hearing. How? Why? Sandra turned her head slightly toward the door, but couldn't speak.

"Who...what..."

The buzzing came back so forcefully that she was motionless to do anything. Her tongue felt as if it was three times its normal size, and she could no longer comprehend the basic commands her brain sent to the rest of her body. She was stiff.

"Does the sight of me shock you in some way? I'm not a favorite by most inmates' standards, but I've never been looked at so appallingly before."

She wanted to come up with a game plan, something to turn the tables around, but what? She couldn't even get her mouth to close.

"Were you expecting someone else? A woman, perhaps?"

Her mouth leaped into action. "Yes...well...I...it..."

"I understand. If you're not comfortable, there is a female psychiatrist on board here at the facility as well."

"Uncomfortable? He should be the one who's uncomfortable. He must have no idea what we are capable of! Who the hell does he think he is? We fear no one! Tell him to kiss your ass! Spit in his arrogant face! Choke the very breath from his body! Find a bag! Kill his pompous ass!"

"No!" blurted from her mouth with a gust of air.

"Okay then. Let's get started."

He busied himself with getting situated on the other side of the desk, and she sat there numbly, wondering where the voice came from and why? She hadn't heard it for months, and she mistakenly thought she had rid herself from it because she had been functioning on her own. She thought it was all a bad dream. She knew she had killed her mother and Bill, but she didn't really believe that a subconscious voice had helped her along the way; until now.

"Okay, now we can get started. I'm going to close the door, if you don't mind."

Close the door? She was on edge. She didn't want to be in this tight box with him, or with any man, for that matter. Was this a test? Surely he had read her file. He was the doctor. Why would he want to close the door with her history? She knew now, without a doubt, that this was a test, and she also knew she was going to pass.

"No, it doesn't bother me at all, but may I ask a question?"

"Sure."

"Why are you closing the door when there are people looking at us through that mirror over there?"

He let out a small laugh as he got up and walked to the door.

"Well, you are a female inmate, so it is for your protection as well as mine. They want to make sure I'm not doing anything inappropriate and also that I am not being harmed or harming you in any way, but the door is soundproof. I demand that I am able to keep client conversations private, so they are able to watch, but not hear."

"Yeah, right! He's closing the door because he wants you alone. He wants to…"

The longer she sat silent, the louder the voice became. She almost repeated out loud what she was hearing. She had to flip the switch and take over. She wanted to silence the voice and prove to the doctor that his gender didn't put her on edge, so she began to awkwardly flirt. She had seen it done countless of times in the soap operas as well as movies. Men are easily thrown off track when faced with a flirtatious woman. She had never needed to put these skills to use before, hell she didn't know if she even had it in her, but she was desperate, so she tried. "Okay, so you are doctor…"

"Wesley. Dr. Charles Wesley."

He took his seat again on the other side of the desk, and for ten minutes he didn't utter a word as he flipped through her file. Sandra was becoming anxious again and didn't like the quiet of the room.

"Do you like what you see, Charles? If I would have known how attractive you were, I would have done my hair."

Other than lifting an eyebrow, she got no reaction from him. He continued to appear as if he were deeply involved with what he was reading. When he finished, he closed the folder and peered across the table at her. "Charles? Are you comfortable on a first name basis?"

"Why not? That is your name, isn't it? I'm Sandra, but you can call me anything you like."

Dr. Wesley noticed that she was stuttering over her words, and her eyes twitched back and forth at a rapid pace. She was very unsettled to see that her therapist was a man, but she didn't want to disclose that and was instead overcompensating, coming across as eager, even happy to have a male therapist, which was definitely not the case.

He had seen this happen many times before in patients with rape and molestation in their histories. They would try to pretend that his presence wasn't a bother to them because they wanted to believe it themselves, while they also believed that if they were to say something about having a male psychiatrist, that somehow it would hinder them when or if they were ready to be released into society, which wasn't the case at all.

"Shall we begin?"

"In what position?"

She was shocked by the words that continued to come from her mouth. It was not what or how she was thinking at all. It seemed as if she didn't need to hear the voice anymore. She was the voice.

"How about we start with your childhood?"

Sandra didn't utter a word as the buzzing once again consumed her.

"Who does he think he is? Let's talk about his childhood! Who was giving it to him at the age of eleven?"

"Well, it seems you enjoy talking about a lot of things, but obviously your family isn't one of them. Is that a soft spot for you? Something you'd rather not touch?"

"I'll show you what I want to touch, asshole! Kill him!"

The voice continued raging inside of her, and she had to admit, she was getting quite annoyed herself. She had no idea he would start out right at the center of everything. Surely they could have begun with how was she adapting to the prison, if she had any friends, etc. This blunt approach was not for her. Attempting to defend herself, she took on her façade again.

"I know there's more we can discuss than cemetery stories."

"Is that what you call your past? A cemetery story?"

She didn't answer him; instead, a stare-down ensued. He had to think of another angle to get at her.

"Okay, I'll start talking, and if I say something that makes you uncomfortable or hits a nerve in some way, just let me know, and we can move on to something else. Do you understand what I am telling you?"

"Charles, you must have missed something in my chart. They say I'm disturbed, not stupid."

She had no idea that her little comments were being written down as uncooperative and withdrawn.

"First I would like to talk to you about your father."

"Why him? He's not on my list of bed partners. I'm sure you'll be much more interested in my activities with them."

"Ms. Hansley, I'm here to help you. If you are not ready for counseling, then I can reschedule you for some time later in the year. Maybe that female therapist you're looking for will be up for rotation by that time."

Shit. She was not fooling him. He had a comeback for everything she said. He never altered his composure when she said seductive or alluding things to him. He was almost at the verge of kicking her out of the room, and that had never happened to her. She wanted to be able to get a grasp of the situation, but at the same time she didn't need him writing more negative things to be passed on to the next person. Sandra knew she could not afford to leave.

"Fuck him! He's a moron. What the hell does he know? We can leave any damn time we want to, and I think that time has come."

"No, we need him right now."

"It'll be your funeral."

Sandra realized she was now putting herself in the same context as the voices. She had never used the word "we" when she would hear the whispers in her ears, but now she supposed she needed the voice just as much as it wanted to be heard.

"What exactly would you like to know about dear old dad?"

"Let's start basic. Do you miss him?"

"This is bullshit. Let's get out of here!"

"I used to when I was little."

"Did you know your father set up a trust fund for you and that you will receive $275,000 when you are released?"

"No."

"Your father has never forgotten about you. Does that matter to you?" Silence. "What about your mother? How do you feel about her?"

"She's dead."

"And how do you feel about that?"

"Much better, I suppose. She would have killed herself eventually anyway."

"Is there any remorse?"

"None."

"Did you love your mother?"

"Yes, until she ran my father away with her lies and viciousness!"

"I see."

"Do you? For most part this feels more like a question-naire rather than some form of therapy. The only reason I'm here is to dwell on the past? I can do that without an audience."

Dr. Wesley took a breath and allowed himself to be absorbed into the plush leather of his chair. She was going to be another tough case; he had no doubts about that. She really didn't want to be sitting across from him as it was, and now he was digging in her past. No, he was not one of her favorite people at this time, but he also knew that he had to gain her trust somehow in order for her to open up to the idea of therapy.

She was blocking every avenue he went down, and her answers came in quick, sarcastic bursts. He knew that was a sign that something deeper dwelled within, but it was a slow and sometimes tedious process.

"Is there anything you would like to discuss for our last ten minutes?"

Without hesitation, she exclaimed, "You."

Dr. Wesley didn't blink in response. He had heard this answer many times, so he was well prepared on what to say and how to get things from his patients while all the time, they thought they were delving into his life. "Let's make a deal. I'll tell you about myself, and you exchange some information with me."

"Okay."

She was finally on the winning end of this whole charade. She decided to keep her answers to a minimum and meanwhile find out as much about the doctor as she could.

It was natural for her not to trust men, but deep inside, a root had begun to form, and it took her to a dark place where the opposite sex was concerned. Not only did she have a strong distrust for them, she genuinely hated them.

It had taken her months to get used to the sight and closeness of the male guards, and it had taken her even longer to taper the idea of snatching their throats out. They were there to do a job, and as long as that's what they did, she was able to block them out.

They spoke less than a sentence a day to her, and she kept her responses even shorter. They placed the doctor here to shake things up a bit, but she braced herself to handle it. She was off-balance at the initial sight of him and with the sudden session, but she gathered her strength and was ready to let the games begin.

"I'm Dr. Charles Wesley. I live in Aurora, Colorado, and I've been here for the last seven years. I'm originally from Chicago, I'm married with no kids, and I have been working for Winsor Correctional Facility for four years. Now, your turn."

He had told the most basic things about himself, as he normally did. This was the opening of the gates. Once the client got started, he was an expert at keeping them going.

"My name is Sandra Hansley. Born and raised in Boulder, Colorado. Only other part of Colorado I've see is my jail cell. I'm not married and never want to be. Kids are definitely out of the question. I've never had a job in my life, unless you count prostitution as some form of career."

Sandra flopped back in her chair, feeling exhausted and vulnerable. The last person she had to share her life story with was no longer a part of her life. Mrs. Washington did the best she could under the circumstances to get her the least amount of time possible, and Sandra knew she would never forget that. No matter how horrendous the crime, she'd remained by her side, and that did mean something in the bottom of her heart.

"Now we are getting somewhere. Why did you stop?"

"I told you what you told me."

"Well, time is up anyway. You will start off in our next meeting, so think about some things you would like to discuss before you return. Unfortunately, they only allow thirty minutes per session, but I will try to get the time increased before your next session."

"When is that?"

"Friday."

"Day after tomorrow?"

"There's a lot that needs to be discussed, and I feel you're not being totally open with me about most things. I know that takes time, so I may have to shuffle some patients or pass a few to the other therapists, but whatever the case may be, we will be having steady sessions during the week."

Sandra became instantly agitated and annoyed. She wanted to jump across the desk and attack him. The thought that this may be some form of test was pushed to the back of her mind. She wanted to tear something up.

"I don't need an extended timeframe. Whatever we are going to talk about, it can be done in thirty minutes!"

He could feel her rage boiling up, and he caught the heated flashes in her eyes. She didn't like what he had told her, and her demeanor was letting that be known. He wasn't afraid of what she may do to him, but he knew if she acted in any way violent in his office, it would land her in solitary confinement, and they would cancel her sessions for at least the next six to nine months.

He wanted to be able to get through to Sandra. He didn't want to be just another person who let her down, so he pushed the button under his desk that alerted the guards.

She hesitantly obeyed them when they came to shackle her, and she left the room quietly.

*

Sandra couldn't wait to get to her cell. She was fuming on the inside, and she was not able to calm herself down. She had to have a plan. She couldn't let things just go as they were. She was being shuffled around, and she had no say in the matter. A plan was definitely in order, and fast! Walking briskly back and forth in her cell, Sandra fumed. "A man! How could they do that? This is a women's prison, for heaven's sake! He thinks he's so smart with his perfectly trimmed mustache. I would love to take a razor to it! I will be ready!" Sandra spent the rest of the day telling herself one in the same thing; she needed to be prepared.

CHAPTER 27

The patient seemed to be very reluctant to speak of herself or her family life at this time. She tries to control all conversations and steer them in the direction she is comfortable talking about. At times she believes she is smarter and more intelligent than the doctor himself.

She talks freely and openly about sex, using it as a form of shield. Men in general bring out the worst aspects of her personality, and it becomes very difficult for her to rein her emotions back in. Is not willing to open up concerning her mother during the initial assessment.

The exact form of childhood that she has been subjected to is still unclear. I am holding off on absorbing the full extent of her chart at this time. I will go through elements of it as I am able to get her to expose it, and talk about difficult matters. Extended hours are needed to break down the barrier that separates the patient from reality and hinders her in completing therapy successfully. Client is difficult to interpret at this time.

Closing out. November 2, 2008.

CHAPTER 28

"Help! Help!" Sandra lay sprawled out on the cell floor while Barbara screamed for the guards and some medical attention. It took ten grueling minutes before help arrived. She was placed on a stretcher, and taken to the medic room.

She returned to her cell almost as quickly as she'd left, with a diagnosis of nothing. They couldn't find anything seriously wrong with her, other than she had just passed out.

"Are you okay? I was worried. I didn't know what to think." Still no answer. Sandra had not spoken to her roommate since they were placed together, and she definitely had no desire to do so now. The last two hours were lost to her. She had no idea that she had fainted or that she had been sent to the medic room. It was all a blur. She was not able to regain focus until she was in her cell again, and Barbara was yakking off at the mouth. She hadn't been able to concentrate on anything other than Friday, and before she knew it, it was here.

"You can make your bunk when you come back. I need you to face the wall right now." Dropping her blanket, she did as she was told. The walk down the corridor was not the same as before. She was no longer un-aware of what or who she was to face; she already knew, and for some reason, it made it that much worse. The actual process of getting searched and placed on the other side of his desk seemed to go a lot faster than the last time, and that too gave her a sense of dread.

"How are you doing today, Sandra?" No response. She was nowhere near ready for this. She did not want to be doing this right now.

"Aren't we speaking this morning?"

Suddenly she blurted out, "What will happen if I decide to stop the sessions?"

A puzzled look crossed his face, allowing himself to mull over what she had just said, and what she could mean by it. He didn't want to rush into an answer, but he did want her to know the consequences for what she was thinking.

"If you refuse therapy, it will not look good to the parole board. They will see that as a sign of you not cooperating with what they feel is the regimen you should be following. Nine times out of ten, you will be doing the rest of your sentence behind bars instead of outside on parole. The therapists and counselors on the board have read your file and have included therapy sessions to help rehabilitate you."

"Rehabilitate? I'm not a drug addict."

Dr. Wesley allowed himself a laugh as he explained to her that not only drug addicts needed to be rehabilitated, but gamblers, alcoholics, etc. "You are to have therapy, and then toward the end of your sentence you will be attending programs with a counselor in a group setting that will teach you job skills etc. to help you adjust to being on your own."

"I was on my own long before I came here."

For the next fifteen, minutes, they sat in complete silence. Sandra stared at the doctor while he filled out some papers and filed others away. She knew he wasn't concerned about turning his back to her because of the two-way mirror. They would probably have her pinned down and shackled before she could make it to the other side of the desk.

The longer she watched him, though, the more distant the idea of killing him became. He was not there to harm her, nor did he come across as being forceful in any way. He said he was married, so that meant someone loved him. That had to count for something. The one thing she could now and always hold against him was the fact that he was a man, and for that reason alone, he was never to be fully trusted.

She wondered what game he was trying to play, but at the moment she could not figure it out. She had grown tired of just sitting in the chair without moving. Her butt was going numb, so she stood up. No reaction from him. He continued to do paperwork.

She stretched her arms over her head before relaxing them again. Slowly, she walked to the corner of his office to look over the plaques and certificates that hung there. The fact that they were bolted to the wall did not surprise her. She touched one of them, only to find that the original glass had been replaced with plastic. Nothing about him or the room bothered her, but the silence.

"Why aren't we talking? What kind of therapy is this? Ask me some questions or something. Don't just sit there catching up on work."

"Am I bothering you?"

Trick question. Slowly, she sat back down. "Isn't our thirty minutes over yet?"

"Yes, but we have thirty more to go."

"Why?"

"I told you at our last session that I would be requesting an extension in time."

"They granted it just like that? Inmates really have no say so in what goes on in here."

The longer she sat quietly, the worse it got. She did not just want to look at him and wonder why his nails were so nicely trimmed and polished. She continued to look him over from head to toe, and she finally found her icebreaker.

"Where is your wedding ring?"

"In the glove box of my car. It disturbs some of my clients when they see it."

She could imagine that being the case since a very substantial amount of the population was here for some form of crime against husbands and boyfriends.

"Is your wife pretty?"

"Yes, I think she is."

"What is her name?"

"I'm not at liberty to tell you that."

"But I'm supposed to be at liberty to tell you all about me?"

"Well, you haven't told me anything yet."

This was a little better than the silence, so she continued on.

"What do you want to know?"

He stopped shuffling his papers long enough to ask, "Oh, are you ready now?"

"I've never had a boyfriend in my life, and no one has ever cared for me. Is this the sob story you're after?"

"What about your father?"

"He left me behind with a drug-addicted whore."

"Why do you think he left? Put yourself in his shoes."

"Fuck his shoes! He left me to fend for myself!"

Her anger was mounting, and she could feel the heat consuming her. She enjoyed the feeling. She could feel the rage just as she had the day she killed her mother, and it made her feel powerful. She could hardly control the shaking, and at this point, she didn't want to.

"Why did he leave, Sandra?"

Instantly, she jumped to her feet as the chair rolled backwards and tilted over. "Because of my mother! That's why I'm here! She was useless!"

Dr. Wesley knew it was more to her than what she had revealed in their first session, but he had no idea how explosive she could really be. She was seething and at the breaking point, but she kept her demeanor cool and distant on the outside. He was here to work on the inside, to draw out her inner fears and help her face them.

If she were to be released right now, at this point in time, she would be very unpredictable and aggressive. Society would not be able to contain her. His job was to repair what had been broken long before her release date. "You're doing good, Sandra. Let it all out. Tell me your story. I want to know your side."

Damn. He lost her just that fast. She had fallen silent again, but he had to keep pushing through. He wanted her to think of the moments that caused her so much pain. She must be able to talk freely about the subjects in order for them to no longer cause flare-ups.

"Did you know that Bill had a wife and children?"

"Am I supposed to care? He should have been raping them instead of me!"

"He did."

She didn't know what to say to that. No one had ever told her his history. Not even during her court proceedings did she hear anything. It was as if she was the villain and he was the victim. She had never heard a bad word about him until now. It had always been her silent voice and actions against him and her mother's corpses.

"You would never believe me if I told you the things I had to endure. I wasn't born so heartless. They turned me into this monster."

"Monster? Why do you say that?"

"Read the file and tell me what other name you would give me." Dr. Wesley watched her as she turned the chair right side over and sat down. She crossed her arms and legs, indicating she was done talking.

He pressed the buzzer under his desk because her time was up.

Sandra sank deep into her bunk after she returned to her cell. She wished she could take her explosion in Dr. Wesley's office back. She wished that she had just remained quiet and been able to control herself, but she hadn't. Now she wondered what he would tell the board about her outburst or if the people behind the mirror would beat him to the punch.

Barbara sat in the corner of the cell atop the toilet. She watched Sandra as she mumbled to herself. She told anyone who would listen about her current living conditions. The exercise program was one part, but ever since therapy, the mumblings and whispering had begun, and Barbara was afraid to sleep at night. She had put in several relocation requests and had been constantly denied.

Either there was some kind of glitch in the system or someone thought it was very funny to put a psycho in obvious need of medication in the same room with her. She had explained several times over that she was incarcerated for assault and trespassing, not mental insanity, and still they were roommates.

Barbara was more than happy to learn that Sandra's name had come up to start the therapy sessions, but it seemed that she returned worse off than when she left. She prayed that the psycho repair man knew what he was doing so she didn't go insane herself!

CHAPTER 29

The mountains always mesmerized him when he drove home from work. There was a huge United States military base close to his house, but he could just as easily block out the sight of it because it did not harm the amazing view.

Slowly, he turned into his driveway and cut the ignition. He gathered a few papers in his hands and got out of the car. He lived on Florence Street in Aurora and had made the purchase without ever going inside. He saw the mountains when he drove onto the street, and the cathedral style of the house with the whitewashed brick put the ink on the paper for him.

However, he didn't set foot in the house until the day he carried his wife over the threshold. He didn't know what he would have done had she not said yes to his proposal, but all went well.

He sucked in a lungful of fresh Rocky Mountain air as he waltzed lovingly on the path between his well-manicured lawn and his home.

His living room was a little on the massive side, even for his standards. One entire wall was smoked mirrors with an etched water scene taking over the center of it. The furniture was minimal, but the space went on foot after foot after foot.

Keeping his papers in his hands, he sunk faithfully into his favorite wicker-back beanbag chair. He'd purchased it at one of the higher end kids' stores, getting a few laughs from his wife and friends, but it was always the first place they flopped when they came over.

He had a lot of notes to write from his dictation, and he wanted to read over some case files before he took a shower.

He didn't realize he had fallen asleep until his wife tapped him lightly on the shoulder. "Wake up, sleepy head."

Fluttering his eyelashes, he slowly came to, and focused on his wife. "What time is it?"

"According to my stomach, it's past dinnertime. I waited for you at the restaurant for a full hour."

Realization struck him at that moment. He had promised Diane that he would meet her after work. As a matter of fact, he'd promised and pinky-sworn on top of it. The sinking trouble he was becoming familiar with was just getting deeper. "I am so sorry. Come here, baby face." He reached his arms out to her but she backed away.

"I'm not in the mood. This the third time in two weeks that you've done this to me. You've started on a new case, and as usual, the first thing you do is forget about me. You promised that you wouldn't let new clients interfere with our lives, but it's happening again."

He knew all too well what past interference she was referring to. A spellbinding case had landed on his desk during his first week at Winsor's. It consumed him completely with its diversity and complex issues. He found himself staying at the library way into the late night hours, studying behaviors and symptoms, trying to find a way inside of his client's mind, never realizing how entrapped he was.

Whether at home or at work, he thought of Tasha Pierson constantly. She was an extremely confused twenty-two-year-old from Johnston, South Carolina, where she had brutally killed several classmates and teachers.

It had taken him eight grueling months to get inside of her head and communicate with her on a satisfactory level.

He had been all but prepared to write a journal about his success using documented proof that with proper technique, even the most delusional of patients could be restored to a civilized manner. Dr. Wesley was ready to seal the deal and get his colleagues for support statements when a call came into his office days later from the prison.

Tasha had apparently written something addressed to him before she jabbed a fork repeatedly in her neck, slashing into her jugular. She died alone in her cell, with a note meant for him clasped between her fingers.

"You can't fix all things that are broken."

All along he thought he was getting to her, helping her. He began to seriously doubt himself personally and professionally after that.

The warden at the prison felt he needed a few months off to recuperate after the state bombarded him with questions after questions. A few months turned into a two-year slump.

The day he walked back into the soldiery chaos of the prison, he felt revived and relaxed. He began to think that the Tasha Pierson case was just some form of fluke or marginal error of misdiagnosis on his part.

"Nothing is interfering with us. I haven't taken the time or energy to get to know this new client."

"Don't hand me that crap, Charles. You've been reading those damn textbooks and files until three o'clock in the morning. I can't do another episode like Tasha."

"So what are you saying? You knew my profession long before I married you. So when the grease gets hot, you refuse to fry the fish?"

"You know what I mean, Charles. You know exactly what I mean!"

He slumped back into the chair and rubbed his temples. In one aspect, her felt his wife was over-exaggerating in her claims. Diane came from a close-knit family where she was the only child, used to getting everything she wanted in the way that she wanted it, but she also had a good and solid heart. He loved her for that.

She understood his career to a point, but if he was honest with himself, he knew he'd pushed her too far. He also knew he was in the doghouse for missing their dinner date, and he would have to put his papers in a folder and find a way to make it up to her.

Going at her on the defensive angle could only make the wrath he was feeling worse, so he knew he would have to go on the offensive in hopes that he would be forgiven. Dr. Wesley needed to shower her with affection and give her the attention she had been lacking for the last few weeks or so.

He allowed a sly grin to cross his face as he tried to think of something to please her and eradicate his current situation. He knew by him missing dinner, he definitely had some kissing up to do and an angry woman to feed, so as quietly as he could, he left the house.

Moments later he found himself standing in the dead center of the Aurora Mall, heading for the flower shop. He bought a bouquet so big it almost needed to be wheeled out to the car for him. They offered to deliver it because of the size of the assortment he chose and said it would take at least an hour to arrange, but he tipped them heavily, returning in thirty minutes for his purchase.

While they went in the back to put it together, he zipped further up the road to the exclusive wine shop that his wife favored for anniversaries and holidays. You could get a hold of some very expensive merlots, but that was not what he was seeking today. He needed something else, and after explaining to the owner the exact kind of trouble he was in, he was taken to the cooler room in the back of the store where he left with a frosted bottle of Cold Duck. Now the meal.

He was blank about how he would be able to sneak it into the house without her still ranting at him, but then another idea popped into his head. He would use her parents. Telling them that he wanted to surprise their angel with a romantic night would get them on the phone and calling her over in an instant. They wanted to be a part of anything that would make their daughter happy.

After making the phone call, he continued on with the planning of one of his most consuming apologies. He decided he would even go through the extent of pulling out their lace tablecloth and candles that he knew his wife had spent too much money on. Yes, he was going all out!

Halfway home, he made a U-turn and headed back to the mall. He had a selfish moment, where he thought of what his consolation prize for the night should be. He was instantly stimulated with the idea of his wife in any of the items that flooded the racks of Victoria's Secret. He settled on a hunter green lace number with a matching lace robe. Dr. Wesley had thought of everything!

Diane's car wasn't in the driveway when he finally arrived home at eight, so that made it one step down, and a million more to go. Eagerly, he started to put the plan into motion. He was moving around so quickly that he lost all track of time. He didn't want her to come home prematurely, and he had not given her parents a timeframe, so he put the security chain on the door so she couldn't just enter, and catch him by surprise.

By eight thirty, he was dressed in black slacks with a silk black shirt. He looked over his handiwork and had to admit to himself that he had done a hell of a job. The flower arrangement stood magnificently in front of the bay window, setting the tone for the soft glow of the candles that lit the table. He was extremely proud of himself.

Diane had been gone for two hours or more. He kept the food in the warmer and took the chain off the door. When he started to grow a little restless, he was tempted to call her parents but decided against it. He waited patiently for his wife but at eleven o'clock, he popped the bottle on the champagne and began to drink.

Halfway through the bottle, he started to get angry and then wondered if he had a right to be. Frustration turned to fatigue, so he carried the bottle to the bedroom to finish it off.

At half past midnight, Diane quietly entered the house. The sight of the flowers in the window took her breath away. She turned to see the lace-covered table, when she detected the smell of burned food. She walked into the kitchen and took the lid off the warmers. On the inside sat two of the most dried out pieces of meat she had ever seen. She was glad the flame had died out; otherwise she may have been coming home to ashes.

She left the kitchen in search of her husband, and stopped when she saw the light on in the bathroom. A full bath had been drawn with rose petals sprinkled on the cool surface. The most seductive lingerie she had ever seen was draped lovingly over the back of her dressing chair. Two crystal champagne flutes were on the vanity, also surrounded by the beautiful petals. The guilt that welled up inside choked her up. So much effort had been paid to making her happy, and she hadn't come home in enough time to enjoy any of it.

After their brief argument, she'd left the house through their sunroom. She had never received the call from her parents. She had arrived at one of her friend's house long before that.

Diane left the bathroom and continued down the hall. "Charles?" Gently, she pushed the bedroom door opened to find him sprawled across the bed, with an empty bottle discarded beside it. He looked so enticing that she was tempted to wake him up and allow him to take her on the tour he intended to give her, but she didn't. She knew he would try to revamp the meal and run more bathwater, but it would only make matters worse for her to have to pretend. She wouldn't have room in her stomach even if she was force-fed. She was returning from a night of dinner and movies with one of her male colleagues.

CHAPTER 30

*S*andra sat at the table, consuming the tasteless soup that had been served to her, but it was not sitting well in her stomach. It swam around and swished in every direction. She was still unsettled from the last session with her therapist, and she couldn't recover from that. Barbara sat uneasily at the other end of the table, continuing to watch Sandra. She had not been the same since her last return from therapy. She had no idea what had gone on, but it didn't help her current situation in the least bit.

They had never been cordial to each other. Sandra had never spoken more than a complete sentence to her since they had been cramped in the small quarters together, but undoubtedly they understood each other. She kept to her side, and Sandra just basically existed on her side, but for the last six days, she had been zooming with nervous energy. She paced the cell all night and was still able to do all of her daily activities the next day. She was exhausting to watch and even worse to be around. Who knew what she was really capable of?

She was so consumed with Sandra and her change of actions that Barbara hadn't noticed the arrival of Beth and her crew. "This end of the table belongs to us."

Barbara turned around and faced the bully. "Oh, come on, Beth. I can't eat on the floor. Anyway, this is Sandra's table."

Beth glanced down to the other end to see Sandra's reaction, but she didn't move. She just continued to eat. She tried to feel her out a little, but Sandra gave up nothing. It was as if they had never arrived at the table. "That end belongs to her, but this is still mine." One of her cronies stood behind her, grasping Barbara in a chokehold, forcing her to stand up. "Now tell me again: whose table is this?" Beth was feeling surer of herself by this time. Sandra had not said a word to secure her area.

It was necessary for Beth to go back and face her again. She had gotten a lot of flack about the altercation she had with her, and she had to redeem herself. If she was honest with herself, she knew she didn't want to run against the grain with her again, but she had to do something. Barbara was her way to get close to the hornet's nest but not actually disturb it. It would look as if she didn't fear Sandra simply by going up to the table alone.

Sandra could hear Barbara choking but still did nothing. She was deeply engrained in her own thoughts, but the noise at the other end of her table was getting to her. She needed silence.

Barbara began kicking wildly and clawing at the arm around her neck before she broke the silence. "Let her go." It was spoken in a whisper, but Beth would be a liar if she said she didn't hear it. She hadn't taken her eyes off Sandra since their arrival, but she didn't give the signal for them to release Barbara.

"I said let her go!"

Beth let out a low whistle, which let Barbara free from her hold. "I see the loony has found a girlfriend. We'll see who takes her virginity first she-man!"

One of her crew decided to chirp in at that moment and enhance what Beth had just said. "Oh yeah, bitch. We will, and—"

"Shut up, Judy. Let's go!"

Barbara hadn't looked up during the thirty-second spat. She continued to rub her neck and appreciate the air she was now freely consuming. She didn't understand her roommate, but when the time came, she took up for her, and that's what mattered.

She wanted to say something to her, to let her know that she appreciated what she did, but when she raised her head to form the words, Sandra was gone. Barbara scanned the area, but she was no longer inside the cafeteria.

She immediately feared running into Beth and her gang without Sandra around, so she quickly ate her breakfast and returned to her cell.

*

When she was done at her work station, she returned to her room only to find Sandra being frisked against the wall. She was not allowed to enter until Sandra was properly shackled, and she realized it must be time for her to see the shrink, so she decided to wait until she returned to thank her for what she had done.

CHAPTER 31

"Hello, Sandra."

"Hello, Charles."

Pulling up his chair, he took his seat behind the desk but did not speak. He sat for a brief moment and studied Sandra.

"You look a little preoccupied. You want to talk about it?"

"I'm not preoccupied. Have you read my file?"

"Yes."

"Thoroughly?"

"Not quite. I have gotten to a few notes and comments given by some of your teachers and neighbors from your middle school years. Would you like to continue from there for me?"

"What, and spoil your bedtime nightmares?" Sandra was being very sarcastic, but today her therapist was not taking the bait.

Dr. Wesley sat back further in his chair and rubbed his eyes. He didn't seem as cool and relaxed as he had in their past meetings. She wondered if it was the contents of her file that were disturbing him. For twenty minutes she sat across from him, but he never opened his eyes.

"Dr. Wesley?" Slowly, he opened one eye to look across at her. "Are you okay?"

"Why the new name?"

An easy smile crossed his face, before he answered. "Well, I had a long night last night. I actually wasn't going to come in to work today, but I didn't have time to call in and reschedule my meetings, and in cases like that they would automatically be seen by the therapist on call."

"That wouldn't be so bad, would it?"

"Actually, it would. For some of my patients to walk in and be introduced to someone else, it could set our sessions back for months. It's the trust issue that I would have to build back up. Surprises are not good for most patients."

Sandra took this into consideration and spoke again. "So you're suffering in order not to let other people down? Admirable."

He mentally removed himself from the office one more time before snapping back into therapist mode. Dr. Wesley felt that since he had dragged himself into the office today, he should at least do some form of work. He pulled his briefcase from the shelf beside his desk, and removed a manila envelope.

"Today I'm going to be showing you some ink blot cards, and I want you to tell me what you sort of images you see when you look at them. I am looking for the first thing that pops into your head. No more than three seconds per card, okay?"

He stood up to remove his jacket, and Sandra noticed it wasn't a suit coat but more of a sporty looking jacket. He was dressed more casually today. He wore jeans and a crisp white shirt tucked in with a belt. He could have easily been the hottest thing on the next soap opera, and Sandra had never noticed that until now.

The mere fact that she was able to be across from him on so many occasions and not want to continually cause him harm surprised her, but she would guess that a large part had to do with him not appearing as the other men in her life. He didn't smell like sweat and liquor, for one, and in some ways, he reminded her of the dark-skinned man that cried and covered her with a blanket not so long ago.

Sandra noticed a light, airy scent that clung to him, if he were to move around the room. She didn't know if it was crisp air from the free world or the cologne he choose, but either way, she didn't find it offensive.

Dr. Wesley's voice brought her around to the current time, and she wondered to herself if she was daydreaming. "Okay, are you ready?"

"Yes."

Just as fast as she answered, an eight-by-ten card was flashed in front of her. "A man...a bed...a chair...a window...a school...a house...black plastic...a child...a truck... .a bag."

He quickly looked over her answers, comparing them against some of his other patients. Their answers shouldn't be exactly alike, but one or two of them should have been matched with at least one of the other patients. Either Sandra hadn't taken the test seriously, or she was in worse shape than he previously believed.

If everything and everyone she came into contact with formed some kind of bond or memory with her past, then he had to know how she would react to such a stimulus if she was living in the outside world. He had no idea if she was capable of ignoring it or if a deeper piece of her would demand that she act upon it.

"So did I pass or fail?"

"It's not a pass-or-fail test. It's just to pick the brain."

"Oh."

Sandra fell silent and hoped that she was coming across as more open to the doctor. She didn't know what he wrote about her on a daily basis, but she knew it could have a big effect on when or if she was going to be able to be released into society or into a psychiatric facility. It was a balancing act for her. She didn't want to be in a cramped office with Dr. Wesley, or any other man, for that fact, but she had to, and knowing that, she adjusted herself.

She didn't mean to be sarcastic when addressing him, but words just seemed to transplant themselves on her lips before she had the slightest chance to think about them. In her cell, sweat would form a layer all over her body just before it was time for a session. Her hands would shake so terribly that from a distance she could have easily been mistaken as epileptic. The bouts of nausea mixed with the fear of leaving her cell to take the walk down the corridor made her weak every time.

No matter how many times she went, it didn't soothe her nerves at all. What she feared most was that he would be able to see and detect her anxiety level when she was in the vicinity of a man, but so far he had said nothing.

She was hiding herself, and from the looks of it, she was doing a pretty good job. After their first run-in, when the entire situation was a caught-off-guard moment, he had never witnessed that level of anxiety from her again.

Where did the sweaty armpits or the shaking hands go, was beyond her, but once she entered the office, she was as cool and in control as anyone; at least that's what she told herself.

The moment the shackles came off, it was as if the new Sandra came out and ran the entire show. She knew what she had to do in order to come across as sane, which was to taper her anger, and she thought she was accomplishing that.

Her life as she saw it was about trusting no one and keeping people at arm's length. She couldn't picture living single in an apartment or a house. She could only focus on right now and getting through it the best way she knew how, and if it included playing patient to the psychiatrist, then that is what she would do.

"Is it possible for me to leave early?"

"Why?"

"Well, I can see that you are busy writing notes. I could be back in my cell relaxing before my workout. Where do all your little notes go anyway?"

She asked him in a casual manner, but it was something she desperately wanted to know. She needed to see just how much her little sessions meant. "Well, when I feel I am making progress or that my patient is taking a turn for the worse, then I deliver my prognosis to the chief of psychiatry in the prison. We then have a meeting with the rest of the board, and that person is either reconsidered in a few months or transferred to a better-equipped facility. We also decide how long the patient needs to have therapy while they are adjusting to the outside."

"Oh. I guess I'd better stop playing around then, or I may be forced to see a shrink for the rest of my life."

"When are you going to stop hiding and become more truthful in our sessions, Sandra? You are very uncomfortable with me. You automatically start twitching when your time is up. You never look at me unless I am not looking directly at you. If my hands are on the desk, then yours are in your lap. This is our fourth meeting, yet you have told me nothing about yourself."

"Don't worry about it, Charles. We still have plenty more sessions left. You may find out all you need to know. Now press the buzzer. My time is up."

He did as she asked, and watched as the guard searched and shackled her. If he would have turned any faster, he would have missed the wink and smile she gave him as she was led from the office.

CHAPTER 32

"Why aren't you taking me to my cell for count?"
The two guards that were escorting her said nothing. They ignored her, as they guided her toward the laundry facilities of the prison.

"Your station was left totally untidy yesterday. Now, the punishment you should be facing is solidarity confinement, but for you, because you are so special, we are going to let you clean the place instead. You know, a chance to correct your mistakes."

They pushed open the doors that lead to the fifteen industrial washer and dryers. There were twelve work tables and three pressing machines in the room. Beside the machines were loads of uniforms and linen.

One pile sat at least six feet high. She knew all of it couldn't be dirty, but she was also in no mood to argue. She didn't want to fight or struggle with the two lapdogs she had been sent with. She was consumed with thoughts of Dr. Wesley, and if she had made a horrible mistake by not being able to control her actions.

She could care less about why she was being led into the laundry room or if Beth had anything to do with it. They knew she was not going to report them. She spoke only when necessary and wouldn't mention something like this.

She was almost certain that this had everything to do with what had happened yesterday. Beth had somehow gotten a couple of her guard friends to organize something to this extent. From the looks of the place, she assumed she was to clean and fold everything. It really didn't matter. She could do sit-ups and pull-ups while the clothes washed and dried. She had a lot of stress to work off, so in the end, Beth was actually doing her a favor.

When she did a full 360-degree turn in the place, she realized that someone had slashed open all of the supply bags and left new stuffing bags on the counters. Sandra could give two hoots about what they had done or what they expected her to do. She had lived in a house with corpses for days; did they honestly believe that she would cry over dirty laundry and spilled toiletries?

She didn't say one word to them as she walked to the first pile and began loading the machine. They were surprised that she didn't put up a fight or struggle. They were in awe of how she was accepting her new duties and handling the situation. The guards came prepared for her resistance. They went into the secured weaponry room and confiscated stun guns and mace, anticipating a feisty confrontation. They predicted by the time they got to the laundry area, Sandra would be on fire and ready to go. They were wrong; so on their way out, they told Sandra they would be delivering her dinner to her.

Once alone, her thoughts ran rampant about what Dr. Wesley said to her and what it could possibly mean. All of this time she'd been going to therapy she believed that he was falling for her lines as she fed them to him. He never led on that he didn't, so for him say what he did really stumped her, yet she'd winked at him on her way out of the door. Winked, of all things!

She was so angry at herself for not being in control of the situation that the tasks that had been put before her became effortless to get through. The more she thought about Dr. Wesley, the faster she worked. In less than an hour all fifteen washers were running and she was getting close to being half done with the re-bagging of the supplies.

Solitude suited her very well. It gave her mind time to roam free and figure out her next plans of action. She could see things clearer and prepare for life's obstacles. She didn't anticipate Dr. Wesley disclosing the fact that he could see through the thin film of lies she was trying to wrap him in, and it bothered her deeply.

On one level she saw him as different from other men and therefore able to see deeper into her, but she quickly dismissed that notion with the idea that he had gone to school to figure people out, and she just needed to accept the fact that he was good at what he did.

Sandra loaded up the dryers and reloaded the washers again. She completed stuffing the supplies and went across to the bar that ran up the wall and across the ceiling, housing the sprinkler system. She climbed up on the table and jumped up to the bar. Within minutes she was working up a sweat from the chin-ups she was doing. The burning sensation felt good and encouraged her to keep going.

Her arms were beginning to feel rubbery and weak when the door swung open and the same pair of guards were standing in the doorway. Sandra jumped down from the bar, landing on the table with a solid thud. She'd pumped herself up and down so vigorously that her upper body was of no use to her. She had hoped that whatever they were up to didn't consist of being physical. She was exhausted.

"Get down G.I. Jane. It's time to go back to your cell." Sandra looked around at the still huge pile of laundry that had yet to be completed and wondered what to do, but they were holding the door open and didn't mention it, so neither did she.

As she stepped closer to them, preparing to exit, she noticed a slight change in the atmosphere. She was immediately on guard but nowhere near ready for action. She was standing close to the shorter of the two, and she could smell the anxiety and desperation that covered her, but she didn't seem to be in the mood for trouble. It was more like she wanted the night to end as fast as it could.

Once out the door, Sandra turned and faced the wall, waiting to be frisked. "Put your arms down. We are just going to walk nice and calm to your cell. Don't try anything, or I will crack the back of your head with my stick!" This was now the third thing that had been altered today. Sandra didn't like change and wasn't very good at adjusting to it.

One guard walked in front of her, while the other one pulled up the rear. They made it back to her cell rather quickly, but Sandra didn't like the looks of it. There was a blanket thrown over the bars, which hung all the way to the floor. You couldn't see in one way or the other. Something was wrong. Sandra turned around in alarm. "What's going on?" They didn't answer her but instead unlocked the door and pushed her inside.

She was standing in total darkness, and she wondered briefly what had happened to the orange glow light that rested in the far right corner of every cell? In less than ten seconds, she was able to detect that there was only one other person in the cell with her, and that relaxed her slightly. It had to be Barbara.

She didn't bother to investigate the situation about the light. She was too tired. The guards closed the cell and left, and that was all she cared about. The darkness was her friend. She could relax and think clearly when there was nothing before her eyes. Sandra climbed up on her bunk, let her head fall to the brick-like pillow, and drifted. She allowed her mind to open up. If she was relaxed and calm, solutions would start to emerge for her? After a few minutes, she was feeling better and a little bit more confident about her next meeting with Dr. Wesley. The ideas were flowing and…

Sandra heard a noise that put her on alert instantly. She bolted to a sitting position and turned her head in the direction of the sound. She couldn't make out the source exactly until she closed her eyes and held her breath. She'd learned that trick when she was in middle school.

If she wanted to hear what her mom was up to in the living room, then she would hold her breath. Outside noise became crystal clear when you could no longer hear your own breathing. So this is what she did.

It was the distinct sound of sobbing that disturbed her tranquility, and to know that it was coming from her roommate made it that much more irritating. Sandra wanted her to be quiet so that she could slip back into her mode of silence, but it seemed to only get louder as the seconds ticked by. "Shut up! You are always sniffling for one reason or another, and I'm tired of hearing it!"

Barbara continued her sobbing, unfazed by what Sandra had said. She jumped off her bunk and started to feel around for Barbara. She knew she would shut the hell up once she put her hands on her! She was at the point now that she wanted to cause physical harm to her. She didn't want to be crammed with anyone in the first place, but a crybaby on top of it all was getting to her.

It didn't take her long to bump into Barbara, and from the feel of it, she had gotten a hold of her thigh, but it was sticky and wet. Her nose immediately picked up the scent of blood. She waved her hand in front of her face and confirmed it: Barbara was bleeding. She didn't feel an open gash or anything on her leg, but it had to be coming from somewhere. She had heard other female inmates talking about self-induced abortions and things of that nature, but she had never been witness to the bloody horror stories they spoke about.

Sandra patted Barbara and still had no idea where the blood was coming from. She reached for her face, but Barbara began to strike out at her and release a piercing screech at the same time. "No! No! Stop it!" Eventually her hands fell to her side, and she continued to sob.

Sandra pushed off from the squatting position she had been in and began to search for the light. The bulb itself

was not in the fixture, so she began feeling blindly throughout the cell. The space was not that big, and it took her
less than five minutes to locate the bulb behind the toilet.
When the light highlighted the situation, she knew if someone else had found her, they may have run screaming, but
Sandra just stepped closer to inspect the damage.

She knew Barbara couldn't see her well, or maybe not at
all, for that fact. Her eyes were swollen shut. The deep hue
of purple danced heavily with the black outline consuming
the entire top portion of her face. Her mouth was twisted,
and her lower lip hung off-center and slightly to the right.

"Please don't touch me. Please!" No matter how brave
or courageous she was, seeing the entire seat of Barbara's
uniform saturated with blood did cause her to be alarmed.

"It's me Barbara. It's Sandra."

"Sandra, is that you?" She knew now with certainty that
she could not see out of her eyes by the way she swung her
arms out in search of her. She had no choice but to allow
her to touch her. "Oh, thank God! Oh, Sandra, Sandra…"

Once again the weeping started, and Sandra could not
understand one word she was saying. Barbara continued
to go at a steady pace of sobbing, but Sandra had heard
enough. Even in her condition, she didn't expect someone
to cry and whine as much as she was. "They raped me. They
touched me everywhere. I'm bleeding. Three male guards
were there, and they also…oh, Sandra, please help me. I
might bleed to death."

"You are not going to bleed to death. Can you stand up?"

"I think so."

Barbara leaned heavily on Sandra as she led her to the
toilet. She had her hold onto the sink while she crammed
toilet paper inside the hole of the commode. She pushed
the button repeatedly until the cool water was almost to the
rim. "Take your pants off, and sit down." Barbara tried to
do as she was told, but even the most basic of things were
complicated. Sandra found she had to help her more than
she really wanted to.

Once Barbara sat down, she had to admit she felt much better. The cool water calmed down the blazing sensation she had in her genitals. Barbara knew something had to be torn inside of her, otherwise why would there be so much blood? She tried to play the entire scene back to the precise moment when something had ripped, but she drew a blank.

The entire episode had lasted well over an hour, and even making it out alive seemed remarkable at the moment. She knew she would have to go and see the medic in the morning, but she also knew she would be requesting to speak to the warden. She wanted her to know what kind of establishment she was running. She would make her look at her face before pretending she didn't know what went on inside these walls. She had made her mind up to go all the way to the top with what had happened to her, and yes, she would definitely be pressing charges! She would be suing the entire prison system for the things they allowed to go on behind their walls. Jailhouse snitch be damned. What more could they do to her?

Being upset instead of feeling sorry for herself, lessened the pain marginally, but as time went by, she wasn't getting any better.

While the water gently cooled her, she manually manipulated herself with two fingers, gingerly probing inside to see if she could detect the damage. To her astonishment, she didn't feel any tearing. There was still a burning sensation, but she didn't feel out of sync in any way.

She had hoped that it was her menstrual cycle that had come down in the midst of them torturing her in all ways imaginable, but still she was not sure. The medic would be able to tell her if her fears were founded.

"Here. Take this." Sandra held her palm out, and there was a powdery substance piled in the center.

"What is it?"

"Put it on your tongue. It will help you feel better and take away some of your nerves." Barbara was more than tempted to allow the substance to take away all of the things she was feeling at the time, but she was not into drugs anymore, no matter what she was going through. She didn't want to be hooked and dependent on something just to get rid of a problem at that instant. Her latter years in life had taught her that. "I don't do drugs."

"Neither do I. It's a strong pain pill I was given when they pulled my tooth. I've been saving it for the day that I may really need it."

Barbara didn't ask any more questions but held the back of Sandra's hand as she licked the powder from her palm. "Thank you." Sandra washed her hands in the sink and climbed back into her bunk.

Barbara sat on the toilet a while longer before cleaning herself off in the sink and putting a sanitary napkin in her panties. Her body was very sore, and she wanted nothing more than to sleep the night away. She had no idea what the daylight would bring, but she was hoping that she would be able to go to the medic, find out if she was going to be all right, and get something for the headache she knew she would have in the morning.

As she lay on her bed, one part of her mind wanted to drift happily into a slumber and let the medication take over, but at the same time, the other side of her mind repeatedly played all the events that had passed, and once again she found the tears falling. Never in her wildest dreams did she imagine her life would have landed her here.

She came from a good middle class family where her father was a mechanic and her mother was a dental assistant. She was the oldest of three kids and, she felt, the most responsible. Her years in high school were unremarkable but successful enough to land her in the community college.

She finished in two years and was able to land a job as a general assistant in a huge real estate corporation. The money was good, but she had gotten greedy and wanted more access to it than she had.

Within three months of working there, she found herself climbing to the top. She had been outwardly flirting with her boss since her first day of employment, but it had taken her an additional ninety days before it ever amounted to anything. She thought her future was banked and in the bag until weeks later she discovered she wasn't the only one he was sleeping with.

Rumors circulated almost immediately from the office all the way down to the cafeteria about the secret couple, but she ignored them. She believed the other women in the office were jealous of her or just upset that they weren't picked to spend time with him. It wasn't until the words of endearment slowed down and the gifts became less and less expensive that it became obvious to her that she had been used and he had been bedding new employees almost from the day he was made partner in the company.

He waved his position and status around daily and waited for the fish to take the bait. When she knew for sure that she had been manipulated and cast aside, she let her anger get the best of her to the point where revenge was the only thing she cared about.

When he no longer sent flowers or his driver to pick her up for a night out on the town, she started making her own plans in the evening. She followed him for more than fourteen days with no proof of anything going on, which frustrated her and almost had her second-guessing herself, but she did not give up; instead she changed tactics. She began to follow his driver.

She knew he was the one to pick her up and drop her off at destinations selected by her boss, and she also knew that a leopard never changes its spots. He would not do things differently; he was too arrogant for that. Within two days her basic detective tactics paid off.

The woman she had been training for the past week was the one she now witnessed slipping into the plush leather seats of the limousine. She followed them for no more than ten minutes when she realized she was being escorted to the exact restaurant he had taken her on their first date.

Barbara knew she would make him pay for humiliating her, and it took less than forty-eight hours to figure out how she was going to do it.

She went out and bought a high-tech camera that could catch angles and zoom in on distances as far as fifty feet. She photographed the driver picking up ladies and her boss meeting up with them. If she was honest with herself, she was in no way enjoying her nightly escapades.

One month later, when she felt she had enough information, she developed the pictures, making several copies, and sent one set to the office addressed to him.

It was one of the best days of her life. She watched him from a distance as he signed for the package. She wished he would have left his office door open when he saw the contents of the envelope, but she could easily imagine the look on his face. Barbara continued to work diligently for the company, but she had long since given up following him. She knew he wouldn't stop because of the pictures alone, but he didn't even seem to slow down.

One week after the photos came out, she found herself training another lady for the position the first one had been terminated from. She knew then that he thought the one he had gotten rid of was the one responsible for the photos, so she started all over again by tailing the driver and the new employee.

There was no surprise when once again the first date took place at Fu-Lin, an expensive Japanese restaurant. Her first thought was to let the blame of the photos rest on the other ladies' shoulders and keep her hidden secrets as her own, but it seemed in some way that if she did that, he won.

On one side of the equation she allowed her actions to be fueled by jealousy and rage, but on the flipside, she knew she had unwittingly fallen in love with him.

She started from a place where taking the family to the Chinese buffet was considered an moderate outing, to learning how to order her meals in Italian, and French.

He had to have known that her feelings for him were growing as they spent more and more time together. She allowed him to have her in any way he imagined sexually, whether she fully enjoyed it or not. He'd known what he was doing to her, and she wanted him to know that it was her pulling the strings now.

Barbara decided to take things to the next level and take new photos to send to his wife. She attached a note, stating how sad she was for her and that she hoped with the photos in hand she would be able to take him to the cleaners in divorce court.

She waited daily on pins and needles for some sign that his wife had received and reacted to what she had sent her, but there was silence. He continued to date multiple women and seemed even happier than before he received the package.

Barbara had had enough! Nothing was rattling his cage, and he smiled at her every day in that cocky way that said, 'I got into your pants, but it wasn't good enough to keep me interested.' On impulse, she barged into his office and leaped across his desk, clawing at his face and neck, spewing obscenities while airing his dirty laundry.

She threw his imported vase into the window behind his head and was immediately enraged again when it didn't break. Barbara knew she must look like a wild woman with her long black hair flying around her face, but she didn't care. She charged at him again. He wasn't putting up too much of a fight; actually, he seemed to be enjoying himself.

Security was called to his office where she was wrestled to the floor and dragged out of the building. She called one of her friends to bail her out of jail, and she instantly was back on his trail. She didn't send anything else to his house except herself.

She boldly went to the door, rang the bell, and tapped her foot in anticipation. Barbara had no idea what she thought she would find at his house, but it definitely wasn't the gorgeous woman who answered.

She stood approximately two inches taller than Barbara, and she was definitely well-proportioned. She was wearing a short black evening dress that accentuated her toned and slightly tanned legs.

For the briefest of moments, her anger was at bay, as she stood confused on the porch. He must have thought she was in the same category or a close comparison to his wife for him to choose her. Barbara knew she wasn't bad to look at, but in no way would she put herself in any form of competition with the lady who stood before her.

Barbara's hair was still tangled, her skirt was twisted with a torn slit, and her pantyhose had long since been destroyed. In the face of this woman she felt she should have fixed herself up first. Her tongue was tied, and for once she wished she had thought out her plan before reacting. She was so close to walking away that she had actually started to turn from the door when he appeared.

The way he began smirking at the sight of her made Barbara want to lunge at him again, but the words of his wife gave her pause. "Is this the lady that sent the photos, David?"

As calm as a breeze on a summer night, he said, "Yes it is."

"And the one that trashed your office?"

"Yes."

She then turned to Barbara, and spoke. "You are a pathetic excuse for a human being. We have always taken a liking to charity cases, but I must say, you are the most annoying. Did you think you were going to win him over from me? Did you think that perhaps your photos would send me crying blindly to my attorney and I would leave him?"

"I guess she did, darling."

Once again he smiled, and that was more than she could bear. She wondered what sick life him and his wife were into. She wanted to stomp them both to death.

When his wife went to close the door, she put her foot in the way and grabbed a handful of her hair. She yanked the lady onto the porch with her, while swinging wildly at her face. David stepped closer to pull her off of his wife when she bit him on the leg. The commotion carried on for three to five minutes until the police arrived.

Once again she was handcuffed and arrested, this time without bail. Assault, trespassing, and stalking charges were filed against her, and with the testimony of the distraught wife, coupled with the photos and her surveillance equipment confiscated from her apartment, she was sentenced to five years in prison.

It wasn't until she had been raped that she really cared one way or the other that she was in jail. When she attacked them she felt justified at the moment, but the punishment she had now suffered because of it seemed to be too harsh for the crime committed.

$$\bullet \!-\!\!\!-\!\!\textit{ccc}\!-\!\!\!-\! \bullet$$

CHAPTER 33

*B*arbara had been to the medic several times and had been told one and the same thing that nothing had been torn down there. She went the next day after the attack, but the doctor stated there was too much blood in her vaginal cavity to do a thorough examination. Four days later when the bleeding just suddenly stopped, she knew it had to have been her menstrual cycle, and not that she was bleeding internally, but she wanted to make sure, so she went four more times in a two-week span. If something had been ruptured or shredded down there, she damn well wanted it repaired.

They asked her multiple times to name the inmates who had beaten and raped her, but she wouldn't. She could care less about the snitch code in the beginning, but since she had been going to the medic, she heard a few tales of women found hanging in their cells and it being ruled suicide. If you had a problem with someone, then you got them back on your own terms, or you ignored it. You never went to the authorities for any confrontations you may be having. That was the code, and now she was even more afraid than before, so that's the one rule she adhered to.

It had taken her left eye three days to open up, but her vision wasn't obscured or blurry, and she was thankful for that.

If she could pick one good thing that had come from her ordeal, it would have to be the fact that Sandra was now speaking to her. It wasn't as if they were having full-out conversations, but if she said hi sometimes Sandra would respond.

She continued to sit at the end of her table, and since she didn't swat her away like a fly, she figured she was okay with that, too. Beth and her crew smiled, teased, and laughed at her when they walked by until it was just no longer funny. Things were shifting into their normal state of being.

For Barbara, the days seemed to be blowing over rather smoothly, although she still had nightmares from time to time about the rape. She couldn't believe the actions of the male guards who were involved, but then again what was she to expect when they were surrounded with vulnerable women all day who were willing to perform any sexual act for a little compensation on their behalf?

Even though she was less targeted, she still felt open and very fragile in her current environment. Her feeling of loneliness was overpowering.

She knew her boss deserved the things she did to him and his wife, but who did she really hurt? They were still out there recruiting for their couple sex or whatever they were into, while she sat in a dingy, dusty prison with women trying to kill, maim, and rape her all in one night. She should have been able to control her anger at some point to at least keep herself out of jail, but at this time she had to deal with the hand that was dealt, and try to keep herself intact.

*

Later in the night when her self-pity was getting the best of her, Barbara tried to control her tears, but they fell so frequently and harshly that the vocal sobs soon followed.

She didn't know why the outbursts would come on so suddenly when she thought she was getting over her situation. At times like these, she didn't deny herself or try to keep the pain inside. She just let what she was feeling take control of her so she could try to work through it.

"Shut up! Stop that damn crying. I'm sick of it!"

She knew Sandra had to have been awake the entire time; she rarely slept at night anyway. Barbara didn't want to make her any more upset than she was, so she got up, went to the sink and splashed water on her face. She went to climb back into her bunk but just stood there, open, and very vulnerable. She didn't know what possessed her, but instead of flopping onto her low bed, she climbed up top where Sandra lay.

Sandra didn't move when the extra weight was pressed into her bed. She knew from the scent alone that it was Barbara, but what she wanted was a mystery to her until she began to talk.

"I know you don't want friends, Sandra, and you're doing a pretty good job at going at this alone, but I can't. I need someone to help me. I have no one else to turn to."

She continued pleading her case to the stiff lump under the covers. Sandra didn't respond to her, but the fact that she didn't get up and physically throw her off the bed gave her a slight confirmation of acceptance.

When she reached out to touch Sandra, it was then that she realized that she had pulled the cover from her head and was staring directly in her face. Even in the dimly-lit cell, her blue eyes pierced right into Barbara. The ache inside of her, mixed heavily with desertion and the long spells of any comforting contact, gradually propelled her decision making skills. In the next moment, her lips found Sandra's mouth, where she pressed ever so gently.

Sandra didn't show any emotions nor did she flinch. She didn't move or even slightly shift out of position as Barbara began planting kisses about her face.

Barbara continued to whisper all the things she was feeling and the desires she wanted to satisfy at the time.

"I am so lonely here, Sandra. I'm not as strong as you." She knew her next step may be her last, but she was so into the moment at the time, that she risked caressing one of her breasts. Again, Sandra didn't move, but her mind was spinning at a rapid pace.

She didn't know what to do, in all honesty. She thought Barbara would never cross the boundary lines of entering her space, but now that she had, what to do about it was a blank for her. She had never been touched sexually by a woman, and in many ways it was different than being touched by a man. She felt Barbara's tongue, moist and soft across her lips, but she didn't open her mouth. She had never kissed a person open-mouthed, so she kept her lips clamped shut.

Barbara wanted nothing more than to show Sandra that not everybody who touched her would bring her harm, but she also knew she had to take things very slowly and calmly; any rash movement on her part could land her on the cold cement floor.

She didn't want to be rejected at this time because she was so eager to satisfy her own appetite as well as bring Sandra some much needed pleasure.

They were locked in eight-inch-thick walls with some of the most deranged and psychotic people in the state of Colorado. The least she could do was let Sandra know that all of the time spent behind these walls didn't have to be so isolating.

Sandra let her continue on with her seduction as she lay back and thought about how she was feeling inside. Dr. Wesley had just told her that very day in therapy that she should not react to things so suddenly. She should take a minute and think about what was going on, how she was feeling about it, and what would be her best course of action to cause the least amount of havoc. Well, that's what she was thinking about until Barbara reached between her legs.

"Stop!"

Barbara didn't descend her hand any further, but she still used the other hand to stimulate her nipples. She was so needy at this time that she almost forgot about taking things slow. Sandra's breasts felt firm and perky through her T-shirt, making Barbara want nothing more than to knead, mold, and devour them.

*

Sandra would not be her first female encounter. She had been to bed with three other women in her past. The first came from her senior year in high school, but they were very intoxicated and high off of marijuana. She had no idea that she had been kissing her friend until she heard the rumors in class, so she never really counted that experience.

The second came the very next year as she entered college, when a girl approached her about it. She vehemently denied being gay, but she soon learned that having multiple orgasms with a woman in a night does not constitute as you being gay but just very open to experimental sex. At least that's the way it was explained to her when she agreed to join in the all-women orgy night.

Barbara's third and last experience came while she worked for David. They had been seeing each other for about a month or so when he greedily brought up the idea of a threesome. On the one hand she was crushed to think that she wasn't enough for him, but then on the other hand she wanted to know who he would think was suitable enough to join them in the bedroom.

A week or two had gone by, and he hadn't mentioned it again. Barbara guessed he'd dropped it because of her lack of enthusiasm or that the mere idea of it may hurt her emotionally.

One day he sent the car for her, and when she climbed inside, he was already there waiting. It was unusual because he normally would just meet her at the location, but not that night. He was all smiles as she climbed in. They arrived at a nice restaurant, spending majority of the evening sipping wine, eating oysters, and stimulating each other under the table.

As the evening began to wind down, they went out through the lobby and headed for the bank of elevators at the far end of the hall. David was a little more heated than he normally would be, but Barbara had written this off as his reaction to consuming so much raw seafood. They side stepped their way into the room, and David immediately began pulling at her dress. Barbara steered clear of his sticky hands as she made her way into the bathroom. She wanted to freshen up first.

The hot spray rinsed her hair, causing it lay slickly over her left shoulder, covering her chest. David loved to see her wet, and she knew it. Her breasts were a little on the small side, but her backside was more than a handful to hold.

She didn't attempt to dry off when she got out of the shower. She loved the sound of wet flesh being spanked and the sting it left behind; it was her own sense of fun that she added to the experience. Barbara re-entered the room only to find the lights out and two candles lit by the bed. David was nowhere to be found, but there stretched across the center of the mattress was one of the most beautiful women she had ever seen. Her body seemed to shine in the flicker of the candles, and she couldn't help but stare; it was like watching a goddess. She was totally naked and completely oiled.

Every move she made toward Barbara captivated her. All of her limbs seemed to move in sync with each other, and she found this fascinating.

She actually didn't climb in the bed until much later because her company was able to do things that she had never witnessed before, even in pornographic movies, while she stood at the foot of the bed. She briefly wondered where David had gone or if he'd set this up as some form of present for her, and if that was the case, Barbara decided to enjoy it to the fullest.

She knew he had to be somewhere watching, and if this was what he wanted from her, then she was more than willing for it to be done with such a stunning specimen.

When the lady climbed on top of her, it was then that Barbara recognized her as being their waitress for the evening. Obviously David had convinced her to come up to their room, and she was very glad that he had. They played many games with each other well into the night, and just when she thought she was exhausted enough and would collapse, David showed up and wanted everything he felt he had coming.

The two of them worked together for nearly an hour, trying to bring him to the point of satisfaction. Any other man Barbara knew would have been done in fifteen to twenty minutes, but David wanted the best every time. You weren't allowed to give him "lazy sex," as he called it.

*

Barbara continued to kiss Sandra on the lips, and she felt them swell in response to the constant attention she was giving them. She licked her neck and collar bone, but she didn't sink her teeth into her, although she was very tempted to do so. She slid down in the bed and blended kisses down Sandra's side and abdominal area. She was surprised to feel that she had a fully developed six-pack underneath all the clothes she wore.

Sandra's skin was smooth and tender under her touch, and the fact that she still had not moved gave her the encouragement to take things even further.

This was very new to Sandra, and still up to this moment she really had no response for what was happening. It was not something that she would have initiated herself, in any way, but she also wasn't totally disgusted by what was taking place. Sandra was confused that one woman could feel this way about another woman. She had never experienced anything like this. If one were to ask why she thought Barbara was kissing and touching all over her, Sandra knew she would not be able to come up with an honest answer.

She had never felt love or lust towards another woman. She appreciated everything that her counselor tried to do for her, but to say she'd loved her in a sexual way was definitely not the case.

Barbara played the game of multitasking by pleasuring herself and Sandra at the same time. She was getting more and more into the act so that stopping now for her would be almost impossible. Sandra's breaths were coming in shorter spurts, which told Barbara more than words ever could. She may not be helping the situation or participating in any way, but her body was responding to every touch.

Barbara's hair was splayed across Sandra's breasts, and with the slightest of motions, she moved her head enough to let the strands play teasingly against Sandra. She was on her knees now at the foot of the bed with her hands grasped in her waistband.

She was looking down at her, but this time she had some idea of what was to take place next. With a man, he would want to penetrate her at this point, but she had no clue as to why Barbara would want to see her private area. "Raise your hips a little."

Sandra looked into her eyes and saw the raw desire that lurked there. Barbara's eyelids were sitting low, as if she was in a dream state of mind. It wasn't as if she just wanted Sandra to do as she asked, but more so that she needed her to, so once again without question, she raised her hips allowing her pants and undergarments to be removed, but almost just as quickly she locked her knees back together.

"Open your legs a little, please." Sandra didn't speak or ask her any questions; instead, she parted her knees. What exactly Barbara wanted to do down there was still sort of a mystery.

Bill had put his mouth down there several times, but her mind had been shut down. She was totally confused and felt so betrayed that she was just praying for it to end.

When she first arrived at the prison they had given her a pap smear, which she found to be quite uncomfortable, and the only time a woman had asked to see her pubic area. She had been given them every year since then, but it didn't make matters any better for her. She knew Barbara was in no way going to perform a test on her, but she definitely wanted her naked and exposed.

If asked, Sandra would not be able to say why she was allowing her body to be manipulated in such a way. A lot of factors could be playing a role in her decision-making, but she knew she wouldn't be able to point one finger in one area to answer such a question. She was not in a fearful state of mind; she was very calm, actually. An odd sensation flowed through her when Barbara's breast became pressed against her arm, which left a soft impression. Thirdly, she really wanted to find out what Barbara thought she could gain sexually by touching and seeing her naked.

When Sandra's legs opened, Barbara rubbed seductively at her inner thighs, calves, and feet. She kissed everything she touched, leaving nothing forgotten. She couldn't believe how sinfully appealing Sandra was in the nude. Her body was in phenomenal shape from her daily workout regimen. Her thighs were firm enough to crack the hardest of walnuts, and Barbara took extra time in relaxing the muscles there. She massaged, licked, and kissed her inner thighs, until she felt her involuntarily jerk on the mattress.

Sandra's mind was no longer able to figure anything out. She was at a point now where her body was in control of what she was thinking, and there was no way she could shift it back to its original state. Barbara planted her head between her legs, and the amount of heat coming from her mouth shocked Sandra. She wanted to close her legs again. She wanted to make Barbara get up, but there was something from inside of her demanding that she stop fighting.

Barbara wanted to give Sandra the oral experience of a lifetime. She wanted her to never know any better and for her to ask for it again sometime in the near future. She made each stroke of her tongue count for something. She was not going to blow her chance of ever being able to touch her again, so she used everything that she'd experienced about a woman anatomy to guide her every step of the way.

Sandra's legs trembled, her back arched, and she had a fistful of hair clenched in her fingers. Barbara knew Sandra was so close to the ultimate experience in sex. Her body quivered from head to toe while she mumbled incoherently in the air.

Barbara grabbed Sandra under her buttocks and lifted them off the bed, firmly planting her mouth deep inside her. She sucked with firm pressure and followed behind with enough strokes to make a porn star crazy. Her hair was being yanked from roots to ends, but she felt no pain, only the hungry need to satisfy Sandra, and within minutes her womanhood flowed onto Barbara's lips.

She tenderly encouraged every drop to the surface where she greedily drank everything Sandra had to give. She kissed her legs lightly, and then let her tongue slide continuously over each of her nipples. Sandra was still in the state of climax, panting on the bed. She looked into her eyes, but Barbara knew she was not focusing on anything in particular. She was in the settling zone, and her body was beginning to calm down. Barbara kissed her lips lightly and whispered in her ears, "Yes, Sandra. Yes." She inserted her fingers where her mouth had been, and she found her to be very warm and smooth inside.

Soothingly, she bit at her mouth, and massaged her vaginal lips to soothe the electric currents that must be flowing through her at the time. She nuzzled her neck, and covered them with the blanket from the foot of the bed. Barbara wrapped her legs across Sandra, and there they fell asleep.

CHAPTER 34

O ne hour before the wakeup call, Sandra opened her eyes only to find herself tangled up with Barbara. Confusion swept over her, but it was the reality of what had taken place the night before that had her shaking her head in wonderment. With her past, enjoying sex was never to be considered, and especially not with a woman. She'd allowed Barbara to touch her with no consequences, and that puzzled her, but to feel the wetness between her legs and to know that she'd permitted such a thing to occur revolted her to the point where she wanted nothing more than to kick Barbara off of her bed.

She battled mentally for several minutes due to part of her wanting to give in to the pleasure that Barbara had given her. She had never known such tenderness, nor did she know that a woman's body could be so soft and warm, but in the most controlling aspect of her mind, she never wanted her to think she would be free to do that again. She didn't want anyone to think they would be able to control her body to the extent that she had allowed Barbara to do so.

She climbed down from the bed and went to the sink, where she scrubbed herself vigorously until she began to burn. There were so many emotions going through her mind that she couldn't grasp any one thing. She felt like crying at one moment and humiliated and used in the next.

Barbara had seduced Sandra for her own satisfaction and she never stopped her. Realizing that she did not take control and put Barbara in her place brought her anger to the surface so fiercely she almost couldn't contain it. The buzzing started as a distant sound in her mind that threatened to consume her if she let it.

She hurriedly put her clothes on, never once glancing in Barbara's direction. She laid there purring silently on Sandra's bunk with her left buttock exposed, totally unaware that her life hung in the balance of her room mate sanity.

Sandra heard the guards on the tier below calling for wakeup, and she realized that she didn't want anyone to see Barbara in her bed. She walked over to the bunk, and hissed in her ear, "Get up!" Sleepily, she opened her eyes and reached out for Sandra, only to get her hand slapped away. "I said get the fuck up!" From the tone of her voice, Barbara woke completely up and looked at Sandra.

"I thought—"

"Rule number one, never think for me! I have a brain of my own."

Barbara sat up and let her legs dangle over the side, more than a little hurt by what she was hearing. "But you—"

"But nothing! Rule number two, you will never sleep in my bed again. Rule number three—"

"Sandra please calm down. It's not that—"

"When I'm finished talking, then you can talk, and it will only be a yes or no answer. Do you understand?"

Numbly Barbara shook her head. She didn't know how last night could have turned into a military drill situation, but from the look in her eyes she didn't want to test the situation any further. Sandra was pacing back and forth in front of her. Her ponytail that she normally wore pulled tightly in the back of her head had come down, and her blonde hair swished furiously across her face as she spoke.

"Number three, never—and I do mean never—will you touch me like that again."

She used her words to cause Barbara pain because she didn't understand her own confusion over what occurred between the two of them. She had to set boundaries, and this was the only way she knew how.

Barbara was feeling so rejected at this time that before she knew it tears were falling helplessly down her cheeks.

"Stop crying. It's not going to change anything. I can't tolerate that noise."

"I'm sorry."

"Stop apologizing. Just forget about it. You can still sit at the end of my table, but that's it."

She was grateful to know that Sandra was still willing to give her some form of cover from Beth and her crew, but at this point it wasn't enough. They hadn't said or done anything to her since the incident, but who knew what the next week or next month would bring. She needed more from Sandra, and she felt this was a good time as any to ask for what she wanted. "Will you let me exercise with you out on the yard? I need to be stronger, Sandra. I can't survive in here if everyone thinks I'm just some pampered wimp. If they come for me again…"

"They'll wish they were dead before that happens."

"What?"

"Yes, you can exercise with me, and I'll help you if they bother you, but that's as far as we will go. We are not a team, nor are we a couple. Is that clear?"

"Yes."

"Do you have a problem with what I'm telling you?"

"No."

"Then get the hell off of my bed!"

Barbara grabbed her clothes off the bunk and jumped down. She watched Sandra pull at her hair and leave the cell, heading to the showers. She didn't look back.

Barbara got dressed before the guards made their way to onto their tier. She didn't want anyone to see her naked.

She didn't want rumors or small talk going around about Sandra. She'd agreed to work out with her and help her if something bad was to happen to her again, and that was worth way more to her than any awkward relationship they may have had. She'd thought Sandra may have enjoyed what they'd shared the night before, but she must have been wrong. From now on, she would stay on her side and try not to step on her toes.

During breakfast, the sound of Beth and her crew could be heard across the cafeteria. They were intentionally being loud and trying to draw attention to their table. Barbara continued to eat, but Sandra could see she was shaken by what was taken place. They were whistling at her and making sexual gestures, which scared Barbara.

Sandra didn't say a word. She watched the scene as it unfolded, and she waited. She knew Beth would not approach the table, but sometimes someone in her crew tried to stand out or make a name for themselves, and they would risk things that Beth would not. It had been three weeks since the attack, and she felt pretty safe that Barbara hadn't gone to the authorities, but she could not be sure if Sandra had taken her under her wing for protection.

She would watch them from a distance and see if their relationship changed any, and she would probably judge her next move from there. But Sandra knew there would be no next move on Beth's part. Once she saw them together on the yard, she would know that Barbara was taken. Everyone would assume they were partners, which didn't bother her much. She knew who and what they were, and that's all that mattered.

After count, they went out to the yard, and Barbara stepped so closely behind that she clipped the back of Sandra's heels twice.

"What do we do first?"

"Climb up on that straight bar, hang upside-down, put your hands behind your head, and then pull yourself up. This is for abdominal muscles."

She gave her no further instructions, so Barbara climbed up and attempted to do as she was told. As she hung upside down, she tried desperately to pull herself up, to no avail. The pain was dull but constant across her stomach. She'd thought after the time that had lapsed that she would have been healed from what was done to her, but maybe she was wrong.

Sandra stood three feet away and continued to watch Barbara at her feeble attempts. She had not risen up more than three inches from the hang when the whining began.

"I can't do this, Sandra. I'm too sore." Sandra was losing her patience and fast. She wanted to help her be a stronger person, but at what cost? She had no time to deal with someone who acted like a baby. She gave Barbara one last look and then turned and walked away.

Barbara could see Sandra backing off from her and heading over to the weight bench. Barbara didn't want to lose her. She had come so far in getting her to help; she couldn't afford to lose her now. She closed her eyes and put her abs to work as hard as she could. She ignored the pain, and the piercing sensation in her gut and pulled. She did not make it to the top, but she had given it a hearty effort. She breathed for thirty seconds and lifted again.

Sandra heard her grunting and groaning behind her, but she didn't turn around. She lay across the bench, doing fifteen reps of one hundred twenty pounds of iron. When she was finished, she told Barbara to get down from the bar. She could see the exhaustion across her face and the pain in her eyes, but she didn't complain.

She gave her a few minutes to get the blood circulating in her legs, before making her jog a mile of track.

They went at a steady pace around the first time, and she allowed Barbara to walk the second round. She took her to the bench, where she made Barbara do ten sets of fifty pounds of weight. Her arms shook tremendously. Each set became more difficult the last, but she could not stop. She went as long and hard as Sandra demanded. She had to do whatever it took.

They went to their cell to rinse some of the sweat off and drink some much-needed water.

"What am I supposed to do when you go to therapy?"

"Do what you normally do."

"But what if they come back? I've just been able to stand up straight without it feeling like my gut is ripping in two. I know the medic said they didn't find anything, but I swear to God I feel shredded on the inside."

"They are not coming back. Beth watched us work out today, so everybody knows I will protect you. You don't need to worry about them, but they should definitely be worried about us."

"Us?"

"Yes. You will not lie down and be a victim while walking beside me every day! There is a time marked on the calendar for everyone. You will know the day when it arrives, and you will act on it."

Barbara had no idea what Sandra was talking about or what she meant, but at this point, she was more than ready to agree with anything.

She saw the sideway glances she was getting out on the yard, and she knew what everyone was thinking, but she knew the truth. Sandra wasn't interested in any way, shape, or form.

CHAPTER 35

"Well, Sandra, I must say you are becoming quite muscular. I hope you're not going for the masculine appeal?" Dr. Wesley sat across from her with a baby blue shirt she had never seen on him before and a striped tie. His pants were a deep navy color, and from the look of the material she knew they had to be expensive.

"I'm just trying to get in shape, not out-wrestle Hulk Hogan."

"I'm glad to hear that. I wanted to take a minute to talk to you about your release date, and your preparations for that. We do have several halfway houses set up in Colorado for those who have stipulations demanding that they spend a certain amount of time there. As of right now, we haven't figured out what category you—"

"We?"

"Yes, we. I have discussed you in great detail with the warden and the faculty here at the prison. I'm not saying you're getting released tomorrow. I don't expect that to happen for the next twenty-two months or so, but it's never too soon to start discussing it and getting all the facts out on the table."

"Well, when do you think I'll be getting out?"

"Let me take a look at your file. Didn't they tell you when you were in court have you read your papers?"

"Maybe to the first and no to the second"

Dr. Wesley quickly re-read her court reports and realized that Sandra had just gone through the motions. Her file stated that she had not pleaded guilty or not guilty. A court appointed psychologist determined she was not fit to stand trial, but in another section it says she was cross examined. It didn't make any sense. He wondered how did Sandra end up in prison instead of the psychiatric ward? Someone had dropped the ball in her case, but it was far too late to turn the tables back around.

If he were to bring it up now, they would throw her into the system attempting to cover their tracks, but in the end, it would be Sandra who would come out the worse for it.

Her release date was closer than he had realized as well. She had been given a psychiatric sentence but was serving the time in the prison system.

There were one or two ways in which he could handle this catastrophe, and he hoped he would make the right choice. He needed to think about which would be the best alternative for her and society. Without a doubt he had to be sure she was indeed rehabilitated. He would have to spend quality time with her, see if a medication regimen was necessary upon her release, and determine if she could re-enter society without the need or desire to harm anyone else.

There was a lot on his plate, and he was hoping that he would make the right decision. He wanted to give Sandra a second chance in life.

Sandra sat across from him, twisting a piece of thread that had come loose from her uniform totally, oblivious to the decision Dr. Wesley had to make about her future. He looked at her in a different light now. She was not like all his other patients; she had earned a top priority spot in his filing cabinet, and he didn't want to let anyone down in his final analysis.

He knew he was alone in coming up with any kind of conclusion for her. His colleges may go along with his input of not letting the courts and the penal system know of their error, but if something were to go wrong with Sandra, they would be the first to throw him to the wolves.

His hands were tied, but he knew what his decision would be long before he made it. Sandra would have her second chance at life, and he was the one who was going to give it to her. Where the system had failed her, he would not.

He would get her time increased again, and he would give some of the best patient therapy he had ever offered. He needed to reread some of the more in-depth manuals and theories on his shelves. Dr. Wesley knew he had just bitten off a huge chunk of the apple, but he knew no other way. He had become a psychiatrist to heal the mind and rehabilitate the soul.

He truly believed that his patients were not lost causes but misguided beings. Sandra was a prime example of why he chose his field of work. She was mistreated as a youth, and now as an adult she had no idea what to expect out of life or who to trust. He would put her on the right path and help her in any way that he could. He liked to look at himself as someone who gave second chances, and that's exactly what he was about to give her.

Sandra didn't how lucky she was in every sense of the word. If everyone followed the ink on the paper, she would get released on her date and not much else. She didn't have to go before the parole board because she would not be on parole when she got out. She would have to report her current address and therapist to a court appointed officer for the first three years after she returned to civilization. That was her only requirement.

It was incredible to him how her case was so mismatched. The sentence was imposed by the judge, but where she was to do her time was not. Yet in the back of her file it stated that she was to be under the care of a psychiatrist for three years after her release. He had never seen such a horrible miscarriage of justice in his entire career.

"Well, you haven't said anything for ten minutes. Does it say when I get out or not?"

"That date should be embedded in your head. Your not counting down?"

Sandra was about to come up with a flippant answer, but for some reason, she held back. He was looking at her differently now since he had gone through her file again. Something had changed, and she was quite aware of it.

"Well, I've never lived on my own, but I do know about paying bills and such. I can get a job and go to a community college somewhere. I'm sure you know locations close to schools, don't you?"

"Yes, I do, and we can discuss that later. Tell me what you would be going to school for and what kind of work you will be looking to do."

Sandra didn't have those things planned out; she had been caught off guard by the direction the questions took. She used a girl's life from one of the television shows she had watched and babbled on about it as if those were her own thoughts. Dr. Wesley seemed to buy it from the moment she began to speak it, so she kept at it.

Something in her file had disturbed him and brought a new atmosphere into the office.

He hadn't told her what he had found, but all of a sudden he wanted to discuss her plans for her immediate future, and that scared her. She developed a very quick temper since being incarcerated, and all the time she had spent across the desk from him had not curbed that. Sandra had learned new techniques to calm down mild flare-ups, but inside she still felt the boil of in-justice simmering within her. She didn't actually want to harm anyone, and she found as long as she was left alone, she was quite happy with herself.

She enjoyed reading, doing crossword puzzles, and working out, but she also realized she couldn't live on that alone.

She picked up a few skills in the half-hearted program they put her in once a week, so she knew how to type and file etc. She hoped it would be enough for her to blend in when she got out. She didn't want to stick out like a sore thumb. She needed to learn how to be social.

"That's very good, Sandra. I want you to give more thought about your future plans and start to write them out. From now on I want you to bring notes and ideas with you to the sessions, and we will discuss them. Also, I want to get you started on a medication that will help you relax a little and break out of some of your barriers."

"I don't do drugs, Dr. Wesley. You are going to have to come up with something else. I am fine the way I am."

"We will talk about that further during your next visit. For now, just write the notes, okay?"

"Yeah."

Sandra turned and let the guards cuff her and lead her out of the office, but she had one last question. "Dr. Wesley do you know the name of the lawyer who is handling the money my father left me?"

The question seemed to have come out of the blue, but when he looked into her face he knew she had been thinking about it for some time. She had been thinking of her future, and this made the choice that much easier for him. "Yes, I do, and we will discuss that when you come back. I will see you Monday."

She turned to be escorted out with a smile on her face. She didn't know if she was really happy for the money or if she would rather have had the love from her father. To think about it too much brought a buried anger to the surface, and she couldn't afford that right now. The last time she allowed herself to dwell on her father, it had taken three days for her to calm down and two weeks for the holes she bit into her cheeks to heal.

Sandra practiced the deep breathing exercises Dr. Wesley had taught her all the way to her cell. The letters had been coming to her for over a year, but she had been disregarding them until now. She had to face the music and the outside world sometime, so she pulled all the notifications from under her bunk and went through them.

Her father passed away one year after she was incarcerated. He left her the beneficiary of a life insurance policy, with a letter attached to it. Apparently, he had some things to say to her, but he was not man enough to face her. The life insurance company left the money and letter in care of an attorney to handle the matter.

He was able to locate her four months after she was put behind bars, but he stopped writing when she didn't respond. Was he sick and his guilt made him seek out his forgotten responsibility? She guessed he had to do more research in order to find out if she was the correct Sandra Hansley from the news reports.

A year later, the letters continued to come again, but she never opened them. She continued to pile them under her mattress as bunk cushions, but now was the time for her to read them in detail.

Sandra never considered what the letters were about, originally, but everything was exposed to her when she decided to open the first one. She had almost missed her opportunity. She went through the postage dates to the very last envelope sent, and it was almost six months old. The law office had indicated that they would no longer be sending letters concerning her policy with Welling Life Insurance Company. She was to contact them either by letter or by phone and use the identifying code on the bottom in order to be referred to the attorney who would be handling her case. She knew if they were not going to write her anymore they had decided to move on from her and focus on more current claims.

Whatever the case may be, she didn't want to lose out on the money she had coming to her. She had a sizable trust fund, and a insurance policy. She needed it to move forward in life, and she wasn't about to let it slip through her fingers. When she returned to her cell, she used the tablet that Dr. Wesley had given her and composed a letter. She wrote out her full name, the name of the prison, and the code on the bottom.

CHAPTER 36

"Another long day, Charles?" It wasn't hard to tell by the sound of her voice that Diane was trying to be sarcastic. Truly, he didn't want to answer her, but she would just keep at it if he didn't say something soon. "It's always a long day when your job is as stressful as mines."

Dr. Wesley went into the room and changed into a jogging suit before heading to the basement to play shuffleboard. The man who had owned the house before them must have been either in the retirement age bracket or had a life just as out of whack as his in order to take the time to have the game built into the flooring. He got out the pucks and sticks just to push something around for a while. He needed to unwind. Things had been crazy for him at work, and to find out that Sandra was misplaced by the system had him just about pulling his hair out.

Dr. Wesley set up the board and then went to the other side of the basement. He'd had a massive wet bar installed within two months of buying the house, and the stiff bill the contractors left him with was well worth the price. He reached for the bottle of brandy and realized he was not alone. His wife continued to nip at his heels.

"A double brandy before dinner? She must have your full attention."

"She? Who is she, Diane? Please don't start. You seem to love making artificial problems lately."

"Artificial? Friends have invited us out over and over again, but we have yet to accept an invitation. We no longer share meals with each other, and let's not mention the bedroom, shall we? I'm your wife, but I haven't made love to my husband in over a month! Is that also artificial?"

Quickly he downed his drink before hustling over to the other side of the basement. This is where he went to get away from the office and from his wife when she was in moods such as these, but today she was relentless in pursuing him.

"Diane, please give me a few moments of alone time, and then we can talk about anything you want. I just need a little space right now. There are some serious things that are going on in the office, and I have to figure it out somehow."

"Are you sleeping around on me? Are you no longer attracted to me? What is it? I think I deserve some answers, Charles, and I want them before you start pushing that damn stick!"

"I'm just trying to unwind, Diane. I don't see the harm in that."

"Is that all you have to say?"

Charles turned his back to his wife and started to play. He could feel the daggers being thrown into his back by the seconds. Diane was ready for round two, and he wanted nothing more than to diffuse the situation. She was standing no more than five feet from him, and she was steaming. The toe of her shoe was being tapped against the floor at a rapid pace, as she leaned against the wall with her arms crossed. She wanted him to say something, anything, but he just couldn't find the words to give them both what they wanted.

Diane had been jealous of his career from the day she noticed most of his clients were female. Whenever she felt he wasn't giving her enough attention, then his job would come into play. If he had to stay at the office late, he would come home to find her with her mouth poked out. No matter what the case may be, she had found it very convenient to blame the bulk of their problems on his clients.

The scenario had worn itself thin, but not the love he had for his wife. He would move heaven and earth to make Diane happy, but at times like these, the effort seemed never-ending.

Diane was tired of kissing up in order to make up, and she wanted him to know it. She had been feeling neglected for too long, and he was not moving an inch to help solve the problem. Everything he did was tied to his job, and she was more than fed up with it. He was making her doubt their marriage in more ways than one, and it was becoming very draining.

She longed for the close connection they once shared and the tight hugs she could always come home to. There were so many things missing that it seemed as if someone had stolen pieces from the jigsaw puzzle that made up their life. Frustration is an evil tool in the hands of a weary wife, as she used it to dig deeper into him.

Diane pushed away from the wall, closed the distance between them, and hissed in his ear, "I'll let you play your game, but before I go, tell me this, Mr. Professional. If you know women so well and can read their thoughts and ideas like children's books, whose bed will I be warming because ours has grown so cold?"

Charles reached out and slapped his wife harshly across the face. "Shut the hell up, Diane!"

She didn't flinch at the pain he had caused her; it only fueled the anger that had simmered inside of her for so long. "What's the matter, doctor? Did I hit a nerve? Do you want to make love, but your body is unable to rise to the occasion? Tell me, Mr. Super Psychiatrist, so I can give you a proper diagnosis!"

Without saying another word, he snatched her by the collar of her shirt, dragging her to the other side of the basement, and threw her onto the sofa by the bar. He was furious with his wife for the little blows she had been throwing his way all week, but now for her to challenge his manhood and taunt him like a third grader kicked him into a entire different persona.

He didn't see his wife's face or the fear that spread across it like a wildfire. He was going to show her just how much of a man he could be. He was going to teach her to shut the hell up. "I'm no longer a man, huh? Then what the fuck am I?"

Rage and fury burned through him as he forced himself on top of his wife. Diane was so frozen with fear she couldn't speak. Never before had she seen her husband like this: demonic and unreachable. He raised her skirt, and fiercely began tearing at her stockings. "No, Charles! Stop! I…"

"Shut up, Diane!"

Quickly he released himself from his pants but was momentarily disgusted to see he had reached a full erection from their struggle.

He dismissed the idea that something may very well be wrong with him if he was able to be stimulated by such acts. He was not about to lay blame for his wife's behavior at his feet. She wanted this, as she had so vividly spoken of it earlier, and he was responsible for giving it to her.

Charles emptied in less than five minutes, and then stood to straighten his clothes. "Are you happy now? Your husband just slept with you."

Diane was startled by his coldness; she jumped to her feet and began swinging at his face. "You bastard! I hate you! Don't ever touch me again!" When he felt her nails dig into his flesh, he grabbed her by the wrists, and slung her back unto the sofa. "Don't worry about me touching you again, Diane. The thought never crossed my mind!"

She sat paralyzed on the couch wondering when her husband changed into the uncaring monster that had just raped her. She felt as if her soul had just been ripped right out of her body. She wanted to get up and remove all her clothing in hopes of cleaning up what had just taken place between them, but the sound of the door slamming only shattered her more.

She knew she had been on his case a lot, and by all sense of the word, she was nagging him day after day, but nothing she had done deserved what she had gotten. She didn't know what to do from this point on. Charles had crossed a line than should have never been crossed. No woman deserved to be forcefully pressed upon, husband or not. But could she really sit there and condemn him as if she had no fault in it? She didn't readily have the answer to that, but she did know where she could go and get peace to find it.

CHAPTER 32

*D*uring the last thirteen months or so, they had formed a misshapen bond and a full understanding of each other. It was a routine, and it worked beautifully for them. Sandra barked the orders, and Barbara followed them, but as time went on, the need to give out direct orders decreased.

Barbara had gotten with the program, and she knew what Sandra expected and what she did not like. It wasn't very hard to do; everything consisted of giving her space and quiet time. On the days when the weather was bad, Sandra would let her go on and on about her family, high school, boys, etc., but she never wanted to hear a story repeated.

She had grown to love Sandra in a way that was difficult to explain to anyone. She would lay down her life for her and would not hesitate to do anything she asked of her. Many of the prisoners were calling her Sandra's puppet, or her slave, but she didn't see it like that. They couldn't see why she had so much respect and love for Sandra, and if she tried, she knew she wouldn't be able to get the words to come out right either, but it was there, and it was strong.

In the mornings, she made sure she endured a rigorous workout, and it was mandatory that she complete twenty reps of ten count crunches a night. Sandra didn't want to shower at the same time she did, so she always went in first, but when Barbara went, Sandra would wait close by just in case someone tried to do something to her. It was very comforting just to know she was there.

It was impossible for her not to love someone who constantly gave her so much security. She couldn't really say that they were close friends because Sandra had never disclosed anything about herself. She never talked of a brother or sister, and the one time she asked about her mother was the last time. Sandra's eyes flashed so violently that Barbara knew it was a no-question zone without being told.

The story around the prison was that she was a nut job who had killed her entire family. She didn't know if it was true or not, but as time went on, she also knew that she didn't care. Sandra never mistreated her, and if you understood her in any form or fashion, you would know that she was true to her word.

She promised Barbara that no one would ever hurt her again, and no one did. With Sandra by her side, Beth and her crew had moved on to the new inmates, leaving her as a forgotten story.

"What's the matter with you? I haven't heard your non-stop chitter-chatter for three days now." Barbara didn't answer. For the first time since knowing her, Sandra found her deep in thought. It wasn't as if she were trying to focus on an idea or remember a name; it was more than that.

Barbara held on tightly to the bars because she could not turn to look at Sandra. Her heart felt as if it was being shredded, piece by piece.

The emotions pulled at her, and no matter how much she knew Sandra hated it, she cried. "I'm going to miss you. That's all."

"Miss me? What did you do? Are they moving you?"

This caught Sandra off guard, and it was her turn to be silent. She had no clue why they were going to separate them, but she knew she didn't like it. To say that she was fond of Barbara would be stretching things a little bit, but she knew she definitely didn't want a new cellmate. She had grown comfortable around her, and Barbara respected her boundaries.

She didn't like to carry on long conversations, but on the days she would listen to her go on and on about her wacky family, it made her feel somehow lighter inside. She never laughed out loud or asked questions, but just to hear her go on and on in her squeaky voice of excitement made the rainy days a slight more bearable.

Barbara became a force to be reckoned with on the yard, and people began to take notice of the muscular beauties. On days when Sandra was not feeling her best, Barbara would push her to finish a set or go the extra mile. They just somehow completed each other.

Barbara turned to face her, trying to swipe the tears away as she did so. She let a small smile cross her face, but her eyes betrayed her. Sandra knew it was more than a solitary confinement transfer. Something bigger was going on, and it was killing Barbara to talk about it.

Sandra ran through everything that had occurred within the last two weeks, but nothing significant popped out at her. She was baffled and not sure if she wanted to hear the problem. If it was a family issue, she was coming up short on how she was supposed to respond to someone being sad about losing a parent or an aunt. She would just go with the flow. She hoped Barbara knew her well enough to know that family was not something she liked to talk about, nor something she cared much about.

"I wish I was being relocated, but I'm not. They gave me papers seventeen days ago. I'm getting out in three weeks." This caught Sandra by surprise, but she didn't let it show. Of course the day would come where they would both be free again, but she had never really put too much thought into it until now.

"You're sad over that?"

The comment brought a little sting to her feelings, but she knew Sandra was just not the compassionate type. She probably wondered why she was sad when she was about to be a free woman, and in all aspects of the situation, she was right.

"What are your plans for the outside world?"

"Don't make light of this, Sandra. I'm not as strong as you, especially on my own."

"Yes, you are. Who are you going to live with?"

"I don't know. I just wish I could stay here with you until you are released."

"What about your parents? Didn't you say they were still alive?"

"Alive, yeah, if that's what you want to call it. I told you a lot of stories, but I never told you the one that ended with my mother being committed to an institution."

"An institution?"

She didn't really want to get into the subject. She was more concerned about being without Sandra, rather than her family history.

*

When her parents were married, they had Barbara, then her sister Carolyn. Her mom was more than satisfied with having just the two of them, but her father wanted a son. He promised her mother Lisa that if she would try one more time to give him a son, then he would not ask her about it anymore, and she would be able to go to school or do whatever she wanted to do with her life.

For three years they tried, and nothing happened. In the beginning of the fourth year, she got pregnant, and her father was very happy. Lisa was excited about the new baby as well because the constant pressure to give her husband what he desired was over.

The pregnancy was much harder on her than when she had her first two children, but she braved it out. Barbara would come home from school sometimes and find her passed out on the floor. She spent a lot of time in the hospital.

In her earlier months because was she so sick, she wanted to know the sex of the baby because if it wasn't a boy, she wanted to abort it, but her husband wanted to be surprised, so they didn't get the test done.

Seven months later, she had a premature baby boy. He was small, but he was healthy. Lisa on the other hand, suffered from a stroke and became paralyzed on the left side of her body during the delivery. She couldn't walk without a cane, and she had to wear diapers for the first eight months after Alex was born. For years Barbara's father took the blame that her mother laid on him. He did feel genuinely guilty for pushing her to have another baby.

Lisa started immediately closing herself off from the family. She would pop in a microwave dinner and go straight to her room with it. Her father was no longer able to share the bed with her; she had put him in the lounge before the baby turned one. He would offer to take her to the hair salon to cheer her up, but she never wanted to go. He bought her new dresses to wear, always careful that they didn't have too many buttons or a zipper she couldn't manipulate herself, but Lisa would never wear them.

It soon got to the point where she wouldn't step a foot outside the front door. She said she looked like a monster because one half of her face was drooping so badly. Lisa was so consumed with appearances and depression that she couldn't see what it was doing to the rest of them. They lost her when she withdrew inside of herself, but she unknowingly took their father with her. The one son he always wanted became Barbara and Carolyn's responsibility. He never had time for him or the girls.

He could be heard sneaking into their bedroom at night, begging to make love to his wife, but she wouldn't let him. She would scream like a lunatic, saying he was trying to kill her. He put himself through tormenting rejection for two years before he stopped trying.

Barbara couldn't wait to get out of the house; it was like a horror movie gone wrong. Everyone was saying how lucky my mother was to have such a devoted husband, pretending they couldn't see that he had aged thirty years over the last five.

*

"Just before I got myself locked up, my dad called me to say he had finally relented and put my mother in a psychiatric facility. I was wondering if he had gotten himself a bed as well because he needed it.

"My sister lives in Nebraska. She took Alex with her when she finished her associate's degree in accounting. I haven't seen either one of them for over five years, and I am not walking back into my father's loony world, so I have no idea where I am going when I leave here."

It took Sandra a good moment to take in the information. She knew she had not lived the ideal family life, but Barbara's life sounded almost as bad. Sandra began to see that they were alike in more ways than it had originally appeared.

Barbara had no one to go to when she was released, and Sandra didn't know how to go about getting things done once she was out. Without hesitation, she asked her, "Do you need money?"

This made her look at Sandra in the most perplexed way. No one had ever come to visit her, she never received any mail that she knew of, and she never went to the commissary to buy snacks. The thought that she would ask her if she needed money as if she had some to offer was baffling to her.

"Why are you looking at me like that?"

"I just never…"

"Well, I do. We'll talk about it some more as your time gets closer, but right now, we need to make sure that you get what you've got coming to you."

CHAPTER 38

S ix days later Sandra spoke to her for the first time in the cafeteria. "Hurry up with your breakfast!" Barbara looked down the other end of the table at Sandra, seeing the cool, remote trance on her face. She drew a blank on why she needed to rush, but when Sandra gave her an order, she didn't question it.

Scooping up the last of her cereal, she dumped her tray. Sandra was close on her heels, as they made their way toward the cells. Before speaking, she checked the area carefully. "When you go to your station tonight, bring back something small and heavy. It has to be solid, nothing lightweight."

"What do you mean small and heavy? Like what?"

"Use your imagination, Barbara. You can't be that fucking stupid."

She didn't want to upset Sandra in any way, but she remained dumbfounded as to what she wanted her to do or why.

It had been almost a week since they had their conversation about her getting out, and Sandra had not wanted to talk about it since. Now she demanded that she go to her station and come back with a small, heavy object. "Why do—"

"Look at yourself. Are you blind?"

With one quick motion she pulled Barbara's shirt over her head. "Take a good look at yourself. Hold out your arms." There was nothing to be seen but beautifully tight sculpted muscles from her shoulders to her fingertips. Her stomach was as solid as a human washboard could get. She had more definition in her abs because she was a smaller frame than Sandra.

Barbara seemed surprised at her form, but Sandra had been watching her from day one. "There's no need to look at your legs. You've been squatting over two hundred for the last month or so. You're as ready as you'll ever be." Fire was blazing in Sandra's eyes, and she seemed so focused.

"Ready...for what?"

Sandra blew out an impatient breath, and nearly wanted to slap some common sense into her. "Revenge Barbara. Revenge. That's what it's all about!"

She had totally forgotten about Beth, her crew, and the whole entire incident when she had received the papers about her release date. Her days were so close now that she didn't want to do anything to jeopardize that, but she also didn't want to say no to Sandra. She had been her protector for so long that it only seemed right that she would want to finally come down on the people who had caused her harm in the first place.

Sandra didn't want to go after Beth for any other reason than the way they had treated her, and it would be simply chicken-hearted if she didn't want a taste of it for herself.

"Okay, Sandra. I'll do my best."

"No, Barbara, not your best; you will complete the task."

They carried on with their day as normal, and the subject was never brought up again. As far as Sandra was concerned, she'd said what she had to say, and Barbara knew what she had to do. They didn't need words in order to understand each other; they just knew.

*

"Okay, ladies, count is over, let's get to it!" A single file line was formed, waiting on the guards whistle to blow, indicating they were to start moving, and when that happened, they went their separate ways in different areas of the prison, never glancing in each other's direction.

Barbara walked into her station, extremely jumpy and looking wired. She just knew she was being watched from every corner of the room. She intentionally dropped things to see if they would come rushing at her, but they didn't. This gave her a small relief allowing her to relax a little.

Her job in the repair room was at the sewing machine. She would sew uniforms that had been torn and sometimes hand-stitch the numbers across the front. She had been looking around for an hour or so, but she couldn't spot anything like Sandra had asked her to get, and she was getting worried. She didn't think that she would psychically harm her, but her silence alone was enough to make Barbara want to keep looking.

She could remember Sandra had found her talking with another inmate inside of their cell one day, and the fury that emanated from her was frightening. She didn't do anything to Barbara per se, but she knew never to bring someone to their cell again or get that much fire pointed at her from Sandra.

*

Time was gradually slipping away from her, and her palms began to sweat. She could think of nothing to take but the sewing machine itself, and even it was bolted down. She glanced around again, this time non-too shyly, but only came across needles, thread, material, and a few buttons here and there.

She wondered about her chances of getting anything at all and having to face Sandra when the needle slipped from her hand onto the floor. She got down on all fours to find it and hit the jackpot. One of the steel bars holding the table together was rusting in the corners, and she was sure she would be able to pry it loose with a few solid kicks. The table was already bolted to the wall, so she wasn't concerned about it falling, but she did wonder how she would keep it from making a loud noise when it hit the concrete floor.

Barbara got back in her seat and dropped two pair of pants beside her. She didn't stuff them under her table immediately, but after fifteen minutes of shifting, they were pressed in the back, under the table, by the leg she was about to dislodge. The material would smother the clink the bar would have made if it were to hit the naked ground.

"Come on, ladies. Hurry up. You have ten minutes to clean up your stations!"

Barbara was sweating as if she was working in a unventilated area. She was solely concentrating on the task at hand. When the metal finally landed on top of the pants, part two lingered over her head. Where in the hell was she going to put it?

"Time is up. Step away from your stations and face the wall."

With one quick motion, Barbara tucked the pipe under her pant leg, and into her sock.

"Stand against the wall. Come on, this is not new information here, people. After you are searched, go to hall B and line up." Her time for pat down was getting closer and closer, and she prayed harder and harder that she did not get caught.

"One zero three seven six three C"

Hesitantly, Barbara moved forward, turned towards the wall, palms flat.

Leslie, a well-known lesbian guard, pressed herself firmly against Barbara's back while her hands none too discretely grabbed her breast. "It looks like your girlfriend wants you to play the man. You're solid as a rock."

Leslie hands traveled leisurely down her thighs, continuing to explore lower and lower. Barbara began to panic. She had to do something, and fast.

"I hope you've satisfied yourself, Leslie, because the next time, Sandra will break your fingers one by one."

The story of Sandra was a well-known one. She had been a wildcard when she arrived at the prison. One guard had almost lost an ear when she tried to manipulate Sandra. She explained to the warden that she was still in between cells when the bars slammed on her. Never did she point the finger at Sandra because then she would have to explain what she was doing in an unauthorized area, so it went unreported officially, but the rumors told it all. You really didn't want to step on her toes or aggravate her unnecessarily.

Leslie didn't know if the lines of gossip were true about Barbara and Sandra being lovers, and she didn't want to find out, so she shoved her to the front of the line. "Cunt!"

As she walked to her cell, Barbara felt tense and excited all at the same time. She felt the weight of the bar against her shin, and she knew Sandra would be satisfied with what she had accomplished.

CHAPTER 39

*G*ently, Diane reached across the table to hold Charles's hand, but she was rejected. He continued to scoop eggs into his mouth as if he were sitting alone. He had yet to forgive her for the harsh words she'd spoken to him several days earlier, or forgive himself for the actions he had taken.

He stood up from the table and took his plate to the sink to rinse. "Charles…"

Drying his hands, he went to the room to retrieve his suit coat, operating as if he were in the house alone.

On a last desperate effort, Diane dashed to block the front door. "Charles, please. Please. I'm so sorry. You don't know how sorry I am. I never meant to say those things."

He blew out a frustrated breath, searching for patience. "Was it supposed to be a secret that you wanted to…let me see…warm someone else's bed?"

"You know me better than that. You know me! I just…"

"Just what, Diane?"

She had run out of words. All of the things she had planned on saying to him were gone. Her mother told her it was not right to push a man with so many things on his mind. She couldn't help the tears that rolled down her cheeks, even though she tried to stay strong. She looked up at him and knew he wasn't going to bend. He was fed up, and she was losing him fast. She still blamed the prison for absorbing the man she had fallen in love with, and she had to fight herself to overlook that.

She couldn't compete with the job he loved, especially when it seemed as if he didn't love her anymore. Diane had run out of options, so she stepped away from the door with her head bowed in defeat. Her body ached for him to touch her, to embrace her, but she said nothing.

Charles reached for the door but then hesitated. Instead, he put his index finger under her chin, asking, "Are you giving up so easily?"

Just the feel of his flesh gently on her skin brought on a new wave of tears. He still loved his wife, and the sight of her being in just as much pain as he was tore through him endlessly. With his thumb, he brushed back the fresh tears.

"What do you want from me, Diane? I'm being pulled by all sides here. You have to find a way to be patient with me. I love to be with you every second I can, but when I come home, it feels as if I need time to let the job dissolve off of me. I don't want to bring clients into this house, into our marriage. Let me relax a little, and I will be free to do whatever you want, but when you start getting on me as soon as I walk in, I just want to keep working to block you out, and I don't want that to be our life."

He could see the doubt in her eyes and knew she had every right to feel threatened, but regardless of the fact, he needed space.

"We can apologize to each other with a kiss"

Bending down, he planted a friendly peck on his wife's cheek."

"Not like a school girl, but like your wife whom you love unconditionally."

"Diane…"

With her breath bouncing softly across his face and her full lips grazing his, he felt a longing for his wife that he'd thought was all but gone. Hungrily, he pressed her against the door with the force of his mouth. This time he was not acting like an animal but a gentle lover who wanted nothing more than to satisfy his mate. He let his jacket drop to the floor and reached up and played with the freshly relaxed strands of her hair. Diane tilted her head back, allowing his massive hands to massage her scalp. She hadn't felt her husband this way in a long time, and once again it brought tears to her eyes.

Her neck held the gentle scent of the last fragrance he'd purchased for her, and he knew that he would not be able to stop moving forward. Neither one of them wanted to come up for air, but Diane broke the trance; out of breath, she asked, "Will you be late to work for this?"

She took a step back and revealed a jet black teddy that stopped deliciously at the top of her thighs.

He was at a loss for words. He had no idea he'd sat across the breakfast table from such a sight. Diane's shapely legs enticed him to no end, and she knew he would not leave her wanting.

She went to pull the pillows from the stuffed chair, and when she turned around Charles had already reached his full potential. There was no material covering her backside at all. The nightie was one–sided, and she wore a very thin black g-string that highlighted her assets.

Before she had the pillows on the floor, he had his phone in his hand, calling his office. There was no way he would just be late. He needed the entire day off for the work he had to do in the house.

By the time his call had been transferred to the right department and he had explained which clients could see the fill-in therapists and which should just be cancelled until he came back, Diane lay on the floor with her legs spread. She stroked herself while softly purring his name. She licked every finger she used, and this was making him crazy.

Charles dropped his phone to the floor and stripped the rest of his clothes off. He wanted nothing more than to please her, which he knew brought him the greatest of pleasures. Diane was very receptive of his seduction, so in turn she was his greatest lover. She knew him well, and that always pushed him to do more than the last time. He desired the element of surprise every time.

The feel of his body was another automatic turn-on for her. His body was extremely solid and sleek. She could feel his sculpted arms wrap around her legs, and it caused her to raise her hips to a face she knew was waiting, but he didn't give in; instead he started from the top and kissed every part of her. Her eyes, nose, and cheeks were the first places he went. He wanted to calm her down and soothe her at the same time, but Diane was in a different zone.

She pressed his buttocks, and arched her back in an attempt to have him submit to her, but he wouldn't. Charles continued to do things his way, and that drove her crazy. By the time he stopped holding out, she was all but exasperated. She had been touched, teased, explored, and bitten in all areas of her body.

Diane felt her nerve endings sending mixed signals across her body, making it jerk and shiver on its own accord. Every time she reached for her husband he would back up and restrain her.

Charles paced himself perfectly. He wanted his wife to remember why she had married him; he needed her to know that she was the only one for him. He expressed his desires with every touch and didn't stop until he knew she had caught on to the meaning.

They lay with their bodies intertwined as his suit coat sat crunched under Diane's thighs. She was sound asleep. He could hear her breathing softly as he nestled himself in the side of her neck. He was a little drained, but not tired.

He slipped from her side and went to get a blanket. She still had not stirred by the time he returned, so he covered her and headed for the shower.

He'd thought about starting a light lunch of pasta and salad before having a second go at it, but instead he went to his office, and pulled his clients files. There wasn't anything that needed his immediate attention, but he also knew his mind wouldn't totally let him throw in the towel for the day.

Charles went to the kitchen, made himself a BLT, and went back to his files. He took light notes on each client and then opened the file on Sandra. There was nothing different from the last notations he'd made, but there was a yellow Post-it flagged on the last page. Someone had left him a note in the back of her chart, and he had not seen it.

Charles peeled the Post-it and read it. It was from one of the senior psychologists in the prison, and apparently he had been following Sandra's case pretty closely as well. The note indicated that Sandra's roommate Barbara Whittler was due for release in the next few weeks or so.

It had been left as a simple reminder to be aware of changes in the patient. When inmates were housed together for extended periods of time and one was due to get released, it could cause a major relapse for the patient. Change was not something that they usually handled well. Charles recalled talking to Sandra about her cellmate briefly from time to time, but he could not remember her as being a significant part of Sandra's life.

However, if his memory served him right, Sandra had been inquiring about receiving her father's insurance money more often lately. She brought it up in a blasé fashion, but now that he let his mind dwell on it, it had been a constant subject over the last few sessions. He didn't want to jump the gun and assume anything about a patient, but he did have to ask the silent questions.

Charles checked his daily schedule again and realized that Sandra was one of the patients he was due to see today. One part of him said to let it go until her next session, but another aspect was telling him to act now or it may be too late. He had no idea why he thought it was so very urgent to get answers from her, but he couldn't let the feeling die.

Major things had gone wrong for him on many levels with two other patients, and it had set him back professionally for a long time. He had no idea if it was due to him overlooking something or just not being good at the one thing he'd always wanted to do, but whichever the case, he couldn't sit on his hands, and not do anything.

Dr. Wesley dressed in a walking suit, grabbed his case, and headed for the door. It wasn't until he entered the living room that the sight of Diane's frame cradled on the floor slammed him into his other reality. Damn! He had forgotten that quickly about the make-up sex he'd just had with his wife.

She looked so beautiful lying there on the floor wrapped in the comforter from their room. Her hair had fallen across her face and tangled innocently with her eyelashes. He didn't want to mess this up. They were finally going to be able to talk and work things out now that the sexual frustrations they shared were out of the way.

He imagined himself showering with her when she woke, and the mental picture made him want to tap her on the shoulder. He turned to face his reflection in the mirrored wall, and what he saw bewildered him. He looked like a man who had no idea what the hell he was doing. Charles turned away and glanced again but saw the same thing.

He didn't want to hurt Diane, but at the same time, he didn't want to let Sandra down either. He needed to know if she knew about Barbara's release date and if she did, how she felt about it. This was to be a crucial time in her treatment. This was a good test to determine if she would be able to handle outside situations and dramatic changes in life.

They talked about it extensively, but it was far different if you were living it. Sandra had always told him that she was attached to no one, and on the surface that seemed true, but even if they were not social in any aspect of the word, she still could very well suffer from separation anxiety.

Sandra's appointment was for eleven this morning, and if he hurried out now, he could make the forty-five minute drive in enough time to see the patient right before Sandra and then her. He would have to call his office, explain the situation, and let them know that he would be coming in after all.

He turned silently on his heels and headed for the back door. He didn't want to cross to the front door because if Diane woke up, everything they had just accomplished would be thrown out with the trash, and they would be arguing in no time. He knew this even as he put his car in neutral and let it coast down the driveway.

If he had to do all this, he briefly wondered, was it really worth it? Couldn't he have found another way? Why didn't he just call the coworker who was going to be filling in for him, give him the heads up to either keep the conversation light and airy or cancel her appointment altogether? There were more options he could have chosen from, but there was only one he took.

Sneaking out of the house and off the block seemed deceitful to him in one way but necessary in another. He tried to rationalize his motive for doing the things he was doing, and he was able to sum it up as he was getting the best result possible for both situations.

He would drive to the prison, see two clients, and rush home. On the drive back, he would order pizza for delivery and arrive approximately at the same time. He didn't expect Diane to stay asleep the entire time. He knew she would wake up looking for him.

She would be furious if she knew he went to work anyway, but he had to wonder if she would still be upset if he had only been gone for a couple of hours. He didn't think she could be too angry after all of the attention he had given her this morning, but then again, thirty-three days of no intimacy couldn't be compensated for in forty minutes.

Dr. Wesley decided to take the chance on everything being okay when he returned home. His subconscious continued to shout that he was making the wrong choice, and once again he pressed it far into the recess of his mind. He was going to deal with a couple of clients, nothing more.

He would be back home in time to relax with his wife and hopefully have another round of excellent make-up sex.

He continued his drive on the freeway, and his thoughts flooded to the surface again, but Charles was not going to be persuaded. He had made up his mind, and he was going to act upon that. He was halfway to the penitentiary and knew he would not be turning back, so when the negativity entered his mind again, he tuned it out with his favorite radio station.

CHAPTER 40

"So I have a note here stating that your roommate is due to be released. How do you feel about that?" Sandra sat cross-legged in the chair with a light smile touching her lips, her eyes were harshly frozen.

Dr. Wesley held the look of a sexually pleased man. He had been very stiff and straight to the point in their last few meetings, but today he had on a light and airy suit, carrying a relaxed demeanor. He was leaned back into his chair, and he, too, had his legs crossed.

This knowledge triggered something in Sandra, and to her, the atmosphere in the room changed. Within seconds she was transported back to her childhood. She could see the face of the men as they caressed her after raping her. No matter how long ago it was or ever would be, she knew she would not forget the look of their eyes: the heavy lids, the dilated pupils...those were all signs that they had used her and were satisfied with what they'd received.

The forever-near buzzing sound was trying to break through and take control of the situation, but she couldn't let it. If Dr. Wesley knew for one minute that she would like nothing more than to leap across his desk and castrate him, she would never be allowed to see the light of day.

She had to think positive, just as he had been teaching her all of this time. She couldn't live in the past. She had to strive for a better tomorrow. Dr. Charles was married, and despite her past, having sex is quite normal in a marriage. She remembered the things he taught her when she began to become frustrated, and it helped. The little sayings were childish in some sense, but she had been silently chanting them for several months, and she found that she was soothed by them.

She would find herself getting frustrated over the minutest of things, and she would mumble the phrases until she would start to feel a little better, which is exactly what she did at that precise moment.

Dr. Wesley felt she was taking the time to weigh out her response to his questions, and he took that as a good sign that his program was working for her. She didn't rush to judgment, and that would be a helpful tool for her when she was released.

He didn't base her recovery on his forms of meditation alone; he knew there were many other elements in society that could outweigh that. His regimen for Sandra would be meditation coupled with medication. If he could get her to stay on both tracks, he knew he was looking at a viable success story.

"Well, I say kudos for Barbara, don't you?"

"That's kind of a shallow answer, Sandra. I would have expected more from you at this stage."

She gave him a puzzled look before answering, "And what stage is that, Charles?" She had resulted back to sarcastic answers, and he now knew enough about her to determine that when this occurred, she was covering something instead of revealing it to him. A brief hint of irritation crossed his face, and Sandra quickly changed subjects.

"I've been meaning to ask you something about the life insurance my father left me. I know I will be able to get the money from the attorney when I get out, but is there any way I could get some of it released to me now, or tap into my trust fund?"

"Why would you want to do that?"

He was trying to trip her up, and she felt it instantly. He began the session by asking questions about Barbara, and now he wanted to know why she wanted to get some of her funds released to her. If she thought about it, she guessed anybody would be able to see that something was going on. She hadn't purchased anything for herself since she had been incarcerated, and now she wanted a lump sum released to her just before her cellmate was due to leave.

She hadn't thought this far in advance and was now upset with herself for not seeing the end of the road before getting there. She turned things around as best as she could and prayed she looked convincing. "The attorneys have been writing me, and they want the case to be over with, I assume, so I wrote back and told them I would find out if large sums of money could be put on a person's property list or if there is a limit to the amount of money a prisoner can have. I didn't really want to ask anyone else, so I waited for my session with you. I figured you would be the most honest and have nothing to gain from knowing I was going to be receiving money."

Her explanation was logical, but was it legitimate? "So what are you planning on doing with the money? Do you know the total amount you will be receiving?"

"They told me a little over $415,000 because of the interest." Dr. Wesley was surprised to hear the ending balance. Not to say that it compensated in any way for her father not participating in her life, but he had done more than many others who had left their kids behind.

"I don't think they will put money like that on your commissary books, but what you could do is ask them to mail you the paperwork, and you can sign the release forms. Where you will be releasing the money to, I would have to look into that." Sandra looked at the clock on the wall as she stood. Her time was up, and she was exhilarated.

Figuring out how to get some money to Barbara was the biggest dilemma she was facing at the time, and her doctor had come through with a solution. He was going to figure out her financial plans for her. She knew he would do what he promised; it helped knowing their conversations were confidential between client and therapist and she wouldn't have to share what she had planned with anyone else.

If he wasn't supposed to extend himself to the point that he had, then she knew for a fact that he wouldn't go shouting off the rooftops that he was looking into a banking situation for her. He would find a solution, so that was one less thing for her to organize.

Her mind had been going crazy since the day Barbara said she was leaving. She didn't really care about it in the beginning, but that night as she sat on her bunk, she realized that she didn't know all there was about being out in the world and living on your own.

She'd heard stories from the women talking out on the yard, but she had never lived it herself. She didn't know the first thing about getting "the right landlord." Some of the women said you knew the nosy ones right off the bat, and if you planned on doing things against the law, the last thing you would want was the landlord coming by anytime they felt like it. She heard that neighbors were the reason some of the women were there, and so on and so on.

She didn't know if the landlord she had as a kid was the "right one" or not; she couldn't be sure. There was talk constantly about watching your back and never letting the right hand know what the left hand was doing. The majority of the inmates were wise to the outside life, and Sandra hated to admit that she was not. She knew about men, their desires, and her hatred of them, but her mind went no further than that.

She didn't want to acknowledge that she needed someone, but it was true. When she was younger she'd thought paying for the laundry to be picked up and going to the corner store were big things, but she didn't know the half of it.

She had never given being free much thought. She lived her life day by day. She had grown used to the routine in the prison, and she was almost fearful of what the free world would offer her. There would be no more guards telling her every move. She would have to decide that on her own. From getting up in the mornings to what time she bathed, these would be decisions of her own accord.

How would she blend in? Barbara knew these things, and they didn't frighten her. She had knowledge about getting a job and doing normal things like everyone else, and Sandra knew without hesitation that she could use her to help do the same.

The last thing she wanted to do was become joined at the hip with anyone. She battled with that notion for several days before giving in. Barbara was her way back into society, and she had no choice but to use her for that purpose.

CHAPTER 41

*B*arbara was smiling like the cat that ate the canary during lunch. Sandra knew she had accomplished what she'd sent her out to do. There was no need to tell her to follow her out of the cafeteria; she had been doing that ever since Sandra assigned herself as Barbara's protector. When they made it back to their cell, Sandra said, "Okay, you can stop grinning like Chester the Cheetah and almost blowing your cover. What do you have for me?"

Barbara was almost giddy with the satisfaction of getting away with the merchandise. Pleasing Sandra had become an important part of her life, so to actually accomplish something she had sent her out to do gave her a thrilling sensation from head to toe. She walked over to her bunk and none too discreetly pulled the bar from under her mat.

Sandra shifted it in her hands and was slightly disappointed by its weight but knew it was sufficient.

"Pretty good for my first time, huh?"

"Your first time? I know you're not standing in prison telling me that stealing this pole is your first crime."

Barbara's pride was crushed. She'd thought she would receive praise of some sort, but instead, what she had done was tossed aside like an everyday occurrence. "That was totally different, Sandra. I thought you—"

"You thought what? That I would clap my hands and jump up and down? Grow up Barbara."

She went quietly over to her bunk and sat down. She looked like a sulking child. Sandra knew she had hurt her feelings, but she refused to dwell on that. Barbara was more than a little weak, and she needed to toughen up for what she had in mind.

"Look, there is no time for this; we are very close to being ready." The purpose of stealing the pipe was finally going to be revealed to her, but she wasn't sure if she was prepared to hear it. She felt Sandra was turning on her, and she wanted no part of anything she wanted to do, but at the same time she knew she would jump at the opportunity if she asked her to do something else.

For the next three days, they followed routine as usual for the most part, but Sandra had skipped being in the yard, but told her to continue to work-out. What she had been doing all that time was held tightly to her chest, but Barbara figured it was all about the "big plan" so she didn't think too much about it. She kept the majority of the details to herself putting Barbara on a need-to-know basis. "Lights out, ladies!"

Following the guard's words came the loud bang as the bars were being shut, securing the prisoners in their cells.

Barbara knew today was supposed to be the day, but as she heard the lock mechanisms click into place, she wondered if the plan was really fool-proof.

Sandra lay on her bunk and counted off the minutes in her head, when she reached fifty minutes, she jumped down silently to the floor. "Sandra, the bars are locked. Maybe…"

"Shut up. Put your shoes on."

Sandra paid no attention to her cellmate. She continued to prepare herself for the evening. They would only have one hour to do what she had orchestrated, but she would have to make do with that. Scheduling was a top priority.

"What's in the pillowcases?"

"Be quiet and stand next to me."

It ran through her mind that Sandra was planning a prison break, and it made Barbara that much more jittery. She was due to get out next week; there was no need for this. Sandra's release date was not far behind hers, maybe a year or so, so why risk it? It didn't make sense. Her mind teased her with the notion; her eyes caught the beam of a flashlight coming down the corridor, making her back away. "Someone's coming Sandra, lay down."

Her warning fell on deaf ears. Sandra remained at the bars until the beam landed dead on her. "Be quick. I can only give your forty-five minutes before we start routine checks." Barbara couldn't believe she was looking into the face of the guard who escorted Sandra to her therapy sessions. She had always believed that she was the only person Sandra spoke with, but she could see now that she had mistaken.

She wanted some form of explanation of how it all came to be. Not only was she apparently speaking to the guard, they seemed a little friendlier than necessary. Barbara was about to voice her opinion, but her mouth froze wide open. Sandra was allowing herself to be kissed on the mouth. She had even gone so far as to massage her breast in the midst of it.

She wanted to object and scream to the top of her lungs, but a direct order came first. "Let's go. Stay close to me."

The trio moved stealthily down the dimly lit tiers. The guard took up the front position, apparently knowing more than Barbara about their destination. She had been concerned about getting caught trying to escape and them tacking on five years to her seven days, but without a doubt their escort would be facing more than that if they were to be seen. To know that she was risking her career as well as her freedom for Sandra infuriated Barbara.

They stopped at the end of a hall, and she turned to them, keeping the light facing the floor. "Now here is the key. It's number 432. Go straight down the hall. We've already discussed how you would return the key to me. Good luck."

Before she turned to go, she pulled Sandra by the arm. They shared another kiss that scorched Barbara's patience. She felt surely she had more rights to touch Sandra than some damn prison guard. She none too gently pulled them apart. "Keep your priorities in order, Sandra!"

She had never spoken harsh words to her before, but she was beyond herself at that moment. Sandra had told her to never touch her again. She believed now it was because she was involved with the guard. "I have my priorities straight, Barbara." She turned and gave their guide and open-mouth kiss.

Barbara felt the sting of tears threaten to build, so she walked off. "To hell with the both of you. Have your girl-friend help you with your mission. I'm going back!"

She was about five paces away before Sandra's voice stopped her in her tracks. "Don't turn coward now. This is your battle, remember? Kim was just showing us the way."

Barbara could not be consoled at this time. Her jealousy had trumped anything Sandra said. "So you mean to tell me that the destination is down your throat?"

Kim spoke up and asked, "Sandra, how did you end up with such a childish companion?"

"Childish?"

In two steps Barbara was at her throat with a powerful forearm. Swiftly, she stuck her leg out and sent the woman tumbling to the floor, making the flashlight fall from her hands. The sound seemed to vibrate through the halls, causing Sandra to speak up. "Get up, Barbara!" But she did not listen. She continued to bang Kim's head on the floor.

"Now! Don't make me say it a third time!"

Reluctantly, she released her. "Let's get something straight right now. Neither of you own me now, nor will you own me later! Let's go. We've wasted enough energy here. Kim, keep the time."

Sandra wanted to retaliate for Barbara just as much as herself. Being with a woman was just a small price to pay to get what she needed done. Kim had been whispering love carols in her ear longer than she cared to remember. Sandra knew she liked her in much of the way Barbara did, but she never spoke about it.

As she was escorted, Kim would state that she would do anything to see her naked and so on, but it fell on deaf ears until Barbara's release date became a subject. She knew she would have to take Kim up on her offer in order to kick her plan in action.

She found it rather odd that for three days Kim just wanted to kiss and oil her body. Sandra didn't know if she would allow much more than that and she was glad she didn't have to find out.

They proceeded down the corridor and stopped next to a darkened cell. "I'll tell you what to do when the time comes. Just follow suit."

Barbara now began to feel tiny prickles running up and down her arms. She knew she had plenty of chance to run, but then what? Her need for acceptance from Sandra was stronger than the desire to flee.

Barbara didn't want to jeopardize her freedom that was sure to come in a matter of days, but what was she to do? For Sandra to know that she had her back in all situations was of ultimate importance to her. This was the time to prove her loyalty, not cower like a mutt. She had to stand up for the one person who stood up for her. She would not bail. She would not hide; she was ready for whatever Sandra had in mind.

She was not a spur-of-the-moment kind of person, so surely some form of escape had been planned out. Sandra would see them to the end no matter what, and Barbara wholeheartedly trusted that.

Sandra entered the key into the lock and put her finger to her mouth, indicating that Barbara should be quiet. Now was not the time for questions. On tip-toes, they went to the bunks where two bodies rested.

Sandra mutely placed the pillowcase on the floor before digging out three feet of rope. Calculating very carefully, she slid it under the indention the sleeping woman's ankles made on the mattress. Beth didn't jerk up until she felt the burning of the rope being tied to her flesh. She attempted to scream, but in one quick motion a piece of duct tape smothered out her sounds.

The smile on Sandra's face was nowhere near pleasant, and that terrified Beth. Her roommate started to wake up, and Sandra kicked into action. The maneuver she used when she entered wouldn't work for her again, because the other lady was sitting up. She hissed in her ear. "Do you want this the hard way or…?"

The hostage filled her lungs with air, preparing her vocals, when she was punched squarely in the esophagus. Before she could even gag, she was bounded and tied like Beth.

Sandra left her on the top and jumped down, instructing Barbara in the process. "Pull that manly bitch to the floor on her hands and knees. I think that's her favorite position, isn't it?"

There was no reply, and Barbara did as she was told. When she looked over at Sandra for approval, the iciness of her features frightened her again. She was locked into another mode, one that she had never seen. There was coldness about her, and she now knew why she was one of the most feared women in the prison. There was no way you could look into her face and not feel terrified.

She didn't experience anger inside of her the way that Sandra did, but she knew she should have. She was the one who had suffered at the hands of the very bitch she was standing over, yet Sandra was the one pushing for revenge.

The mere fact that she was in Beth's cell, prepared to cause her an insurmountable degree of pain, made it simple to forget the transgressions Sandra shared earlier with the guard. She felt something for Sandra at that moment that she had never felt for another human being. Barbara was truly in awe.

Everything seemed to have flashed right before her eyes, and she felt ashamed and determined at the same time. Sandra had asked her a while ago if she needed money and then she told her to bring a weapon back to the room. Barbara had never given it much thought until now. Sandra had been planning this from day one. Ever since the day she had given her something for pain, she'd waited for the day to make Beth pay for what she had done, and she wanted her to be at her side when she did.

Sandra looked across at her and whispered, "Give me the pillowcase." Again, she did as instructed, and she watched her lay everything she had collected out on the floor. "Beth belongs to you, and I will take this injured specimen here. You need to think back to the things they did to you, and remember every last detail. It's lesson time for these two."

Barbara could recall it very well; she didn't need much persuading. She could see the day as clear as if it was showing in a movie right before her. The two weeks it had taken for the burning to stop every time she urinated and the permanent scar under her eye that would laugh at the attempt at cocoa butter were her reminders.

Yes, she could visualize it all too well, and as she did, it took her intensity up to another level.

At the moment, she didn't see herself as a demonic animal or anything close to that, but that is how they'd acted when they had her in their grasp, and nothing less.

She glanced across at the things that Sandra had brought, and once again found herself hesitating. She was conflicted and stuck at the same time. "We have seventeen minutes! Has the pain escaped your memory, or did you enjoy the tearing of your rectum? Are you sure you're healed on the inside? Do you even know? Or are you not ashamed to show your mutilated body to the next man you encounter?"

Sandra knew she was being harsh, but she had to kick her into motion so she could use the remaining time to their advantage. They deserved everything they had coming to them, and she would not be sorry for it. They had destroyed Barbara mentally, and in many ways she knew what that was like. She had never dwelled on what she did to her mother or Bill after her first few years of incarceration, but when the smoke began to clear, with the visions of her life dancing before her eyes, she knew what she had done could be called nothing less than justice.

She didn't have to wait on the courts, nor did she have to be entered into the Department of Children and Family Services, which she knew only came to help after the damage had been done. She had taken matters in her own hands, and she'd ended what had been an extremely grueling life by anyone's standards.

Barbara had to be able to function when she was out on the streets again. Sandra's livelihood in many ways depended on it. She couldn't afford to have her traumatized and sitting somewhere balled up in a corner, wondering why she had been a victim.

She knew she still gave energy to the trauma she had gone through, and that is why she had set this evening up for them. She didn't want the last thing she remembered to be some man or woman ramming something in her private area, but instead how she made someone suffer at her own hands for what they did to her.

It eased her mind at night just knowing that her mother no longer breathed the same air she did. She didn't have nightmares like Barbara. She could hear her crying in her sleep several days a week. She needed to get over it; this was actually something she was doing for the both of them. Barbara needed to be stronger, and Sandra's immediate future depended on it.

"What do you want me to do first?"

Sandra paused briefly and stated, "What is the first thing she do to you?" Barbara allowed her mind to focus, clearly and unobstructed, on the night in question, and there she saw Beth's face appear above her as two men held her down.

She picked up the makeshift switchblade made from shaving razors and tape, Sandra had brought and started cutting off Beth's pants. She bucked and squirmed under her touch pretty much the exact same way Barbara had, so she matched what had been done to her and kicked her squarely in the face.

This didn't stop Beth from moving; she continued to try rolling over and getting some form of leverage. When she reached the ankle of the pant leg with the blade, she noticed seconds too late that Beth's restraints had come loose from around her legs.

Beth sailed a brutal heel right into her breast, which sent her flailing. Sandra pounced on her within seconds and had her secured before Barbara had a chance to cough for air, but when she did, she was livid.

She jumped to her feet and slammed Beth's head into the cement floor. Barbara was furious at this point. She had been on the receiving end of Beth's brutality, and now she was still trying to do her in, whether she thought she had a chance of winning or not.

Sandra leaned back into the bars, and watched them. Barbara was so enraged at this point that spittle could be seen flying from her mouth even though the only light source was the dull beam from their flashlight.

Beth tried her kicking tactics again when Barbara reached for the rope, but she was more than prepared for her this time. Barbara sat on her back and tangled her legs with her own in an attempt to tame them. When Beth was securely fastened, she once again looked over the items that Sandra had brought, and her eyes fastened on the knife that appeared to have been stolen from the kitchen. She went over to retrieve it. "Look here, Beth. A knife! Almost identical to the one you used on me, you sick bitch!"

Barbara returned to sit on her back, and Beth was all but insane with terror. She knew exactly what was coming next but could do nothing about it. Barbara was in control now; she could only hope that she would show a little mercy.

Sandra watched in fascination as Barbara cut away the little muscle controlling the opening and closing of the rectum. Beth's face was so red she appeared to have stopped breathing, but her punishment continued. "Why are we taking the time to cut little pieces of skin? We have eleven minutes left."

Barbara was in her own little world of horrors. She didn't hear Sandra as she spoke to her and could only see the night she spent with Beth as a reminder of all the things to do.

There were men with them when her rectum was penetrated; they were the villains that happily performed that act, but since it was only her and Sandra, she would have to improvise with Beth. She chose the pole that she had gotten from her work site and securely wrapped another piece of tape around Beth's mouth and the pole. She looked across and saw that Sandra was watching and waiting. This gave her all the encouragement she needed to go on.

As Beth lay on her stomach, Barbara got down on her knees between her legs and, with a firm grip, plunged the pipe halfway inside. She knew Beth had to be in excruciating pain, and she loved it. She rammed it a few times and then passed it on to Sandra. It was worse for Beth's roommate Amy. Sandra didn't care about the little tissue that closed the rectum; she used her own brutal force to get the same results, and this caused Amy to pass out.

Sandra mirrored Barbara's every move, only adding slight adjustments to the regimen. She enjoyed watching Barbara act outside of herself. She had never seen her so violent. She knew she had accomplished what she had set out to do, and that was to leave a lasting memory in her mind other than the night they sodomized her.

Barbara would remember this night; sometimes it would make her shudder in disbelief, and sometimes she would smile in appreciation. The inability to wrap her mind around what she had done to another individual would play with her in her dreams, but she knew she would only vaguely see the night that had started all of this.

"We have four minutes, Barbara. It's time to wrap this up."

Sandra had been so lost in her own scene of fog that Barbara's movements were momentarily lost upon her. She wouldn't have believed it if someone had written it on paper, but Barbara was smearing blood from Beth's ass across her face.

She watched for sixty more seconds and then crossed the room, straddled Beth from behind, put the pole under her neck, and pulled for leverage. Her head flipped back so quickly it came as a surprise. Sandra sat on her back using the forearms she had worked on for years and effortlessly broke Beth's neck.

Barbara bolted up from the mattress, looking both wild-eyed and sedated at the same time.

"Why did you do that? Why…"

"I'm sorry. I wasn't aware that she had become your girlfriend."

Barbara was totally out of her element at this time. She knew now that she was at the point of no return. Sandra had killed Beth in the most horrendous way, and she was now a witness to it. She watched as Sandra yanked Beth by the hair and slung her to the floor in the most dismissive fashion.

Barbara could feel the trembling in her feet seconds before her entire body felt as though it was pulling away from her insides. She began looking for her way out of the cell. It was Sandra's voice that brought her to a slamming halt. "Where in the fuck do you think you're going? Are you going to leave this bitch alive?"

It was only at that moment that Barbara realized Amy was still very much alive writhing on the floor.

"You leave no one behind to tell their story. Your story is the only one that matters. Kill her. We have forty-five seconds." Barbara didn't know what to do. Her mind was racing. She looked back at Amy and realized what Sandra said was true. She was less than a week away from being released, and there was only one person in this room who could take away that possibility.

Sandra didn't speak another word as she held the knife out towards Barbara. "Do it! Thirty-one seconds."

Puzzlement filled her as she wondered if she was operating on her own accord or if her body was merely an extension of Sandra's hand, but she swiftly crossed the room, exposed Amy's throat, and sliced her from ear to ear.

The arterial blood sprayed her hands, her feet, and the bottom portion of her pants, but it went unnoticed. Sandra removed the knife from her hand, packed up their tools, wiped everything down, and led her out of the cell.

The guard met them at the end of the hallway, and Sandra handed her the pillowcase. She removed Barbara's clothes, all except her panties, and put them inside the sack as well. At that moment, Kim wanted to back out of the agreement.

The look on Barbara's face alone was saying fifteen to twenty years. She was not talking, and it seemed as if she was unable to focus either. "What's wrong with her? She looks as if she was in a fucking massacre!"

"Don't worry about her. Just do what you're supposed to do! I don't want to hear my name in the morning."

When they made their way back to the cell, Sandra was more than prepared. She removed dampened cloths from under her mattress and quickly wiped off her face and hands. Barbara still had not come around to speaking or making any movements, and Sandra wanted to do nothing more than to break her neck as well.

For Barbara to now show weakness infuriated Sandra. She grabbed her by the hair and hissed in her ear "Clean yourself up, or you will not be getting out of here until you're damn near fifty!"

It was only then that Barbara began to move, but in a stiff way. Sandra pulled out the fresh uniforms she had for them and dressed herself and Barbara. Barbara still said nothing as she climbed into her bunk and pulled the covers over her head.

CHAPTER 42

The alarm bell rang at six o'clock in the morning. All the cells were opened, and everyone was ordered to line up on the tier. There were eight guards and a swarm of police officers and agents walking the units. It had taken less than thirty minutes after wake-up call for the news to circulate about Beth and Amy being found.

The lead detective was screaming into a megaphone to get everyone's attention.

"If for some reason you ladies believe that we will not find out who is responsible for these horrendous crimes, you are wrong. The person or persons responsible will be held accountable for their actions. A full investigation is underway, and we will not stop until these merciless killers are found. Anyone with any information leading to their arrest will be held in good favor with the parole board. I will see to it..."

His speech was never-ending. They would be in lock-down for the rest of the day, and there would be no yard activity for fifteen days. The warden started to speak daily about punishment and consequences until it seemed as if they were listening to nothing more than the radio.

She tried to look forceful and confident in the eyes of the media and the families of the victims, but everyone on the inside of the prison knew that Warden Halt was just putting on a show.

She repeated the words "full investigation" every time they were in the cafeteria, but no one saw any other staff being hired, and the police were only granted limited access to certain files and inmates.

Some of them wondered if she really wanted the homicide solved. This was not the first murder she'd had to deal with since her seven years in Winsor, but it was by far the most gruesome. Three days after the bodies were sent to the morgue, the warden found out that the white flakey substance on the cheek and lips of one of the women was vaginal fluid. They did a quick inmate DNA scan only to find out one of her officers were the owner of the residue. Pandora's Box had just been opened.

Beth and the women she hung with made many several enemies over her thirteen years' incarceration. She had no idea if this was the work of an inmate or one of her own staff members. A full internal search proved the employee had a tight alibi seeming as though the crime occurred after her shift, but because of her termination due to an obvious sexual relationship with a prisoner and explosive media coverage, wishing that Beth cleaned up after sexual escapades was an understatement.

At least eight members of her staff had been terminated last year alone for being romantically involved with inmates. Fights had broken out several times between staff members over a prisoner. It was more than common if she cared to admit.

Where she would go from here was definitely a dilemma. She couldn't seek too much outside assistance from her peers because they had been dead set against her from the day she was elected. She had gone through the proper channels and had the right educational background in addition to a ten-year history in the police force herself, but when it came down to men versus women for high stake positions, she became instantly unfavorable to her male colleagues.

Halt's first two years in the system had been spent deflecting intentional sabotage. What anyone could imagine to do to her, it was done, from stealing files to setting tier fires. Some nights she went home to an empty house with her tail between her legs, ready to give any willing participant her job. On other nights, she would go home so angry, that drinking three to four shots of tequila and shooting multiple rounds into an empty drum out by her barn, was normal activity.

*

"They're going to find out, Sandra." Barbara zipped and paced around the cell with nervous energy. She popped up and down off the bed like a jumping bean, constantly ringing her hands and pulling her hair in the process. Sandra had had enough. Ever since the warden had demanded a lockdown, Barbara had been going stir crazy in the confines of her cell.

"Sit the fuck down." Sandra made this statement in a nonchalant way, but the meaning was understood.

"I'm sorry. I guess I'm getting on your nerves, huh?" Barbara flopped down on the mattress, defeated. "Do you think they will question us personally? Your friend won't snitch us out, will she?"

"Get over here and exercise. You are getting on my nerves." Sandra continued to count as she did full military sit-ups on the floor. Once in the zone, she didn't like to be interrupted, and Barbara knew that.

She was becoming more of a nuisance than a help. She needed some kind of space put between them. She was still in sit-up mode when a guard approached the room.

"Get off the floor, GI Jane. It's time for your counseling session."

Sandra allowed herself to be escorted through the corridor of the prison. As she did, she noticed the others were doing one of three things: lying across their bunks, playing cards or some other game, or just watching as other people walked by. In Sandra's eyes it was all delightfully depressing. She figured lockdown couldn't last that long; it had to end sooner or later.

CHAPTER 43

"You seem a little agitated this afternoon. You want to talk about it?" Sandra continued to rock silently, and bite her nails. She wouldn't look Dr. Wesley directly in his eyes, but watched him nonetheless as he wrote notes. "Well this is not going to be a productive day, I see. You obviously have something on your mind but are not yet willing to talk about it, so I will have them return you to your cell. I have ten additional patients to see because of this whole lockdown episode."

Dr. Wesley leaned over to press the buzzer, and then she spoke.

"It's my roommate."

He seemed a little surprised by her outburst but even more so by what she said. Sandra seemed to always have a cool head and definitely was a loner, so to hear her now speak directly of her roommate was surprising.

She never let anyone get inside of her deepest thoughts, and to see her act this way about a roommate not only intrigued the doctor but also made him anxious to know just what was going on. "I'm listening."

Sandra knew she had to be quick on her feet. Dr. Wesley was no dummy. He had seen his fair share of nut cases and could decipher acting and authentic behavior with ease.

"I keep having dreams about her."

He was taken aback by the comment but did well to conceal it. It was pretty common in institutions that the same sex would eventually become attracted to each other, being in close proximity to one another on a daily basis, but what had him baffled was that it had taken Sandra almost six years to open up about her attraction.

"It's quite natural to have dreams of intimacy about a person you are so close with. You—"

"I cant stand being locked up with her day in and day out is taking its toll on me."

Dr. Wesley was on instant alert. He had seen an incident like this one occur not too long ago, but the men were disgruntled lovers, and when their prison was closed for a lockdown they went at each other's throats. Something had to be done about Sandra's situation, and he wasn't waiting until tomorrow.

"Is Barbara okay? Do I need to send a guard to your room?"

Bingo! Sandra had him on the hook, but she had to make sure she was able to keep him there. She broke out of her trance-like state to say, "Just forget I said anything. I will use those techniques you taught me, and I'm sure I will be okay."

He wasn't having it. Sandra had a violent history that she had been able to keep at bay, but who knew what it took to bring it back to the surface? Barbara buzzing around her cell agitation Sandra in such small confines with no where to escape, couldn't be good.

"Do you want me to talk to the warden? I'm sure I can get one of you guys an hour or two outside until this dies down."

Sandra began flexing her wrist and fingers simultaneously, causing her knuckles to crack.

"If I begin my meditation when I return to my cell, do you think it will be enough?"

Sandra began running her fingers through her hair again and again until her scalp sizzled from the feel of her nails. She knew she had earned his attention, but was he fully on board for what she needed done? She had to make sure.

"Sandra, can you stop twitching long enough to explain what you are feeling right now?"

Instead of doing as she was asked, she added additional movement to her body by shaking her leg. "It's like an exciting energy I feel whenever I'm around her. I can't control it."

"Does she know you feel this way about her? Have you mentioned this to her?"

"No."

Every limb of her body remained busy until Dr. Wesley had no choice but to use the vial he had stored in his drawer. "I'm going to give you something to help calm you down, okay?" No response. Sandra was looking straight ahead, eyes glazed over.

He couldn't believe she had slipped so far back into herself. She'd been doing so well, and he rapidly convinced himself that if he was able to immediately remove the irritation from her cell, she could bounce back in no time. He had gotten so far ahead with her, only to see his work crumble right before him.

She didn't so much as blink when he inserted the medication into her arm, making him want to shed tears of disappointment. He had to report his findings and be sure something was done about it. This was not another one of the "brush under the rug" occasions; this needed an immediate solution.

Absently, he pressed the buzzer for them to come and get Sandra. They arrived ten minutes later, during which time her twitching had subsided substantially, but she still looked out of sorts. The door clicked shut after they exited, leaving Charles alone with the silence. He caught himself running his fingers across his head as he thought about Sandra and stopped instantly.

He knew he couldn't sit idly by and wait for the catastrophe; he had to act now and get something done. Snatching the phone from its cradle, he called Warden Halt's line. "We need to meet."

Barbara was released two days early after their conversation. The warden didn't want any more heat, and Dr. Wesley didn't want a major set-back. They came in agreement that Barbara had been a seemingly model prisoner, and her crime was not violent enough not to consider a forty-eight hour release, so it was done.

CHAPTER 44

S andra woke in her cell with a slight crick in her neck from lying in an awkward position for the majority of the day. Her cell was dim and quiet; at the moment, so was the tier. It wasn't quite time for supper, so she laid back down and relaxed on her bunk.

It had been eleven months since Barbara had been released, and she was doing just as she had been told. She had used someone else's name and address on all of their correspondence, and she sent a letter last week indicating that she had found a better apartment than her last choice, and was out buying furniture.

Sandra instructed Barbara to keep her posted on her progress but not to send too many letters as to draw attention to the fact that they were communicating with each other. She used Kim to get her letters through unopened because she couldn't trust that Barbara wouldn't make a mistake. Her time for release was nearing, and she had to make sure all her ducks were in a row.

She had Barbara open a bank account in her name, and she was the go-between for herself and the lawyers. She signed all the necessary release papers through the mail so that she could return them to the insurance company.

Sandra's last session with Dr. Wesley was coming up next week, and she was more than ready to get it over with.

If she admitted it to herself, she was having more than a mild case of anxiety about stepping out into a world that she had not seen in more than six years, but she knew the time was now or never. She needed Barbara as her anchor and guide through the toughest part of adjusting, but by her father leaving her money to live off of, she was told it would make her transition easier.

Sandra had never held a job, and she knew that was all included in fitting in with society; but being so consumed with her rage, hatred of men, adjusting to life behind bars, and dealing with a male therapist consumed her every thought. She had no mental capacity left with which to think of basic things.

Barbara sent her sort of a questionnaire in the mail, wanting to know what some of her favorite things were so that she could stock the house, and three weeks later Sandra still held onto that paper. She had no idea what her favorite shampoo was; her mother always used bar soap, and she couldn't remember the one her father used to buy her from childhood. She asked her what size clothes she wore, and even that was a guess at best. She had visibly gained weight from working out, and their uniforms were in small-medium-large formatting, so that's what she wrote on the paper: medium.

She didn't have a favorite color. Sandra no longer liked the bright pink, blues, or yellow that she wore as a kid. In her mind those were the colors that attracted predators, and that's the last thing she wanted to be faced with when she was released. So she wrote the colors that she saw every day: grey and black.

Sometimes she would get frustrated with the paper and toss it to the side, but now that her release date was less than two weeks away, she was compelled to fill in the blanks so that Barbara could have something to go on in helping her look more normal.

She didn't know if the things she was being asked were necessary or if Barbara was just being curious, but whatever the case, Sandra did her best because she didn't want to mess up. She had no plans on returning to prison, even though it really hadn't been so bad.

Some of the ladies complained about missing their favorite food or the touch of a man, and Sandra could not relate to any of that, so she never longed for it. The one thing she did remember, but didn't long for exactly, was Rocky Road ice cream. She remembered that she was supposed to have enjoyed some with her counselor before all hell had broken loose. That is the one thing she told Barbara to get for her, and plenty of it. She had never tasted it, but she knew anything from Mrs. Washington could be nothing but good.

She thought about her counselor often after the first two years of incarceration and now even more than ever with her release looming overhead. She wondered if she still worked at the school or if dealing with her had driven her to quit. She couldn't say she blamed her if she did. It must have been like a scene from hell to see the two dead people your student cad killed.

Sandra never gave much thought to the corpses in the closet. Dr. Wesley asked her if she was interested in knowing where they had buried Dorothy, but the look that flashed across her face made him put a definite no, in her file.

When he asked her about her father, her disposition was a little softer, but not by much. Dr. Wesley asked if she would like to know where he was buried, and Sandra replied that she would like to know. He jotted it down as having a positive reaction to the father figure, not knowing that the day she went, if she should ever go, she planned to urinate on his headstone and spit on his grave.

"Mail call, ladies. It's someone out there who still gives a fuck!" Open and inspected mail was passed through the slots, but Sandra's was still sealed and intact. She opened the envelope that contained her new address and directions on how to get there. Once again, Barbara had not let her down.

Everything was in place, and she was ready to smell the air on the other side. It had been explained to her that she would still be under the order of the courts for the next three years. Sandra would have to keep her appointments with a certified psychiatrist and have them continue to send in the appropriate papers. The last part came as a direct recommendation from the chief psychiatrist of the prison, the warden, and Dr. Wesley himself. She had no idea that he would add his support to that sort of stipulation or that he had the power to do so, but it was printed there in black and white for her to read over and over again.

She didn't want to sit across the desk from anyone again and have them analyze who or what she was or what she should become. She was completely irritated by the gesture, but she didn't tell him that. As a matter of fact in their last session, she was just as happy and as bubbly as she was expected to be. He didn't keep her for the entire hour, and she was glad of that. Her face had been masked in phony smile mode for so long she thought she may need a chisel to put it back in its normal position.

He wished her well and signed all her necessary documents to be processed. "So are you ready for your big day? There is a lot going on in the world out there. You have to be careful and alert at all times."

"Yeah, I know. I am always on alert for the big bad wolf."

Dr. Wesley came from behind his desk for the first time since she had been seeing him, and he escorted her to the door. "There are some really nice people out there, Sandra. Not everyone is a wolf."

"Not on the outside."

He shook her hand and watched as the guard searched her. Everything seemed to be moving in slow motion for him, and he realized that he would be sorry to see her go. Any psychiatrist either in the practice for years or just getting their feet wet would love to have the chance to dip into the recesses of Sandra's mind. She was cunning yet vulnerable at the same time. She needed someone to care for her, yet she didn't really understand love.

He doubted if she would ever be able to have an affectionate heterosexual relationship or if it would be possible for her to love someone of the same sex either. From the time she and Barbara became roommates, he had gotten a whiff of the rumors circulating through the prison about them, but he didn't see any proof of that when he saw Sandra or when he asked her about Barbara.

He remembered not too long ago that he believed they should be separated. Sandra looked so consumed with destruction at the time that he really did fear for Barbara's safety, but now as he looked at her with the painted smile on her face, he could only wonder what else had she not been truthful about.

———————

CHAPTER 45

The cab pulled up in the front of the facility to collect Sandra; making Barbara once again true to her word. She did anything and everything that Sandra asked of her, and it wasn't simply because it was her funds that she was doing it with. She knew she had grown physically and emotionally attached to someone she hoped one day would feel the same way about her.

Sandra walked to the cab with nothing more than the clothes on her back and a small paper bag with prescriptions and a three-day supply of medication as she reached for the front passenger door of the vehicle.

"What are you doing? Fares belong in the backseat. Have you been in there that long?"

Sandra felt an instant flare-up inside of her but did everything she could to control it. She had gotten no further than the parking lot, and already the urge to beat someone to a pulp threatened to consume her. Silently, she opened the back door and slid across the seat. The driver then asked where she was going. She wasn't totally sure she would be able to answer without being thrown out of the cab, so she held a piece of paper up to the Plexiglas for him to read. "Are you a deaf-mute or something?"

He seemed to think he was the funniest comedian of all time with his greasy hair and stained clothing. He couldn't suppress his laughter as he pulled out of the parking lot. Sandra's cheeks were numb for the duration of the drive because of the constant pinching sensation her teeth caused as she bit into them.

He continued to make lesbian jokes and lewd comments about what she was going to be doing with her tongue for the rest of the week. She desired nothing more than to show him exactly what she wanted to do with her tongue, but staying free overrode the eagerness to teach him a lesson, so she stared out the window as the traffic and people flew by.

When she was younger, she loved to see women dressed up in fancy dresses and business suits, visualizing her mother in such attire, but now the sight seemed to taunt and tease her as if to say, "Look at what you never had."

"That'll be $42." She never uttered a word as she excited the cab. "Hey, bitch! Hey! I said—" Barbara reached through the window and tapped him on the shoulder, handing him the money. He didn't see the other woman when she appeared at his side, and it startled him momentarily.

"Watch your mouth, prick."

"Oh, it's my lucky day. I've finally met the one with the tongue, huh?" He turned sharply in his seat and placed the cab in gear, but not before yelling more expletives at Sandra. He had no idea how difficult it was for her to ignore him, but she did.

She calmly walked into the apartment with the number eleven on the door without saying a word to Danny Palomino. She remembered the company's name, the nametag on the dividing window, his face and the license plate. She had no immediate idea what she would do with the information, but she stored it in her memory bank anyway.

"Where is all your stuff?"

"Stuff?"

"Yeah, you know, from the jail?"

"Why would I take anything from there? I'm shedding a new skin. Do you know how to cook? Because I'm starving."

"Yeah, sure. I just went shopping so everything would be fresh for you. I bought a lot of nice smelling bar soaps and shampoos so you can wash the stink off. I know I did as soon as…"

Sandra put her hand up to silence her and asked, "Did you buy some unscented Ivory soap?"

"No. They gave us that in liquid form while we were in prison. I thought you might like—"

Sandra turned around to face her with ice in her voice. "Whatever happens between us from this day on, Barbara, don't ever think for me because I guarantee you will continue to be way off base."

Sandra went to the kitchen, grabbed the dish soap, and headed for the bathroom. She didn't want to start off her return to freedom like this, but from the episode in the cab to Barbara telling her what she wanted, it was all getting to be just a little too much for a first day. She turned on the shower and tried to relax.

She leaned against the wall as she allowed the hot beads to rain down on her. The reality of being out of prison and free to do whatever she wanted was still slow to sink in. Having no clue of what to do next, she referred back to something Dr. Wesley had told her, and that was to make out a list.

She didn't know where to begin, but if eating good food was considered something to do, then she would start her list out with that. She did know for sure she would not be returning to anybody's school. Sandra figured it was a waste of time to obtain a degree in anything because once a felony popped up on her record, including the details of the felony, she would spend the rest of her life looking at doors closing in her face.

Her criminal history basically stopped her from socializing in any workplace, and she wasn't certain if she minded much at all. She knew she wouldn't be able to tolerate the multiple personalities and mood swings on a daily basis despite what basic skills they taught her in prison.

She figured from her earlier years at school and watching television that people got along all the time and worked out their problems in orderly fashion, but there was nothing orderly about her. On most days, she didn't feel normal inside. There was something ticking from deep within her core, almost as if a raw, unguided energy possessed her.

The feeling had always been at the base of her, she supposed, but as her release date from prison drew closer, it seemed that it controlled her every move. She didn't discuss it with Dr. Wesley for fear he would somehow be able to extend her prison term or come up with some other recommendation. She had not gotten used to the feeling and therefore wouldn't have been ready to try to explain it anyway, but she was free now and ready to brush the whole thing off as anxiety.

She was told that she needed to find a therapist when she was released and had approximately sixty days in which to do so, and she put that on her mental list as well.

Dr. Wesley had an office outside of the prison, but she didn't want to continue a relationship with him. He knew too much about her and would not be easily fooled if she had a reason to lie about something. She needed a fresh source, one that she could find on her own, someone she felt comfortable with, not someone who was pushed on her whether she liked it or not.

As she washed herself in the shower, she felt a new energy come over her, one that was calm but steady in her gut. She liked the feel of it and understood what it was: constructive thinking. When she had something to do and had it all planned, she seemed to be calm. She guessed the other feeling came when she was out of focus. She wasn't sure, but she knew she had to keep busy to keep everything positive for her.

Sandra briskly dried herself with the towel and called, "Barbara, where are you?"

"I'm in the kitchen. You said you were hungry so…"

"Come here!"

Barbara rushed in the bedroom for Sandra. "What is it? You look wild-eyed."

"Wild-eyed? I need a phonebook."

"We don't have one."

Sandra didn't say another word but just stared at her. Barbara caught the meaning immediately. She turned off the skillet and left the apartment in search of a phonebook as Sandra went to the closet in search of something to put on.

The longer she searched, the more disgusted she became. Row after row of skirts and dresses lined the closet. She checked the sizes and quickly realized they had been purchased for her. She thought she had made it clear that she would not be donning any frilly shit. Those days were long gone for her. She would never be vulnerable to a man's glare or allow herself to become a target. She would fight with everything she had before a man would ever take advantage of her again.

Sandra found a pair of jogging pants in one of the dresser drawers and put them on, along with a T-shirt. Her golden locks fell in ragged strings down the middle of her back, and she played with the strands while gazing at her reflection. Her blue eyes blazed and sparkled against her dilated pupils, and she guessed she did look a little wild-eyed.

Sandra hadn't had a good look at herself in years. The metal tin that was screwed to the cell wall did a poor job in the way of a mirror. Your image would always flash back distorted and off-centered. Some of the women learned how to master their reflection in the metal, but Sandra never cared enough to.

She rifled through the vanity cupboard in search of a hair dryer before realizing that the space was too small. She found it under the sink. The heat felt good on her scalp as she methodically brushed her hair. Within minutes, her tangled locks were drying into to a beautiful golden mane.

The palest of streaks flared boldly out against the darker ones. After years of basic washing and trims every now and then, she still commanded a head of hair that beauticians try to mimic daily.

Sandra paused as the golden locks cascaded from the crown of her head to the indention below her shoulder blades. She knew that a transformation was taking place right before her eyes. She was no longer looking at Sandra the inmate but a free woman with the world at her feet. On the outside she would be able to keep the attention of anyone she passed, but along with that were the unwanted stares and whistles. She would become prey to the average man, and she could never allow that.

"I'm back. I found..." Barbara's words clogged her throat like a morning mucus plug that restricted her airway. She couldn't get a word out no matter how she tried, and clutching at her throat didn't seem to help. Sandra moved towards her and relieved her of the parcels she was carrying. Swiftly she moved to the couch and flipped through the guide.

Barbara took a few tedious steps behind her, but she was not given a second glance. It wasn't until she raised her hand to touch her that Sandra acknowledged her by quickly reaching up, grabbing a hold of her wrist, and twisting in one single motion that brought Barbara to her knees.

"Ouch! Damn it, Sandra. I was just looking at your hair!" Sandra released her grip on her and turned back to looking at the yellow pages. "Where is your hair?"

"On the floor."

"You know what I mean. Why? Why did you cut it?"

"I was hungry and bored. You don't like it?"

Barbara took a moment to stare at her side profile, and she couldn't believe the transformation. At that moment Sandra could have easily been mistaken for Tommy.

CHAPTER 46

"I can't sit in this house another day. I'm going stir crazy. Come on. Let's go out and get some air, get a couple of drinks, or something."

Sandra rose from the floor where she had been doing several reps of abdominal crunches. "You go ahead if that's what you want to do, but I'm staying inside tonight."

"Tonight and every night since your release."

Sandra had found a therapist in town who was willing to take her case, and she took a cab to her office twice a week. As a matter of fact, she took a cab everywhere to keep from walking amongst what she considered the garbage of the world. She made special arrangements with the cab company so that the same female driver picked her up when she needed to go somewhere.

She was more than content to listen to the old lady babble on about politics and the injustices of the Social Security department. If she picked her up on Monday, she would repeat the same story to her on Wednesday, but it didn't bother Sandra at all. She had established a daily routine, and just like when she was incarcerated she wouldn't falter too far from it.

They have been sharing an apartment for six months now, and Barbara had been showing more and more signs of agitation over the last couple of weeks. She came from a different background than Sandra; she enjoyed being surrounded by different people and things, where Sandra felt more stabilized by routine.

Barbara had wanted to go out since day one. She wanted to shout from every rooftop that she was free, but she'd stayed very close to the apartment since the day she found it. Sandra told her that under no circumstances were they ever going to have company in the house. She was not allowed to bring men in at all. She had been given specific instructions not to mingle with the neighbors or anyone else, for that matter, and she stayed on course for the most part.

She would allow herself a flirt here or there when she went to the grocery store, but never more than that.

She had only been intimate once since she had gotten out of prison when she met a guy at the bar. She'd had way too much to drink and basically told him her life story over empty sex and cold tacos. He'd wanted to know more about her, where she was staying in the area, etc., and her loose lips almost sank her ship. The instant he started to attach himself, she realized that she had broken one of Sandra's rules, so in response to that, she gravitated to the other side of town to search for another apartment, never to disclose her error to Sandra.

She knew Sandra would never frequent a place like the one she met the man in, but she didn't want to take any chances on running into him in public if she and Sandra were ever to go out together. She didn't want to know what, if any, consequences she would have to suffer for betraying her trust. Sandra had never been violent towards her, but she had already witnessed what crossing her line could mean.

"Can we go out, Sandra? It'll be nice for you to hang loose for a while. We can have a martini and listen to some music—you know, get into the groove of things."

"No!"

She cut the words so sharply that Barbara could only blink in response. "I'm sorry."

With a bowed head, she ventured in their bedroom. "Wait." Sandra was on her feet, toweling off the sweat that had accumulated on her abs. She didn't want to take the mother role over Barbara, but she also didn't want her roaming around, allowing herself to be attached to the vermin in the world.

There was still so much she needed to learn and adapt to. Every day was a mental task for her. No one knew or understood the daily battles she fought in her head. She took everything in steps and tried desperately to stay on course of her new life while simultaneously drifting away from her prison habits. She only gotten as far as staying in bed for ten additional minutes and eating breakfast later than she was used to, and now Barbara wanted her to go outside.

She did everything she could to ease the fierce case of nerves and doubts that swept through her as she said "Where do you want to go?" Barbara was so stunned she almost didn't have an answer.

"Uh, just down the street, I suppose. I noticed a bar sign on the side of the building. It might be country, but the beer should be cold."

Without further hesitation, Sandra stated, "Let me get dressed."

Barbara clapped her hands in glee like a little kid as she bounced up and down on the bed.

Sandra allowed herself a brief smile as she went to shower and change. This was all part of the process, she kept telling herself. She knew eventually she would have to mingle with people in order for her not to be seen as some form of freak. "Take a step in the right direction, and you won't regret escalating to a higher, more independent ground. Trust me." That was the famous Dr. Wesley quote she repeated as she showered, but the buzzing sound that crept upon her threatened to take over. She shook her head repeatedly, but the sound had smoothly transformed into her voice of reason.

"You trust the good old doctor that much? Are you really ready to walk out into the arena? Trust me! Trust me! Ha! When was the last time you heard those words? While nice Uncle Bill thrust himself repeatedly into your innocence, shredding away your pride, your dignity, your self-worth! You don't have to prove anything to that slut! Let her go, and be rid of her once and for all!"

"No! No! No!"

It was moments later when she realized that Barbara was wrapping her hand in a cold towel because she'd destroyed the vanity mirror. Shards of broken glass reflected, diamond-like, on the tile floor, creating their own illusion.

"Sandra...Sandra...talk to me, please. What happened?" Sandra appeared to be in shock and immobilized. She continued to stand at the sink, unmoving, as Barbara rushed to clear the floor of the sparkles made from the glass.

"Let me move you to the bed, okay? I need to get this up and..."

Her sentence was again cut off from the sound of Sandra's voice. "I'm still getting dressed. You wanted to go to the bar, didn't you?"

Barbara didn't answer. How could she? A drink was only the tip of what she really needed. She could use a line or two to help her get over the jitters that were consuming her body. She hadn't dabbled in the drug scene since she was arrested, and she vowed never to do it again, but a nice line of white would help her be able to deal with Sandra and the mood swings.

CHAPTER 42

The Coyote Sun was dark, damp, and musty to boot. Christmas lights were strung from one side of the room to the other, but it only helped in making the place appear more depressing.

All eyes were on them as they stood just inside of the entrance, wondering if they should continue to venture in or just go to the liquor store for a beer.

Mind made up, Barbara turned for the exit, her arm linked with Sandra's.

"Come on in, honey. We don't bite, do we, fellas?" There were a few distant whistles from the dark corners, and Barbara knew she didn't want to see the owners if they looked anything like the bartender. Not only was he clearly a hundred pounds overweight, inebriated, and missing a couple of good ones in the front of his mouth, but his shorts were well hidden in the creases of his abdomen.

She wanted to find a new location where a night out on the town didn't include the best hillbillies Denver had to offer. Her mind tried to capture a picture of another bar or night club close by, when Sandra took six sure strides across the floor and plopped down on the stool next to the door greeter.

This was not where Barbara wanted to be. She wanted to dance with someone who at least looked as if they had taken a shower in the last few weeks. She wanted to be told how beautiful her smile was and how they always had dreamed of meeting someone like her, and she just didn't see those opportunities there. The oldest operating jukebox planted in the corner belted out its next song....country, of course. Great.

Barbara reluctantly dragged herself to the stool next to Sandra. "I'll have a double of the good stuff." Then under her breath she wondered if such a thing even existed where they were.

Toothless was on the move by the time they purchased a second round. "So what bring you two fine damsels out to the Coyote?" Barbara looked as if she was internally battling herself against swatting him like a fly or pouring a drink over his head, and Sandra just looked dead ahead with the coldness of a snake.

Barbara began to feel as if this whole night was a big mistake. She should have followed her first instinct and left Sandra at the apartment, gone into town, and bar-hopped. She could feel electrical currents spinning and jumping off of Sandra, and she was two bar stools away.

After an hour had gone by, they were receiving even more unwanted attention from the newcomers. Sandra hadn't so much as gotten up to use the bathroom, let alone shift positions on her stool. She continued to stare at her image across the bar as if fascinated by the sight.

She downed her first beer without coming up for air, but she seemed to find comfort in slowly peeling the label off the second one.

Dr. Wesley weighed heavily on her mind, and she began to wonder if she would be able to control her inner anger, instability and sanity long enough to conquer her demons. She knew now with certainty that is what her past had become: floating demons. The episode back at the apartment drifted through her mind continuously at a manic pace.

She knew even with the help of a therapist she had yet to come to terms with her past. She didn't know if she could ever get over the betrayal of her parents, Uncle Bill, or the slew of degenerate molesters that followed. They'd feasted on her young flesh until there was no more of her to give. She wondered if Dr. Wesley really thought she could just "move on with her life," or any of the other popular slogans that were thrown around in situations such as hers.

Those were just words that did nothing to soothe her breasts that still felt sore from being pulled, bit, and manipulated by strangers. Sometimes at night she swore she could smell the men on top of her. She began bathing three times a day to ease the burning she imagined was still aflame between her legs. Not once was she asked "Are you okay? Am I hurting you, little girl? Am I too big for you?"

Sandra slung her bottle across the bar, shattering her second mirror of the day. She rushed outside of the building, not only to get some air but to get away from the screaming and racket that followed her. She spent several moments dry heaving and trying to catch her breath at the same time. She had to focus. All of the calming techniques she had been taught over the last several years had escaped her when she needed them most.

She didn't know why she'd flared up like that, and in front of so many people. She saw Barbara on her way out, and it seemed as if she was being detained by some of the men inside. Maybe they thought she had left and was holding Barbara responsible. She didn't know what was going on, but when she was able to pull herself together, she had to go back inside and face the music.

"You know that mirror is going to cost you, little lady." Sandra looked up as she wiped the back of her mouth with her hand. She instantly knew the man before her was just like any other man she had encountered. She could see it in his eyes. He complained about the damage she had caused to his establishment, counting each dollar as he stared lustfully at her breasts brimming at the top of her tank top, making Sandra instantly stand up.

"I'm sorry about what happened in there. I'll just go get my friend, and we will be on our way. I'll leave more than enough to cover the price of the mirror." She briskly began to walk past him, but she was grabbed by her upper arm.

"Do you think that's all you owe me? I tired of you masculine bitches who have no idea how to act like a lady. Now your friend in there, she's cozied on up to the bar and settled herself right on in for a good time, so I thought, being the gentleman that I am, that I would take it upon myself to show you the same. You know, put a little woman back in you."

He said all of this with smug satisfaction, not once releasing his grip on her. Sandra didn't want to flip out and do something worse than she had already done, but she did want to go home. This outside world was not for her, and she wanted nothing more to do with it. Sitting in the apartment and listening to her cab driver were more than enough.

Spinning on her heels, she asked, "How else do you expect me to pay you back? I don't wait tables, and I don't serve drinks."

The owner tilted his cowboy hat back, looking eye to eye with Sandra. "Oh, honey, I wouldn't dream of anything that sweet." With that statement, he jerked her to the other side of the building that was completely blackened out. There wasn't even a slight illumination from a street lamp. She couldn't see anything for a moment or two, but the powerful stench of urine was unmistakable.

He roughly pressed himself into her with his mouth, viciously clenching her lips in his teeth, while his lower region pumped and pressed her against the wall. Sandra could feel his savage energy bulging in his pants. The involuntary muscle begged for stimulation and release. Sandra wanted to vomit, but her mouth was consumed by his tongue and teeth, forcing her to swallow it back.

She didn't resist his advances as he pulled at her jeans and panties, didn't show any emotion as the material gathered around her ankles. Her sight was blank and out of focus, but she calculated his every move. "Turn around, you stiff bitch. I want some ass for my merchandise!"

She found herself submitting as if this lewd act was being performed on someone else. She couldn't grasp the reality of what was being done. Not here, not now! She had no answer for his advances, until he penetrated her.

The action flashed a image so vivid in her mind that she saw herself as the helpless little girl from the past. The pulling and tugging of her buttocks brought her back many, many years. She was no longer Sandra the twenty-six-year-old but Sandra the teenager who had finally said, "Enough is enough!" Her short hair was being roughly jerked back and forth, which constantly scraped her face against the brick surface of the building. The pain of him entering her faded off into a deep, almost sedated moment of calm as she pushed herself off the wall, breaking his uneven stroke pattern in the process.

His breathing was shallow, which told her that he had exerted a valuable amount of energy during his performance.

"Your turn, cowboy."

Sandra bent down as if to better accommodate him and deftly removed her belt from her jeans. She bounced back up with the force of a wind tunnel, landing the buckle squarely across the bridge of his nose. The force split the skin and cracked the bone instantly, sending a spray of blood into Sandra's face.

"You bitch!"

One of his hands held the gash in his face while the other one reached for Sandra.

Swiftly, she stepped out to the side, wielding the buckle again. The solid thump stunned him enough to give her the vantage point she was looking for. She stepped out of her clothes and continued to work on him. She never gave her nakedness a second thought as she looped the belt around his neck in a noose fashion, pulling the flap that caused a crushing pressure to envelope his windpipe.

The spitting and gurgling began to echo loudly in her ears, causing her to pull even tighter to silence the sound. The cowboy's eyes bulged several times their normal size before turning off. Even in the dimness of the alley, Sandra could see the telltale signs of death in them, so she released her hold on the belt. His body began to slump backwards against her, but she carelessly moved and let the urinated alleyway become his crutch.

Sandra knew she had just failed herself and her vow to society. She didn't know why she allowed things to go this far or how she so easily gave up the little freedom she had just earned. She waited a brief moment to hear the police sirens blaring, but there was none. Did anyone know he was coming outside to find her? He more than likely didn't mention it because he knew his intentions when he saw her at the beginning of the evening.

No one had seen them together, and that gave her a small glimmer of hope.

Sandra began consciously cleaning up the crime scene. Tediously, she removed the condom for his now less-than-intimidating shaft. She realized that he'd already put on protection before coming outside to see her. His mind was set on one track, and now it was to be his last.

She knew she couldn't leave the incriminating evidence behind, so she stuck it in the back pocket of her jeans. She removed her tank top and began wiping his hands, thighs, and any other part of him that may have been in contact with her.

She balled her shirt up and scrubbed vigorously at his genital area, hoping to dissolve any traces of her DNA. She would not get caught! The idea of killing him and not going to jail for it brought an almost gleeful moment to the surface.

Her muscles burned as she lifted him under his arms. She knew that all she needed was a little more time, and she would be okay. She had no plans on staying around like she did with her mother. She had no sentimental memories here; this was an act of self-defense with a twist. Sandra was mentally detached and outside of herself on this one. She didn't think of him as anything more than an obstacle in the way of her future, one she needed to rid herself of.

Honestly, she felt no remorse for what had just taken place here today or eight years ago. Dorothy allowed men to feed and prey on her daughter for the sake of her own high, so…fuck her, fuck her, fuck her!

A throbbing pain was shooting up and down her arm before she realized that she was repeatedly bashing the cowboy's face in with a brick. She hadn't realized she pulled him behind the dumpster or why she had no control over herself or the situations she seemed to always be in. Now there was even more blood for her to try to clean, and this made her even angrier. Her knuckles were bleeding, and she began to see the light fade in the tunnel. If they investigated far enough, there was no way they would not find her DNA all over him. Damn it!

Sandra stood up and stared down at the heap of man on the ground. She was going to get caught, and she knew it. She expected to be found by tomorrow and be back in prison by the weekend. Before she could finish a bowl of cereal, the police would have her cuffed! Once again she blamed her fate on the man who lay at her feet.

A blinding sense of defeat consumed her as the slideshow of her immediate future played before her. Eight more years of Dr. Wesley peering into her soul didn't sound very stimulating. Another thought that didn't go down well was the prospect of a life sentence.

Without any motivation from the corpse, she began to stomp the heel of her bare foot into his already lifeless body. Violently, she grabbed hold of the dumpster for leverage, allowing herself to get lost in the momentum and savageness of it all. She decided she would dance on his parade until the police came marching in.

"Sandra? Sandra?" Hearing the sound of her name broke into the storm of torture she was in. Sandra looked into Barbara eyes but didn't recognize her for several moments. "What happened here?

Releasing the dumpster, she turned to fully face her. She figured she must look like a maniac at the time, but the expression on Barbara's face said she had to be looking a little worse than that.

Blood ran from her calves to her feet, creating a red web between her toes, while tiny splatters consumed the rest of her unclothed body. As she licked her lips, she tasted the sticky droplets that must have formed there.

She didn't care about anyone at that moment except Barbara. She didn't want her to think she was some form of monster or that she had just deliberately set out to kill this man. She was trying to blend in, she wanted to know life as Barbara knew it. It was important to her to try to get reason out of the situation and explain herself. "He...he..." In a childish way she continued to point at the heap on the ground.

"Get your clothes on. Hurry!"

She tossed her the clothing that had been discarded by the building, but Sandra didn't move, just stated, "Go home, Barbara." They stood there facing each other, sizing up the situation, their bond, and the trust they must have for each other in order to see another day.

Barbara knew she had to make a choice. She could turn and run or stay and risk incarceration again. It would take her less than twenty minutes to clear her things out of the apartment and be on her way. It wouldn't be hard to get lost; she had fifty-some odd states to choose from. Sandra had padded her bank account fairly well, and she definitely had enough to start over, but her devotion to Sandra was once again stronger than the risk.

"Get your clothes on! We don't have much time."

We. The deciding word. The ultimate two letters that would sear them together now and forevermore.

CHAPTER 48

Before entering the apartment, each woman removed their shoes and clothes. Sandra remained out in the hall as Barbara went to retrieve a couple of garbage bags. Diligently, she wrapped up each of Sandra's hands and feet. She also placed a bag over her closely cropped hair. Sandra never spoke a word but simply repeated the steps on Barbara. They didn't want to touch anything in the house and risk transferring blood to any surface. After they picked up the body, put him in the dumpster, and covered him with trash, Barbara was just as bloody, if not more so, than Sandra.

Sandra was the first in the shower, where the bags were cut off of her hands. Barbara went next and then cleaned up after them. She used so much bleach she nearly passed out from the fumes in the small space. Sandra was still operating in "space mode" as Barbara called it. She was like this once before, after their incident in the prison. She stayed zoned out for hours. She knew it was useless to ask her anything at this time because she would not get an answer.

Barbara let her settle down, but she continued to move. She knew she had very little time to get things back to their normal state. All traces of their night out on the town had to be erased. They would remember two ladies being there, but never would the police think his death was the work of a woman. He was nearly a complete form of pulp when they lifted him. Barbara poured beer on his genitals to rinse away anything Sandra may have left behind. He was fully clothed, and badly beaten. The cowboys would be blaming each other long before they considered them.

She went into the hall with a duffle bag and put all clothes, including their shoes, into it. Everything had to go, even the bottle of beer she drank on the way home. The plastic bags she removed from their hands and feet went inside as well.

She dressed in a casual jogging suit on top of a pair of fresh jeans and a tank. She would strip them off as well after she found the perfect place to burn the items.

She wasn't taking any chances; their very freedom depended on how well she did tonight. She knew that just as well as taking her next breath. She would not let them get caught from a careless mistake on her part.

Over the years of confinement all you heard were stories of how women ended up behind bars from one little error: didn't wear gloves, buried the evidence in the back yard, kept bloody items in the house, confided in a friend, etc. Mistakes had cost them years of their lives. Well, she had taken notes and was not about to slip up now.

Barbara exited the bus with her duffle bag in tote, checking and re-checking to ensure no part of her was left on the seat or in the aisle of the bus. She pulled her cap down low on her head and headed to "Cradle City." She knew a little bit about this area; in her hay days she would come here to get a fix or two before hitting the club scene.

There were a few low-end prostitutes out, as well as bums who littered the street. There weren't too many lights this area, which made it a prime location for what she had to do.

*

Back on the bus, Barbara rethought every step, every nook and every cranny she may have come across since finding Sandra in the alley. There was no doubt in her mind that the cowboy they lay to rest deserved it, but did it really have to come down to that? He was a little over six feet, but definitely on the skinny side. Sandra could have taken him down without so much as busting a sweat, but why didn't she? Why would she allow him to get the upper hand? If they were going to be in this together, which after tonight they definitely were, then Sandra would have to open up. Barbara decided that all the cards would have to be on the table if she was to go on the run with her.

On the run? Is this what it had boiled down to? They obviously couldn't stay in the same area, even if no one figured them for the crime. They would have to move, but not suddenly. Another frequent mistake made by criminals was changing locations too fast. If the police were to come sniffing around, you shouldn't leave the beginning of a paper trail with your landlord by breaking the lease instead of sticking around to answer questions. You were basically putting a red flag on your back when you left an area, residence, or job directly after an incident, especially if you broke a lease.

They were two ex-cons who were not supposed to socialize with each other, let alone live together. Red lights had been flashing in the back of her mind since the day Sandra was released, but Barbara was willing to take her chances with her.

She knew overall she wasn't bad to look at, being a five-foot-six, curvaceous brunette, and she could probably land a husband at the next big event to hit town, but she just had no desire. She wanted to wait for Sandra to be released so she could help her acclimate back into society. In fact, she was more than eager to do so. She enjoyed picking out things she felt she would like, even though she was way off base with the skirts and all. She loved being the one to set up shop and give her a place to call home when she was free.

If Sandra went down for the cowboy, then so would she. This solemn promise she made to herself as she burned everything in a dumpster that greatly resembled the one they'd buried the tavern owner in.

No matter what temperament she had to deal with or what lines she had to cross, she knew that she would never leave her side.

"Sandra, where are you?" Barbara walked into the kitchen but heard the water splashing from the back of the apartment. "Sandra?"

She found her sitting in a tub of water, scrubbing herself vigorously with a kitchen sponge. The water could not have been warm because her body had a light blue tint to it, and her lips were shivering uncontrollably. "Sandra!"

Hearing her name being practically shouted in her ear broke the repetitive state she was in, and she turned to look at Barbara. "What are you doing, Sandra? You can't go on like this. Whatever happened, happened, but we must stay focused. I need you. I can't do everything by myself. You have to break out of this." Barbara was sitting on the side of the tub. She wanted to be in close proximity to her. She had to get eye contact and try to help Sandra focus. They were not going to get far if they continued this way. She had to be able to communicate with her at all times.

"Sandra, get out of the water."

Barbara stood up and held the towel open for her. Wordlessly, she let the water out, stepped out the tub, and allowed herself to be dried. As Barbara reached her arms around to dry her back, Sandra surprised her by speaking. "I'm sorry, Barbara." Those three words vibrated her heart like a world class earthquake.

"I know you are, but you need to tell me what happened, okay? I need to know why you did this."

Sandra allowed herself to be guided into the room, where she sat on the far corner of the bed and began to talk to the only person who mattered to her. No one else would do what she had done. Barbara risked her life and future to help her. Even in her most tortuous state of mind, she could see that.

"My mother sold me for drugs when I was eleven…"

Barbara had no idea how horrifying her past had been. This was definitely a step up from any "mommy dearest" story she had ever heard. No wonder she couldn't function in society properly. She'd never had a chance.

Sandra went through detail after detail of every man, every episode, ever scene of herself being used. She quickly skipped over the part of how she killed her mother, but nonetheless her life was a horror story.

Barbara felt compelled to do something but didn't know exactly what. She wanted Sandra to know that not every touch was a bad one and if nothing else, she loved her. Gently she reached across the bed and grabbed her hand. Sandra looked at her but didn't move away. Barbara brought her hand to her lips, gently grasping her fingertips.

"Do you trust me?"

Sandra didn't answer. Barbara needed to show her how much she cared and that she would stick by her through anything. At that moment, she was willing to go to hell and back for the wounded woman who sat across from her.

CHAPTER 49

"Good morning." Barbara opened one eye to the sight of sunshine and Sandra holding a plate. "I made you breakfast. Go wash your face and rinse your mouth out." Doing as she was told, she kicked her feet from under the covers and headed for the bathroom. She glanced back at Sandra before turning to face herself in what used to be the mirror. They should have called in someone to repair that already, she had to get it done before they moved.

Sandra was in a seemingly high-spirited mood, and she was calm. Definitely a change. Barbara wondered if any of this was stemming from their talk. She hoped she was able to get through to her, but she also knew that dealing with Sandra could easily be compared to flipping a light switch.

She was busy setting the nightstand as a table when Barbara emerged from the bathroom. "You want juice of coffee?"

Barbara stretched her arms above her head. "Coffee, definitely. I'm still sleepy." Sandra walked past her on the way to the kitchen with long purposeful strides.

"So what do you want to do today?"

"Do?"

"Yeah, let's go see the sights. I haven't been out in a while. You can show me some stuff, like how to bargain shop!"

Barbara didn't feel it was right to be seen outside so soon. It had only been two weeks. But then again, she didn't want to spoil her good mood; they were few and far between. Sandra rambled on constantly while they ate, which caused Barbara to continue looking awestruck. What in the hell was going on? Her personality had done full 180-degree turn in the last couple of months. Sandra had gone from silent, to speaking a few words to the party girl. This could not be normal behavior. Something had to be ticking in that pretty little blonde head of hers, and Barbara wasn't too sure if she wanted to know what it was.

*

Their year lease was up, and the transition to a new house went by without a glitch. Sandra no longer wanted to live with neighbors', so they hunted for a small house. It seemed as if the house had to have specific qualifications, so Barbara left the choice exclusively up to Sandra, which landed them in a small two-bedroom, two-bath ranch-style house with a finished basement.

It sat on a half-acre of land, but Barbara couldn't figure out why the most appealing part to Sandra seemed to be that the landlord had a P.O. box for the rent to be mailed in. She was in her late sixties and stated she was only in town three to four times a year, but she readily gave them the number to a maintenance company if any problems occurred. They were instructed to take the repair costs (if any) out of the rent and send the remaining balance and a copy of the receipt to the P.O. box.

"Well, this is it. Isn't it perfect?" Barbara looked around, not too sure what to think. The inside was nice enough but also very dingy because of all the woodwork. Dark oak wood led up from the floor to the middle of the walls, where it ran dab smack into matching paneling, which consumed the rest of the walls.

The white ceilings were the only features that announced they weren't standing inside of a tree. The kitchen was directly behind the living room but was not defined by much but a stove, a refrigerator, and a few spaced-out cabinets and countertops. It all blended together flawlessly, especially the prehistoric appliances.

There was a firewood pile on the floor near the stove, and Barbara prayed they didn't have to burn it in order to cook. The first bathroom was right off the kitchen, stopping the wood flooring abruptly. What took over was a mint green explosion.

The tub, toilet, and sink were a 1960s version of "happy green," and someone had taken the time to paint the vanity an excruciating amber gold. The floor and wall tiles were black and white and appeared as if they had gotten off at the wrong subway stop. Barbara tentatively stepped around Sandra to introduce herself to her separate living quarters.

The second bedroom, which was hers, was considerably smaller and held a damp, moldy smell inside of it. It held a slightly stained red shag carpet, but she felt it was doable, considering the walls were white. Barbara scanned the ceiling only to find half of it was consumed by spider webs and a giant wet spot. "Oh, I think we will need that maintenance company. The roof looks like it leaks."

Sandra joined her in the room to inspect the damage. "Well, you'd better call them now because we're not having visitors any time soon after that." Sandra left the room, giving Barbara a wink and a quick pat on the ass.

A slow but warm smile covered her face as she let the words sink in. No company? Did she plan on officially making them a couple? Did she finally decide it was okay to love? Barbara had no real idea what her words meant, but she was more than willing to hang around and find out.

"Okay, that's the last box. You want to go get something to eat?"

"Nah, I think we can survive the night. There's eggs, cheese, and a couple of other things in here. Why don't you make those omelets you're famous for, and we'll wash it down with a glass of the good stuff."

"The good stuff? We only have a $4 bottle of zinfandel."

"Well, it'll be good tonight! I'll be back after I shower in our retro bathroom." She bounced out of the room, leaving Barbara at the sink cutting green onions.

*

Sandra emerged wearing only a towel on her head. Her body still held the moisture of the shower, and minuscule beads of water danced happily down her stomach. She had been completely removing the hair from her most delicate area ever since the bar scene, and from the smooth glow of her skin, she wasn't planning on letting it grow back again.

"Either the eggs smell incredible, or I'm just starving." Without a hint of feeling exposed, she poured herself a glass of wine and plopped down on the couch.

Barbara was at a loss for words. She had never seen Sandra this open or raw. She usually slept in two or even three layers of clothing. She didn't believe in nightgowns so no matter the temperature, she kept panties, shorts, and pajama pants on her while she slept. To see her now as if she were flaunting her nakedness was a true flip of the coin. Was she just feeling absolutely relaxed to be away from the cowboy episode?

Barbara watched as she sipped delicately from the glass, as even the most subtle of movements caused her body to flex and ripple in different areas. She was beautiful. The desire to touch every curve, every indention became overwhelming. She had never thought of a woman sexually in a partnership kind of way, but the magnitude in which she lusted for just a simple touch from Sandra controlled her every thought and consumed her dreams, but she wanted Sandra to want her, too.

"Dinner is done." Sandra turned and watched as Barbara plated the omelets and rice.

"Rice?"

"Not just any old rice. This is rice with butter!"

"Ooh, now I'm impressed!" Sandra sat at the table, not hesitating to tear into the omelet. She was rinsing her mouth with her wine when she caught Barbara staring at her.

"What?"

"You were really hungry!"

She looked down at her plate where only a few isolated grains remained. "I guess I didn't take time to inhale, huh?"

Both of the women laughed as Sandra took her plate to the sink. Barbara continued to eat until she felt Sandra standing next to her. She looked up, not knowing what to expect, but a kiss on the cheek wasn't it.

"Thanks for dinner."

"I love you." The words tumbled from her mouth, spilling themselves at Sandra's feet.

Sandra became confused almost instantly. Barbara was putting her in a category she didn't want to be in, trying to make her come to terms with something she knew nothing about: someone's feelings and love. She had no concept of the word or how to compute it in her brain. She knew people spoke of love all the time, and she watched all the lovey-dovey shows on television, but what you were supposed to feel inside when that occurred came as a bit of a mystery for her.

She was feeling a little light-footed after establishing a new house that she found basically on her own. She knew what to look for and she searched high and low until she got it. Barbara was seeing a brief opening of her emotions, and Sandra felt she was using it for her own advantage.

She understood hate and how at times it was capable of sweeping her out of a moment and placing her into a totally blank environment, but that was as far as emotions went for her. To see the open look on Barbara's face registered no response on her part. She had no idea what Barbara wanted to hear, but the animalistic look in her eyes reminded Sandra of the many men who looked upon her as prey. She found Barbara's gaze to be a little softer, but it held the same intensity.

"Do you want to touch me? Sandra asked."

"Yes."

"Why?"

"Why?"

"Yes. What is it about me that you want to touch?"

Barbara's mouth was dry. She couldn't come up with the right words. She didn't want to destroy how close they had become, but she was also tired of sleeping with someone she couldn't touch or being around someone she loved but being afraid to express it. "I want to make love to you, Sandra, not just touch you like an object."

"Make love to me? You're a woman, Barbara. Get a hold of yourself!"

With that said, Sandra turned and began washing her dish at the sink. Barbara was livid. Saying she didn't want to have sex with her was one thing, but she but she would not be walked over for having a heart.

Swiftly, she grabbed Sandra by the arm, spinning her around. "I have a hold of myself, thank you! I can't keep going on like this! You're hot one minute and cold the next."

"Hot? When have I ever been hot for anything, Barbara? You're the one who has feeding yourself this imaginary life we're supposed to live. I never told you I would love you now or later. We are room-mate's, and maybe friends, but nothing more."

Barbara was furious, and stunned, at the same time. How could she have been so dumb? Why did she let herself fall for Sandra? She could have been getting her life together instead of incriminating herself in a murder and loving the hopeless murderer. She had really messed up.

Barbara knew her life had taken a turn for the worse, but she'd be damned if she would continue down such a dark and drab path. Putting herself back on the right track would have to become her top priority, not chasing some-one she would never be able to catch.

No longer would she be Sandra's doormat or co-conspirator. She needed space. She needed time, and she needed it now.

"I will always love you, Sandra, because of what you taught me and the way you stood up for me when I thought I was alone, but I can't keep doing this. I need more from you. I deserve more." Barbara walked to the closet to retrieve her jacket.

She kept her back to Sandra the entire time, not wanting her to see the hurt across her face that transformed into tears running down her cheeks. She thought she mastered that much successfully as she walked across the blurry front lawn to the garage.

As she climbed into the Toyota that Sandra had just bought her, the tears blended with her runny nose. She had never before felt so used and discarded. Barbara wondered why she always found herself falling for the wrong kind of people, men or women. She needed to clear her head and think, which was impossible for her to do being in the same vicinity as Sandra.

She glanced back in the direction of the house; the vision became foggy and distorted just like their relationship. She quickly put the car in gear before her emotions betrayed her yet again. Barbara took off with no specific destination in mind, but a new start was in her heart.

*

The sound of the closet opening and closing, the sight of her putting on her red jacket and walking across the living room and out the front door did nothing for Sandra like the sound of silence she left behind. She didn't know how long she sat on the sofa or how much time had lapsed before she realized Barbara was not coming back.

CHAPTER 50

*D*ays later, Sandra began snapping herself back into shape. It took her a little more than forty-eight hours to come to the conclusion that she had been deserted. During that time, she listened to every sound in the house, thinking it was Barbara coming back, but two sunrises later, she knew it was over.

She quickly surmised that she didn't need the dead weight around her neck, constantly demanding some form of emotional stimulus out of her. She was a solo artist. Always had been. The only thing that hindered her at this point was her immobility and not knowing how to drive. She realized she would have to correct that problem immediately.

She didn't particularly like public transportation because of the smells and drifting body odors, but Barbara had taken the car she bought with her. She couldn't sit in the house and dwell on it; she had to get things going, so she got dressed and went in search of the perfect location for what she needed.

Approximately four miles from her house she found the driving school that was listed in the yellow pages and right smack next door was the office of Dr. Bridgett Springler.

She called to make an appointment, which took nine days before she could be seen because of all the red tape associated with her therapy. Dr. Springler had to get payments authorized through the system, get a copy of her file from Dr. Charles and her previous therapist along with discovering where she was to send her report and findings. That took all of nine anxious days.

Sandra hoped that nothing would go wrong. It had taken her a nice amount of time to find such a suitable place. She didn't like moving around much, and if she only had one location to go to, it was less likely she would encounter strangers and be put into a situation where she was expected to say and do "normal" things. She wasn't ready for that. Carrying on meaningless conversations was not one of the tasks on her list, so if at all possible, she would rather avoid the situation totally.

Her buzz cut had grown out a little more, and she gelled it down on the sides, giving her kind of a punk rock look. This caused Sandra to reflect a crisper, even younger appearance. She tried to hide behind her clothes by wearing baggy sweats and T-shirts, but since it was eighty degrees outside, she had to wear jeans in order to blend in as much as possible.

The denim was a little on the baggy side, but it took no imagination to see she was beautiful and shapely. She purchased a dark pair of sunglasses from the gas station across the street from the school, and they provided the shield she needed. She could see out but, no one could see her eyes. They were the windows to the soul, right? Well, her soul was covered!

Sandra entered the coolness of the doctor's office and went to the reception desk. "I'm here for my ten o'clock appointment."

The elderly lady didn't raise her head, just slid a clipboard across to her. "Fill out the top two sheets and keep the third to read at your leisure."

Sandra sat with the clipboard in her lap reading question after question. Damn! They wanted to know everything about her from kindergarten to how she thought she would die! She decided she would answer only what she wanted to and leave the rest blank.

"Ms. Hansley?" Sandra bounced out of her seat, and followed who she assumed was Dr. Springler across the hall and into the back room. "You can have a seat anywhere you like. Can I have the forms you filled out?" Sandra handed in the forms and then looked behind her to choose a seating option.

The couch was definitely out of the question. She wasn't some nut job in need of hypnotizing. Instead, she chose the chair sitting right in front of the desk. She would look her dead on instead of cowering in the chair positioned in the corner.

The leather of the seat was supposed to be comforting, she guessed, but due to the air being on full blast, it was rather cold and stiff. She noticed that Dr. Springler used all of the "mood-lifting" colors Dr. Wesley had talked to her about in therapy. The lower half of her office was pink, and the top layer was yellow with a white ceiling. If the sight of the room didn't cheer you up, it would definitely put you in the mood for some lemonade.

She used all dark brown leather to tone the colors down a little, but when it was time for her desk, she must have realized that she left out a calming color. She went the full nine yards in purchasing a beautiful oak desk, sanding it down, and painting it a pale sky blue.

There was a green fern growing wildly over one corner of the desk and a group of photos facing Sandra on the other. She rather quickly caught on that the photos faced the patient in hopes that they would ask her questions about her family, where in turn, she would began to ask them duplicate questions. Sandra wasn't falling for it. She could care less about the doctor or her family. All she wanted were the notes to go to the proper authorities, indicating that she was in therapy and attending the sessions, and she hoped it wouldn't take Dr. Springler all day to write it.

"I see you've decided to skip most of the questionnaire." Caught off guard by the softness of her voice, Sandra's eyes flashed a guarded blue.

"Yeah."

"Okay. I'll ask the questions, and when you answer, I'll fill in the blanks."

"Get it out of my file. I'm sure Dr. Wesley sent it to you." The ice in Sandra's voice threw her off guard, but she tried to stay on track and not agitate her patient too much.

"I don't like following other people's opinions. I like to come up with my own profile and judge the situation from there."

Dr. Springler looked dead into her eyes. She waited to get a flinch or anything to give her an opening, but she got a blank stare in return. "Okay…so…let's start with your date of birth. You left that blank, but surely we can fill that in."

"What is your problem? I said I'm not going to fill in your questionnaire. Do you have anything else on the agenda today, or are we done here?"

Dr. Springler's eyes flicked. She had let the patient take charge of the situation, and she wasn't quite sure how to get the ball back in her court. This was her first year out on her own. Sandra was her first client from a penal institution and her third client in total. She was determined not to fail.

"I have to have something to report to the courts and the state. Those were the conditions of your release. I can't just leave everything blank. Tell me something…anything that we can go on. I'll let you start wherever you want to."

Sandra decided to test her honesty level from the start. She said she hadn't read her file, and that is the same line that Dr. Wesley fed her in the beginning, but she knew he told the truth. He didn't begin to read what the courts had to say about her until they were almost six months into their sessions. She wanted to see just how sincere she was.

"Well, my brother and I robbed convenience stores for five years until we were finally caught."

"Oh, has your brother been released as well?"

Dr. Springler was jotting down notes as she talked, looking very earnest in her work.

"He died in jail last year."

Her head quickly jerked up and her liquid brown eyes beamed into Sandra's.

"I'm so sorry. When did you find out? Just recently, or were you incarcerated at the time?"

She didn't make any rash decisions because she didn't know anything about her. Another honest therapist?

Once again Sandra was stuck and didn't know how to handle the new situation, so she shut down.

The quietness in the room became very unsettling to Dr. Springler. Sandra had gone quiet, and she didn't know how to open her back up. "How long were you in jail?"

"Seven years."

"Did they let you out early for good behavior or was that your original sentence?"

This brought a smile to Sandra's lips, and a childlike sound followed closely behind.

She couldn't remember the last time she'd experienced tightness in her stomach from laughing. Physically, it felt like contracting abs during a workout, but the timing and action was all involuntary. It took a little effort for her to regain her composure, but she finally answered, "No, Dr. Springler. I have no good behaviors." A small but negative shadow crossed over the doctors face, which instantly had Sandra switching moods.

"Oh. Is there anything I should know about—"

"No!"

Sandra then crossed her arms, taking on a defensive pose. She was putting up the barrier again, but not before the next question was aimed at her. "Do you have any other siblings?"

She was starting to lose her composure and didn't know how to gain it back. Everything was slamming into her at once, and her mind began flipping through the channels involuntarily. From Barbara leaving, to having to encounter life on her own so abruptly, snapping was an action close at hand. She didn't want to lose her footing in this office. She needed this lady to write up the proper documents, but no matter what, she could not get a hold of herself. The familiar buzzing came like a vengeance as she rose to her feet.

"What is this, a fucking job interview, or what? I come here for therapy, and you don't know a damn thing about me because if you did, you wouldn't have your Mary Poppins family photos facing me so that I can stare at them my entire session! Learn how to do your damn job! You know what? You should attend one of Dr. Wesley's seminars to find out what a real psychiatrist is supposed to do! Start by reading the file, that's why it was sent to you!"

Sandra smashed every frame on her desk against the bright walls. She couldn't take the confinement anymore. She would not sit in a chair and be picked apart like a specimen.

The secretary ran full steam into Sandra as she entered the room. The elderly lady was startled and bug-eyed by the scene. She had difficulty catching her breath as she clutched the faux strands of pearls at her neck.

Calmly, Sandra patted her on the cheek, leaving a bloody streak just below her jaw line. "It's okay. No need to be alarmed. That's why I'm in therapy."

*

Sandra's head buzzed with the sound of a million voices. She thought it was a good thing at first that the doctor hadn't read her chart, but as she continued to try to figure out her method, she concluded she was just a lazy ass who saw her as an easy check.

"Well, let's see how easy I am now!" Sandra went on a mumbling rampage for over an hour. It wasn't until she had found herself in the dead end of a cul-de-sac that she began to try to regain focus.

She turned around in three circles, trying to get her bearings, but she had no idea where she was. "Fuck!" She walked back to the end of the street, but it yielded no clue as to her location. The stoplights that were practically on every corner by her doctor's office were now missing from where she stood. She continued to look side to side as if a yellow brick road would magically appear, but it did not.

She was so upset with herself that she didn't see the man approaching, until he was right beside her. "Are you looking for a specific address?" He was too close. His breath practically danced across her scalp. Her nerve endings began shooting all over the place.

There was a feel of static electricity flowing up and down her body, running the full course repeatedly. Her fingertips felt as if they were being filled with kinetic energy.

Sandra turned slowly to face him, taking a step back at the same time.

"I'm trying to find the bus route."

"The bus routes? You're more than fifteen blocks off. Is there anything I can help you with?"

"No, I just need the bus route."

"Well, it look as if you need a Band-Aid as well. You have blood all over you hand." She didn't know she had injured herself when she lashed out in the office.

She briefly wondered what Dr. Springler was thinking about her at this moment. "I can let you rinse your hand and give you a Band-Aid."

"I just want to go home." Sandra was looking dazed and out of sorts. She was on full alert but calm at the same time.

"I can give you a lift home or to the bus terminal, if that would help you out."

"Where is your car?"

"Right over there. It's in my garage."

"Okay."

She hated herself for needing a stranger, but she was still mentally out of whack and wanted nothing more than to be in the comforts of her home.

A million things flowed through her head as she watched him turn off the water hose and head for his front door, but she never spoke. "We can go in the garage from the kitchen. I left the opener in the drawer." Like a knight in shining armor, he held the door open, allowing her access to his home and his family's personal belongings, and without a thought, she followed him inside.

Everything was museum-clean and touched with every shade of brown there was. From the foyer to the kitchen there was light tan carpeting with dark chocolate furnishing. Sandra paid no attention to the artwork or accessories lining the shelves. She was not there to decorate, although she would say that his wife needed a little help in that department. She aimed straight for the kitchen and waited beside the back door. A deadbolt without the key stopped her from going straight out to the garage. "You can rinse your hand if you like."

Wordlessly, she turned toward the sink and began rinsing the dried blood from her palm and fingertips. Turning the water off, she felt him once again at her side. His body was pressed slightly against her, and there was no denying the firm object against her hip.

"Here's a towel."

Gently he draped it over her wet hands and proceeded to dry them. Storming signals raged through Sandra's head. The mere idea that he believed she owed him something for letting her rinse off the dried blood, grabbed a hold of her and wouldn't let go. Although, as her subconscious considered it, the thought of her being just an object for him to force his devilish desires upon had her welcoming the new prospect with wicked delight.

She never wanted to go back and relive her past, never wanted to revisit the demonic torture she endured, but life constantly threw her into a situation where she was always standing on the victim end of the stick; but not anymore! Fuck them all! She would no longer play the role picked out for her. She would now play what was and always had been intended for her.

"You are so beautiful." Sandra stared him dead in the face, waiting for the moment. His eyes were closed, while his hips moved rhythmically with Sandra. He wasn't rough with her, nor did he force her to straddle him on the kitchen floor, but she never stopped his advances; in fact, she encouraged him. She allowed him what he wanted with no resistance.

He was supposed to take her home, help her realize that there was someone in this world who looked out for the little people, but instead, he chose to see if he could get his rocks off with her first, use her and then take her home. Hell, he probably wasn't going to offer the ride once he got what he was after, but none of that mattered now. What he was going to do or should have done was of no consequence to her now.

Sandra was in full control and in the moment. She increased the rhythm and squeezed a little tighter with her thighs. His words were no longer coherent and came across as short gasps mixed with gurgles. A light sheen formed around the corners of his mouth casting a moist glare upon his lips. He was ready. His release consumed a large part of his strength, and he would not be able to gain it back instantly.

She managed to quietly pull the empty garbage bag out of the can, jerking it over his head in a matter of seconds. He tried to twist away, but her athletic form kept him planted to the floor. His next line of defense was to throw wild, blinding punches in the air, hoping to land one that would release the plastic from around his head, but she dodged every one while twisting the excess bag under his neck.

His air supply was more than limited. His lungs began tingling in the lower lobes until the pain became more insistent and desperate.

The sheen of sweat swelled and became more pronounced across Sandra's knuckles as she clutched her makeshift weapon with all her might.

He bucked wildly off the floor as his hands grabbed hold of her upper legs, clawing viciously at her flesh. She could feel the stinging as it crawled over her thighs, but she didn't lose focus. She kept her movements swift and deliberate until he went silent.

CHAPTER 51

"This is Dr. Wesley. How can I help you?"

"Hello, this Dr. Springler, the psychiatrist handling the Hansley file." Wesley immediately sat up and looked alert. The hair on the back of his neck swayed with nervousness. It had been a little under a year since he had seen Sandra, and just hearing her name stirred him.

"Yes, Dr. Springler. What can I do for you?"

"Please call me Bridgette. I hope I didn't catch you at a bad time, but I was hoping to discuss a few behavioral issues with you..."

He didn't like the things he was hearing from someone he considered his colleague. Sandra had gone to her office and scared the living daylights out of her. She was requesting his help in any way that he could give it, and he wanted to do nothing more than to help her out. He knew what it felt like to be the new kid on the block, but to have Sandra as one of your first clients must be near earth-shattering. She didn't really go into detail about what it was that had sent her into such a rage, and from the sound of it, she didn't have much of a clue anyway. The only thing she was able to clarify was the fact that Sandra was out walking around without any medication.

"I'm free for the next two days. What part of town are you in?"

"My office is located Pueblo, but I am willing to meet somewhere closer to you. I have a 5:00 appointment, and then I'll be free."

Dr. Wesley felt the jitters take over his speech, causing him to ramble on and on like a man on a first date. He was nervous and excited at the same time. "Okay, let's meet in Denver right off the eighty exit at the Chatter Steakhouse. Can you make it by about seven o' clock? You might run a little later depending on traffic from your side, but I'll leave my name at the front for you."

"Okay, that'll be good. See you soon." She wanted to be able to stand on her own and show the world that you can achieve your dreams if you work hard enough, but when it came down to the bare bones of the situation, she had to admit that she didn't have what it took to help Sandra. She was in way over her head but smart enough to know it.

*

Charles watched as a young, very nervous, but intelligent-looking woman approached his table with a heap of pamphlets and notebooks neatly stacked in her arms. Would they be discussing Sandra so deeply that she need classroom time? Chatter's wasn't exactly a bring-your-work-to-dinner kind of place. If he would have known a little more about what she wanted from him, he might have suggested a pancake-and-coffee kind of establishment. "Bridgette?"

"Yes. Nice to meet you, Dr. Wesley." Charles stood up to help her with her tower of printouts and getting into her chair. She was settled in but obviously had a lot on her mind, and he couldn't wait to hear about it. "Would you like to order something to drink or...."

"Yes, a gin and tonic."

"Wow, you really are wound up."

She smiled in response but immediately started in on the business at hand. "I have talked to Sandra twice so far, once on the phone and very recently in my office. Let me just say there was a significant difference between the two. During our phone encounter she was very brassy and arrogant but closed-up at the same time, whereas the day in my office, she just looked blank whenever I asked her something she didn't want to answer or couldn't answer. No reaction. It was like someone forgot to turn the lights on."

"Did something happen? Is she in a relationship of some sorts?"

"I'm not sure; we haven't really talked about anything like that yet. She doesn't think I am qualified to do so, for one. She was the one who suggested I contact you."

Dr Wesley froze as the waiter arrived at the table. Taking the advice of a patient was the truest sign of being green behind the gills. They are never to direct the flow of therapy, or you could find yourself on the couch, so to speak.

He quickly ordered the cocktails before turning his attention to his companion across the table. "Please tell me she has no idea that we are meeting."

Bridgette looked a little offended by the suggestion but understood his reasoning. "No, of course not. I just wanted your insight on the situation—you know, peek through the window with your eyes. I need some leverage here."

He allowed himself a sip of the warm amber liquid of his drink to soothe the flutters in his stomach. She said she wanted some form of insight, but how much did she really want to know? In some ways he had to be careful about what he said. For him to reveal too much too soon could send her running off with her tail between her legs, and that would definitely not be the best outcome for Sandra.

Dr. Wesley wanted to help her as much as he could, but he must always be professional and put the client first. "So where do we start, Bridgette?"

"Well, Sandra was very explosive when she found out that I had not read her file before seeing her. In the beginning, as I later found out, she started out by lying to me. She told me she had a brother and that they had robbed convenience stores. I jotted down notes and asked a few questions periodically, but basically I figured I would wing it for our first few meetings, and that idea backfired terribly. She had a fit and started throwing things in my office."

"I will be surprised if she comes back for a second visit. With me, she was in a forced kind of environment because of her incarceration, but with you, she could just as easily move on to someone else. I don't see why she would return after that outburst."

Dr. Springler was a little put off by the direct revelation placed before her, but if she was honest with herself, that is why she asked to meet him. She needed to hear another opinion, someone to bounce ideas off of, but more than that, she needed to be prepared for Sandra. Dr. Wesley said she would not return to her office, but if she did, she wanted to be more than equipped for it.

To have a patient throw a tantrum was not out of the ordinary in her field, and in the end it was always better than a patient who chose to draw inside of themselves, but to see someone who was able to display both emotions at the same time was not something she had ever seen in her textbooks. She needed help from someone who had played the field longer than her.

"I was hoping you could shed some light on the situation for me. I mean, have you ever seen these behaviors from her, or am I special? Is she playing mind games with me? Does she just want to control the situation?"

The history of Sandra Hansley was not hard to conjure up in his mind. He had read her file so many times it played smoother than his favorite melody. "Well, so far there's only one thing that you have told me that bothers me."

"What, that she destroyed my office?"

"No. What was her mental state when you saw her last? How long has it been since your initial consultation?"

"Well, she has missed three appointments so far. I was going to call in and report her, but I felt slightly guilty about how everything had turned out, so I would say three weeks."

"Wow!"

Dr. Wesley couldn't believe how naïve Bridgette was, and he couldn't help but think that was one of the reasons she had been chosen by Sandra. She claimed to have read her history the same day that Sandra had torn through her office, but she had let three weeks go by without contacting anyone. Her chart alone should have sent up the red flags when she didn't make her next appointment.

Proper procedure would have been to call the officiating authorities at the courts to send a unit out to do a wellness check. If she couldn't be located at that time, then the reporting officer was to wait forty-eight hours to see if a qualified replacement would notify Dr. Springler indicating that she had taken up therapy with someone else.

Under the court's ruling, they were not allowed to change their therapists more than three times during their entire course of treatment, and they had to stick with the appointments given to them or risk immediate hospitalization or imprisonment and fines. Dr. Springler had followed none of the rules. In the end she may have ended up doing Sandra more harm than good.

He wouldn't stand on a podium and say she was miraculously cured while in his care, but he could say that she had been stabilized. He was able to discontinue all of her medications except the two she was to take for anxiety attacks. If she ever felt like the walls were closing in on her or things were getting out of hand, then the pills would be able to get her to a much calmer state of mind rather quickly. He felt the medication was working well for her. She had only used four to five pills in the last year or so, but after she was released, she may have needed to be placed on a schedule instead of the as-needed arrangement.

She may very well be in need of a refill, and that could be what was causing her rash behavior. The first thing he would recommend is to get her on track with her medications, and then try and follow up from there. "So what medication is she currently on? Did you follow up with the pharmacy to see if she has been getting her refills?"

He was firing questions at her in rapid succession. She wasn't ready to be judged by him. She thought he came to provide insight, not lay her out on the cross to be analyzed. "I never gave her a prescription. I spoke with her for maybe twenty minutes in my office and a five minute conversation on the phone."

"Well, what did the previous doctor prescribe?"

"I don't know."

Dr. Wesley blew out a breath of impatience. She could not be this dense. Sandra would need a new therapist. He had already made his mind up that he would be placing some very much-needed phone calls when he got home. "Don't you have any follow-up notes from the first psychiatrist she saw? Sandra has been out of prison for almost a year. You can't be the first…"

Shock and confusion stopped his babbling tongue. Sandra had not been under any form of therapy since her release? The question in his mind was did she dodge therapy all of this time? Dr. Springler has still to clarify that and if so, why now did she now seek it?

Did she do it because she didn't want to get caught and risk being sent back to prison, or had she finally sought help because things were getting just a little too rough for her? Was she reaching out in some way? Dr. Wesley was more agitated that he cared to admit.

He had no reason to get more involved than being a sounding board for a colleague. He should have simply told her to call Sandra's court officer and take it from there, but instead he jumped in with both feet planted in the rapidly sinking quicksand while his wife's voice boomed in his ear about his commitment to her and how nice their lives had been.

CHAPTER 52

S andra strutted up and down the street like a zombie. She looked totally zoned to the average passerby, but up close you could see the intensely alert look in her eyes. She had been in and out of this area for the last two weeks now, and she felt comfortable with the idea that she knew all she needed to know. She was functioning on an extremely imbalanced mixture of exhaustion and revenge. The walls had more than closed in on her; they had simply tumbled down. Her mornings switched to night without any warning or promise of seeing tomorrow.

When she was able to see herself from the outside, she knew she had lost all touch with reality, but she did not regret it. She was suited for this kind of life, and there was no chance of her trying to turn it back around. She vowed to herself that there would be no more appointments, no more talking to inadequate, undereducated fools! She was her own boss now. She didn't need a textbook or a stuffy suit to tell her that life had screwed her repeatedly since birth; she was living proof of that. Had anyone ever reached out a hand to help her along the way?

She paused briefly at the thought. There was only one person who had tried to be there for her during the bad times and toward the end. She knew Barbara really did care for her, but Sandra had been afraid and mistrustful of her deeper intentions. She'd laughed in her face and mocked her until she'd had enough and pulled the stopper out.

As she explored deeper, she knew her first instinct had always been to put her guard up since the first day she was incarcerated. Being with Barbara was an unknown territory for her and something she was not eager to grab on to.

When Barbara touched her in prison, her first instinct had been to choke the life out of her, but the tenderness she used with her, followed by the newfound warmth that seeped throughout her body, sent her down a different path. Fear. Did she enjoy being touched? Could touching ever be an enjoyable sensation? She had never known a mouth to be so soft. They had always been pressed upon her with such brutal force that her lips were often punctured by her teeth.

With Barbara it was different, new, and something she was very much afraid of. Why did she want to still be around her after what she did? She knew every dark secret of her past and present, but yet she continued to want to be with her. The entire revelation was an experience within itself for Sandra. She didn't know how to address it or even from what angle to start.

"Hey, baby, you looking to score?" Sandra turned and faced the driver of a sleek new BMW. She must have unknowingly been standing in the same spot for quite some time. He coasted on the side of her, waiting on an answer.

"Score what?" The street lingo she had yet to master, which made things a little difficult for what she had in mind.

"What's your flavor, darling? Coke? Meth? Heroin?"

Heroin? The name alone flashed her back to her preteen years, back when she had no idea what the drug was, but now the meaning was all too clear.

"I don't have any money."

The driver put his car in park and turned in the seat to face her. "I know that, honey, but you do have other means of paying for what you want."

Sandra stood on the sidewalk, rubbing her arms up and down like she had seen many of the other women doing. "You have to bring me back here."

"No problem."

The driver leaned over and opened the passenger door. Sandra walked around the back of the car and hoped the Cheshire cat smile that crossed her face was long gone as she climbed into the front seat.

CHAPTER 53

"No, I am not her primary therapist right now, but I was when she was incarcerated. Look, I just need to know her whereabouts."

"Fill out the proper request forms and send them in with a copy of your license and I will try and have the information released to you, but to be honest, I don't see what you have to do with my client in the first place." Dr. Wesley gripped the receiver even tighter, trying to force calmness he didn't feel.

Sandra's court officer was playing hardball with him when the truth of the matter was he had no idea where she was. She could have moved to Timbuktu by now, and he would still be stonewalling him with his thumb up his ass. "This is a matter of urgency, sir. I need the information of her last known address."

"That may well be, but I have a job to do mister…"

"It's Dr. Wesley. You can download my profile from the institutional website, and I will fax you a copy of my identification, but I need you to jump on this information for me immediately."

"Once again, when I get what I need, you'll get what you want. Until then, have a nice day, doctor."

Officer Allen leaned back in his chair clamping his hands behind his head. He would get whatever documents he desired as soon as he returned from vacation. Right now his only focus was the Las Vegas Poker Tournament that has been calling his name all week, and he didn't want to think about anything else. It's not like the guy was her primary doctor anyway, so what did he want with her personal information? Officer Allen gave it about ten more seconds of thought before dismissing the entire situation. There was a lot of that behind bars. Falling in love with your patient… the story was as old as history itself.

*

Charles paced the living room back and forth, brimming with frustrating. How the hell could this have happened? Where was the continuity of care? Something had to be done! Sandra could have already taken a turn for the worse, or she could very well be headed in the wrong direction and seeking help. Anything was possible at this moment. Dr. Wesley was more than anxious to find the right answers. He began calling one number after the next, throwing his name and position around in hopes of shaking an olive from its branch. Nothing.

Beyond the point of control, he slammed the phone down, cracking its entire base and sending it crashing to the floor. "What's going on?"

Charles turned to see his wife watching him. "Sandra's missing!"

Instantly fear registered across her face, swiftly imbedding itself in her eyes. Her mind had quickly skimmed its way through the family, coming to rest on her great-aunt Sandra Mae. "What! What do you mean missing? When was the last time anyone saw her?"

"I don't know. No one seems to have any answers."

"Well, she couldn't have just vanished into thin air, Charles. We have to find her. Does Renee know how long she's been gone? She lives the closest to her."

"Renee?"

"Yes. She moved near her about three months ago. Who called you?"

Charles quickly regretted opening his mouth. He was so caught up in the moment that he didn't take the time to think first. Diane would turn it into a "me against the world" argument if he wasn't able to sidestep her. "I don't know who was on the phone, actually. They sounded a little hysterical and said, 'Sandra's missing.' I automatically connected that to be your aunt Sandra, but maybe I'm reading too much into this. We should definitely call Renee before we decide to send out the search party."

Diane looked down at the broken phone and then up at her husband. He was visibly agitated, and at the time she was, too, but she felt something wasn't right. She knew when Charles wasn't being totally honest with her, and this definitely marked one of those times.

"I'll use the phone in the bedroom to call Renee." Charles stated. He ran his hands across his face, exhaling his pent-up frustration.

"Why?"

He turned to see his wife watching him from the doorway.

"Why what? We have to find out what's going on and what that mystery phone call was all about."

"Stop! Stop it Charles! You're talking to me as if I'm stupid or as if I haven't spent the best years of my life learning exactly who you are. I was so caught up in fear for my aunt that it didn't immediately register to me at the time that I never heard the phone ring. You've been in here making calls since you came home, but instead of talking to me and telling me what was really going on, you chose to lie to me. I don't think I need to tell you how that makes me feel…we've been down that road before."

Charles knew he was supposed to say something, react in some kind of way, but nothing happened. His mind was so consumed with the lack of progress he had made in finding Sandra, that his wife's feelings became a secondary notion.

He was the kind of doctor who liked to follow through. What was so wrong with that? He wasn't about to explain.

The more the incident ran through his mind, the more he convinced himself that his wife should be on a need-to-know basis and nothing more. It didn't matter that she was his wife. Patient confidentiality would always take precedence with him and this was nothing more than him trying to help a patient.

"Don't pull out the violin so soon, Diane. I haven't done anything wrong. As a matter of fact, I did receive a call from a colleague of mine stating that Sandra was missing. I was simply making a few follow-up calls, but I kept running into dead ends, and it ticked me off a little. That's all."

Charles was talking as if he were giving an opening statement at a trial, but he was very convincing when he needed to be. He knew he had just gotten over the hurdle and back into her good graces not too long ago. He didn't need another breakdown like the one they went through when Sandra was a client of his. Diane was the glue that held his sanity together, and he needed her.

"You deliberately allowed me to believe that you were talking about my aunt."

"No, you made that assessment all on your own. You didn't give me a chance to tell you who I was talking about. I was going on about one person, and you were thinking of another. Our signals got crossed, and to read more into it than that would be a mistake we can't afford."

She wanted to ask the question of why he told he was going to go and call Renee if their signals had just gotten crossed, but she didn't. She did feel as though she jumped to conclusions when he said Sandra was missing, and given the chance to catch his breath, he might have come clean.

The name Sandra rang a bell as an old case of his, and if she was correct, it was one that had totally consumed him, but it was an old one nonetheless. Someone had called him, and he got a little upset, nothing more, Charles didn't normally go looking for trouble.

CHAPTER 54

S andra glanced back over her shoulder one last time before closing the door with a gloved hand. She was physically sore inside and out. The driver of the car who later called himself Big Rick turned out to be more than the downright bastard she had taken him for. He pulled into the hotel parking lot, which relaxed Sandra slightly because for what she had in mind, she didn't want it to be an outside episode like the cowboy.

He told her to wait in the car while he went to pay for the room, and she chalked it up to him being embarrassed by the company he was with. She hadn't paid attention to see if he really went into the office or not. She sat patiently in the car, mentally going over her inventory in her plastic bag.

This was a major step for her in a new direction, and she didn't want to mess up. She was knowingly and without any form of persuasion going to take another person's life. She felt thrilled to know that she was in charge of her actions. She didn't hear the buzzing in her ears or a voice in the back of her head. This was all her, and she was exhilarated. When the real desire to pull something like this had come to her, she didn't know, but she had no intention of disregarding it.

She had been wronged several times over, and no matter what she did, it just continued to happen. She had never considered herself a victim since the day she had taken care of her mother and Bill, and there was nothing more important to her than proving that.

The tap on the glass made her nearly jump out of her skin. Big Rick stood outside of the car, waiting on her. Sandra carefully rolled her bag up and got out of the car. "All set?"

"I need to get paid first."

She knew from watching and listening to the women in the area he picked her up from that this was the way they talked. They said to always get your money first or you might find that you had been screwed twice by the same man. She wanted him to think nothing more than he had picked up a drug whore, so it was very important that she came across as knowledgeable in her craft.

"You'll get paid, bitch, as soon as we get inside. I don't do business in the streets."

Well, surprise, surprise. The smiling gentleman just jerked the personality meter all the way to complete and utter asshole. He had already sealed his fate, and at that time Sandra could care less about what he said. She had turned on a mode that brought a calmness over her, increasing her focus level. She was very, very ready.

They entered the room in total darkness. He stopped at the doorway and pushed Sandra further into the space. A new sense instantaneously overwhelmed her, one she was not prepared to come to terms with but knew existed. The fear she felt caused her palms to itch furiously, but she ignored it. Her first instinct, which came naturally, was the fight or flight response. She knew she should listen to it, but the desire to kill Big Rick was too strong. She sidestepped all of the warnings and ventured further inside.

Her nerves caused her knees to shake slightly, and her bag all but slipped from her grasp when the buzzing began. It came so fiercely she jumped literally off of her feet.

She felt herself relaxing and letting it take over. The power of it soothed her, and she was no longer afraid. The room was filled with violence and manipulation. She would not be able to face it alone, and she was thankful she didn't have to.

"This bastard will pay dearly for what he tried to do to us. He is the scum of the earth, and he needs to be taken care of. Do your job, Sandra!"

Sandra wasn't the least bit surprised to find two additional men in the room. They were sitting on the bed as the light came on. The driver slammed the door behind himself, announcing, "It's time to play, boys!" He had no idea how precisely right he was. It was indeed time.

*

Sandra had not cried deeply since the age of twelve, but filled with an incomprehensible void, she let out the most gut-wrenching sound imaginable. It manifested from the bottom of her soul and poured itself out through her eyes. She clumsily held onto her bathroom sink to keep from falling. Her very being was crumbling beneath her. She began to choke so violently that her chest burned like a fire running through her body, until Sandra could hold on no more and collapsed on the floor.

CHAPTER 55

B arbara typed quickly at the keyboard, enjoying the feel of it beneath her fingertips. She had been working temp jobs since she left Sandra five months ago. The dentist she was now working for had his own private office and was desperate for help. His wife had been working side by side with him for years until she decided she wanted to start a family.

Six months into her pregnancy, she was placed on bed rest, which left open a prime position for Barbara. He didn't ask her very many questions at the interview, and since she could type, answer the phone and she had a good outward appearance, the job was hers. The work wasn't hard, and the hours weren't long. Barbara kept to herself and didn't ask very many questions. She knew she was still acting as if she was locked up, but she couldn't help it.

She found a small one-bedroom apartment, and she was happy with the arrangements. She missed and worried about Sandra daily, but she knew she had to try to focus on herself. Visions of seeing Sandra's body tormented her dreams, leaving her frustrated and exhausted most nights, and not being able to actually see her drowned her spirits, but she had to push forward and keep going. If Sandra had bothered to get a phone installed was a mystery within itself.

"Excuse me. Are you Barbara Whittler?

She looked into a pleasant set of eyes and felt that she should know the person, but she didn't. "Yes?"

In an earlier time she would have been the one to open the conversation, but now she never answered more than what was asked.

"How are you doing? I'm Dr. Charles Wesley."

He made this grand announcement as a smooth, well-manicured hand was extended her way. Dr. Wesley. *The* Dr. Wesley! Oh shit, oh shit, oh shit! Her mind instantly ran to the night with the cowboy, and she hoped like hell she was holding her composure. Somehow he must have connected the homicide to Sandra, and he had come there to question her about her part in the whole ordeal.

Her mind was running and processing faster than the PC she was working on. Dr. Wesley took the seat across from her, adjusting his slacks, she briefly wondered where the police were. Why didn't he have an escort? Something didn't feel right about his whole pop-up visit. Sandra had taught her well. She had nothing to say to him but prepared to listen very closely.

Charles didn't know where to start. He had to play his authority role to the best of his ability and not come across as desperate as he felt. He came for answers, and he wasn't leaving without getting them. "So I see you are current with all of your parole appointments. Staying on the right path makes that a plus, right?" He let out a nervous laugh that set Barbara on edge. Why was he acting like this? She now felt that he had come to tell her that something was wrong with Sandra but didn't know how to get around to it. "What is this all about?"

"Yes, well, the reason I am out in your area today is the connection you have with Sandra Hansley."

"Connection?"

"You guys were a little more than friendly, if my memory serves me right."

"Did Sandra tell you that?"

She hated herself for asking the question, but she desperately wanted to know if Sandra ever considered her to be more than just helpless Barbara.

"No, she didn't say that, but rumors travel fast, as you well know. I am wondering if you have seen or heard from Sandra since her release."

"And when was that?"

Dr. Wesley leaned back and looked intently at the woman he was sitting across from. She seemed impossible to penetrate, almost as if she was protecting Sandra, but from what? Or who? "Come on, Ms. Whittler. Let's not play games here, okay?"

"Look, Dr. Wesley, I don't think you're here on official business in any capacity, so let's cut to the chase. What do you want?"

It was his turn to feel uneasy at this point. He didn't know what to do or say. He wasn't even sure if coming here was a good idea now that he was finding himself on the other end of the interrogation. In all actuality, he was ready to just walk out the door and leave Dr. Springler with her own problems.

Barbara didn't blink as she stared at him. He had tracked her down for a reason. Something obviously had come up about Sandra, but from what she could tell, it was nothing major. There weren't any lights blazing or orders being barked, but he wasn't there for nothing. She wanted to extract some information from him and at the same time remain distant. "Dr. Wesley, is there something I should know?"

Charles decided to give her something in order to get something. She knew Sandra just as well as he did—hell, probably even better. He saw no reason not to tell her the truth of his visit.

"Well, Sandra's new therapist got a hold of me, stating that Sandra's behavior is off the charts, so to speak. She trashed her office on their first visit, and hasn't returned. It concerned me enough to try to locate her and see what, if anything, I could do. No one seems to know where she is, and she hasn't checked in with her court officer either, so that's kind of what led me to you. You were much easier to find."

Jail was the last place she wanted to see again, so she did check in frequently for every move she made before she made it. She wouldn't return to a life of fear simply from not being accounted for. The fact that Sandra had not checked in at all was news to her because that was their number-one plan after they moved. She'd wanted to get her on the right track, and Sandra had agreed at the time.

She'd never mentioned trying to see another therapist, and Barbara couldn't help but wonder if the argument they'd had triggered her to go seek help. But if so, then why the explosion in the office? Why the change in behavior? The doctor must have done or said something that irritated Sandra. She always lashed out when she found herself being cornered or if she felt she was being forced to do something that she had no desire to do.

From what she was hearing, Sandra was all over the map emotionally, and Barbara blamed herself. She knew what kind of unstable creature Sandra was, but at the same time when she couldn't or wouldn't provide her with the kind of relationship she desired, she'd walked out on her, leaving her to fend for herself.

Sandra had never lived alone or had to deal with the ordinary humdrum of the world everyone else was accustomed to, but Barbara had to admit that she did give it a good try most of the time. She refused to let her mind wander to the what-ifs of Sandra, especially now. Dr. Wesley was tearing her apart layer by layer with his specific wording and twisting of sentences. She had to get rid of him and take some time to think.

If Sandra needed her, there was no way she wouldn't help, but she had to make sure that that was what was going on and not that the system was trying to trap her for a minor misdemeanor. "Well, your guess is as good as mine,

Dr. Wesley. I haven't seen Sandra since my release date. It's not like we live together."

He chewed up her words, placed and calculated them swiftly. The fact that she said "live together" raised his antenna. He had never asked her that. He phased the questions in a way to see if they have had any form of contact with each other, but she had just supplied more than he had bargained for. Without a doubt she had seen Sandra, and more than likely they were living together now.

He had no time to change the line of questioning; he knew she would pick up on it. Her body language alone let him know that she was bringing the conversation to a close. He would have to find out about Sandra another way. "Well, I must say I am glad to see that you have stayed on the right track, Barbara, and I really do hope the same for Sandra. You know as well as I do that she needs constant therapy. She has been able to keep herself into a calm state of mind, but I don't think she is experiencing that right now."

With that said he stood up; giving her his business card. "My personal cell number is on the back. If you hear from her, please give me a call."

Barbara skeptically took the card. She felt as if she was being drawn into a web, with no clear notion of how to escape.

Dr. Wesley parked down the street for the next hour or so. He knew that if she did know where Sandra was, she would find a way to get to her instantly or place a call to have Sandra come to her.

Time ticked away as dusk became the back drop of the day. Barbara hadn't made a move, and he was feeling embarrassed and a little stupid. He was chasing a ghost that didn't want to be found. He had a wife at home who was beginning to worry about his own mental stability, yet he sat stalking someone who had nothing, in any way, to do with him. He had to get a handle on the situation and himself. He couldn't continue to jump into situations so deep that he couldn't paddle out of them. Feeling like the world's biggest jackass, he pulled off with his wife on his mind.

He was all out of excuses. Why was he really hunting down Sandra? Was it the fear of failing? The idea of having his name associated with a loose cannon? No, it was more than that, and he knew it. This wouldn't be the first time he dove headfirst into such an unorthodox case.

During his earlier at a private office, years before working at Windsor, he found himself close to being terminated with his license permanently revoked. He had drifted into the role of more than just a therapist to Latoya Morales. He began believing the vivid imaginations that twisted and blurred in her mind. When she came to him as a patient, her file stated she was being released from prison after serving eight years for the murder of her husband. The details of the crime weren't that gruesome, and according to the court document, she continued to plead self-defense throughout the trial.

As he treated her, not once did he take notice on how increasingly seductive her clothing became or how inappropriately their conversations continued to drift as time went on. His marriage had once again hit a state of vulnerability due to his cases and their multiple unsuccessful attempts to become pregnant. No clinic could seem to help them with their problem, and they began to drift apart. She was going through the phase where she wanted to be alone and wallow in her own self-doubt, so he slept on the couch for over two months. Charles considered himself a patient man by far, but sixty days without the feel of your wife was enough to drive a sane man crazy.

It seemed as if Latoya knew his struggles from deep within and fed on them. One day she arrived ten minutes early for her appointment only to find him lounging on one of the sofas designed for family meetings. She eased into his office unbeknownst to him and planted a kiss so softly yet tenderly upon his lips that he never opened his eyes or gave what he was about to do a second thought. He simply pulled her on top of him, allowing her to feel the need inside of him growing uncontrollably. She only had two sessions left with him, and would no longer be under his care. She passed all his tests, hadn't she? Truly she was rehabilitated. Or so he thought.

On her knees, she exposed to him a breast just right for suckling, and he was eager to oblige. She mounted him swiftly, and Dr. Wesley was so totally lost in his urgent needs that the consistent chant she spoke was lost on him. It wasn't until the start of round two where things went very wrong. To look down and see himself being fondled by one of his patients sent a nauseating jolt to his very core. As he was dragging her off of him, he knew he had just flushed the last eleven years of his life down the drain.

It didn't help matters any when his secretary entered the room because of the loud shrieks Latoya forced out. The scene was ugly: panties on the floor, his pants down low enough to reveal himself, and Latoya screaming, "My doctor raped me!"

She quickly and repeatedly declined the secretary's offer to call the police. She simply leaned over, wiped her mouth with his shirt, and left.

He took an immediate leave of absence, wanting to avoid eventually being handcuffed at the office. After two weeks of silence, he wrote a letter to her parole officer that cleared her from therapy, and thankfully, he never ran across her again. He wished the next man luck and never thought any more about it, except when Diane brought it up occasionally.

He confessed to her as soon as he bolted in the door from the office that day. He later realized it was definitely not the best thing to have done, considering he was judged by that incident frequently. If he so much as mentioned a client more than once Diane's radar would go into overdrive.

Charles didn't know if he was trying to test his internal restraint when he took the position at the prison, but somewhere within himself he wanted to find out what went wrong in the Morales case. Was it just a fluke, or was he really vulnerable to women in need?

For the first four years he was on staff there, he sailed his way through. There were a few times he found himself mildly stimulated behind his desk, but that's exactly where he stayed...behind the desk.

Female inmates would resort to all sorts of things when they were in the presence of men. Some of the guards fell prey to their seduction and quickly became unemployed husbands and fathers.

Even with a guard outside of his office door and the two-way mirror, they would flash him or begin to masturbate right in front of him, but there was a panic button installed for him, and he would press it long before the moaning began.

CHAPTER 56

*T*he length of time she had been on the couch watching the night become delicately submissive to the day or how many times the cycle repeated itself was lost to her. She felt so drained that getting up to face another day of the garbage that flooded the streets of every corner, in every corporate office and planted itself at the head of the table of the most devoted Christian families was almost inconceivable...but not quite.

One day she knew this would be all over and she would meet her demise head on, but until then, she felt a sense of profound obligation to destroy the men who preyed on women in need, the ones who took advantage of women who were just looking for a little help, someone to assist them through a difficult part in their life or a troubling situation.

For every soul-sucking leech she ran across, Sandra vowed to take him swiftly to meet his maker. There was no regret to be had in her quest for vengeance. Did they ever regret? How about the many men who sinfully sought pleasures in the touch of their own daughter's flesh? Did they ever regret? Did the fear in her eyes register in his mind as he sat pompously across the table from a wife he no longer desired to touch?

Sandra allowed her life to play in front of her like a continuous reel until she felt the kinetic energy begin to resurface inside. She went into the bathroom and lingered in the shower until the hot water ran cold. Finding something to wear was not a problem. She donned the same outfit every night.

There was nothing different about her routine. The women who walked the "red zone" never complained about her being in their territory, considering she was more than eager to take the troublemaking johns nobody else wanted or who they were afraid of. Even the routine clients who came by and gave the women a hard time were right up Sandra's alley.

On slow nights, they would tell stories of being raped with foreign objects or beaten or having men slam themselves so viciously into their mouths that a few of them ended up with tonsillitis or torn mucus membranes.

Sandra always knew when one of the worse apples came onto the scene because the women would begin disbursing and acting busy, and they wouldn't approach the car. That was all Sandra needed to see in order to justify her next move.

Some of the women began to notice that the worst of the batch never returned, and they began to look at Sandra in a different light, almost in a hero-worship fashion. She was brave enough to approach them, and obviously fierce enough where they wouldn't return. A few tried to get friendly, but Sandra would pretend to drift off into her zombie mode as if she were high. There were only two things she wanted them to know about her: her name was Cyndi, and she was a drug user. Anything else was of none of their concern.

*

When her body became numb from the shower, she emerged, dried off, and then faced the mirror to apply brown eyeliner under her eyes, smearing it in to appear as if she hadn't slept in days. She used the lightest shade of foundation the store sold so on first glance (which was all most of them gave the women anyway) she came across as undernourished and weak. The lipstick she kept bold and bright, taking her appearance to an even paler and shallower height.

Sandra slowly pulled the worn halter dress over her head while the rest of her attire was placed on in a mechanical way. She put on her dirty, worn gym shoes last. They were actually new, but she'd kicked them around in the dirt before putting them on. She didn't want old shoes to be a reason why she wasn't able to run if she ever had to.

Her appearance was what the men liked to prey on. She appeared desperate and docile at the same time, and if the streetlight hit her just right, she even looked innocent.

With a baggy long-sleeved jacket on over her dress, no one could see the solid definition of her biceps and forearms. Her shoulders could easily take the heft of an object three times her size if it ever became necessary to lift and move someone. Her quads, core, and shoulders would all work in sync to accomplish whatever needed to be done.

She never slacked on her workouts no matter how fatigued she became. Staying fit was her top priority. She knew it could be the difference between life or death for her, and she would be damned if one of those predators got the best of her.

She checked herself once more in the mirror, proud of the transformation. Needing no keys and fearing no one, Sandra pulled the door closed and left the house with her back slumped over in the perfect slouch to enhance the appearance of it all.

She made her way to the back of the house, cutting through overgrown fields that would take her three blocks away from the bus terminal.

Sandra sat patiently at the bus stop and picked at the bugs that clung to her socks. She allowed no more thoughts to enter her mind when she was in transformation, which actually was a blessing When she would sit at home, tired from a day out, she would always wonder if she should do it again or just walk away while she was still free, but then the buzzing would start up right along with the voices. They would call her a coward and make her get up off the couch and do their bidding.

She had no control over the noise or the voices; it was as if they ruled her body and she was just allowed to borrow it from time to time. If she didn't move when they said move, then she would get no rest. The hissing would be in constant battle with the buzzing, and she would do just about anything to make it stop. The constant reminder that she had a job to do and a role to play was a daily nag. All day every day it would antagonize her until she picked up the eyeliner. Transformation took place, and it brought silence.

Outside, she had to stay alert and on her toes but stay visibly blank at the same time. As the bus neared, Sandra instinctively reached for the bag that she always carried with her, and for the first time in her adult life she was visibly shaken. Frantically, she looked on the ground and behind the bench but found nothing. The doors to the bus opened, and this time the wildness her eyes was not rehearsed. She needed her bag. It had become an extension of herself, and she didn't want to move without it.

"Are you getting on, ma'am?" The driver was a little more patient with her because he knew her to be a regular. It wasn't hard for him to know a drug addict when he saw one. His sister had been strung out for the last fifteen years. "Come on now. People will get upset if I wait any longer." Her decision was made. Without looking back, Sandra boarded the bus.

Her first three hours in the zone went by in a blur. Sandra was very unsettled, and unfocused. Men were continually pulling over for her, but she was unorganized. She knew she had to make the choice of either getting her act together or going back home to regroup. She couldn't afford to half-step while she was out there. It could mean the difference between walking away and coming out on the losing end.

Focus, Sandra. Focus. The clarity that she needed was not there. Her mind wandered senselessly over the smallest things and refused to cooperate with her. She just couldn't do it. Everything came and passed in waves, giving her a feeling of vertigo. There was no use in her just standing around; she had to retreat. She looked down the street one last time, declaring to every man out looking for a good time that he should feast well tonight and pray he didn't run into her tomorrow.

"Hey, hey, hey! Where are you going? I've been honking for damn near five minutes. I had to pull over and get out!" Sandra didn't know she was being addressed as "the horse," so she continued on to the bus stop and home where she could use her familiar surroundings to get a hold of herself. She was crumbling internally. She knew that, but could she quit? She would have to think hard about what she was going to do. It was extremely difficult for her to hold a train of thought, but she had to try. If she was beginning to stray from her pattern, then she may very well be putting herself at risk. She had to do better than the rate she was going at. It was either all or nothing.

"Are you seriously trying to ignore me? See, you're the type that needs a man to put you in your damn place." He grabbed Sandra roughly by the arm, spinning her around to face him. "I've seen you around here for a while, looking as though you own the street or something, but I can break that arrogant shit right out of you. From now on you'll answer to me and only me unless I say different. Understand?"

Sandra continued to give him a blank look, which infuriated him. He had women who bowed down and feared him from one end of Marshall Avenue to the next. For him to run across Sandra acting as if she didn't even have the slightest clue who he was brought him to a point he chose not to ignore. "Get your motherfucking ass over here!"

Roughly, he pulled her into the alley, causing her to nearly sprain her ankle. They were in the garbage lane for all the stores that faced the other street, and it had that same hint of decaying fish and urine as the dumpster she was behind with the cowboy.

Once in the dark, he slapped her so viciously across the mouth that her lip split instantly.

"You see, bitch, this is what you need. You hear me now, don't you?

Sandra snapped out of the state she was in as the buzzing became demandingly insistent. She had shut herself off from what was going on around her, and now to be humiliated and treated like trash was too much. She had actually been rethinking the whole idea of being out today. She didn't know how much longer she could go on.

She hadn't suffered such rapid spells of anxiety when she was in prison. Maybe she should have committed some small-scale crime to have extended her sentence. She was deeply into her new persona, but it didn't put her at ease.

"Don't be a coward now! You know who and what we are! There are no social tea parties for us. We eliminate crime! Your face should be on the damn wall of fame! No one but us has been able to see these vultures for who and what they truly are, and we cannot abandon that! They think we are weak, and this is why they slither our way!. They see us as less than human, something placed on earth to wipe their feet upon, but day by day we reveal ourselves and watch them squirm and beg for mercy! You cannot walk away from who we are. They made us this way, so give them what they're asking for!"

These men had picked her for some reason. This was to be her calling; her sole reason for existence. Sandra's unstable capacity gave up on trying to find another way. She began to fully embraced this new revelation.

"He thinks we are some common street whore he can push around! He has no idea who we are or what we are capable of! Cut his fucking head off and spit down his throat! Castrate this bastard!"

Sandra was furious. Once again she hadn't done anything for him to display the amount of hatred toward her that he had, but there was a reason he was in front of her: to be killed. She would take full credit for what she was about to do, and then she could rest. They would handcuff and process her in no time, and she would be back where she started. All she had to do...

"Return to prison to live like a caged animal? We are needed here and now! We are not a victim. We are heroes! He is not worth a second thought. None of them are! Do what must be done!"

Yes, the voice was right, of course. This incident was exactly why she did the things she did. Men found pleasure in being the rulers of women, and she didn't think she would ever see the day when it would be any different. There wouldn't be a day when their off button would come into effect and they'd begin to rethink the avenue they have traveled on or for once consider a woman's feelings.

She remembered several women in prison were there for murdering their spouses or lovers, some in vicious attacks, some in more subtle ways, but she never blamed them or looked at them any differently, knowing that whatever the circumstances, they deserved it.

Sandra was fierce in her conviction but growing very tired. How could she solve the problems of the world? One man at a time? Impossible. No matter how many men she became responsible for eliminating, there was always another and another who needed to meet the same justice. But she was just one woman. She would need a tribe or an entire village of women to bring down such putrid men.

Her mind was no longer trying to help her figure out the next steps or her next move; for the last couple of months she had been operating on autopilot. Sandra had a routine, and it worked. She had no idea if she held the strength or the capability to change now. For who? It was all so exhausting.

Her gag reflex brought her squarely back to the situation at hand as she realized her assailant had a handful of her hair and was roughly trying to thrust himself down her throat. She began to choke and almost vomit.

Pebbles from the pavement embedded themselves into her knees, which became unbearably painful. Sandra had not made her mind up if she would die for the cause or let the cause die. She would try to think on it a little later, but what she did know right now is that this makeshift pimp had reached his expiration date.

She maliciously calculated his next thrust as he lay his head back against the brick wall. She waited until more than half his manhood was engulfed before clamping her teeth. She never imagined how tough the sheath of muscle was until that moment. She pressed and pressed until she felt her teeth meet and began shaking her head and pulling backwards like a delusional pit bull. His screams could be heard for blocks as he punched her furiously across her head with his fist until seconds later he passed out.

Sandra continued to dismember his now flaccid manhood with the strength of her jaws and teeth. She was enraged beyond any measure, and she wanted the world to know it. She gathered no second thoughts or remorse as she used the switchblade that dislodged from his pocked to slice his throat.

Sandra had no gloves on or a change of clothes, and people were beginning to come out the back of the restaurants to investigate the commotion. She had nothing to cover herself with, so she ducked her head and ran. She used the adrenaline, her athleticism, and hopes of not being caught to carry her to the field by her house, where she collapsed from exhaustion.

*

Barbara wondered if Dr. Wesley was following her himself or having her followed, so she took a slow and deliberate route home; stopping at the grocery store, filling up her car, and even going so far as to get a pedicure, ensuring that she was not trailed. Her first instinct was to go flying to Sandra's house and lay it all on the line, doing whatever it took to get her back on track but her insecurities got the best of her midway through her plans, which led Barbara straight to the front door of her own apartment.

She sat on the couch, chewing her nails, for more than an hour. What could she do? She couldn't call. There wasn't a phone installed in the house. Barbara now regretted not handling such a mundane task before they moved in, and she was more than sure that Sandra hadn't gone out of her way to get one. Barbara continued to weigh the pros and cons to decide if she really wanted to step back over the threshold with Sandra again.

Did she think she could endure the heartache and sacrifice it took to be near her? She had gotten along so well these last few months…no stress, no worries. She went to work, came home, ate, and more often than not would turn to the workout channel and get twenty to thirty minutes of cardio in. She wished she could have stayed more diligent in her workouts and been able to keep up with the routines Sandra had her accustomed to when they were in prison, but it just wasn't in her genetic makeup to exercise for two vigorous hours in addition to five hundred abdominal crunches on a daily basis.

Barbara continued to rethink everything they had been through together and how Sandra had basically saved her life in prison. She would have never made it through that ordeal without her, but did that mean she had to continue to stick her neck out for the rest of her life? Did she owe her for all eternity? She didn't know if she had enough gusto for another setback. Dealing with Sandra could be mentally draining and tedious on many different levels, but at the same time, there were good days.

She could easily smile at the day Sandra tried to make a cappuccino in the espresso machine and all the foam splattered on her face or the day she'd thought she stopped up the tub and went and gathered up all her belongings only to return to an empty bubble nest. She got in the tub and for the life of her couldn't figure out where the water had gone.

There were many occasions where Barbara found herself walking Sandra through the most simplistic of situations, baby-stepping the entire way, and at this moment she was at war with herself, trying to gauge if it was worth doing all over again.

*

Sandra made it to her house, limping and dragging herself on wobbly legs. She plopped on the sofa, full of jitters unable to move. Minutes ticked away to hours as the blood on her hands and arms began to dry. Dazed and out of sorts, she found herself peeling the flakes off one by one, creating a translucent burgundy pile at her feet.

Night had turned to day, yet she did not sleep or move from the couch. Exhaustion came into play but was easily disregarded. She was numb and confused. Her mind refused to either replay the past hours of her life or focus on what her immediate future should be, so she just sat slumped there, emotionless, transfixed on her hands.

*

She could hear the footsteps long before they landed at the front door. Her sense that she was in danger was the first bodily function to return. It alerted her, demanding that she respond to its source. She heard the car easing its way up her drive sixty seconds before it came to a stop.

They had come for her. They followed the blood trail and the witness statements until they reached the end of the rainbow. She felt cornered, betrayed, and furious at the same time. It was finally going to end.

Trying to right the wrongs of mankind would now rest on someone else's shoulders. If she didn't see it, then she wouldn't have to deal with it, and that's how she had been content enough in prison. They were no outside distractions, no need of making everything right or seeking revenge in every man who had wronged her.

On borrowed time, Sandra calmly accepted her fate. She hadn't done so bad. She had rid the world of eleven highly deserving scumbags. She would let society do the rest. She was only one person, and that was not enough to start the fight, let alone win the war. But why should she surrender when her survival instincts told her otherwise? Why should she be cast out from society while allowing vile predators to remain free? Where was the justice in that? Where did the law come into play when the innocent or misguided needed to be protected? They failed them continuously! And why? Because the world had conceded that men were the rulers of all things and may manipulate and dispose of them as they wished?

Well, they would not dispose of her! She was not going out without taking a few more with her! The next time a man met a lady named Sandra, be it at work or in a bar, he would think twice before proceeding, and that was glory enough to take to the grave. Men would remember that at one time or another, a woman held power over their lives. Their next breath was solely at her discretion, and quite often she made it their last! Yes! A legacy of sorts. She would be the one to interrupt dreams instead of being scared to sleep. The media would cover her story for days, and she would smile sinfully for the camera. It was her time, and she decided to end it on her terms!

Sandra was exhilarated. She let an unguided excitement take control of her that made her eyes dance and her feet move quickly into action. Before the knock could sound at the door, she retrieved a large butcher knife and removed her shoes, standing alert at the door. Quietly, she turned the lock mechanism to the vertical position, unlocking it.

She figured if she didn't answer soon, they would try the door. Men felt they owned everything, so without a doubt her house was included.

Sandra backed into the corner and waited. The opportunity would present itself, and she would not falter. The knocking stopped, but the threat remained. Sandra could sense it, almost smelled it through the solid wood frame of the door. They were still out there, and she couldn't afford a mistake.

Her eyes focused entirely on the knob as she noticed the twisting motion that took place. The handle took a sudden and direct turn to the right while the door simultaneously opened. Sandra's back was fully arched. Her toes held slight cramps from carrying her weight for the last six minutes or so. Her triceps stayed pulled and tucked over her head as she prepared to bury the entire blade into the back of the intruder.

She would wait for them to take two steps inside, and she knew that would be her perfect opportunity to strike. Their lungs should begin to fill with blood as soon as they were punctured. Every strike thereafter would be swift and calculated. This was a totally different killing compared to the others. They all deserved to die, but if she were to kill the detective who was at the door, what did that make her? An animal just the same? It seemed as if this killing would eliminate the meaning for the others. It made her briefly wonder if she would be able to lay in jail content with the things she had done, or if this moment would haunt her. Would it take away all the wrong that she made right? Sandra was losing her edge. Her drive to get rid of the unwelcomed guest was dissipating at such an alarming rate until she wasn't sure if she should kill the person on the other side of the door.

She wanted to be able to get away without having to harm them or get caught, but how? How could she get out of the corner without being seen? If she moved now, she would be detected quite easily, so she waited. Sandra would have to see how the cards presented themselves.

"Sandra?"

It was not a man's voice, but it was still unexpected.

"Sandra?"

She could now see the back of Barbara's head as she entered the house. She took seemingly cautious steps inside, and she didn't close the door behind her. It was as if she was frightened to enter. Sandra remained hidden and confused. What was she doing here? Was she here to trap her somehow? Had the police sent her? She watched as Barbara crossed the room and entered the kitchen. She took small steps in looking for Sandra, but didn't seem as if she really wanted to find her. "Hello, stranger." Sandra kicked the front door closed and locked it.

Barbara jumped nearly a foot, sending the dishes on the counter clattering to the floor.

"Sandra! Oh shit, you scared me!"

"Did I? Well, imagine my surprise when I heard someone entering my house unannounced."

She crossed the room with the knife in her hand, but held down low, and stood right in front of Barbara.

"What are you doing? Why are you looking at me like that, and why do you have that knife?"

Sandra couldn't answer the question of how she looked. She knew she had been sitting in the same position since she arrived home. She hadn't so much as taken a drink of water, as she now realized the thirst that consumed her. But how she appeared at the moment wasn't relevant to the current situation.

Barbara was considered an intruder at this point. She had stormed out of the door and left her, but she still felt as if she had the right to just enter the house? No. She'd just showed up out of the blue as if she belonged, but she didn't!

Sandra raised the knife to Barbara's throat in one fluid motion while using her free hand to pull her hair back, granting her clear access. "Sandra! What are you doing?"

"What am I doing? I should be asking you that!"

White froth formed in the corners of her mouth and flew into Barbara's face with every syllable. Momentarily, she noticed the bloody flecks that streamed through Sandra's hair, along with the wild brush clinging to her shirt. She smelled horrible, and she looked deranged.

Barbara couldn't believe the transformation that had taken place in her so suddenly. Her actions alone spoke volumes. She didn't need a therapist; she needed to be in isolation until she calmed down and some of her paranoia was decreased.

"Shall I kill you, Barbara? You smell like a cage—the very same cage they want to put me back in, but I'm not going! How many are there? Are they surrounding the house? Are they going to come in with guns blazing? How many did you bring here?"

Sandra had gone completely mad! Barbara was stunned. Sandra's psychotic mind had taken a turn for the worse, and the longer she looked into her dilated pupils, the more she thought that there was no one who could help her. "Back off, Sandra."

She leaned forward and pushed her back slightly, but Sandra resumed her position before she could breathe.

"You came to bring me down?"

"Bring you down? Are you crazy?" She asked her the question even though the answer was quite obvious. Sandra was off her rocker. "I came here because Dr. Wesley tracked me down and showed up at my job. He was asking about you."

"So you brought him straight to me, huh? Where is the prick you speak of?"

"I didn't bring him anywhere. Get off of me!"

Sandra didn't move but she did lower the knife from her throat. Barbara took that time to smack Sandra so hard in the face that red welts showed up in seconds.

"You need help, Sandra, and I'm not talking about sitting in a chair and talking about your feelings! You obviously need medication, and plenty of it! Look at the house. You were always neat and tidy without a hair out of place, and now look how you are living! There are bugs flying around your dishes, and the house smells spoiled!"

Sandra didn't utter one word but went across the living room to peek out of the window as she slid the knife in her waistband.

"It'll be better for everyone involved if you just tell me where he is."

"There is no one here, Sandra."

"I'll check."

She removed the knife again and slipped quietly out of the door.

Barbara couldn't wrap her mind around what had taken place in the short months she had been gone. Since Sandra, she had moved on with her life, followed her parole officer's orders, checked in on time, found a job that she actually liked, and even moved into a nice one-bedroom apartment. She was well on her way to blending back into society without Sandra, but to see her now being so buoyant in the mind and obviously having trouble separating reality from delusions caused her great pain.

Sandra didn't love her the way she wanted to be loved in the time frame that she wanted it, so she'd left her. Not once did she consider how unstable she would become in her absence or how and if she would be able to manage on her own. None of that had occurred to her when she shut the door on Sandra to pursue her own life.

Her emotions were raw at the time. She just didn't think she could survive another blow of rejection, but the situation as she saw it now had her wondering if she was to blame for the turn of events.

She was lost in thought inside of the house as Sandra circled the outside. She began to clean the kitchen, shedding tears as she did. When she removed the dishes from the sink, she noticed that the plates on the bottom still held dried egg remnants from their last meal together. The eggs were glossy yellow in color and clung to the plates and forks for dear life. They would need to be soaked.

Barbara ran all hot dishwater and piled the plates and silverware inside. She found herself swatting at flies and gnats, which brought a fresh bout of tears to her eyes. What had she done?

She knew deep down inside that there was no chance that Sandra would be able to make it on her own, and she'd left anyway. Despite how she may fail in life or find herself in horrible situations, Barbara had left her behind to fend for herself. If Sandra would have done the same to her in prison, she didn't know if she would be alive to think about it. But she didn't. She never walked away from Barbara, even though as a loner, most of the time she didn't want to be bothered.

Even living as close to each other as they did in prison, days would go by without Sandra saying anything to her, but she knew without a doubt she kept her in her sight. It was almost as if she was the babysitter watching the baby she didn't want to be bothered with. They could go for days on end without speaking, but she would always feel Sandra's protective glare in the cafeteria or wherever they went. She'd protected Barbara when she needed it most, and it pierced her deeply to know she didn't do the same.

Barbara ventured into other parts of the house that needed attention, noticing clothes lying around in disarray. She silently picked them up and carried them to the dirty hamper in the bathroom. The sink alone was enough to make her want to back out. There was makeup smeared in the face bowl and lipstick stained on the mirror. When did Sandra start wearing makeup? Was she seeing someone? A man?

She quickly dismissed that idea given Sandra's current state of mind, but she still could not figure out why she had decided to change her appearance. She began unfolding the clothes in her hand to get a second look, and the stockings with the holes in them were the first thing to catch her attention, along with a filthy halter dress that smelled as if it had been stored with barn animals for the winter.

What was she doing with these clothes? Was someone else staying here? Could she have possibly found someone to take her place? Jealously engulfed her as she found herself going through the closet in the bedroom. The clothes she left behind were still in boxes, as were Sandra's. She had no idea what was going on, and she was even more afraid of finding out.

"Do you always rummage through other people's belongings, Barbara?"

"I was cleaning up, and I saw those other clothes. I thought—"

"Oh, good. Tell me what you think."

"Sandra, I don't like the way you are looking at me. I came here to help you, but if you feel like I am intruding in your life—"

"Sit down, Barbara."

"No, I think I have had enough. I don't know what's going on, but I do know you have made it quite obvious you don't want me here."

She stepped away from her, heading for the bedroom door. Sandra didn't budge. She no longer held the knife, but if looks could kill…

"Sit down!"

She didn't want to fight Sandra, but she did want to leave.

"Why did you come here?"

"I told you Dr. Wesley came to my office."

"What did he want?"

"He said you haven't been to therapy in quite some time, and the last time you showed up on the radar you destroyed your doctor's office. I told him I haven't seen you since I was released. I didn't think he believed me, so I waited and covered my tracks to make sure I wasn't followed here. I wanted to see if you were okay…if there was anything I could do…"

Her tears turned into a dramatic bout of despair as Barbara slumped to the bed, covering her face.

"That bitch is no therapist! She disrespected me!"

"Sandra!"

"You don't believe me? I tried the whole straight arrow thing, and you know it! It's not for people like me! I am here to find predators!"

Sandra began a mad pace back and forth in the room, rambling on and on about correcting the wrongs that God had created.

"I have been on my feet for days, trying to end the corruption that stalks the streets, and you know what? One, two, three down and nine million more to go!"

Barbara bolted upright, covering her mouth. "Sandra, no! What have you been doing?" She grabbed her by the arm, stopping her rhythmic pacing. "What are you doing, Sandra?"

"I'm correcting God's errors."

"That's not your job, Sandra. You can't fix the world."

Barbara's mind quickly put the pieces together and realized she had in more ways than one admitted to harming, if not killing, innocent people. The clothes, her mental state, everything had been altered. From the first time she had witnessed it in prison to the scene outside of the bar until now, she saw the pattern. She had convinced herself that Sandra had acted out of self-defense at the bar, that she had not intentionally brought undeserved harm to anyone, but now she wasn't so sure.

When she thought about the knife, the dried blood in her hair, the smelly clothes, and a host of other things out of place, she couldn't help but wonder if she was posing as a bum on the streets and killing people as they walked by. Barbara was terrified by the prospect.

She had been on her own long enough for things to swell and blur in her mind. She obviously couldn't jump back into the swing of things by herself; someone had to be there to break her out of a cycle when she fell into a bad place. Her counselor had come to the house as a life preserver initially, and Barbara had been beside her for the other two incidents, but now in her own isolated world, she didn't carry a magic rubber band to pop herself back into reality, so she continued to live and breathe what she believed to be right in her eyes.

"You know, I don't think we need to carry on with this conversation. Leave."

"I'm not going anywhere until you tell me what the hell you have been up to, and if it's what I think it is, we need to also find you a way out. I left you before, and I know now more than ever that I shouldn't have done that, but it's going to take hell's fire to get me out of this house tonight."

Sandra looked down at Barbara as she sat stubbornly on the bed. Her eyes were red-rimmed, and the salt of her tears had dried on her cheeks.

She was here to help. But help who? Sandra had given up on the idea of being rehabilitated quite some time ago. She felt there was no one she could trust. Every corner presented an obstacle, and every obstacle turned into a tunnel of darkness. How could she ever see her way out? Her brain seemed as if it was split in two, and was slammed back together again in random order.

Sandra wanted to be rid of Barbara in one breath but wanted to thank whatever divine spirit that had sent her to the door in the next breath. She knew she couldn't go on much longer and that death would be the only thing that would be able to put a stop to what had become of her.

The change to come about her was slow, and in no way deliberate, but a part of her concluded that she did not want to die. She wanted to feel normal inside and do all the things that women her age should be doing.

She looked at Barbara again and noticed the glow of her skin. She had been doing very well for herself. She appeared fresh. There was life in her eyes. The natural highlights in her hair danced sensuously with the amber in her eyes, indicating she had sat in the beauty shop recently and treated herself to a professional day of pampering.

She was moving on in life without hindrance. Why couldn't she? Where they really so different? Was her future really based upon her choices? Did she even have a choice? Was it written in stone that she had to continue on this path of destruction and solitude? She blamed her parents for what had become of her, but for how long could she point the finger everywhere but at herself?

The intolerable impulses she had about men, could they be controlled? Could she learn to overlook them, maybe shadow them out somehow? She didn't think so. Every step she took in the right direction seemed more difficult and mind-consuming. She had to think about what to say and who to say it to. Did she do this right? Did she stick out like a sore thumb? What could she do to blend in? The battle was constant and tiring.

On the other side of the spectrum, life in general was a little bit easier for her. No thinking, just acting on impulse and internal rage. If a man stopped his car to pick up a prostitute to use at his disposal, then he deserved what he had coming to him, simple as that! There were no excuses for it. They were sick and vile humans who hid their true selves in the day but expected all of their perverted fantasies to be satisfied in the night.

"You know, I normally don't do this but my life is…"

"My girlfriend cheated on me…"

"I just got out a bad relationship…"

They must have all purchased the same book of lies. Sandra wanted to make sure there would not be a sequel made.

"I'm tired, Barbara. Just leave"

"You want to take a shower and tell me how you got that blood on your hands?"

"Yes, to the shower. The blood is self-explanatory"

Barbara didn't ask any more questions but went to the bathroom and began to run the shower. All of the towels were still pressed tightly in the boxes, except the one she had obviously been using repeatedly. There was no way to get the crusty layers of dirt out of the fibers, so she threw it in the trash. "Your water is running." Sandra glided past her and headed for the shower without glancing at Barbara.

She felt embarrassed, humiliated, and angry all at the same time. She wanted to give it a try and really put forth the effort this time to have some form of a life without the bloodshed and the rage, but she was just too ashamed to put it in words. Barbara must think she was some kind of maniac. How could she not? The house was filthy, and her body smelled of the streets and the waste of many men.

The odor of Mr. Castration clung stubbornly to her, which caused her to replay the scene with him again and again every time she inhaled. No, she didn't want to live this life any longer. She wanted out!

*

The lamp was set up on the bedside table, fresh linens were laid crisply across the mattress, and her house shoes with the huge fur balls on the top were at the foot of the bed. The scene dipped her back to a better time when they were sleeping in their first apartment and Barbara surprised her with the house shoes. They seemed a little too girly for her at the time, and she would have ordered her to take them back, but for some reason when she wore the furry foot covers it made her feel better, lighter, somehow.

Barbara always told her that if something in life makes you feel good, go get it and keep it. So she did, and now here they sat in plain view, her feel-good shoes. She could hear Barbara rummaging in boxes nearby and it brought a sudden calmness over her. Things were shifting into another place without much hesitation, and she could feel her mind trying to rest. It was as if the last few months of living in the cast of a female *Rambo* were over, and if she had to admit if only to herself, it felt very calming. Her scalp no longer sizzled as if her brain was frying, and she gave credit for that to no one but Barbara.

She went through the last couple of weeks on fierce bouts of energy. She had eaten very minimally during her spree, using the neighborhood store for egg sandwiches in the mornings. They were prepared in the back on a make-shift grill, but the owner caught all the customers who took the bus to work or other destinations. Daily, she would wash the sandwich down with a Coca-Cola and wait for the next dead man to stop by.

When she returned home, she rarely ate again. The electricity would be too vibrant, too strong. It would take over her body and leave her with raw numbness that blocked all her other receptors. She could only manage sleep in two hour intervals, then exercise for an hour, lift weights for another hour and constantly check the perimeters of the house for enemies. This is what had become of her life. She would get the six to eight hours of sleep that her body would require, but it would be broken up into short intervals.

Barbara returned to the room to find Sandra still standing at the foot of the bed. She had not moved to get dressed or do anything else, for that matter. "Here, let me help you." She got the lotion from the shelf in the closet, put some in the palms of her hand, and began oiling Sandra's arms.

"Do you love me, Barbara?"

She stopped what she was doing and sat on the bed. She had to be very careful how she answered the question. Sandra had calmed down significantly, but she was still in a wired state. She didn't want to send her back off on a tangent, but she also knew that she would be able to decipher if she was telling the truth or not. Very calmly, and without putting the tension she felt into her voice, she answered her. "Yes, I do, Sandra."

"When did that start? After I took up for you?"

Barbara let herself laugh and drift momentarily back to the days when they were incarcerated. "No. I was more scared of you than anything. You were so frightening. I didn't close my eyes for the first eight or nine nights with you in the cell."

A smile crept across Sandra's face, and it seemed to brighten things.

"I developed feelings for you in a slow-motion kind of way. I thought at first it was because we spent so much time together, you know with the workouts and sharing a cell, but then over time I realized I missed seeing you when you went to your therapy sessions or when we went to work. I always wanted to be around you. I guess you could say I admired you."

Sandra thought about what she said and then asked, "Do you want to know what I've been doing?"

Barbara thought about it, but couldn't answer. She didn't want to see Sandra in a different light than she was in right now. Since the time she pulled into the driveway, Sandra had gotten more in control of her emotions. A big part of that was because of the way she handled the situation.

Barbara had been afraid of her when she first arrived, but she knew she couldn't show it. She hoped that the time they had spent knowing each other would be enough to bring Sandra back to reality. But she wasn't ready to bet the bank on it. She had never seen her like that, and it took everything in her not to bail out and head for her car.

She briefly wondered if Sandra would have followed her and hunted her down like some sort of animal. Would she have been able to leave freely, or would she have killed her? She was in a deep delusional state, and Barbara didn't know what, if anything, she could do to keep her mind at rest.

"No. I don't need to know what you were doing unless you want to tell me. Do you still have those pills that your doctor gave you? You know the ones in the little plastic packets? You were supposed to take them until you saw a new..."

She cut the sentence off. She could see Sandra's eyes starting to shift right in front of her. It threw her off guard for a minute, but then she realized that Sandra was more than angry at the psychiatrist she had gone to see.

Barbara didn't know if it was even safe to mention Dr. Wesley's name at this time, so she didn't. "Do you still have the packets? I think you packed them in your toiletry bag from our last apartment. Have you used them?"

Sandra didn't answer her, just stared blankly into space, focusing just above her head. Barbara took the chance of sliding off the bed and going into the closet to look for the box marked "bathroom". After pulling off the tape, she opened it to find the pink bag of toothpaste, deodorant, and medication right on the top. As she unzipped the pouch, she could feel tension in the air around her. Sandra had moved, and she could not see her in her peripheral vision.

Quickly, she grabbed the pills, zipped the bag back up, tossed it in the box, and pushed it in the closet. She turned around in one swift movement, only to find Sandra standing behind her with a glass of water. She nearly jumped out of her skin at the sight of her. "Oh God! You scared me half to death! I didn't know where you went."

"I need water to take the pills. They are supposed to help me right? I guess I should have taken them before all of this started."

"It's okay. What's important is that you are taking them now."

Barbara handed her the pills and like an obedient child, Sandra swallowed them.

"I'm going to take a shower. I'm so tired. I had to work all day, and I was on pins and needles about you the entire time. It kind of wears you out, you know?"

She grabbed a towel and headed for the shower. As the water began to flow over her, she let her tears mingle with it. She felt deep sorrow for what had become of Sandra. She didn't believe for one moment that she deserved what happened to her, nor should she be blamed for the things that she had done. Life had been so cruel to her.

She cried for not being there when Sandra had needed her the most; she wept for the rooted feelings of being alone and the possibility of not being able to help Sandra in any way, but she was not giving up.

Dr. Wesley had given her his card for a reason. If she could convince him to write her a prescription, she could take Sandra to get it filled. That would hopefully be enough to stabilize her until she was ready to try another therapist.

Eventually, she would have to be willing to sit across from somebody and tell them about her nightmares. Not only would it be good for her emotionally, but she was required by law to do so. Barbara figured she had to come up with a plan immediately. She could no longer wing it with Sandra. Things needed to be structured and in some order if they were to precede any further.

Tomorrow was the first day of the rest of their lives, so to speak. She had a lot to think about, such as her job, for one. She couldn't just walk out. Maybe she could convince Sandra to come to her apartment for a while. So many things ran through her head that she had an intense migraine by the time she left the bathroom.

Once again she dug into the box designated for the bathroom and found some Tylenol for the rapid pounding in her head. Sandra had already climbed in the bed and appeared at first glance to be sleeping. Barbara dried herself off and applied an ample amount of lotion. Sandra had not been taking care of herself lately, and from the looks of things, Barbara knew she wouldn't be able to focus on herself for quite some time. She put on a set of pajamas and headed for her side of the house.

"Will you stay in here with me?"

She turned to see Sandra gazing at her with the face of the hopelessly innocent, but Barbara knew she didn't want to be in the same space with her at the time. Her heart was too open right now, and if she was honest with herself, she had not thought her next plans all the way through. She vowed to Sandra earlier on that it would take hell or high water to get her out of the house, but would it? If she had more time to think through her plans, she may very well be going to get the bread in the morning and not coming back.

Sandra asked again if she wanted to know what she had been doing, and the answer still remained a firm no. She didn't need the gory details. She knew what Sandra was capable of, and she also knew it took less than a second to change her moods. If someone had done something to her in the streets, there is no way they lived to tell anyone about it.

Sandra didn't know how to talk her way out of situations. She didn't know the words to diffuse anger in another person. She just wasn't made that way. She walked a straight line, and if something obstructed its path, she would remove it in the worst way imaginable.

Dr. Wesley did the best he could in trying to enhance her social skills, but the sessions were just not computing fast enough with Sandra. She remembered how she'd behaved initially in the bar. She was quiet and kept to herself, and her behavior was less than approachable. She wasn't ready for the outside, and Barbara knew she shouldn't have forced the issue. She should have pressured Sandra into taking her medication long before she urged her to go outside.

She had come home with them in addition to a current prescription for a refill, and she never said anything. She was very much in control when Sandra first came home, yet she did nothing to keep their lives in order. She let Sandra go about her day doing whatever she wanted, and not once had she mentioned a doctor to her.

She took one more look across the bed, allowing her guilt to make the choice for her, and relented to her wishes. Walking across the room, she slipped into the bed with Sandra.

"Can you tell me about your job, Barbara?"

She turned to face the window because she could not look at Sandra. Knowing who she was continued to split her decision about what she should do with the information. "Barbara, are you mad at me?"

Her voice had taken on a sluggish tone, and she knew the medication was kicking in. "No, Sandra, of course not. Just get some sleep."

Sandra was quiet for a minute longer and Barbara let her mind wonder about tomorrow. She had never been in a position like this where the balance of someone else's life hung in her hands. She didn't know if she could truly trust Dr. Wesley with the information that she had about Sandra. Would he become a friend or foe? Would he run to the police, or would he try to help them out? Barbara didn't know the details of what Sandra had been doing, but she wasn't totally ignorant to it either. Maybe, she thought, she could leave most of the details out and just convince the doctor to get her some help. She didn't have to tell him everything, but just enough to kick him into action of finding her someone who really did practice by their credentials.

She knew there was a possibility of Sandra being committed to the hospital for a seventy-two hour observation, but she also knew that she needed it. They would regulate her medications and help her in dealing with outside therapy. It has to be done. It was the only way they would be able to live some kind of normal life.

To even think that she was still not ready to leave Sandra after all things considered came as no surprise to her. She had always been an "until the end of time" kind of person, pretty much like her father who never gave up on her mother. If there was even a small morsel of hope for her to have the outcome she wanted, then without a doubt she would stay and try to get it. She wasn't a quitter and never have been, and above all else, Sandra needed her.

She tried to settle down and get some form of rest, but it was not easy when all she could think about was Sandra bouncing out of the bed at any given moment and stabbing her or pressing a pillow over her face. She turned away from the window and lay on her side to face Sandra. She looked so serenely beautiful that it forced tears to fall from her eyes again.

Gently, she took a finger and traced the outline of her face, and Sandra didn't stir. She was in a deep sleep, which her body had been craving for quite some time. Part of the dream state she was in came from the medication, but the other part was from pure exhaustion.

She had let her hair grow, and it now rested softly across her cheekbones. She still felt a longing when she looked at Sandra, and her heart still faltered when she was next to her. Barbara planted a kiss on her forehead and closed her eyes.

CHAPTER 52

*B*arbara woke to blue eyes facing her. Sandra was dressed in the filthy clothes she had thrown in the trash with the same knife as the night before tucked into her waistband. She was standing over her, and feeling her presence must have been what made her wake up. "Come on, Sandra. Not again."

"It's time to leave ."

"Leave? To do what? Where are you going?"

Barbara slid herself into a sitting position and cleared her head. Her watch stated it was three o' clock in the morning, but Sandra was full of energy. She had to have been up hours ahead of Barbara. The medication must have only caused drowsiness because it had done nothing for her state of mind. She was still prepared to go out and continue doing whatever it was she doing before Barbara arrived.

"I have to catch the bus."

"Do you have to go today? I came all the way over here to see you. How about you rest for one more day, and when I go home tomorrow, then you can go back out?"

Sandra stood rocking back and forth as if she was listening to her favorite music. Her anxiety level kicked back up, but it wasn't nearly as bad as earlier. Barbara felt she had a chance to get her to calm down much faster than she had before.

"She is trying to stop us from doing what we set out to do! It is our mission to get rid of the dirt that walks the streets, and now she brings her prissy ass in here telling us to stay in the house? Are we grounded? Look at her in your bed! She is no better than the ones we find outside. She wants to touch you and play with your damn tits! Will she love you after you have given her what she wants? No! Kill the bitch, and be done with the whole thing! We…

"Sandra? Here, take another pill. It will help you."

Barbara knew she wasn't focused on her but on something that neither of them could see. It finally dawned on her that during the times Sandra would sit in a trance for long periods, it was because she was listening to something or someone else. She didn't think Dr. Wesley had given her any form of medication for that, but she knew that was exactly what she needed.

Sandra appeared to be daydreaming, but at the same time her eyes were all over the place as if she were watching the dance of Christmas lights. She called her name several times, but she did not respond. Only after she had gotten the last of the pills out of the closet did Sandra seem to snap out of it.

Barbara put the pills in Sandra's hand, but before she could hand her the water, she threw the pills across the room and headed for the door. "You take them. I don't need them."

Barbara lunged from the bed, extending herself across the doorway.

"Sandra, please! Please. Don't make me call for help. If you walk out of that door, I'm going to call the police and have them drag you back in. Please don't make me prove it!"

For the tiniest of moments, Sandra looked as if her feelings were hurt, and Barbara seized the opportunity. "Let me make you something to eat first, and then you can tell me what you do out there all day, okay? We will rest a little, and if you still want to go outside, then you can go."

Sandra seemed to be contemplating the idea as she sat on the bed.

"I really don't want to go outside, Barbara, but something inside of me says I have to. They're pulling me in every direction, and I can't let them down. They need me to finish what I started. But I get tired, and I really wish they could find someone else."

"Coward! Coward! Coward!"

"They won't stop until I'm done, so the sooner I get it over with, then no more voices."

She was almost afraid to ask, but she knew she had to find out what exactly she was being forced to do. She wanted to be on an even playing field, and the more Sandra told her, the more she would be able to combat what her thoughts were trying to get her to do.

"Where do you go when you leave here?"

"The bus stop."

"And you just sit there all day?"

"No. I get on the bus, and get off eights stops down."

"Always eight stops?"

"Yes."

"Then what do you do?"

"I go and get a sandwich from the corner store, and when I'm finished, I wait."

"What are you waiting for, Sandra?"

"For the men."

Barbara had caught the meaning, quickly and clearly. From the clothes, to the old looking shoes, to the heavy makeup, Sandra was out posing as a prostitute. The knowledge of it almost took her breath away. How could she have done a total about-face like that? She hated them with a passion, and now she dressed for them?

She couldn't imagine Sandra lying on a filthy mattress, allowing men to do with her as they pleased. It was enough to make her vomit. Why would she subject herself to such behavior? And why all of a sudden the new lease on life?

Barbara's eyes flicked quickly to the knife Sandra pulled from her waistband. She laid it on the bed beside her and was removing her shoes. Barbara mind skipped, as she realized she was in the room with the person Colorado police and state patrol was looking for.

She'd caught bits and pieces about what was going on due to the small glimpses of the news she heard when she was at work, and some of the clients who came in freely opened discussions about the killings, but she hadn't given it a second thought.

Men were being murdered on the streets, and they assumed the suspect was male because of the obvious strength it took to overpower some of the victims. All of the men were found in the lower end of town and were killed during or right after sex had been initiated. They concluded that the rash of killings could be an act of a sick and twisted pimp. No one in their right mind would ever figure it to be one on the most beautiful women they had ever seen.

There hadn't been any claims of witnesses or leads to speak of. Some patients who walked into the office felt the killer was a hero. Women said that if the men were on that side of town (which was well-known for drugs and prostitution) in the first place, then they deserved what they got, while others still had pity on the victims.

The reason the story was catching a little more heat than any other headline was the method used to kill the men and the fact that one of the more recent casualties happened to be a prominent businessman in the Colorado area. He was known to give big donations and support many of the fundraising programs in and around the city. His death, though it appeared to be by the hand of the same killer, was quickly swept up to appear as if he were robbed while doing some form of charity work in that area. No one dared to delve further into the crime to ask what form of charity took place in a motel room. They just wanted to catch the man responsible and bring him to justice quickly.

Sandra continued to get undressed and put her pajamas back on. She didn't say anything to Barbara when she climbed back into the bed, but she did pull the covers back for her. She seemed to want to keep her close, almost as if she didn't want her out of her sight. Barbara didn't know if she felt safer with her being there or if in some way she was trying to keep her eye on her. Did she not trust her?

Still unable to decide her next move because of the gravity of the situation coupled with the driving need to do something but not knowing what, she slipped back into the bed. Sandra slid very close to her and simply rested her head on her shoulder.

"I want to be free like you Barbara. I don't want to hear these voices. I don't want to hurt those men. Well, I do, but I don't, and that is what I don't understand."

She sounded like a child confessing her innermost secrets, and Barbara could feel herself wavering under the spell of it. She knew it was not Sandra's fault that these things were happening to her. She had been through disastrous things in her youth, and that could only cause a sense of misdirection in her adult life. That had to be exactly what Sandra was going through. Barbara felt that she wanted help. She had just asked her in an offhanded kind of way for it. She deserved a chance at normalcy, some kind of balance in life. She deserved a shot in trying to achieve that.

"You have to go to the doctor, Sandra. You have to get some help and start taking the right medication. It's the only way for you to make it. I think they'll have something that will stop the voices.

"She is trying to control you! Don't listen to her. You're lying with the enemy. She will betray you in the end, and then you will be looking for us to help you out. Get rid of her!"

"My head starts buzzing, and then it takes over somehow. I don't really know what is going on until it is too late. I didn't know it was voices I was hearing at first. I assumed it was my inner thoughts and ideas that I was acting out. It wasn't until I wanted to do things the right way that I realized I didn't have the power to do so."

Barbara turned over and looked at Sandra. She had never been this close to her face where she could detect the smallest pattern of freckles across her nose. Her eyes looked almost cartoonish in their purity.

"I'm going to be there every step of the way, Sandra. I'm not going to leave you. We will get you some help, but you have to be willing. Are you serious about trying to leave your dark past in the past?"

She didn't answer her, but she did nod an affirmative. Barbara looked into her eyes and saw the uncensored hurt and fear there, but she also saw someone who desperately wanted to get out of the slump they had found themselves in.

"Let's try to get some sleep, okay? In a few hours we can eat and maybe go for a drive."

"I don't want to go outside. It's what they want, it takes over when I'm outside."

"Okay. Then girls' day in. I will run to the grocery store and get a few things. You only have bread, and I don't trust those eggs."

"All right."

Sandra seemed satisfied about what was going to take place, and she didn't want to ruin it by telling Barbara what the voices had been whispering to her. Listening to them was disturbing, but not damaging. It was the buzzing that took over her every thought, and right now there was silence, so she slid further down into the comforter and tried to sleep.

CHAPTER 58

*T*hey sat on the couch watching semi-funny TV shows
as they ran one after the other. It was getting close to
lunch time and they were both tired of eating toast and
drinking coffee, but Sandra had convinced Barbara to wait
until nightfall to go outside. She felt the night was safer
from prying eyes, and she didn't want anything to happen
to her.

The voices had been in her head all day, telling her to
hop in the car and leave, kill Barbara, drown her in the tub,
etc. It became nearly impossible to focus on the television
because everything ran together. At one point the voices
were in her ear, and seconds later they were actually coming
from the television.

"I'm going to go in the room to lie down. Will you come
with me?"

Barbara didn't hesitate to answer her. "Sure."

She had been watching Sandra out the corner of her
eye, and the agitation she saw there was extreme. She felt
sorry for her. She didn't really know what she was going
through, but the battle had to be mind-boggling.

Sandra went straight to the room as Barbara cleared the
dishes and turned off the television. She ventured into the
room that was supposed to have been hers and retrieved

the box that held all of the books and magazines she had read and the newer ones she left behind. She toted the box with her into the room, and Sandra had the covers pulled over her head. "Are you okay?"

She didn't respond, so Barbara continued to dig into the box until she came across a magazine she didn't recognize. Even though the articles were several months old, the information about the celebrities was still news to her. She sat on the edge of the bed, thumbing from one page to the next, until her eyes began to run the letters together. How she could be as tired as she was when they had gotten up no too long ago was a mystery to her, but she crawled in the other side, also deciding to take a nap. She slipped in the bed thinking about what she was going to prepare for dinner. She wanted it to be something nice but also simple. Her mind was resting on pasta and a salad until she felt something hard underneath her feet.

Barbara bent down to retrieve one of the pills Sandra had thrown down earlier. She looked across at her, wanting to make her take the medication, but then she thought better of the idea. They were going to eat dinner, watch a little more television, and then go back to bed. She was almost rushing the sun to come up the next day, because she would be taking Sandra to the hospital. She would be able to call Dr. Wesley in the meantime to find out where to go from there.

This time he will get to know his client for whom and what she truly is. She wouldn't be able to sugarcoat her way through this one; Barbara was going to be there every step of the way. If Sandra didn't speak up, then she would be the one to tell them about the voices and the things that had occurred in her past.

She was going to make sure she received the right medication and that she was taking it, no matter what. It was going to be an uphill battle, but she was more than prepared to stay. She would not walk out on the one person who stood beside and in front of her.

She felt Sandra slide over when she settled in the bed but she still kept the covers pulled tightly over her head.

"What's the matter, Sandra? Remember when we said we were going to talk to each other and let the other person know what's going on? I can't help you if you won't let me."

Her voice was muffled by the blanket, but her words were clear. "You can't help me with this."

"Is it the voices?"

"I don't think anyone can stop them."

Barbara pulled the covers back and saw that Sandra had been crying. Her face and pillow were still wet from the residue.

"Come here. It will be okay. We will find a way."

Barbara nestled herself in closer and wrapped her arms around Sandra. Gently, she rocked her back and forth, and for the moment it seemed to have smoothed her. She stroked her hair and softly dried the tears from her face. Sandra kept her eyes closed and didn't say a word. After some time, she released her and turned over. Barbara needed to rest just as much as Sandra did. She didn't know what to expect from her, but she did know that she wanted to be ready if something was to occur.

She allowed her head to sink into the pillow, thinking about nothing in particular when she felt Sandra's arm encircle her waist. Her body became stiff but alert. Unsure of what her next action would be, she waited with a closed fist, holding her breath. If she tried to harm her in any way, she would have to be prepared to fight it out with her and run for help if necessary.

She knew Sandra was going through some kind of psychotic episode, but she was not going to just sit idly by and become a victim. She didn't know what method she used on those men that who were surely stronger than her, but she was going to give it the best she had.

Sandra had not moved since she had wrapped herself around Barbara. They seemed to be waiting on each other, when Sandra took her free hand and gently stroked the back of Barbara's head. She leaned in to take a whiff of her shampoo, and felt her resist the gesture.

"I was smelling your hair. It's soft."

Barbara didn't know what to make of the whole ordeal. It felt as if she was caressing her, yet she knew in all likelihood that could not be the case. "Try to get some sleep, Sandra."

"I'm scared, Barbara, scared of the outside, scared of tomorrow, scared of everything but you. I don't know how to treat people or allow them in my life. When I go outside and see the men out looking for women, I feel powerful because I know if they choose me, they won't be able to hurt another woman. They say mean things to me and smack me around, but I play along because I know the end result. This whole world is dark to me except you. I've never felt pain with you until you left. It was as if something splintered inside of me, but I couldn't identify exactly what it was or why it disturbed me. If I made you mad or hurt your feelings, I'm sorry."

Barbara was almost too stunned to turn around. She had never heard her speak so openly about anything since they had been together. It was impossible to penetrate Sandra's thoughts, and in this moment she had learned more about her than she ever did.

She waited a little longer to see if she had more to say, but Sandra kept quiet. Barbara didn't know what, if anything, she should say on top of Sandra's endearing words, but she did know that her confession was something very difficult for her. She hesitantly turned over to face her.

"I don't want you to think that you can't talk to me. I'm with you, and no matter what you have done, it won't make me feel any different about you. I am not a judge."

Sandra looked her dead on for nearly a minute before leaning in and kissing her on the mouth. Barbara didn't close her eyes to the sensation, nor did she respond. She didn't know Sandra's full intentions, but she did know better than to jump the gun with her.

She pressed her mouth even tighter while making awkward attempts at thrusting her tongue out. The effort was a little painful, and Barbara could feel her teeth grazing her lips. She gently pushed Sandra away. "What are you doing?"

She didn't answer her, just leaned herself in for another kiss.

"Why are you doing this? What's gotten into to you?"

"I've never been kissed by someone who loves me. No one has ever loved me. You came and helped me when you didn't have to. You told me you like touching me."

Barbara was softened by the gesture, but she didn't want Sandra to think she owed her for anything. She didn't want her to regret it later, or worse yet to look at her like a man without a conscious.

"You don't owe me anything, Sandra. Let's just get ourselves a nap, and we will take it from there, one step at a time."

"Is sex always rough, Barbara? Do they all pull at you and punch you? Some of them ram their private parts in your mouth until you choke. They pinch your arms and breasts all the time. Some of them like to twist your nipples until you almost pass out from the pain. They—"

"Stop it! Stop it! They are not normal, Sandra. Something is terribly wrong with them. It doesn't have to be that way, and when you start taking your medication and seek therapy, it will help you see that. Not all men are monsters, and not everyone you come in contact with wants to hurt you."

"Do you love me, Barbara?"

Barbara didn't know if she had simply forgotten that she had asked her the same thing earlier or if she was trying to test her in some way, but it didn't matter. Her answer would never change.

Sandra gazed into her eyes and knew she was telling the truth when she said, "Yes." for the second time.

Sandra reached under the covers, grabbed one of Barbara's hands, and brought it up to her breast. Then without warning, Sandra pressed her lips firmly against Barbara's, making her front teeth catch her bottom lip.

"Ouch! Sandra, you don't have to use so much force to kiss somebody. Is that what you want, to kiss me?"

"Yes."

Sandra turned to lay flat on her back, and she put her hands to her sides. Barbara once again felt as if she was taking advantage of her, and it almost made her change her mind, but the desire of wanting but never being able to have Sandra consumed her. She knew it was selfish to make love to her during such a fragile time in her life where her emotions were all over the board, but her need for the closeness dimmed those hesitations from view.

She propped herself up on one elbow, and with the back of her hand she traced the contours of her face. Many things flashed through Sandra's mind and surfaced in her eyes as she watched her. Barbara could see the uncertainty, doubt, insecurities, and pleasure all at the same time. She was battling herself from one extent to the other.

She went painstakingly slow with every move she made, constantly asking if she was okay. She did not object to the removing of her shirt or pajama bottoms. She kept her eyes focused on Barbara's face the entire time. She never asked a question but she did comply with everything Barbara asked of her.

She knew she would only have one chance at this, and it took everything inside of her not to devour Sandra on site. Her body was simply exquisite to behold. Her skin still held the scent of the shower she had taken earlier, which aroused Barbara intensely, but she knew if she moved too fast, it would ruin everything, and Sandra would truly start to believe that there was no difference between a man's and a woman's touch.

No matter what the outcome of their future was, she wanted to make this day a day of awakening for Sandra. She knew she would have to keep things simple and gentle. She didn't want to expose her to the many forms of sex that could be held between two women; the basics were all that Sandra could endure, and she would push her no further.

Although she must have had sex in many different forms, considering her current line of business, she didn't want their lovemaking to remind her of anything a man may have done to her.

She leaned down upon her close enough for their lips to just brush against one another. Gently, but ever so slowly, she applied pressure, and closed her eyes. When she opened them, she found that Sandra had done the same. She repeated this two to three more times, and each time Sandra closed her eyes when she did.

"Do you like it, Sandra?"

"I don't know."

Barbara continued to kiss her and tenderly licked her bottom lip. She was moving so slowly that she felt a cramp begin to form in the arm she was using to hold herself upright. She subtly shifted positions and allowed her fingers to flow down into the crevasses of Sandra's arm.

Her skin was so soft and beautiful to Barbara. She reached down further and clasped her hand in hers. She felt a slight trembling pressure as Sandra responded to her touch. For her it was as if a green light was glowing above her head and the sky was opening up. She was at a place where no one could reach her. She wanted to show her every positive aspect of lovemaking.

Sandra tried to express her feelings to her while trusting that she would be the person to show her that the world was not such a bitter and cold place. She was doing things that Barbara knew her mind was screaming for her not to do. She wanted nothing more than her touch to become a healing factor for her, something to silence the screams of her demons.

Barbara wanted to erase all of the internal scars, all of the years of abuse, isolation, and pain from Sandra's heart. Her intentions were to bring a light into her life and share every step with her.

She had never been in a one-on-one relationship with a woman, but she knew without a doubt that is what she was signing up for by being intimate with Sandra. A man would never be able to enter their life in a sexual aspect or any other aspect, for that matter, and she would never let Sandra find her with a man. It would set her back mentally and perhaps destroy everything they were working so hard to build. She knew she was giving up any means of ever being in a heterosexual relationship by making love to Sandra, but it was all worth it to Barbara.

To lay with Sandra now felt more gratifying than any feeling she had ever had with a man. Sandra had stripped down all of her barriers and placed her trust in her. She had never felt so responsible for another human being.

With men, they seemed to always be in charge. It was sex on demand when and where they wanted it, and at most times whether it made the woman comfortable or not. Sex was something that she had enjoyed in her life, but there was a distinct difference with Sandra. It mattered greatly to her if the recipient of her advances was pleasured as a result.

Barbara kissed her full breasts as she kept her hand clasped with hers. She nuzzled the fullness of them and couldn't imagine someone doing anything but loving one of the most tender parts of a woman. She looked into Sandra's eyes as her tongue explored the firmness of one nipple and then the next. She felt as if she held the world's most precious rosebud between her lips.

Sandra jerked involuntarily, almost as if she was waiting for the pain to come from her breast being touched, and it made Barbara pay that much more attention to her. She released Sandra's hand and wrapped each one of hers around the soft mounds. Her nipples were beginning to respond to her touch, and her face was relaxing slightly. She concentrated on what she was doing while trying to imagine how Sandra was feeling at the time.

She stroked the sides of her body and smoothed her palm across her midsection. She was giving her a massage, in a way, trying to bring her a sense of relaxation and pleasure. When Barbara moved her hand further down to Sandra's pubic area, her wrist was immediately seized in a tightened vise grip.

Sandra watched her for a response, but Barbara didn't say anything. She kissed her over and over again on the lips and even more softly on her breasts and shoulder area. She used her free hand to rub and knead her neck as she continued to suck on her earlobe. She could feel the grip on her relax some, and she felt relieved that she wasn't stopped all together.

Barbara trailed her side with kisses until she had reached her navel area. She stuck her tongue inside and Sandra shivered as if tickled by the motion. She did it again and confirmed that indeed Sandra flexed in response. A light but airy sound escaped her, and it sounded miraculous. She had actually giggled.

She didn't know Sandra had a playful area on her body. Hell, Sandra probably didn't know it either, but it made her happy to know that she was the person to have found it.

Barbara removed her clothes and let Sandra get used to their skin touching. She wanted her to feel the heat that radiated from her pores just from being near her. The sight of Sandra coupled with the enormity of the venture they were about to take together was enough to bring Barbara to her highest peak. It took every ounce of willpower she owned not to start stimulating herself. This time would be devoted purely to Sandra, and she was not about to put her aching desires before that.

She knew she may not be able to make Sandra reach an orgasm on their first night of real love-making, but she did want to make sure she would be the one requesting a return visit.

"I'll be right back."

She got out of the bed in search of the baby oil that was still packed away in one of the boxes. When she returned to the room, Sandra still lay in the same exact position in which she had left her. Her eyes were a little blank, but she did turn her head toward the doorway when she entered.

In a way it made Barbara feel as if she was taking advantage of a child; almost as if she was forcing her into a situation that she was totally unaware of and uncomfortable with. She eased onto the bed beside her and just stared down at the woman who had grown to mean so much to her.

"We don't have to do this, Sandra. We can just take a nap. I don't want to make you—"

"No, I'm okay. I was just listening. It was okay when you touched me. It felt like feathers. It wasn't rough."

Barbara couldn't have been happier if she had won the lottery.

"I'm going to give you a massage and help you relax, okay?"

"All right. I really want to give you something that you want too Barbara. You have always helped me, I kinda owe you."

That statement stopped her from applying the oil to her legs. She stood at the foot of the bed and felt empty. She didn't want Sandra to think she owed her for anything. She thought she had initiated the whole thing because it was something that she wanted as well and now to know that she thought she was doing her a favor caused her to feel hurt and confused.

"You don't owe me anything, Sandra. This is something that couples do. This is what people who love each other do, not as a favor or trying to show an act of kindness. I can tell you that I love you, and this is a way to show you as well. When someone who loves you touches you, it feels very nice. It has the power to take your mind off all other things. You get lost in that person, and you don't want to be anywhere else."

Sandra raised her head and looked at Barbara standing at the foot of the bed. She seemed as if she was on the verge of tears, and Sandra knew she had caused such a thing to happen. She didn't know how to show Barbara the things she wanted to see. She had never been in love. She had no clue which questions were the right ones to ask and which were not.

She was trying to give her something that she knew she wanted from her. Wasn't that the whole reason they had separated in the first place? Because she didn't want to be seduced by Barbara? She didn't want her to leave again. She needed her to help in the next phase of her life and maybe beyond that.

When they were in prison together, she was in charge all the time. She thought she would be able to continue that position when they eventually lived together, but things had taken a dramatic shift, and she was on the other end.

"I just want you to see that I am willing to try to change. I want my new life to be with you, Barbara. You are the only one I can trust. I feel like everyone is out to hurt me. My mind is always foggy, and I can't see the good side of anything. I want to try this, not just for you but for me, too. I'm tired of being on the outside of where everyone else is. You said this is what couples do. I never looked at you as an intimate partner, but I guess there is no other name for it. I feel like I need to give you what you want, but at the same time, I'm hoping that I will be giving myself something as well. Do you understand? I know my words don't come out right when there is a little buzzing in my head."

The tears flowed down Barbara's cheeks, and her vision of Sandra was now blurred. She had never heard such beautiful words being spoken. It opened her heart and ripped at her emotions. She loved her at that moment more than she ever had.

Sandra got to her knees and met her at the foot of the bed. She did exactly what Barbara had done for her earlier and wiped the tears from her eyes. Barbara stood naked and still in front of her, afraid to make the wrong move. Sandra wanted to show her that it was okay, that she was open to explore any and everything she had to give.

Sandra kissed her on the lips and was surprised that she felt warmed inside by the softness of her mouth. Barbara kept her hands to her sides, with the oil clutched in one of them. Sandra retrieved it from her and popped the lid. Her eyes held questions as to what the purpose was, but then she voluntarily dripped some in her hands and applied it to Barbara's breasts. She rubbed them and hoped she was not hurting her.

Her nipples perked in response almost immediately, and this made Sandra smile. She glanced up at her and saw that Barbara had closed her eyes. No one was watching, which made her feel a little bit more confident to advance into her next move, which included playing lightly with the little peaks. She rolled her tongue around and around in the same form used on her, concentrating very hard on not clamping her teeth, and it seemed to bring some form of satisfaction to Barbara, so she kept doing it.

She put a few more drops of oil in her hands, reached around and rubbed it across her bottom. Barbara moaned and looked down at Sandra. She held her hand opened and Sandra poured some oil into it.

They spent several minutes with gentle caresses and shaky hands. Barbara leaned down and sucked on Sandra's mouth. She licked and pulled at her lips until they were pouty and swollen from the attention.

Sandra lay back, and Barbara climbed on top of her. She moved her hips in a circular motion, which momentarily eased the tingling between her legs, but she dared not touch herself.

With her knees she nudged Sandra's legs apart and found herself cuddled softly between her thighs. She rocked them in a slow rhythm, never taking her eyes off of Sandra. She hadn't said a word, but the look on her face was priceless.

She was already beyond her wildest dreams, but she wanted to take Sandra with her. She put more oil into her hands and gently slipped her fingers down to Sandra's nest.

The warmth surrounded her fingertips and took her to new heights. She continued to kiss Sandra while sliding her fingers up and down the smoothness of her womanhood.

When she felt her legs part ever further, she was encouraged by the gesture. She kept rubbing her breasts and stoking her body as she smoothly let her mouth replace her fingers.

Sandra's back arched, and her eyes made her look like a deer caught in the headlights. Barbara stroked her thighs to try to calm her nerves, but Sandra sat straight up. Her legs were still open, so Barbra pushed her face deeper and started a trail of butterfly kisses.

Sandra eased back on her elbows but continued to watch Barbara's every move. She had never felt something so soft and moist on her, and she had to admit that she found it quite extraordinary. It put an end to the buzzing in her head while bringing temporarily peace to her mind.

She flopped back when her arms began shaking and her elbows could no longer support her. She felt Barbara's hands lift her by the buttocks, and she couldn't help but to move her hips in sync with her mouth.

Barbara focused on the job at hand as she nuzzled herself into her. She used the light pressure of her tongue to seduce her. Sandra's legs began to shake as she became more excited than her. By increasing the pace, she was welcomed by the warm flow of satisfaction. It seeped through her fingers and smeared itself over her lips.

Barbara tasted her in her mouth and loved the sweetness of it. She could see Sandra's breaths coming in short bursts, but she did not stop. She went in with more determination which had her name being whispered from Sandra's lips. The movements of her hips increased, making her second downpour become far more powerful than the first. Barbara was saturated with it.

Sandra's body was shaking while her eyes stayed shut. Barbara climbed to the top of the bed and smothered her face and upper body with kisses. She ran her fingers through her hair and continually professed her love to her.

"I love you so much, Sandra. Thank you for letting me have this moment with you."

She opened her eyes and freely kissed Barbara's moist lips. Tears sprouted from her eyes, but they both knew it wasn't from pain. Sandra had been released in many ways. She had been touched in the most precious of places, but it did not sting. It didn't burn, and in the end she had not hated it. She would never forget what Barbara had just done for her.

They wrapped themselves in one another's arms, falling easily asleep, and Sandra, for the first time since childhood, slept without dreams as peacefulness engulfed her.

CHAPTER 59

*S*andra woke to the sound of the shower turning off. She had no idea how long she had been sleeping, but she could see out the window that the sun was long gone.

She rolled over and felt a small amount of peace within herself. Although she could hear small voices like a distant echo trying to come forth, they weren't strong enough where she couldn't ignore them. As soon as Barbara was able to find her a doctor and the right medication, they voices would stop; at least that is what they were banking on. She didn't want to be a hopeless case or someone everyone had given up on. She wanted to change, and Barbara helped her to see that it was more than possible for her to do so.

As a matter of fact, Barbara had shown her a world of things. Sandra's ideas of love and companionship came with a new meaning now. She has seen the other side of the coin, and it was all due to Barbara.

She believed her when she said she loved her. No one else would have gone through what she did. She was nearly killed when she arrived at the house, but it did not stop her from trying to reason with Sandra.

She had been so wired and on edge that she couldn't see straight. She knew the only reason she was in a semi-calm state at this time was because of the medication that was slowly wearing off, and the determination of Barbara.

Sandra got up from the bed and headed for the bathroom. When she opened the door, she found her standing in her panties and wiping the steam from the mirror.

"Oh, you scared me. Do you want to shower?"

Barbara quickly scanned her face, searching for some form of wildness in her eyes that she now knew to be associated with psychotic behavior, but she didn't see any indication that she was feeling out of sorts.

"I...I love you, Barbara."

The words came out choppy, but it was clear she meant them. Before Barbara could say anything Sandra had her pressed firmly against the vanity. Her kisses were not as rough as before but they were placed forcefully upon her mouth.

Sandra's hands scoped her body and stopped at the elastic waist of her panties. She pulled at them, and Barbara wiggled her hips to oblige her. She draped her arms around her neck, giving Sandra just as much as she was getting.

She told her she wanted to try to make her feel the way she did earlier, and Barbara was speechless. This was more than she could have ever asked or hoped for. She was pleased beyond belief at their earlier attempt at lovemaking, but to have Sandra now return the favor was almost too much for her to soak in.

Sandra placed her on the lid of the toilet and stood before her. Barbara encircled her waist and kissed her from her stomach to her thighs. She wanted desperately to put her mouth on her again, but Sandra stopped her. She dropped to her knees, and opened Barbara's legs to manipulate her internally.

"Am I doing it right, Barbara?"

"Yes...yes..."

Sandra kept at it, transferring her mouth from her breasts and back down, repeatedly, as was done to her. She slid her fingers to her layered area, and it made Barbara say things that she didn't understand. She felt she was doing what she was supposed to by Barbara's reaction alone.

One leg was draped over the corner of the bathroom sink, and Sandra held the other one tightly in her grasp. She was leaned back against the tank of the toilet as her hips worked in a frenzied pace against Sandra's mouth and hands. As Sandra used her mouth, Barbara legs jerked all over the place.

When she gave in from exhaustion and release, Sandra tenderly ran her tongue up and down the length of her.

The odor that came from her was different than that of a man, and it didn't leave a bitter taste in her mouth. This was new to her, and she was more than happy to see that being with Barbara in this way did not remind her of being with a man.

She didn't feel dirty or degraded for what they had just done, but was more relieved than anything else. Everything Barbara had said was true, and things did not have to be as bad as they were.

Barbara said that she was in love with her and this was what lovers did, so she concluded she would get used to doing such things in order to keep Barbara in her life and make her happy.

It was her only goal now, next to getting on the right track with her medication, and she was satisfied in knowing that she had something and someone to look forward to.

No one would come between them, and she hoped to never again push her away. She felt comfort in her arms almost in a protective kind of way, and it soothed her innermost being.

Barbara leaned forward and kissed Sandra on the mouth. They hugged each other and shed a few tears, knowing they had just discovered something they had been searching their whole lives for.

*

After they emerged from the shower, they went to the room in search of clothes. Sandra grabbed another set of pajamas, while Barbara managed to dig out a pair of jeans and a T-shirt.

Sandra still didn't want to venture outside to get the groceries with Barbara, so she waved at the door and locked it firmly behind her. She had to admit at this point she was fearful of what could happen if she was left alone again, but she had to try to convince herself that she could do it, and she didn't want to worry Barbara too much either. Sandra knew she would have turned around and chosen to go hungry if it meant helping her, but at this point in time, she needed to help herself as well and not become a liability.

She needed to keep busy and try to occupy her mind with something. She didn't want to turn the television on for fear of hearing the voices that may project from it.

Sandra went into the bedroom in an attempt to unpack all of the things that were neglected since she moved in, starting with one of Barbara's boxes first. She stared for a while at the photo of Barbara riding a bicycle. She placed it on the nightstand and tried to return to the task at hand, but when she moved, she could feel the eyes of the picture probing into her.

It didn't take her long to figure out what was going on, and she also knew there was no way to keep it at bay for long. She kept moving in hopes that she could use her mind to focus on other things and drown out the images and words that threatened to overpower her, but none of Dr. Wesley's techniques were working.

A small clock radio sat in the bottom of the box, and she had the idea to plug it in to drown out the buzzing that was growing more and more consistent by the second.

Sandra liked the idea that she could try to do something about the noise, so she disregarded the other items in the container and began looking for an outlet. She bent down and searched behind her nightstand, but there was nothing.

Briskly she went around to what she would now like to think of as Barbara's side of the room, yet she could not find any form of an electrical outlet.

Sandra stood in the middle of the room and glanced around. Her train of thought couldn't wrap itself around the notion that maybe a socket was simply not in their room, only other parts of the house, so she continued to search.

She knew she was becoming too consumed with what she was doing and that maybe she should seek another plan while she still was in some sort of control, but the pull on her mental state far outweighed what her common sense was telling her.

One by one she pulled articles out of every box in the room. There was no reason for her to think that she would stumble across an extension cord they never owned, but that is exactly what she was looking for.

The buzzing hit her so fiercely it caused her to tilt back and stumble to the floor. For a second she could do nothing more than blink and try to get her bearings. Within seconds she thought of the pills she had knocked out of Barbara's hand earlier. They had fallen to the floor, hadn't they?

On all fours, she crawled around the bed in search of them. The radio in her hands was dismissed, as it became an object of intrusion. Sandra wanted to do whatever she could to keep it together. She knew it shouldn't take that long for Barbara to come back and...

"She's not coming back! Why would she after you let her touch and molest you? She's laughing at you now. You gave the whore what she wanted, and now she is gone!"

"No! No! Barbara is not a whore. She—"

"Shut up! Get off the floor and get dressed. We are late! Frolicking around like horny teenagers. You will never be able to scrub her stink off of you."

"Please. Please. I don't want to do it anymore. I want Barbara. She is going to help me. She will call Dr. Wesley and he—"

"Dr. Wesley? He is an illiterate pervert! You like the way he watched your breasts and smiled at the print of your pussy in your prison garb? He is a predator who preys on the weak. Get dressed!"

Sandra cried the tears of the wounded as she fought the war but lost the battle. She tried to win and somehow protect everything she had just grown to love but found it impossible to do. The force, combined with the need to comply was too strong. The inconsistencies were all psychological, and it left her nothing to fight. She was not made to live happily ever after. She was simply a tool used to do the bidding of justice, nothing more.

Minutes later, she found herself in the bathroom, applying heavy liner to her eyes, becoming one with the ritual. Her street clothes were not where she would normally leave them, and it baffled her for quite some time. It seemed that since her normal way of doing things had been altered, she was now lost for what came next. She always got dressed after the makeup. Things had to go in order.

"You see what that bitch has done? She stole all of our stuff. Wear what you just had on. Those sick bastards wouldn't care if you arrived in your Sunday best. Hurry up!"

Sandra moved into the room and put on the pajamas she had just taken off. Every step forward came in painfully slow increments. She was not moving as she normally had in the past when it was time to go out. Her steps were more hesitant this time, as if she were trying to delay the inevitable.

Sandra didn't know if she wanted to be saved at that moment, but she did know that she didn't want to walk out the door. Her feet were as heavy as cinderblocks, which was a direct reaction brought on by her subconscious. It tried to get her to wait around in hopes that someone could come along and make the right decision for her, but the only thing barking orders was her mind.

"Put your shoes on. That'll girl. Now get our little blade, leave the bag behind. We are stepping it up a notch!"

She twisted the locks that she had just fastened an hour ago and swung the door open. She felt like she was split in two as tears pierced her vision and the crooked grin of the insane pressed itself upon her lips.

She took off in the same direction as always, never bothering to close the door behind her. When her feet hit the pavement, it shredded all doubt as she became who she had always been. Any hesitation she may have had was replaced with accuracy and concentration.

The house that grew smaller behind her no longer existed. She could only see forward, so that is the way she walked. She couldn't take the bus because she left the house with no money, just instability and a weapon, so she walked the eight stops without complaint.

CHAPTER 60

Barbara's stomach balled into a twisted knot that wouldn't let her go. The chills that consumed her had her dropping groceries as she entered the house. To see the door standing wide open from the driveway was a horrible sight. She knew Sandra had left, and she also knew where she had gone.

Digging in the bottom of her purse, she searched feverishly for the card Dr. Wesley had given her. She needed someone to help her at this point. She considered what state of mind Sandra would be in when and if she stumbled upon her. She didn't want to face another episode like the one she walked into yesterday. Barbara needed help, and he was the only person she trusted and believed wanted Sandra to be stable as much as she did.

Her hands shook as her fingers grasped and held on to the card. She pulled out her cell phone and missed dialed three times before the number came across the screen correctly.

It wasn't until the ringing began that she thought about the hour in which she was calling. She prayed he was not asleep or out to dinner with his wife, as it was almost nine o'clock.

As the phone rang, she exchanged her flip-flop sandals for her gym shoes and headed back out to the car. She was totally disheartened to hear his voicemail click on the line, but she had to keep moving. Quickly she rambled off their address and the fact that he needed to bring some kind of medication with him if at all possible until they could get Sandra to the hospital.

Gravel flew from her tires as she sped out of the driveway in search of Sandra. Her nerves were getting the best of her as she tested the speed limits up and down the deserted streets.

CHAPTER 61

*D*r. Wesley got up at ten o' clock due to the urgent demand of his bladder. Diane was out to her co-workers bachelorette party, and he had fallen asleep in front of the television after consuming three beers.

When he returned to the couch, he searched for the remote control in between the cushions but came up with his phone first. He sat it on the table and plunged his hand again for the remote.

Satisfied with the retrieval, he sunk deep into the sofa, preparing to channel surf when he noticed his phone blinking. The screen indicated he had missed a call during his nap, but he didn't recognize the number. He was about to dismiss the caller and the message they had left, but something told him that he should at least check it out.

It could be from one of the ladies who were with his wife; maybe they were trying to notify him. Something could have gone terribly wrong at the party, or she may be in need of a sober escort. Charles smiled at the notion that his wife may be sitting at the bar, singing out of tune and waiting on him with the rest of her friends.

He clicked his heels on the coffee table and started to go through the few messages in his phone to get to the most current one. What he heard last made his blood run cold.

The fear in Barbara's voice put him on instant alert. She sounded absolutely terrified.

Charles jotted down the address and went in search of his emergency bag. He made it a habit to keep a little case of emergency vials and tablets with him at all times. It was a practice widely used by the majority of the doctors in his field. He was taught to always be prepared for anything, and at this time he was glad he'd paid attention to the advice.

He wasn't familiar with the address, but he knew what side of town it was on, so he snatched his keys off the hook, grabbed his little black pouch that contained what he felt he may need when he got there and locked the door.

*

Charles knew he was in the general area but nowhere near the right street. He pulled into the gas station, showed the acne-riddled attendant the address, and was made aware that it was a little cottage that sat back from the street next to the big field.

Dr. Wesley thanked the attendant and headed that way.

He had to pull into the driveway in order to check the address on the house because, like his informant had stated, it sat far back from the street. He let his eyes scan the front of the dwelling until they rested upon a wooden stump that held the numbers 1279. There wasn't a street sign posted where he turned in, but how many more houses could hold the same address numbers and sit next to a field?

He didn't know what he was walking into as he gathered his belongings and got out of the car, but he hoped he was ready to help in any way that he could. He tried to call Barbara back several times, but she didn't pick up. Gingerly, he approached the house and knocked purposely on the door. He waited a few seconds before knocking again.

The house seemed eerily quiet as he reached for the knob and gave it a twist. It turned freely and without notice in his grip. The light from inside illuminated his face.

"Barbara? Sandra?"

His voice rang empty, and he knew no one was home. He decided to venture further inside and take a look around. He needed to know if anyone was hurt in the house or was it truly deserted. Barbara made it seem like a 911 situation, so he wanted to make sure he didn't leave someone inside unattended.

He entered the living room and walked quickly toward the open kitchen area. He could see from where he stood that they both were vacant. He found himself facing closed doors on his left and right, so he went left first.

He stood in a bedroom with boxes neatly stacked against the wall, and a bed with no linen on it. It appeared as if the room had not been used since they the boxes were placed there, so he turned and went in the opposite direction.

When he pushed the door open, he quickly realized he was in a room that had held occupants at one point in time not too long ago.

Charles took in the clothes and miscellaneous items that had been strewn all over the room, but he also saw boxes with Sandra's and Barbara's names scrawled in permanent marker on them. The bathroom door was open, and there he saw more of what he had believed to have been true: they were living together.

That was a very moot point at the time because Sandra was in need of attention. His first and foremost line of business was to find Barbara or Sandra, whichever came first. He wished she would at least answer her phone or call him back. He didn't know what to do, but he felt like an intruder walking through their house, so he backed out of the door, closed it, and left it unlocked, the way he had found it.

Charles returned to his car and anxiously waited to hear word from either of the women he had come to help.

CHAPTER 62

S andra stared down at the man who lay very still beneath her. His skin was still warm to the touch, and she briefly wondered if she blew breath into him, would he wake up?

He was a brutally savage beast that deserved to be killed at least twice. He'd sucker punched her when they first arrived at the motel, which gave her the indication that there was more to come, but she had never encountered someone quite as violent as the monster she now sat upon. Sandra reached around and felt for the patch of hair he'd yanked from her scalp. She was slapped constantly and viciously as she was forced to perform oral sex on him.

She wanted so badly to rip his manhood from its very socket with her teeth, but they told her to be patient, so that's what she did. For a while she thought they abandoned her because of the many opportunities she had to take him out, but they insisted that she wait. She had to endure many acts with him, and she was at the point where she was losing the edge on him and she thought that he was going to get away from her.

He made her shower several times as he climbed inside the stall with her to shove soap in and out of her mouth. He called her names and on several occasions kneed her in the chest. She tried to stay focused on the end product, but she didn't feel the desired energy that she normally did.

It never lasted this long, and she wondered if somehow this man was different or if the connection had been crossed between her and the voices. They controlled her when she was in moments like this, but she felt out of sorts and unbalanced. The buzzing conveniently vanished, leaving her in jeopardy with him.

His appetite for sexual brutality seemed insatiable. He tied her up, and whipped her with the belt from his jeans. He then released her and demanded that she crawl on the floor like a dog. Sandra hesitantly complied with his every whim, only concentrating on the indication that his time had expired.

After nearly two hours had gone by, he had grown tired and decided to place her on top of him. He slammed her down forcefully again and again while yanking her by the hair that scarcely remained on her scalp.

Sandra had gone blank and out of tune with what was going on. She knew the time was coming for him to be done with her, yet she heard nothing. His grip became slack in her hair as his eyes closed. He licked his lips and had a big grin spreading across his face as he emptied inside of her.

His body grew still, but he had yet to open his eyes. Sandra looked to the door and was very tempted to just walk out and get lost in the night. She had never had anything like this happen to her, and she really didn't know what to do with him or herself at the time.

"You see how lost you are without us? You need us. You were so worried about that bitch, and now look at you! It's time to move on before this bastard wants round five. Reach your hand under the pillow; you'll find what you need."

Sandra actually breathed a sigh of relief when the buzzing broke through to her. She immediately took action and felt the handle of the knife protruding from the pillow. When she took the time to put it there, she didn't know, but she was more than thankful they did. She didn't hesitate as she plunged it deeply into his exposed throat. She wanted to pull it out and go crazy with it, but they advised her not to.

His hands clamped on to her thighs, and she quickly grabbed them. He gurgled a little, but seconds later a fine stream of blood seeped from the corners of his mouth. His energy dissipated as his body gave out. She knew it was done.

Step by step they took her through the process of cleaning up and removing her fingerprints from every surface. She was instructed to soap up a towel and clean his genital area, which she did. As she manipulated the flaccid muscle, it took the strength of a thousand for her not to yank it from his body.

She was done with the towels, but she would not leave them behind. She had left the house without her bag, so she dumped one of the pillows and used the case to carry the evidence collected.

Sandra checked the room one last time, made her way to the door, and stopped. She looked back at the man that may have been one of the most hellacious pieces of vermin walking the face of the earth and instantly felt an impulse she could not control. With sure steps, Sandra walked to the dresser, picked up the discarded bar of soap, and stuffed it in his mouth.

She walked across the parking lot and into an alley. Arriving at a dumpster, she retrieved his wallet from the pillowcase and opened it. She had never taken any personal belongings from a scene, but in this case, she did. She wanted to see if there was a family photo or a picture of some significant other he had dehumanized, but there were none. She wasn't too surprised by that or to see that there was only three dollars inside of it. He had never planned on paying her. He was going to use her like a mutt and then discard her without giving up a dime.

It didn't matter now. Sandra took the bills out, wiped his wallet off, climbed into the dumpster, and went down deep for a bag close to the bottom. She ripped the plastic slightly and with her shirt wrapped around it she pushed the wallet inside the bag and covered it with the remaining trash.

Sandra turned down a few more alleyways before emerging on the street. She had no problem blending in, even though she was carrying a pillowcase. It was late at night in an undesirable neighborhood. No one asked questions there, and rarely were you ever looked in the eyes. She made a left at the corner and stopped at a sewage draining system. One by one she dumped the towels and then the case into the drain.

If they were ever discovered, it would be impossible to get any DNA from towels that had been soaked in waste and rainwater. There wasn't a single trace of her left on any of the victims. She entered their lives and exited just as quickly. They weren't able to tie her to anything she had done thus far. She was free to roam again.

Her latest escapade took a lot out of her body, and she was exasperated. Sandra needed rest, and she suspected it also had something to do with the side effects from the meds Barbara had given her. She could usually go for almost three days without sleep, but now being in the elements for mere hours and coming from a medicated high, she was worn out.

She could hear nothing over the buzzing; it became so disturbing that she began to plug her ears with her fingers to decrease the volume. She guessed she must have looked quite out of touch with reality from the stares she was receiving on the bus. She bought a soda with the last of the dollars she had more than earned; the other two went toward her transportation home.

She almost breathed a sigh of relief when she started across the field toward the house. She had done everything they had asked of her, and she was finally able to feel calm. Unwanted images of Barbara suddenly blinked in front of her, and she began to feel different about tonight. There was no way she would disregard what she had done, no matter how torturous the man was. She would ask why she went looking for him. But wasn't it better that she had instead of leaving him for someone who wouldn't be able to handle themselves? It was a conflicting battle nonetheless, and she didn't want to keep thinking about it.

She was just a puppet, here for the taking. When the buzzing revved itself up, there was little or nothing she could do about it. The voices flexed her inner ear to the point of blindness. It would not leave her until she began working at their command. Sometimes she welcomed the voice and the strength that came with it, and other times it felt as if they demanded her to do a job she had not applied for.

She continued on her familiar trail to the house when her eyes caught a glimpse of something shiny up ahead. As she got closer, she could tell two things: it was the porch light reflecting off a bumper of a car, and it did not belong to Barbara.

No one had ever mistakenly pulled into the driveway since she had resided there. She specifically chose a house that sat back from the road and was not easily traveled on by accident. The mailbox was located at the end of the street near the intersection, so there was no reason for anyone to ever turn toward the house.

A couple of times she saw a car that had driven by and then turned around, but never had anyone arrived unexpectedly at her home. Sandra slowed her pace as she closed the distance between herself and the car. She didn't see the frame of anyone on the inside, so she turned her focus to the house.

Had they gone inside? Did someone just abandon their car here? Had they broken down? These questions and a million more zoomed and bounced around her, but no answers came with it.

She stayed careful and aware of her surroundings. She would not be thrown off by the element of surprise. If someone was here to get her, she would not hesitate to show them she wasn't an easy one to be gotten.

CHAPTER 63

*D*r. Wesley almost missed the shadow that passed by his window. He hadn't realized that he'd slumped down in his seat and drifted off or for how long. When the shadow presented itself under the illumination of the porch light, he could clearly see that it was Sandra. What he didn't understand was why she seemed to be sneaking up to the house as if she didn't live there.

He continued to watch her for a few more moments, which gave him a chance to really see what had become of her. She was slightly thinner than she had been in prison, but nonetheless, he could tell that she was still a fit woman.

Her clothes were dirty and a little tattered, but other than that she looked physically fine. Her mental state was an altogether different issue. Even from the distance at which he sat, she looked crazed.

At the time she was pressing her face against the door, and he guessed she was listening for someone or something. On her toes, she made her way to the window, where she then peeked inside.

Dr. Wesley didn't know if he should call her by name or wait for her to enter the house and then knock. If he got out of the car, he knew she would feel exposed; if she would attack him or not was not easily discernible.

He continued to monitor her from his vehicle and became very disturbed by her activity. She walked the circumference of the house once and didn't seem satisfied, so she did it again before entering.

Her behavior was on a scale he had never seen. He looked at his bag and wondered if what he had inside would stabilize her in any way. She was not just having an episode; she was functioning in a full manic state.

Charles thought about calling the paramedics and getting her restrained, but he knew when she discovered the ambulance everything could go haywire.

Slowly, he gathered his nerves and headed for the door. He put one foot in front of the other until he arrived at the porch, but he was no longer feeling sure of himself. This could very well be a dangerous situation he was placing himself in, but he could see no other way. Barbara had called him for help. Obviously things were out of her control, but not so much so that she had to call the police, so he found a little comfort in knowing that.

Dr. Wesley tapped on the door, not harshly as to startle her. Easily the sound would carry throughout the small house. He gave it a few minutes and tried again. He didn't get a response, but he knew she was inside. Throwing caution into the wind, he tried the knob and found that the door was not secure.

Charles turned the knob completely and pushed the door open inch by inch. He tried to stick his head in to peek around when the force that came from behind it almost caught his fingers in the frame. Sandra was on the other side of the door and had been prepared for whoever had been lurking at her house.

After getting over his initial shock of what happened, he quickly composed himself. He knew he had to try to gain entry, and he hoped their past relationship would grant him that access.

"Sandra? Sandra? It's me, Dr. Wesley. I just stopped by to check on you."

The sound of his voice startled her. This is not what she expected. Sandra quickly latched the door and leaned against it. What did he want? How did he find her? She knew for sure he had brought the police with him and that she would have to fight to get away.

She could feel the anxiety clinging to every pore in her body, but for some reason, she was not afraid. She tried to weigh her options on the best way to go about handling him being right outside her door and how to get away from him without being caught.

"Sandra, I'm here to help you. Barbara called me and asked me to stop by. I brought you some medication. I really just want to talk to you and make sure that you are okay."

The words came out as a whisper, and she felt as if she had been betrayed.

"Barbara?"

She wondered if that was the reason she was not at the house when she arrived. If she'd called him to come and help her, then why wasn't she there waiting on him? Everything began to blur together, and she was giving it her best shot to try to keep it together.

"I told you she was a traitor bitch, but you wouldn't listen! She led the enemy to the door! If you let him in..."

Sandra clasped her hands to the sides of her face, attempting to block the voices from entering her head. She needed to trust Barbara. She had called Dr. Wesley for her, and neither of them had ever done anything to hurt her, yet they were insisting that they were both out to get her.

Her head became silent for mere seconds and in that time, she reached out, unlocked, and yanked open the door. What she should do next was impossible for her to figure out. She placed her hands back over her ears and stared at her doctor.

Charles first noticed the many emotions jetting through Sandra's eyes, and they all seemed to battle one another for center stage. She had on a pair of dirty pajama pants, and a just as dirty matching shirt.

He didn't waste time lingering on the porch or try to break the tension with a simple attempt at conversation. She needed to be treated immediately, so he stepped inside and closed the door behind him.

Touching her at this point was out of the question. Charles walked past her and placed his bag on the table. He never let her get completely out of his sight, but he didn't want to appear uncomfortable in her presence either.

Patients who were in a manic state could often decrease points of anxiety significantly when their surrounding environment was relaxed. If he was to show the fear that walked the walls of his intestines, without a doubt she would react to it. Just a hint of abnormal activity on his behalf would feed her mental state into believing that something was not right about the person or persons in the room with her, and all hell would break loose.

Right now the most important thing was to keep the energy at a minimum. She was wound very tightly, and he didn't want to enhance that.

Dr. Wesley turned fully toward her, but he still did not speak or try to approach. He simply observed her from where he stood. Sandra had not advanced toward him either; it was as if they were in a standoff, weighing each other and what their next move should be.

Sandra was afraid to take her hands from the side of her face even though she could start to hear the whispers of the voices seeping in. The longer she stood there, the stronger they became, urging her to do something about the intruder who stood just a few feet away.

Look at him. he is staring right through you. He wants to fuck you. That's why he is here. What do you think he has in that little bag of his, medical supplies? He is going to tie you up and make you take it like a dog! The good old doctor is imagining what color panties you have on right now, and he is getting very excited! What are you going to do, lie down and take it? You have to move now before he gets the upper hand. Do it! Do it now!"

She wasn't convinced she was going to act on the things they were saying, but just by the off chance they were right and she needed to be protected, her eyes skimmed over his body, stopping where the legs of his pants met.

Her stance instantly became one prepared for battle, and this was not missed by Dr. Wesley. He took his hands out of his pocket and readied himself for impact. The moment the atmosphere changed, he knew it was not going to be an easy talk-down situation.

Sandra's hands formed fists at her side, and she looked at him dead on. The entire vibe was different. She no longer appeared to be confused by his presence; as a matter of fact, she was no longer looking at him. Her head was tilted slightly to the left as she began to nod her head in agreement.

"Sandra, do you want to talk about what's going on?"

Her head whipped around so quickly he was sure it had to have made her dizzy. With dedicated steps she advanced on him, closing the space that separated them. She wasn't exactly aiming for him, but more to the left, as if she was headed to another room.

He watched her for a few seconds, realizing almost too late that she was headed for the kitchen. Quickly, Charles rounded the counter that separated them and grabbed Sandra in a bear hug.

"Sandra, I want to help you. Please let me help you."

She kicked her legs and continuously flung her head backwards in an attempt to cause him harm. Placing one foot on the cabinet, Sandra pushed with all her might, trying to knock him off balance. Dr. Wesley was just as physically fit as she was, maybe even more so. None of her antics moved him. He bent down and brought her to the floor with him.

Sandra screamed, yelled, and began to spit at him. He couldn't get her to listen to him or come to reason. Charles looked at his bag sitting on the counter and wished it wasn't so far. Sandra's strength was enough to give any man a run for his money, and being in the state she was only intensified that.

Her voice had reached its full potential as he tried to drag her to the living room. The progress was slow and tiresome, but letting her go was not an option.

Dr. Wesley's foot slipped from under him, which left his leg exposed and within range of Sandra's mouth. She did not miss the opportunity. She sunk her teeth into the tender part of his inner thigh with a menacing grip, wanting to tear the flesh from the bone. His cry of agony seemed to bring about a frenzy in Sandra. She shook her head from side to side like a rabid dog, and the power in her jaws was relentless. He had no choice but to try to pry her mouth away from him, and to do this, he released her arms.

When she felt his restraint loosening, she went all out. Charles didn't want to cause her physical harm, but he had to get her off of him. He called her name several times, but she didn't acknowledge it. Sandra had plans for him, and she wasn't going to stop until she had completed what she set out to do.

"Sandra!"

Barbara's voice rang out across the room, getting Dr. Wesley's attention. It seemed as if Sandra hesitated, but only briefly.

"Get her off of me!"

Barbara rushed to the floor of the kitchen, wanting to diffuse the situation. She got down on her knees, leaned her face down so that she was looking her in the eyes, and spoke. "Sandra, let him go. Don't do this. We only want to help you." She continued her gentle cooing in her ears, hoping to block out the other voices that were present.

He could feel her releasing him, and the relief was remarkable. Charles didn't move or speak the entire time Barbara talked to her. Under no circumstance did he want to reinitiate the battle between them.

Barbara's soft whispers were getting through to her. Not only was he grateful, but surprised as well. It was nearly impossible to talk down a patient who had reached a full psychotic episode, yet right before his eyes an untrained civilian was doing just that. He marveled at what he was witnessing, which made it crystal clear just how in tune with each other they were.

Barbara began stroking her hair, and Sandra clung to her for dear life.

"Help me, Barbara. Help me."

Sandra was afraid of her next steps; terrified of what they would demand her to do. Her mind was whizzing at a tornado pace, and she couldn't shut it down. She knew she was holding onto her lifeline, but that did nothing to console her.

Dr. Wesley waited a second more before he got to his feet and went directly to his bag. Sandra needed something to calm her down and try to gain some form of stability. He withdrew the needle from the satchel and returned to the kitchen. Sandra's head was still embedded in Barbara's chest with her back to him. He made eye contact with Barbara, indicating that he wanted to administer some medication, and she nodded.

Sandra didn't so much as flinch when the syringe pierced her skin. Charles returned to the couch to examine his wounds while Barbara continued to rock her on the floor. He could feel a dry trail of blood on his leg, so he excused himself to the bathroom to get a closer look.

When he dropped his pants, he couldn't believe the damage. The skin was broken; with the print of at least nine teeth that had deeply cut through his flesh. He grabbed a washcloth and ran it under cold water. He pressed it upon his skin and he let out a small yelp as the stinging sensation ran up his thigh.

The animal that attacked him was not the same person he saw in the prison. One part of him didn't want to return to the room where the ladies of opposite backgrounds were sitting, merged as one. The entire scene was something only a film director could conjure up.

Sandra lay in her clutches, crying and mumbling, while Barbara continued to try to console her.

Charles gathered himself none too quickly and ventured back into the kitchen. They were no longer on the floor but had relocated to the couch. It was very obvious to him that the medication was taking an effect on Sandra. Her sobs were considerably decreased, and she was speaking in simple sentences. He still felt that she needed to be hospitalized and started on a rigorous medication program to pull her fully out of the state she was in. He had given her a mild sedative, but she needed severe psychotropic treatment as well.

She looked up at him as he came into view in front of the sofa. The most naive and misunderstood child in the world could not have posed for a better picture. She was the poster child for the innocent. Her big blue eyes beamed at him with unshed tears lingering in their corners. Her bottom lip still held a slight tremble, and it made him want to do nothing more than wrap her up in a blanket, promising to make it all better, but the pain in his thigh told him something else altogether.

"How is she?"

"She is doing better; she's calming down a little."

Barbara continued to stroke her hair, and he wondered how their bond seemed to be so strong from a penitentiary relationship. Neither of them fit the bill of dedicated lesbians, so he dismissed the notion of any form of a sexual bond, but he had no idea what their relationship actually was.

"You know she is going to need immediate medical attention. What I walked into cannot be solved with just the injection I gave her. It will wear off, and the cycle will start all over again. She has to get help.

Dr. Wesley pulled up one of the kitchen chairs to sit directly in Sandra's line of vision. He needed her to realize that before he left their house, she would be headed toward treatment.

"Sandra, it's Dr. Wesley. I need to talk to you."

Her voice came out in a whisper, but it was discernible. "You want to talk about the men?"

He was confused for a moment and believed that she was speaking from another place and another time until she interrupted his thought process.

"He was mean to me tonight."

Charles took this to mean only one thing so he asked, "Are you dating someone, Sandra? The man you are seeing, is he mean?"

He didn't pick up on it at first, but the line of questioning seemed to be more disturbing to Barbara than Sandra. He was confused about what really was going on between the two women, and he was more on guard about his safety in the current situation than trying to counsel Sandra.

"He tied me up and beat me."

It was only then that his eyes were directed away from her face. He saw the marks across her legs, along with the nicks and scrapes surrounding her wrists and hands. The longer he looked, the more evidence revealed itself of the situation she must have been in before she came home.

Maybe that was the reason she checked all of the windows before she entered the house. Maybe she believed her attacker had made it back to the house before her. He had no idea how long this was going on, but from the looks of things, this was not a first-time occasion for Sandra or the perpetrator. This could explain her frame of mind from the time he arrived. She may be a victim of rape and obviously even more, which would definitely be enough to cause mental instability, especially considering her past.

Dr. Wesley knew he was too close to the situation to be of much therapeutic help to Sandra, and he was not even halfway tempted to venture into that role, but he did want to gather as much information from her as he could so that he could pass it on to the doctors at the hospital. He wanted Sandra to go for immediate attention and then on to a facility from there. She needed to have a place to allow her to rest, receive proper medication and eventually wean her way back into society. He needed to call the hospital, explain the situation, and hopefully be put through to the doctor who would be assisting in Sandra's care.

Charles's mind ran through each and every scenario step by step. He didn't want to drop the ball this time, at the risk of losing another patient.

"How long has this been going on with Sandra?"

Barbara looked up from the floor to answer him.

"I don't know. This is the first time I have seen her in some time."

"You don't live here?"

Barbara realized that he must have noticed more than just one person's belongings in the house. She didn't know if his line of questioning was to help Sandra or to land them in more trouble than they already were in. She decided to feel him out and see where he was going with this.

"I used to, when Sandra first got out. I showed her a few survival techniques, and then I moved on."

Charles wasn't buying her story, but that wasn't for him to decide. He wanted to focus on Sandra right now and getting her some form of treatment. The fact that they were living together was secondary to the current situation.

"So when did you get back here?"

"Yesterday afternoon."

Dr. Wesley looked incredulous at her, "You've been dealing with this all day, and you just decided you needed reinforcements?"

"Yes. She was sleeping when I went to get us something to eat."

"So what brought all this about? Why the outbreak?"

"She said she hears voices."

This came as a surprise to him. He was expecting to hear a sob story about an abusive boyfriend, a jealous lover, or even stretching to envision a stalker lurking about, but hallucinations was a whole other ballpark. She had never mentioned anything of the sort. He was finding out more today about Sandra than he ever did in their extensive consultations. She had been more than able to pull the wool over his eyes, and he felt duped yet again.

His past flashed before him and his mistakes seemed unending. This would be his third patient who was able to feed him illusions, and he bought into them hook, line, and sinker. No matter how much credit he gave them for being able to deceive even the best of them, he still could not let it go. He had degrees upon degrees hanging from his wall, and he should have been able to detect the slimmest hint of deception, but he did not. It was always when it was too late and things were far too gone that he realized he should have made a left when he made a definitive right.

Charles had thoughts of going back to teaching, but now he was convinced that was where he would be able to perform at his best. He needed to work on the minds of the healthy and help guide them in the right direction. He no longer needed to be behind a desk trying to figure out the truth from fiction. He was growing very tired of the misleading and puzzle-solving. He would see this thing out with Sandra, but as soon as she was established in a safe and secure environment, he would happily drop the ball in someone else's lap and leave it there.

He had been offered a position earlier in the year at the nearby university in Boulder, and he was now eager to grab it. He would place a few calls tomorrow and see if the position still existed. If not, he would go about seeking other avenues to get into some form of teaching. His letter of resignation with the prison will hit the proper desk in the morning. If he had to start back off at a community college, so be it, but analyzing live cases versus textbook theories was no longer a dilemma for him to consider.

"What I gave her is going to put her to sleep, so maybe we should try to get her to the bedroom."

"Did you bring enough for a few days? I'm going to try to get her settled before going to look for a therapist."

"Barbara, she needs immediate hospitalization. Her condition can't wait a few days. Giving her injections and the few pills I was able to get my hands on will not stabilize her. She needs around-the-clock medical and psychological staffing."

"Yes, of course she does."

Dr. Wesley helped lift Sandra from the sofa and he was surprised to see that she was still able to stand on her own. It had been almost thirty minutes since he had given her the sedative, she should have been groggy at best.

"How are you doing, Sandra? Do you feel better?"

Sandra looked into his face with eyes clear and blue as Caribbean waters. "I killed every last one of them, Dr. Wesley."

"Killed who, Sandra? What are you talking about? Can you tell me?"

At the moment he figured she was going through a mental ramble until Barbara's actions set him on edge. She tried to hurry Sandra into the room and usher him out of it, but there was no mistaking the things she continued to say.

Charles planted himself firmly in the doorway, letting Barbara know he wasn't going anywhere until he could decipher what Sandra was talking about. She was speaking in a monotone voice, but it was clear with very few slurred words.

"Every time I go out I would hope that no one would stop for me, but they always did. Not one of them was nice…or kind…in any way. They all just wanted to use…me and soil my soul, and I let them, every one of them, because I knew my time would come to…clean the slate. Some liked to bite, and…others would punch or kick me. I ran across a few that just wanted basic…I guess ordinary sex, but I had to get rid of them too…because I was soiled."

Dr. Wesley took the time to once again look over her body, and the picture that was taking shape in his mind scared him to his very core. There had been stories running for days on end about men being reported missing by their families or found dead in hotels and alleys. If what Sandra was saying was to be believed and she wasn't just conjuring up a story that she'd heard on the news and deciding to make it her own, then she was in need of far more than just an ambulance ride.

"Sandra, why do you do this? Why go out and hunt these men?"

He tried to change his line of questioning to see if she would be shaken up or fall flat of answers, but she looked up at him again and said, "I was hunted once, too, Dr. Wesley."

He knew then he was staring in the face of someone the police, as well as the media, had been looking for. There was no physical description of the culprit. The FBI had profiled the subject as being a man and was concluding that the victims had been somehow caught up in a homosexual lure. Their suggestions outraged the families. They could be found daily on the morning talk shows defending their husbands, boyfriends, brothers, etc.

The second known victim was what changed the game for the profilers when a distraught wife stepped forward and spoke about her suspicions that her husband was bisexual and that she believed that he may have been killed by his lover.

The story was ran so much that Charles had to admit that he started to come to the same conclusion as everyone else. Nothing was ever taken from the victims, which ruled out robbery as a motive, and although they had been found in a less than desirable area, only half of them tested positive for drugs, also ruling out a drug-deal-gone-bad angle.

Sandra's angle was much more believable to Dr. Wesley, and it would fit with every man they had found. The motels were all within a few miles of each other and weren't very far from where he was now standing.

He knew that Sandra would never be able to have a normal relationship with a man no matter how she tried to play the flirting role with him in his office. He could see instability all through her, but never did he see then what he was seeing now.

There could be a lot of truth in her story, but it could also be just mental fantasy on her part. He had to clear up what was real and what was fiction long before he ran off and alerted the authorities. He didn't want to be a star guest on one of those daytime shows as the delusional psychiatrist with egg on his face.

"Did you know these men, Sandra? How did you meet them?"

She was lying on her side now, with her head propped firmly in Barbara's lap.

"If you know one, you know them all, Dr. Wesley. They take…advantage of women. Look what that monster…did to me. So I did it to him, too."

Charles still wasn't quite sure about Sandra or her slurred ramblings, but he decided to push forward, no matter how uncomfortable Barbara looked. He felt he was on the edge of something, and he would not back down.

Sandra was in a relaxed and open state of mind, and he planned on taking advantage of it.

"How did you kill this animal you ran across?"

Barbara pushed Sandra to the side and jumped up.

"That is enough, Dr. Wesley! I will not let you badger her as if she were on the witness stand!"

"Should she be?"

"I think you need to leave! I appreciate what you have done for us, but I can handle it from here. I will see to it that Sandra gets what she needs."

He was being verbally evicted, but it only drove him further to find out the truth. He needed to know what Sandra had been doing since her release from prison.

"I stabbed him."

Both of their heads whipped around simultaneously when Sandra said this. Her head was propped up, her chin rested in her palm. Her eyes were drooping, but she was trying to fight the medication. She wanted to keep talking, but her next words were totally inaudible.

He didn't need to hear anything else from her tonight. She had said enough. None of the victims had been stabbed. The police had not released the exact information surrounding the homicides, but they did let the cat out of the bag slightly, when they made that announcement of the men being asphyxiated. That clue alone led most people to the conclusion that they should be on the lookout for a man.

Charles turned back to Barbara as Sandra's head slipped onto the pillow.

"I'm sorry for the way I came across, but I had to know if what she was saying was real or imagined, and I thank God that it has all been a figment of her imagination. You don't know how relieved I felt when she said 'stabbed.' I have been keeping up with the latest developments and news segments pertaining to the unsolved homicides, and I know none of the men were butchered. I'm sorry if you thought I was badgering her or trying to do more harm than good."

Barbara stared him straight in the eyes and knew he was telling the truth. He didn't believe Sandra had anything to do with the recent rash of murders, at least until the profilers came up with a different subject of interest or he took the time to really absorb what Sandra confessed to him. It left them in a lose-lose situation either way it went, but for right now, she had never been so relieved in her life.

There was nothing she could have done to make Sandra stop talking that wouldn't come across as being openly suspicious, which made her crazy with anxiety after each slurred sentence.

He was less than a minute away from calling the police on Sandra; she knew it but could do nothing about it. Barbara let out the breath of panic she had been holding and ran her hands through her hair.

Dr. Wesley grabbed her by the elbow and escorted her from the room. "She is going to need her rest. We can go in your living room to talk about her arrangements."

Barbara allowed herself to be guided to the sofa, but the last thing she wanted to do was answer more questions. She had to think of a diversion or something to take his mind off what he had just learned. She connected with the deeply imbedded need to protect Sandra, and by this time she knew it was by any means necessary.

"Have a seat, doctor, and I am going to pour us some much-needed wine. I brought a bottle back from the store to have with dinner, but I guess we can enjoy it still."

Dr. Wesley could think of nothing he would like more than a glass of wine. He knew he shouldn't indulge at a time like this, but he didn't think he would be able to make it home with his nerves as frazzled as they were.

Barbara returned with two glasses filled with wine, and he happily took the one offered to him.

"This has been a very trying day, hasn't it?"

"Yes, it has."

Barbara kicked off her shoes and tucked her feet up under her. She was facing Dr. Wesley and sipping from her glass.

"Do you mind if I ask you a personal question?"

"No, not at all. I don't think we could get any more personal than this."

"How did you come to be so protective of Sandra? I mean, I know you guys shared a small space for quite some time, and that has the ingredients of creating a bond of some sort, but I think this goes a little deeper than that."

Barbara smiled at him and continued to sip.

"Yes, you are right. Sandra saved my life in prison and became my personal bodyguard. I had some very horrific things happen to me, and she, in a sense, rescued me."

Charles heard many of the horror stories that took place behind the walls of the prison. He didn't dare ask her to go into details about the incident; it would be a sure way to have him placed promptly on the doorstep.

"So you feel like you owe her for what she did for you?"

"Yes, I will always be indebted to her. She has my undying loyalty."

"Wow, that sounds stronger than most marriages. It must have been some ordeal she helped you out of."

"Yes, it was."

"Well we both know that Sandra is not healthy at this point, and what I wanted to recommend to you is that I call the nearest hospital and have her directly admitted. I can consult with a few of the doctors there and make sure she get treated with kid gloves during the initial consultation, and beyond. Then after their recommended discharge, she can be committed to an in-house facility. It will take at least a year or so to stabilize her from what I've just seen. This won't be an overnight trick."

"That's a long time."

"Yes, but it will get you the best outcome."

Barbara seemed to be saddened by the idea of seeing Sandra put away, but he had to let her know what she was looking forward to. Charles took another leisurely drink from his glass when he thought he heard sniffling. He turned just in time to see her wiping the tears from her eyes. He reached over, giving her a friendly pat, but this seemed to make matters much worse. The tears were in droplets as they fell from her eyes.

"It will be okay, Barbara."

He hugged her by the shoulders in a half-embrace, trying to console her, but Barbara's hands were shaking uncontrollably as she tried to take in more of her wine. The contents spilled down the front of her shirt and onto her lap.

She picked up the napkin and tried to blot the stain, but it seemed to only get worse.

"You are going to have to soak that in cold water right away if you want to save it. Once the wine has a chance to set in the material, it's over. I have ruined more than my fair share of shirts, let me tell you. I can remember…"

Charles' words were lost as she pulled her shirt over her head, exposing her breasts.

"Whoa! What are you…"

"I'm going to put it in the bathroom sink."

Barbara didn't appear to give him a second thought as she left the room, soiled fabric in hand. Charles finished his glass of wine and, without thought, picked up the bottle for a refill. He drank more rapidly from the second glass than he did the first and realized a little too late that he should have stopped after the first one.

His head was beginning to swim a little, and he wondered what the alcohol percentage was in the wine.

Seeing Barbara remove her shirt the way she did shook him up and excited him at the same time. He wanted to try to gain her trust in order to find out more intimate details about Sandra, but he did not want to do it by risking his marriage. It had taken him months on end to get things back on track at home, and he was not about to throw it away on a quick night with a bisexual ex-con.

The idea of making it to his feet and leaving was fading in and out rapidly. He would have appreciated a round of nausea so he could release himself of some of the alcohol he had consumed, but that was not going to be the case. The liquid seemed to have built a thick coating inside of his stomach and was happy to lay dormant there.

Making it home was a dilemma that didn't cross his mind anymore. He felt warm and satisfied inside and was no longer in a big rush to get off the couch.

He leaned his head back and basked in the warm glow wrapping itself around him. His feet felt very light, almost as if he could just float across space without any use of shoes. Charles' mind was no longer filled with his cases or the things he imagined he had to do the next day; it had magically been wiped clean, and for the moment, he was thankful for that.

He would not miss the opportunity of asking where he could get a hold of a bottle of that wine. He considered himself an avid wine consumer, but he had yet to run across a bottle that had as much effect on him as the one he'd shared with Barbara.

It would be the perfect stash in the secret drawer of his office. He could be having a bad day in one moment and a laidback experience in the next. Yes, he definitely needed to get some and take it home.

Charles opened his eyes, not realizing that they had been closed, and reached again for the bottle on the table. He wanted to read the label, but he missed the entire object. This brought laughter bubbling to the surface, and he quickly covered his mouth. Why he didn't want to make any noise at the time was lost to him as well. In reality, he had forgotten why he was sitting on a sofa, which was in a house that he knew did not belong to him. Again, this brought laughter, but he couldn't cover his mouth because his arms felt as if a ten thousand pound weight had been placed in each of his palms.

"Are you okay, doctor?"

The sound of the voice was vaguely familiar to him, but he couldn't put a name to it. He let his eyes roam the room in search of the speaker and eventually they landed on Barbara. She was standing just to the side of him with no clothes on except for a flimsy piece of material that had no right to be called underwear.

"All of my clothes were ruined by the wine, so I had to remove them. You don't mind, do you?"

Barbara reclaimed her spot on the sofa but slid a few more inches closer than she had been before.

"You seemed so uptight when you first arrived, and you worked so well with Sandra. I thought it would only be fair for you to have a chance to relax yourself. I took the liberty of putting a couple of the pills you brought in your glass of wine. They did wonders for her earlier on, didn't they? I mean, she calmed right down"

She spiked his drink with his very own medication. Charles couldn't gather his wits about himself. One part of his brain was telling him to try his best to sober up, while the other part of his brain stared feverishly at the peaks of Barbara's nipples. Dr. Wesley blinked a few times, but it did nothing to clear his head and everything to blur his vision.

Barbara grabbed the back of his head and led him to her chest. It was not voluntary, but he didn't object either. Charles reached a clumsy hand up and amazingly was able to latch on to her breast. He let the softness of the skin massage his beard, and this, too, made him laugh.

Barbara began to play with him in ways he had only witnessed in certain movies, and his mind betrayed him again as sexual moans replaced his giggles.

He had no clue at this time that he was married. The idea of being some form of therapist would have doubled him over with laughter, and to know that he should not be a willing participant in what was going on was just downright ridiculous. He was a man, and here was a woman working diligently to fulfill his desires. This is why God made man: to be served!

His thinking pattern was turned completely off, and for the time being he was only able to follow the orders of his body; but moments later, that signal, too, was disengaged.

He wanted to kiss her pouty lips, but his thoughts and movements were disassociated from each other yet again. Charles tried so hard to be mad at Barbara for what she had done to him, but he couldn't. Her scent made him want to forget her every wrong, but something inside of him wouldn't allow that. Something a little bit stronger than the haze of the liquor and sedatives kept breaking through to reach him at the surface. If he could just grasp what it was and what it meant, he knew it could do him a world of good.

He took each mental step deliberately and intentionally. Dr. Wesley put all of his frontal lobe to use when he made his next move and grabbed Barbara's wrists. He had very little strength in his hands or arms, but he held on as tight as he could, refusing to let her go. He tried to lift his head and look into her eyes, but when he did this, his head kept falling until it landed on the back of the couch and he was looking at the ceiling.

She'd laced his drink with the medication he had brought for Sandra, but why? Was her drink spiked as well as his? Did she see this as an opportunity to satisfy some sick sexual desire? Or were her plans for him more sinister than that?

It took every ounce of willpower he possessed to ignore the fact that he had just unwillingly entered Barbara's cavity. She kissed and suckled his neck while rocking him in her very own rhythm. There was no concern for him or what he may be thinking at the time. She was in it for herself and making the best of it.

The fact that he could not respond physically as a willing participant barred no hesitation in her manipulation of him. She grabbed his hands and placed them where she wanted them at the time. She squeezed them when she wanted to apply pressure and let go when she was done. It seemed as if she was well versed in getting what she wanted from the opposite sex.

His body had betrayed him by responding to the touch and caress of Barbara's controlling hands. Her breasts bounced and bobbed continuously against his chin, but mentally he had no interest in them or the other techniques she was using on him.

His subconscious was going at a hundred miles per hour, but he couldn't get his body to function in sync with it. He knew that he was not attracted to Barbara and under normal circumstances he would not have found himself in his current predicament.

Dr. Wesley thought of things he could do to try to combat the effects of the drugs, but he was not in reach of any milk or cold water. He felt so helpless at the time that he was near tears.

He didn't feel the contractions of Barbara's pelvic walls or the heat. He was becoming totally numb and losing all sensation. He tried to remember all of the things he had put in the bag, but he could not. Some of the intramuscular vials were from last year, as well as the pills. He knew he had brought sedatives, but which ones? He couldn't pray for an answer.

He knew by combining them with alcohol, it only intensified the drug. Did she use the same tablets, or did she mix a little here and a little there? That also made a difference in the potency and duration of the effects. He definitely didn't have the mental strength or capacity to try to organize them and judge the rate in which they would reach their peak or decline.

Just to know she had rammed his manhood inside of her without his permission took Charles to a place he never thought he would be: a victim. He was experiencing firsthand what women go through when they are date raped. He may not be able to feel the pain or be able to describe the mental agony of it all, but he now knew what it was like when someone used your body for things other than what you desired.

The clarity of her moans sickened him, but still not to the point of nausea. That would be something to see, her reaction to having his dinner splashed all over her. He wondered then would she keep stroking and licking him?

Charles closed his eyes again because the feeling was a bit more pleasant than trying to keep a focus on Barbara. She moved herself in an exotic fashion and if he was on the outside looking in, he may have complimented her on the performance. As it were, he was not impressed.

Sometime later Dr. Wesley opened his eyelids again, but for an altogether different reason. The electricity in the air had shifted. He still was heavily sedated, and he hated to admit it was even more so than previously. It was almost as if he was functioning in an alcoholic blackout state. He could no longer see her face, but just her physical outline. Her hair crisscrossed against him in such a fashion that he knew she must have turned around and faced the other direction. She didn't seem to tire of him, and she was determined to use him until his body no longer responded to her.

She called out his name and to hear it ring from her lips made his mouth go dry. Barbara let go of his hands and began to function on her own. She was picking up the pace, and her head was now firmly planted next to his. She contorted her body in such a way that she was able to lick his face while facing forward.

Charles once again began to feel more sleepy than sick, but his mind was drumming with a different kind of feeling. The hairs on the back of his neck still responded to the fight or flight mechanism instilled deeply within the human core, and the desire to act upon that was astronomical. He didn't possess the strength to push her from atop him, but he knew it was crucial that he make a serious attempt at freeing himself from her embrace.

He didn't know how long he thought about how to get from under her or what happened to the last crucial minutes, but during the process he must have gone blank for some time. Barbara already changed positions and was once again facing him. She looked down at Charles, but she was no longer smiling from the throne on which she had perched herself. Her glare had turned slightly demented in nature.

"Do you like it, doctor?"

Dr. Wesley didn't answer but instead tried to focus on the avenue he was going to use in order to gain himself some form of leverage. She was definitely under the influence of what she had given him, there was no denying that, but it seemed to make her sexual ways surface at a peak that took control of her. He was sure she had not been a stranger to drugs in her past. For her to so willingly consume something she knew nothing about sounded a little farfetched.

It only made sense that she knew what and how much she had given herself as well as him. Her measured amount made the approach that much bolder, more seductive, while she basically gave him enough to play the role of the lead dummy.

What her true motive was he could not comprehend. Did she find him so attractive that upon meeting him she wanted to jump his bones? Their paths had crossed in prison once or twice, but he never detected anything sinister in her eye contact or movements.

Was she just grateful that he showed up when he did and helped her with Sandra? The ulterior goal of what she was trying to accomplish was lost to him. The only thing he knew at this time was that his body was being used in ways that he was not happy about. Even if he had been intoxicated on the wine alone, he knew within himself that he would have made a few phone calls to make sure that Sandra was handled properly and then taken himself home.

Maybe during his work hours the next day or sometime later he would have checked in at the hospital to get an update on her progress, but nothing more.

Barbara had taken things down an entirely different avenue, and he knew once he sobered up, he would verbally attack her with the disgust he was feeling by what she had done to him. He wondered if she would think it funny in some kind of way or if she would hang her head in embarrassment for the criminal act she had committed.

On a plain scale that's exactly what is was. She took advantage of an unwilling participant. He knew if he ran to the police about what occurred between the two of them and they took one look at her complex yet basic beauty, he would be laughed out of the station, and flashing his credentials wouldn't get him any further. No, this was not something he would share with anyone, but he definitely would tell her firsthand about her actions and be wise enough to keep his distance from her.

As he dwelled on the circumstances even further, he knew that after he helped Sandra, this would be the last he would want to see of either of them. He would look for that new position he desired and wash his hands of the couple.

He was a therapist, not some form of guardian angel. He hated that it had taken him this long and to wind in this kind of circumstance before realizing his mistakes.

He made a lot of blunders along the way, but to see himself whacked out on his own medication was an all-time low for him. He was sure he wasn't the only psychiatrist to have stumbled along the way; he had heard a few whispered tones during his career, but he always prided himself on being different, somehow better than most.

He had a lot of self-reflection to do, as well as self-adjusting. He would support his wife and do anything possible to help her have the baby she had always been craving. They had tried several times, but when their third year came around, he knew things were not right in the equation. It had to be on the part of his wife, but he dared not mention such things. He was more than capable of having children; he knew that from the mistake that had occurred in college before he met Diane.

He was thankful that his partner at the time was also goal-oriented and didn't want to be a mother before obtaining her degree. They mutually decided on an abortion and soon after went in separate directions.

Charles didn't know if she somehow blamed him for what happened or not, but to say she turned very cold and uninterested in him after her procedure would be an understatement. He thanked his lucky stars when he was released from the duties of their relationship.

He would be lying if he said he didn't think of her from time to time and wonder if she agreed to the abortion because he was so gung-ho for it or if it was something that she really wanted. When he started to feel the chill in their conversations, guilt was not the first thing to pop into his mind but confusion and resentment.

Charles felt she wanted him to say more about what she had been through, but the words and emotions escaped him. She seemed satisfied with their decision one day and moody and complicated the next. The break-up wasn't a nasty one or even rude in any way; it just happened. He stopped calling her because he didn't know what she wanted or needed him to say, and in return she decided to do the same because he was unable to cradle her emotions. Either way, it was over and done, and he was free to finish his master's degree.

He had plenty of one-nighters after a brief dry spell, but he never allowed himself to get committed to anyone or sleep without protection, sometimes doubled, until he met Diane.

There was something different about her, and he liked how it affected him. He was one year fresh from schooling and more focused than ever on succeeding and making a name for himself. She began as a phone friend in the beginning when he met her at the courthouse, but he couldn't help but find himself wanting more than that. She dodged him for months and would not meet with him no matter what the venue. He used the address on the business card she had given him and sent flowers every time he received a paycheck, but he never got a reply. By the time she would answer the phone for him (sometimes days later), he was so happy to hear from her that he forgot to ask the about the dozens of flowers he'd been sending.

If he was to admit it now, he was truly struck by the chase. He hadn't so much as held her hand across a dinner table, but she controlled his dreams when he slept. It had taken him nine months to physically bump into her again, so he put his best lines in motion and wasn't taking no for an answer. He had to know if she was just as exotic as the infatuation that swirled nightly in his subconscious.

There was only one way he was going to be able to get her out of his mind, and that was to find out that she couldn't live up to the high standards his imagination had placed upon her, but she did. She turned out to fulfill them and more. Life couldn't get any better for him.

He stumbled across someone who knew what she wanted out of life, and she didn't mind taking her man along to get it. He fell in love with her smile long before he knew the softness of her lips. There was something about Diane that he found genuine and unique.

She encouraged him when he didn't have the strength to do it alone. She advised him when he didn't know which way to turn. She loved him with every ounce of her being. He didn't have to search for it, beg for it, or wonder about it; it was there in the way she looked at him and the beautiful love she made with him. They were inseparable, and he didn't care who knew it.

After three years of walking in sync with one another, he proposed to her.

They shared a house and a life together with all of the responsibilities, and it didn't faze them. Their first hint of trouble brewing was the decision to have kids. He fought it for quite some time but gave in when he realized there was no other face he would rather see grow from childhood to womanhood than his wife's.

It was a mutual agreement, and he fell in love with the idea when he saw how happy it made his wife, but if was deeply honest with himself, he didn't mind so much that it was not happening as fast as she would have liked.

After their third year of a healthy, enticing sexual relationship, protection-free, when she still hadn't so much as missed a period, she allowed herself to get caught up in the market of buying self-help books and listening to quack doctors on the radio stations.

Every day he came home from work she had a new remedy for him to try. It was do this or do that, and he always complied because he didn't have the heart to tell her that it was not him with the problem. She figured that out all on her own when she went to her next annual gynecological visit.

She did have a little blockage in each of her fallopian tubes, but he saw no other reason why she wouldn't be able to conceive after everything was taken care of.

Not only was Diane fearful of the procedure because of the greater probabilities of what could go wrong, but she also felt she didn't have her husband's backing one hundred percent. So they sat stagnant on what and when their next steps should be. It was not an open discussion or topic that they approached frequently because she felt somehow she was a failure as a woman; once again, he didn't know what to say or tell her to make things any better.

But in his current situation he knew without falter that when he was able to wash this incident from his immediate consciousness, he would take Diane to get the procedure done. He would be with her every step of the way and make sure the doctors were doing what they were supposed to be doing and to the best of their abilities. He would not let her down this time. He no longer wanted to run from the one thing he thought would hinder him; he would now embrace it as another chapter in the many chapters they had left in their lives.

He couldn't wait to get home and share this new found revelation because he knew she would be happy to see it in him. And for the first time in a long time, he knew that was what life was all about: completing yourself with the one person you knew would walk over hot coals for you.

CHAPTER 64

Barbara watched Dr. Wesley closely for any hint that he may be coming out from the narcotics she placed in his glass, but he still was not able to hold his own. She wouldn't say that she was not enjoying what she was doing on a small scale because he did feel powerful inside of her, but to have a sexual romp with him was not her initial goal.

She was quite impressed with the way he came in and took control of a situation that was far beyond her grasp; it made her notice him more as a man than just a therapist, but that was not why she decided to spike his drink. She did it for leverage.

Once Sandra had begun to tell the tales of her life, she knew it would only be a matter of time before he would be able to put the pieces together. He would not shelter her from the authorities but more or less throw her to them.

His decision to place her in some kind of nut farm didn't sit well with her, but she would allow it if it meant that they would be able to be together afterwards. What concerned her most was the look across his face when he believed Sandra was responsible for the homicides that had taken place in neighborhood. He quickly switched from the doctor on call to lead detective of the FBI. He would not let it rest.

Basically, he badgered a woman whom he had given sedatives to. It wasn't fair in her eyes, so she decided to come up with a way to even the score.

She skillfully placed her phone on the counter and pressed the record button when she went to the bathroom. Anyone who paid half attention to the video would see him willfully helping himself to a glass of wine and even smiling.

The camera was now directed at them and sitting flush with the arm of the couch. She recorded every movement and started it over and over again every time it shut off. They would see him holding her breast in one clip and his fingers manipulating her womanhood in the next. She didn't know how sloppy it would come across because he was so out of it, not even able to even hold onto her, but she knew with what she had, she would be able to convince him that he didn't want the story out.

She'd blackmailed a man before in her day, but nowhere near this level. She'd never had this much at stake. Sandra's freedom and their future depended on the clarity and conviction of what she had managed to do.

When he was alert enough to start making demands and pointing the finger of blame, Barbara would happily play back the little tryst they'd just shared on the couch, whether it was voluntary on his behalf or not.

She planned on spinning the story so well that he would have no choice but to bow down to her requests. She would see to it that he feared the outcome of her allegations.

Telling him that she would send a copy to his wife was just the tip of the iceberg in terms of her deception. If he still was not cooperating on the scale in which she felt he must, then she would next go after his career. She would play the tape for the prison warden and hit her with a scandalous threat, and if that didn't work, she planned to go to every newspaper in the Colorado region until her story was picked up.

Hearing that a psychiatrist of the state was somehow involved with the inmates that he treated would leave a nasty stain on his reputation, his field, and more importantly, his marriage.

She was prepared to go all the way with what she had, but she hoped that he would see things as they were and back off.

The connection she had with Sandra was one she had never experienced before. She guessed in some ways it was comparable to a girl always falling for the "bad boys" but it just so happened that in this case it was a "bad girl."

She wanted to get closer to Sandra and actually find out what made her tick. She was more than ready to sacrifice herself to be at her beck and call. She possessed a power that most men spent a lifetime trying to obtain, but for her it was naturally instilled in of her. She didn't put on big shows or do anything to bring attention to herself; no façades existed in Sandra. When she needed to act, she was more than prepared to do so.

Barbara couldn't exactly say that Sandra didn't go looking for trouble because that's exactly what she was doing by walking the streets at night, but she didn't harm people in general. She was getting rid of trash that needed disposing of, and Barbara admired her for the courage to do something about it.

She would have loved to have wiped her boss and his wife off the face of the earth, but she didn't have the full volume of rage instilled in her to do so. If she had known Sandra then, things may have turned out differently for her. She wouldn't have been locked up, and they may have even gotten away with what they would have done to the two most sickening people she had ever run across.

She was beginning to feel physically turned on by Dr. Wesley's stamina as well as the equipment filling her. She decided she had enough video for what she wanted to achieve, but there was no need in letting the moment go to waste.

She clamped her thighs tightly against his, grabbing the back of the couch for leverage. She moved in ways that plunged him deeper, and she could feel herself responding to the maneuver.

Charles was looking up at her with such hatred that she nearly lost her momentum, so she closed her eyes and visualized herself with Sandra. Barbara began to growl as the images and the reality of the pleasure she was receiving merged into one. She was so close to an awe-inspiring experience that she nearly didn't detect the shift in the air.

Sandra stood in the doorway of the room and watched what transpired between the two of them.

Her doctor had a hold of Barbara's thighs as she pumped and rocked him. How it came to be or who came on to whom she didn't know; the only thing she knew was that she didn't like what she was seeing.

When she woke in the bed, there were no clues as to where she was or what had transpired between the time she had gotten home and finding them on the sofa. She remembered her last escapade, but nothing more until she walked into the living room.

Barbara held the look of the guilty, and her doctor didn't seem to be aware of her at all. She felt tenderness in her arm and rubbed the spot where she had been injected. Small fragments began to play back in her mind, and she realized Barbara had held her down while he administered the shot to her.

Did they think she would never wake up? Did they plan this from the start? She did recall Dr. Wesley telling her that Barbara had placed a call to him. Why didn't she meet him elsewhere if they wanted to have a roll in the hay? Why did she bring him here?

Things were coming back in bits and pieces, and she stood patiently while her mind tried to categorize and sort through the entire scenario. Barbara had not too long ago professed her love to her, yet in a matter of hours she had managed to climb on the first man in sight.

Jealously was not the first thing to pop into her mind, but the feeling of being betrayed was strong. She'd thought

Barbara was there to help her in some form or fashion, but it was not to be. She had no real feelings for Sandra, and the idea of being made a fool of was not one to be easily dismissed by her, but what she should do about it was the immediate challenge on her part.

Should she demand that they both leave the house? Ask for an explanation? Her next course of action was not clear. She wanted nothing more than to return to the bedroom and forget that she had ever run into such a deceitful setting, but then what?

No, she would not play the role of the wounded, not even for a woman. Barbara's gender somehow changed things for her, but she knew she could not let her go unscathed for what she had done and was doing. She would viciously pay the price like all the others who had crossed her.

Her ears began to ring, and she did nothing this time to stop them. She didn't want to. It was the only thing in the room that could possibly understand what she was feeling at the time, and she needed them.

Getting rid of Dr. Wesley would become her first priority because he was a man, and because of his size and strength alone. She knew she could overpower Barbara with no hesitation, and with her, she would take her time.

"I told you she was a whore, and now she has proven that! They planned this from the beginning and wanted you to find them here screwing on your sofa. Your sofa! She has brought nothing to the table since the day you met, and now she goes and does this! It's a slap in the face and a laugh behind your back. But we will see who gets the last laugh now, won't we? Do what you must!"

Sandra left the spot in which she was standing and headed to the kitchen. She pulled the drawer open in search of the proper knife but closed it on second thought.

Moving robotically, she opened the cabinet under the sink where the used plastic bags were kept and fumbled through them for one to her liking but was unsatisfied. They were all too thin and easy to tear. She needed a strong bag that could hold up to the force she was about to put upon it.

She continued to look around until she spotted her bag of supplies peeking out from the bathroom floor.

Without a second thought she went and picked it up.

Sandra could feel Barbara's eyes on her, but she didn't lose focus of what she was doing. She was swinging into her rhythm now and didn't have a need to make eye contact with either of them. She was prepared to get back what they had tried to take from her, and that was the only thing she was interested in.

She left the kitchen area but didn't walk fully into the living room. She turned a sharp right to stand at the back of the couch. Barbara looked as if she was prepared to speak but didn't.

Sandra sat her bag on the floor and bent down to find what was all too familiar to her. Just to have her tools in such close proximity brought a lightness and admiration for what she had been able to do with items people thought were ordinary and served a basic purpose in life.

When she stood up, she held the plastic she had been using for the last few victims. There were traces of blood on the handles and even inside of the bag. She licked her lips in anticipation of what was to come. She had a job to do, and it was one that she was more than good at.

Charles swallowed the lump that had formed in his throat the moment he knew Sandra was standing behind the couch. Barbara had him weighted down, and he began to push feverishly at her thighs to get her up. The strength in his arms was wavering as his biceps shook from the effort. His body would not wake up and respond to his demands, although he kept trying.

*

Barbara saw the transformation slowly as it occurred. She watched her every move but didn't like what she was seeing. Sandra was focused on the both of them, and that is not what she wanted. She had to let her know that truly at this moment what she walked into was not as it appeared.

"Sandra, wait."

Dr. Wesley was wiggling even more now, and she was losing her balance. She didn't want him to get up, but she also didn't know if Sandra planned on swinging at them from where she stood. Barbara noticed the plastic in her hands and watched as Sandra wrapped the handles tightly around each wrist. What she was going to do with such an object confused her until she no longer had to question.

*

Charles jerked when he realized his face was pressed firmly in the sack. It was then that he knew Sandra had not lied to him. She had done all of the evil things confessed earlier. Every time the news mentioned the serial killer on the loose or he discussed the latest developments with colleagues, he found himself agreeing the victims were homosexuals and had been caught in a deadly sexual game of some kind. How else were they able to explain the fact that some of the men were in shape and seemingly capable of taking care of themselves. No one in a frightening death experience would allow it to come so easy without a fight.

Drugs were considered when the news of what was going on first hit the screens, but after the third victim tested negative for any form of street or prescribed pharmaceuticals, the end conclusion was that they were looking for a man or men who was able to overpower the victims.

He now knew how they fell short. He was getting a grasp firsthand at what Sandra was capable of and the expertise with which she operated. Why she chose to do what she was did came as no surprise to him. She felt violated and used by men all her life. As she'd said to him before, she was hunted.

She was getting back at all the men in her past and the ones she believed didn't deserve a future. Her mental makeup was all wrong, and he'd failed in seeing that from the day they first began. He should have studied her file and been on point when she became his patient, but he took it lightly.

He pictured her as a run-of-the-mill patient who needed a little one-on-one conversation and a very mild dose of anti-depressants, although if he was to admit it now, he would have had a change of heart toward her release date after reading her file in its entirety.

Dr. Wesley wrote prescriptions and attached them to the list of things she would need to pass on to her next therapist.

He had no idea how unstable Sandra really was because he didn't do his job as he had been trained to do it. He'd let her down as a patient, and he'd failed to protect the citizens of Colorado by knowingly releasing someone like her into society with a simple note of instructions attached to her lunchbox.

He had taken many wrong turns when it came to Sandra, and he knew from where he sat this was to be his last.

*

Barbara grabbed at her wrist and tried to force reasoning into her, but it was not to be. Sandra released one handle and smacked Barbara with a doubling force, but she did not give up. She attempted to pull the bag off Dr. Wesley's head and was met with a single crisp elbow to the cheek for the effort.

"Sandra, it's not what it looks like. I did this for you, for us!"

With her free hand Sandra bent Charles' fingers back until she heard the significant crack of bone. He let go of the bag, releasing a suffocating yelp from the pain. She was handling both of them sufficiently.

"Sandra, he was going to put you away, but I stopped him. I drugged him and then recorded us on the couch. I was going to blackmail him into leaving us alone! Sandra, please!"

She continued to twist until his air no longer inflated the plastic. His feet were kicking, but Barbara wouldn't let him up. She didn't want to find out if he would be able to take them both out at this time. He didn't feel as if he was functioning to his fullest capabilities because she was still able to hold on to him, but she also didn't dare take the chance to find out he had an adrenaline reserve tank.

Reaching Sandra was her only concern.

"Sandra! He's dying!"

As she said this, she knew she would not be able to change her course of action. The bag was as tight as it could be, and Dr. Wesley was no longer trying to put up a fight. His body moved sideways and seemed to involuntarily shiver every now and them, but he had nothing left to give. His hands slipped from their current position of cradling each other, and she could feel him sag deeply into the couch.

"Sandra, listen to me. When I said I loved you, I meant it. There is nothing I wouldn't do for you. Sandra!"

Barbara clumsily found her way off of Dr. Wesley and stood in front of what once was a vibrant man. Sandra released the plastic and came around to stand in front of her. Barbara reached out her hand to get some kind of bond to surface between them, but it was knocked away.

Sandra's eyes twinkled in a way the most devious of killers' did. They were standing at a stalemate, but she knew that would change soon. Sandra was nowhere near calm or reason, but Barbara knew that was the only weapon she had.

"I recorded us. I was going to show it to his wife if he sent you away. I didn't know what else to do, Sandra. You told him what you have been doing, and I saw the determination across his face. He was ready to call the cops on you. This is the only thing I could think of to stop him. I would never hurt you. You know that, don't you?"

Sandra smiled, and it cut Barbara to the core. With one hand she pushed her over the coffee table and watched as she landed on the other side. Her head bounced off the floor, but she dismissed it and quickly bounced to her feet.

Sandra advanced her way and took a swing at her face. Barbara ducked and continued to stand her ground.

"Sandra! Please, Sandra, don't do this. I didn't know what else to do. I'm telling you the truth. Please!"

She tackled Barbara to the floor and found the softness of her neck to press her thumbs into. She bore down with enough force to fracture, if not crush, her windpipe. Barbara clawed her arms in an effort to lessen her grip and even fruitlessly reached for Sandra's neck in response but came up short and disadvantaged.

She had nothing but her eyes and hands free to help her come up with some form of a defense when they beamed in on the wine opener lying a few inches from her fingertips.

The lack of air or the desperate need for it became secondary to grasping the object. She used her nails to dig into the floor in hopes of crossing the centimeters necessary for her success.

The cork hung askew from the tip but was on firmly enough to move the entire opener when she latched on to it.

There could have never been a better feeling than the sensation of her fingers closing around the coolness of the metal opener. She looped her thumb into the handle, knocking the cork loose, and slid it firmly into her grasp. She knew she had no intentions of killing Sandra, despite what she was going through, but she had to change the scenario, and quickly.

Her chest began to heave from lack of oxygen, which initiated a burning sensation incomparable to any depth of heartburn to crawl throughout her body. Her eyes watered as she looked up at Sandra and plunged the tip of the corkscrew into her hip area.

Sandra peered down at her and then at the wound inflicted upon her. Back and forth her eyes went as she let go of the grip she had on Barbara in order to remove the stinging object from her hip.

Barbara coughed and tried to prop herself on her elbows for more air when she felt Sandra's weight slip from her abdomen to her thighs. She breathed a sigh of relief and continued to slide from under Sandra.

Everything moved in slow motion as they stared at each other. A small blotch of blood stained Sandra's pajamas as she got to her feet with the corkscrew in her hand. Barbara's success was short-lived as she realized that Sandra now held the very weapon she had used against her.

She wanted to get to her feet, just in case she was more than prepared to finish her, but she also feared that making another move may agitate the situation even further.

"Sandra, what do you want me to do? I'm sorry that you found me like that, I really am, but I was all out of solutions. Please look at me. I love you."

"You have the leverage; now do what you need to do. Don't let this whore get into your head. She is a liar!"

The voices continued to torment her every thought, but it was fading out. She could hear the command, but the strength in which they came across was weak and brittle. The buzzing was at a minimum, and Barbara's voice penetrated through it. The decision was now her own. She could give power to either side, and when she saw the truth in Barbara's eyes, it silenced the voices that much more.

She didn't want to kill her now, and she was not so sure if she'd wanted to do it when she had her by the throat, but she also knew if Barbara hadn't gotten a hold of the opener when she did, she could easily have been a corpse emptily gazing up from the floor.

"Can I stand up?"

Barbara decided to ask instead of make the move on her own. She could see that Sandra was coming in and out of her haze, and she wanted to keep her steady and focused on her. How she was able to bring Sandra back from her manic episodes was unknown to her, but at the time she didn't give it much thought, just remained grateful that was the case.

Sandra didn't respond to Barbara's questioning because she was still trying to determine what she should do about the situation. She stared off into space but was still quite aware of her surroundings. She watched Barbara pick herself off the floor, yet she did not respond vocally or physically.

It was a grainy film of confusion that she was emerging from, and the clarity that she was becoming faced with startled her. Barbara stood less than three feet from where she was planted, looking disheveled and just as discombobulated as she felt. She knew what had transpired between them, but what she didn't know was what she was going to do or say about it.

Barbara rubbed her neck and advanced on Sandra. She closed the space that separated them, no longer fearing the outcome of such a maneuver. Getting her to recognize her as being the one on her side became her quest.

"Are you okay? Let me take a look at your leg."

Sandra still couldn't find her voice, but her body language suggested that she was not going to harm her. Barbara pulled the band of her pajamas down until the area where she had harmed her was exposed. She didn't think she would need stitches, but she would have to have a dressing of some sort to cover it.

Barbara grabbed Sandra's hand and placed the fingers to her lips. She kissed them lightly, lovingly, and tenderly. The emotions flowing through her at the moment were intense and raw. Her legs trembled as she tried to stand erect and unafraid of Sandra. This was the true and telling moment of their future, and the mechanism was powerful.

She pulled the fabric back up and stared into the eyes of a woman she had more than grew to love. Their future depended on the plans that she would make, and she didn't mind that in the least bit. She was willing to take care of Sandra in every way.

She wanted to guide her into the room and get her into a nice hot bath where she would join her. She pictured herself washing her back, and kissing her shoulders. From this moment on, she vowed to never let another man explore her body for any reason.

She wouldn't come up with excuses for her actions but stay steady on the course of keeping them together. They would have to move, and she was sure that when Sandra had a level head, she wouldn't have any problem convincing her of that. They would start fresh and blow off Colorado altogether.

Barbara pulled Sandra's hand, indicating that they were going to the bathroom, but her steps stopped cold. She didn't move. Barbara turned around to face her and nearly dropped dead in her tracks. Dr. Wesley had a hold of Sandra's leg in a desperate vise grip. He was trying to pull himself off the sofa using her for balance.

They were locked in a soldiery moment in which neither of them was able to find momentum. Sandra didn't try to free herself from his grasp but simply looked at him as if he had appeared magically from the cushions upon which he sat. He was digging his nails into her thigh, only inches from where Barbara had deeply plunged a corkscrew.

His eyes held a determination that she found fascinating, and she couldn't turn her eyes away from. He tried to speak, but the first few words came out in indiscernible gurgles.

Charles found his voice seconds later and mumbled a definite, "Bitch!" in her direction. He couldn't get his footing, so he continued to pull Sandra down to him. What he would do with her once she landed on his lap was not something he considered.

He had lost consciousness when Sandra tried to kill him, and he couldn't believe his luck when his eyes opened up. He saw them on the floor and wanted nothing more than to put a bullet in both of their heads. He knew Barbara had drugged him, and at first he could have forgiven her for that, but to hear that she was going to ruin him with her amateur video took him to the other side of angry.

She'd initially called him into the mess they called a life. He was lounging in the comforts of his home until the phone rang. If his wife had not been out, his phone would have been on silent, and he would have not gotten the message until the next day. By that time he would have been thinking with a clear mind and may have sent someone else in his place because he would have been at work.

He wanted to believe that was the course of action he would have taken, but he knew he may have responded just the same. Sandra was a special case to him, and he felt he had dropped the ball in her care, so coming in to help her would have been a normal reaction. But now the tables had turned and he wanted to do to her what she had accomplished to do to so many others.

He wanted nothing more than to see the life drain from her eyes the way she had thought she had done with him. He was innocent in the whole drugging affair, but he was the one who pulled the shortest stick. Barbara kept trying to talk sense to Sandra, which he was briefly grateful for, but she was not to be persuaded.

She honed in on them and went straight into action. She was in the same zone in which he had found her earlier, and he now realized that Barbara may have been able to talk her out of it without him. They didn't have a need for him, and that was made all too clear when he instantly became disposable.

Charles reflected on what had happened to him over the course of the last few hours, and he pushed that rage to the forefront of his being. Sandra was not putting up much resistance to his pulling and tugging at her, and he used that to bring forth courage. He would get out of their house tonight, and if he had to kill to do it, then so be it!

Sandra had lost her balance, landing pretty much in the same place she had found Barbara in earlier. Dr. Wesley's hands clambered to find a lethal grip on her, but he had not gained back the full dexterity in his hands. They slipped when they were supposed to cling and just would not function at the level he needed, but he was determined.

He used his weight to throw her off balance, and he now had her lying across his lap, looking directly into his eyes. He was almost thrown off by the purity of blue, but not enough to lose focus when his life depended on it.

Sandra seemed unfazed almost amused by his efforts. She hadn't lifted a finger to protect herself, which made him second-guess how much damage he was really doing, but he kept at it. He was going to cause her bodily harm and more than likely see the last breath escape from her chest. It was a him or them situation, and he was not going to be on the losing end of it.

He placed his hands on her throat just as she had done with Barbara, and he squeezed for everything it was worth. His grip was not tight, but he knew it held a little pressure because Sandra's face began to redden. It was the first time she'd reacted to his touch, but she simply grabbed his wrist.

If he was not so shaken up himself, he would have sworn on a stack of bibles that she was pressing his hands into her, and not away. Her eyes seemed to be pleading with him to complete what he had started. It shook him down to his feet to see her like this. He wavered in his touch, but she kept her grip firmly in place. Did she want to die? Did she know he was trying to end her life? Is this what she wanted?

Charles became sickened and indecisive. He had never been so close to taking a life, but here sat one of the most beautiful yet violent women he had ever run across, and that is exactly what he set out to do.

He closed his eyes for a second and squeezed with the feeble energy his body produced. It was not enough to kill a kitten, let alone a human, but he didn't loosen up. He hoped that the diligence he felt in his heart would somehow manifest itself in his hands.

Sandra's eyes watered and then shifted. If he had not been looking at her so intently, he may have missed it. She was no longer meeting him eye to eye but over his shoulder and slightly to the left.

He didn't catch the meaning at first, but then it registered…Barbara.

His neck snapped back, and the grip in which he found himself in was crushing. Repeated blows landed squarely in his face, and he could do nothing to stop the downpour.

Barbara was screaming and swinging simultaneously. A thin crisp sheath engulfed him, and he knew he was again on the losing end. Barbara erupted seemingly out of nowhere and unleashed a fury on him that he had not been prepared for.

Now as he felt Sandra's hand upon him, he knew they were not the encouraging fingers he'd thought they were but vice grips meticulously planted to keep him in place.

Barbara pulled and tugged at the bag until it was the thinnest layer imaginable snagged across Dr. Wesley's face. When she first saw that he had not died she'd been relieved, but uncertain of what to do with him.

When he put his hands around Sandra's neck and set himself with sheer determination to kill her, there was doubt in what she would do. Sandra was incapable of handling him, and she had basically become submissive under him, but when she saw Barbara emerge from behind the couch, her face lifted, and she appeared thankful.

To see her being manhandled and strangled stirred something deep from within her that could not be smothered. Sandra needed her, and she would not let her down. Now was the chance to show her that she meant everything she said. She loved her and was there only for her. Once she locked eyes with Sandra and she knew they were on the same page, he should have considered himself dead that very second.

In a moment's notice, Barbara was willing to tie an infant down on a set of train tracks if it meant Sandra would be safe. He would have to be eliminated, and there would be no coming back from it this time.

He would not walk another day on the streets of Colorado or any other. He would never be able to tell his wife that he loved her or hold the child he didn't know she was carrying. His life as he knew it was over. It would take three years for his wife to come to that realization, and four more before the insurance company paid her and she moved out of the home they hoped to raise a family in.

She would fall apart at the seams from the loss, but her best friend would be there to comfort her, support her, and eventually marry her. His son that he would never see would carry two last names: Wesley-McKenzie, after his two fathers.

His life, career, and dreams ended with plastic wrapped around his face, and blood dripping from his nose and lips. His eyes would have been swollen shut, but the circulation ceased and his tissues failed to fill with telling fluid because his heart no longer pumped.

*

Barbara held onto the bag until her hands knew no other shape, leaving her knuckles white from tension. It was Sandra who untied the handles and laced her fingers with hers. She massaged them tenderly until the color returned to her palms.

She finally released the tears that had been bottled inside of her and they dripped warmly unto Barbara. Neither one of them gave Dr. Wesley a second glace as they embraced and kissed behind his corpse.

They were forever sealed by a bond stronger than any other. Where their lives would take them only time could tell, but on the journey ahead, they would share the footsteps and the demons that walked with them.

Life's hurdles would be jumped in unison by two women who were eternally merged. One mind. One mission. One destiny.